To my Gifted Hope, Emily, Nicholas and Emerson

STORM FORGED

STORM FORGED

THE DARKEST STORM - BOOK 1

PATRICK DUGAN

High school is a breeding ground for loathing, acne, and peer pressure, and that's on the good days. For me, school was more about dodging bullies than red rubber balls. I slid through the crowded hallways, my head down, trying to avoid being noticed.

"Hey, Ward. Where ya goin', Slag," followed me down the hall. *I guess all the mining around town made Slag an insult.* Heads turned, some to watch, some to leave as fast as possible. When you have a collar, you don't want to be a handy target. You wouldn't think having a silver band no thicker than your finger affixed around your neck would cause so many issues, but it did. After a short argument between my male pride and my instinct for self-preservation, I ran, hoping none of the pretty girls saw.

I hitched up my backpack, rounded the corner, and headed for the cafeteria. Depending on the teacher, I might get some assistance. Brunner closed the gap as I ran into the cafeteria. Rows of beige tables stood as mute witness to my pending humiliation. Most of the tables sat empty, but the few students around decided to help. Technically, they helped Brunner by blocking my exit, but I'm not complaining, much. *Great job, Tommy, run into a room with no teachers.* At least once a week we played this game, so I set my backpack on the floor. No sense getting blood on it.

"Mutt, I asked you a question." Brunner, a goon in every sense of the word, cracked his knuckles, the sound proceeding him as he approached. At any other school, he'd have been a star football player, being six-foot-two and over two-fifty. I would call him a Neanderthal, but why insult our ancestors who discovered fire? I doubt those innovative cavemen would be nineteen and still juniors in high school. His fist smashed into my mouth, dropping me to the floor. "I hate to be ignored."

"Who could ignore something as ugly as you," I tried to say, but a size-fourteen Timberland boot stopped anything from coming out of my mouth that wasn't breakfast.

"Stay down," Brunner yelled as he kicked me in the side again. Pain exploded through me, and I felt like I would burst absorbing the punishment. I pulled my knees up, struggling to protect myself better. The crowd, drawn to the scent of blood, encircled us chanting, "Slag," as Brunner continued his onslaught.

I struggled up to my hands and knees—standing would take a lot more effort. I'd be damned if I would let him think he had the best of me. I had a reputation to maintain, however pitiful. If only I didn't have this damned collar, even a crappy power like Firework Farley had would have lit him up. I tensed as his foot swung back to deal the final blow.

"Break it up! Break it up!" Mr. Taylor shouted as he bulled his way through the crowd of students encircling us. "The bell is about to ring, get to class."

The kick never landed as Mr. Taylor grabbed Brunner by the shirt collar. "This time you aren't getting away with it."

"Mr. Taylor," Brunner pulled out of his grip, holding up his hands to protest his innocence, "Tommy fell, and I tried to help him up."

"I was born on a Wednesday, but it wasn't last Wednesday. You'll be getting a week of detention and a phone call to your parents."

"I don't think that will be necessary, Mr. Taylor," Vice Principal Robinson said from behind him. Robinson was immaculately dressed in her usual business suit and heels, of which I had a great view. Her blue-black skin made her look almost statuesque, but the flash of anger in her eyes argued otherwise. "Obviously, Mr. Ward tripped, and Mr. Brunner lent a helping hand. Dissidents tend to be clumsy, after all."

Brunner laughed, his friends rallying around him, high-fiving and slapping him on the back. "You'll get yours, Taylor, you freaking terror-ist!" Brunner taunted. His friends all laughed as they sauntered out of the cafeteria.

Taylor bent over to help me up. "I will not stand for a student being beaten just for what he is."

I groaned as the conversation veered into oncoming traffic and a head-on collision with a semi.

Vice Principal Robinson stepped closer. "Mr. Taylor, I understand your point. The government has worked hard to mainstream Dissidents back into society, but troublemakers tend to end up in The Block, and I would hate to lose one of my best teachers."

Mr. Taylor straightened, his face draining of all color. The Block, one of the maximum-security detention facilities, quelled even the toughest Gifted. Taylor knew she didn't make idle threats. "As you wish. I will take Mr. Ward to the nurse so she can check him for injuries."

I jumped up, fighting to regain my balance. The world spun for a second, but I stayed on my feet, a major accomplishment after being worked over by Brunner. I'd gotten better at avoiding serious damage during these incidents. Mom would be upset if the nurse called her again. "I'm fine, Mr. Taylor." I grasped his elbow as the world slid sideways, my stomach leaping to the back of my throat.

"See, Mr. Taylor, the boy isn't hurt. Please escort Mr. Ward to class and remind him not to be so clumsy in the future. A week's detention should help him think about what he's done."

"He shouldn't need an escort to protect him going to class."

"Mr. Taylor, it's fine. I really do need to be more careful walking to class." I stared into his eyes, trying to convince him to drop it. The last thing I wanted was for him to end up in The Block on account of me. Once a Gifted entered, they never came out again. I couldn't let that happen to him.

"See, the boy understands the situation better than most, Mr. Taylor." She turned on her stiletto heels and strode across the cafeteria.

I waited until the vice principal got out of earshot. I slung my back-pack over my shoulder. "Thanks, Mr. Taylor."

"It's not right, Tommy. You can't help being born with Gifts any more than she could help being born black."

We passed through the cafeteria doors, then my mouth flew to where my brain feared to tread. "Did you have your powers before the Reclamation?" It was considered rude and a bit dangerous to ask about a Gifted's powers, but I didn't have anyone else to ask. All the kids my age had been collared in kindergarten, so we didn't even know what our abilities could do.

Mr. Taylor studied me for a bit before answering. "Yes, I did, Tommy."

I trembled with excitement. An actual Gifted who knew what they could do was similar to meeting a rock star. "It must have been amazing?" I blurted out.

"Amazing, but there are costs for using your Gifts. Still, my life ended the day they collared me, but it also saved me. Gifts are always a two-edged sword." He stared into the distance for a moment before glancing over my shoulder. The first bell rang before I could ask more. Vice Principal Robinson watched us from the school office's entrance, her long gleaming red fingernails tapping on the door frame. Mr. Taylor cleared his throat. "If you aren't careful, they'll cut you to ribbons."

"Gotta go. Thanks, Mr. Taylor." I shoved my arms through the backpack's straps and ran for history class, my least favorite subject.

I slid through the doorway, right before Mr. Powell shut the door. Of all the teachers I had to deal with, Lewis C. Powell was the worst. Ex-military and the Reclaimers' chosen representative in Redemption, Powell bore the scars of hunting down Gifted during the Reclamation War. He hated the Gifted with every ounce of his being and made sure we knew it.

"Why, class, look. Mr. Ward, our resident terrorist, decided to grace us with his presence." His angry sneer twisting the scars. "You know these Dissidents think they can come and go as they please. Well, at least they used to before we collared them like the Mutts they are."

The class laughed. They always laughed. *And here it comes, wait for it.*

"Let's see what Mr. Ward thinks of a week's detention for being late."

The second bell rang announcing class should start. I'd made it in time, but Powell's petty cruelties brought him great joy, and the Norms worshipped him, the Reclamation hero. *Two weeks of detention before first period. Another record for the books set by Mr. Tommy Ward, juvenile delinquent.*

Mr. Powell stomped to the front of the room, his self-satisfied smirk firmly affixed to his scarred face. "Today, we are discussing the aftereffects of the Reclamation. Can anyone tell me why we are so fortunate to have students like Mr. Ward here?"

A couple of hands shot up around the room, but none higher than Wendell Hempstead's. The school nerd, he would have been bully feed if not for the Gifted. Powell's daily assault reinforced the fact of Gifted were the bottom of the food chain.

"Okay, Mr. Hempstead."

He stood up to answer. Wendell's bad haircut, pasty white skin, and Coke-bottle glasses showed him to be the ultimate kiss ass. "Mr. Powell, after the destruction of the major cities of the world by the Dissident terrorists, the Reclaimers had detention centers built in five locations: Siberia, Poland, Brazil, the Sudan, and here. Collared Dissidents are required to live within a two-hundred-mile radius of one of these detention centers; thus, Mr. Ward is here at our school."

"Very good, Mr. Hempstead."

Wendell beamed at the praise as he sat down. *He is such a brown-noser.*

"Why are you required to live within two-hundred miles of such centers, Mr. Ward?" Powell said, a nasty gleam in his eye.

"So you don't have to be too far from your boyfriend?" popped in my head and may have made it out of my mouth if I had felt suicidal. While I couldn't be kicked out of school, this being the designated Dissident school, worse things could happen, and Powell would make sure they did. I decided not to die today. "So we can be monitored and have frequent updates to our collars, Mr. Powell, and after reeducation become a valued member of society."

I am such a wuss.

"That is correct." Mr. Powell turned his back and launched into his real lecture on how the Protector saved us all from the horrors of the Gifted menace, how noble his surrender after all the Dissidents had been captured, blah, blah, blah. I failed history every term, but no one cared if I did well or not. Well, other than Mom. She most definitely cared.

The rest of the day crawled like a slug across broken glass. Pre-Calc ended with a reminder from Ms. Hannah to study for tomorrow's test. I grabbed my backpack and headed to the Dissident Protection Center, built to withstand an uncollared Gifted just in case one of us ever broke free. In the fifteen-plus years the Institute had been educating Gifted kids, detention has been its sole use.

5

I entered what we called the Air-Lock. The room could hold four to five hundred people, even though there are about one hundred Gifted kids going to school here. The door belonged in a high-tech bank, not a high school. Carbinium doors and six-inch bolts were set into two feet of ultra-hard concrete. The walls, floors, and ceiling had been constructed of the same stuff. Rumor had it a nuclear bomb wouldn't damage the Air-Lock. Inside, a wonderland of beige awaited us. The beige walls complemented the light brown floor tile and the off-white ceiling. The lights were some sort of filament tech, no electricity in the lines, just in case. The only "real" thing in the room was an old wooden desk a Gifted teacher sat at during our time here. Most of the kids waited here for the Institute's armored buses to take them to the dorms, but the rest of us, the ones who lived at home, constant "detention" had been implemented to keep us on campus as long as possible.

Jon and Wendi Stevens were already there. Wendi stood out, a rose in a junkyard, with long blond hair and blue eyes; she would have been prom queen, if not for the collar she wore. Her friends clustered around, words flying around like tumbleweed in a windstorm.

Wendi's twin, Jon, stood a head taller than most of the Gifted guys he hung out with. He rivaled any quarterback with the square jaw and wide shoulders. Not that it mattered. Once the collar had been affixed, the label of Dissident, of Slag, applied and everything changed.

I passed by, flashing an awkward half-smile at Wendi, who didn't see it.

"…another Gifted girl murdered, I'm scared," one of the girls remarked, wringing her hands in front of her. "What if it happens here?"

Jon snorted. "We are under guard twenty-four-hours a day. No one gets out of here until they're eighteen."

Wendi smacked Jon's shoulder. "As my rude brother pointed out, it would be difficult to attack anyone here."

His head swiveled to face her, the purple bruise around Jon's left eye, plainly obvious. "Yeah, nobody ever gets attacked here. Tommy got the crap beat out of him by Brunner just this morning."

All heads turned to look at me. My face decided bright red would accent all the bruises developing there. Wendi gave me the puppy dog eyes. As any reasonable sixteen-year-old boy would do, I fled.

I sat down at my desk and took out a book to read. We were supposed to do homework, but none of us ever bothered. Unless your teacher had a collar, you didn't get higher than a C in the class anyhow.

I felt a hand on my shoulder and jumped a bit. Marcel pushed into the desk next to me, sucking in his stomach to accomplish this feat of contortion. He wasn't fat, exactly; Mom called him "big boned." A huge smile crossed his face as he ran his hand through his afro. Marcel's hair could be considered the eighth wonder of the modern world due to the size.

"Hey, Bruh. S'up?" he asked, extracting his Samsung Supernova from his backpack and popping open an app he had written. "I hacked the guards' frequency, and they are going crazy. Someone broke out of The Block."

"Really?" No one had broken out of the Block before. It made Fort Knox look like a tourist trap.

"Yeah, nasty dude called the Grim Reaper. They say he killed twelve guards getting out." Marcel grinned.

"Good for him, bad for us." Whenever problems arose, the Reclaimers cracked down on all the Gifted. Random searches, lockdowns, and emergency practices would be coming soon. When the first of the Gifted women went missing, the Norms freaked out. For a Gifted to have killed a Norm, especially multiple guards, at the world's toughest prison, should be impossible.

Marcel punched me lightly in the shoulder. "Yeah, but Bruh, he got away." He tapped his chin, which indicated a plan in the works, but there was no way out for us, especially without our Gifts. If you tried to escape, they locked you away or put you on TV for *Saturday Night Showdown*. The Norms loved to see us fight in high def.

I decided to change the subject before someone overheard us. "Mom sent in the paperwork to renew your weekend pass."

He nodded, a smile growing on his face. "Excellent. Mom's cooking is a lot better than the Institute's. They served instant potatoes the other night. I mean, who would do that to a poor potato? I guess the spuds must have been Gifted."

We laughed. To the rest of the world, we were opposite in every way. He was tall, big, and black, whereas short, skinny, and white described me, but in our hearts, we had been brothers since the day we met in kindergarten, and things would never change.

The last of the kids filtered in, and the guards sealed the door from the outside. The thump as the Carbinium bolts slid into place reverberated in my chest. My stomach twisted like always because my stupid lizard brain nibbles at the thought: is this the time they aren't going to open the doors again? If everything was normal in an hour or so, we would be released to go home for the night.

High school really sucks.

2

The door banged open. I sat up, startled awake to find my perky, morning person mother standing in the doorway, a huge grin on her face. "I've got some business in Great Falls, so get dressed and let's go."

I groaned and tugged the covers over my head. "I'm not wasting a Saturday sitting around your office. I'll be here when you get back."

"Oh, well, I thought you might like to kick it at The Secret Lair while I worked, but I guess I should let you sleep..." she trailed off as she started to close the door.

"What!" The cover flew off me as I leapt out of bed, wincing as the bruises from yesterday's beating cramped. "You didn't say anything about that!"

She gave me the sympathetic eyes usually reserved for when I was sick. "No, you go back to bed, you're tired."

The door closed. "I'll be ready in ten minutes," I yelled at the door. I threw on the closest clothes I could find from the floor. I rejected the first shirt I grabbed. It didn't pass the smell test. Laundry would be in my near future, one of the chores Mom had passed on to me as part of making me a real adult. I dressed, ran my fingers through my hair, swished around some Scope, kicked on my boots and winter jacket, and ran for the front door.

Mom sat on the couch, keys twirling around her finger. "Now if you could only do that on school days."

She picked up her briefcase, I picked up the two banker's boxes with her documents, and we headed to the car. The boxes slid into the back seat, the top one promptly falling, but I caught it before the lid came off. After I climbed in the passenger's side, Mom started the car, turned up the heat, hit the gas, and we were off.

Mom clicked on the CD player. The Protectorate owned all the broadcasting, and a lot of older music had been banned as subversive. Most people hoarded CDs and DVDs of their favorite artists as you could no longer buy them. Springsteen played as she sang, off-key, to "Blinded by the Light." I could tell she was lost in her own world until the song ended.

She glanced at me with a smile. "Your father and I must have seen Springsteen twenty times before you came along."

I rolled my eyes. "It's like you had a life before me." I tried to keep the smirk off my face but failed miserably.

"*We*," she said. "We had a life before the Dark Brigade. Everything changed after the attack."

We rode in silence. What would life have been different if the Gifted terrorists, the Dark Brigade, hadn't destroyed half of the world in an attempt to take it over? I'd still have a dad and no collar to start.

Great Falls was the closest "city" to us. Redemption sat in the middle of nowhere, and Great Falls, a couple hours west of nowhere, but still within my two-hundred-mile leash of The Block. Once a month, we trekked in so Mom could pick up her caseload, drop off work for the paralegals, and generally bore me to death for an entire Saturday. The big thing for me is after she picked me up from The Secret Lair, we got to eat at a real restaurant for a change. Nothing really nice. Those places didn't allow my type in.

Mom pulled the mini-van up to The Secret Lair's front door. I slung my backpack over a shoulder and tried to hop out, but Mom stopped me immediately.

She grasped my arm before I could jump. "Now listen, Tommy. I want you to stay inside. Don't go wandering the neighborhood." I nodded and tried to jump out again. Another failure.

"I mean it. This is not a good neighborhood. Promise me you'll stay inside."

I checked to see if anyone watched me through the windows. It's hard enough to make friends without being thought of as a mama's boy. "Mom, I will."

"Okay, I'll be back at four, and we can get some dinner after that. I love you."

"You too." This time I got the door open and made it out of the Mom-mobile. I waved as she drove off to work.

I tugged hard on the front door since it weighed a ton. Iron bars covered the cracked glass, which must be bulletproof since none of the cracks had gone all the way through. The smell bordered on intense. Hot dogs, incense, and sweat all mingled together in a place. The interior hadn't seen sunshine in forever. Discolored bean bags dotted on the floor, most with teens and twenty-somethings of all shapes and sizes on them playing video games or watching the feeds from their favorite sites. Tables lined one wall, where a couple of guys played a board game and a few more sat playing *D&D*. The foosball and pool tables were empty, but it was still early.

The owner of The Lair, Blaze, and his assistant manager, Max stood behind the counter. I'd been here enough that I knew the staff, and they knew me.

"Dude, that's your mom?" Blaze asked as I approached the counter. Blaze had to be almost sixty, skinny as a lamppost with a long gray pony-tail hanging down his back to his belt. He owned the place but didn't have a collar. Word around The Lair claimed he had worked with a team before the Reclamation, but since he didn't have powers, he's legal.

"Yeah." My cheeks burned with embarrassment. Even though I'd been here quite a bit, I still hadn't made any friends among the locals.

"Dude, she's hot." A big grin spread across his face.

"Really?"

"Totally, dude. Next time, have her come in and say hello."

"Okay, I will." I had always thought Mom was pretty, but then again, all sons thought that about their moms. That Blaze said it shocked me.

Max chuckled. He had shaggy, dark hair, and most of the girls flirted with him when he worked the front desk. "Blaze, take it easy on Tommy. You never know what powers lie beneath that quiet interior."

I grinned. "Powers? Me? I doubt I could power a light bulb. I'd prob-ably be one of the guys who could pee rainbow colors."

11

They both laughed, but Max studied me seriously. "No, I don't think so," he said softly.

I shrugged. "I'm gonna get some lunch." They both waved goodbye, returning to their earlier conversation.

I walked into the "café," a cross between a 50s diner and a mosh pit. The chrome edge of the lunch counter sparkled around the concrete and glass chips that made up the surface. A hodgepodge of various styles and color, the stools stood around the base of faded teal green and back-lit bands of chrome. Mimi, the waitress, adorned with tattoos and piercings, her hair bright blue on one side and purple on the other, stood behind the counter. Today, she wore a dark blue t-shirt with a "Free Dominion" logo on the front. The only "normal" part of her was the gleaming silver collar around her neck.

I stopped at the bar and waited for Mimi to notice me. "Hey, Sport, whatcha' want?" She chomped on a large wad of bubble gum. A large bubble appeared, which promptly popped.

"Hot dog and a Pepsi, please, ma'am," I stammered out. Mimi made me a bit nervous.

She nodded. "Dog and a pop, gotcha. You call me ma'am again, and I'll punch your lights out, Champ." She shot me a big smile, and her eyes sparkled with either amusement or malice. I couldn't tell which.

I handed her a couple of credits as she handed me the food. "Keep the change," I muttered. She winked and went to talk to Max, who stood at the end of the counter. Mimi's smile faded as they spoke. I made a hasty retreat.

I grabbed a booth with a great view of the TV screen, pushing my jacket and backpack in before me. A couple of bashers lounged at a nearby table, arm wrestling. Three more compared their latest tattoos. A group of girls clustered around a table in the back, giggling and talking together, interested in me more than anything. They must go to school in Great Falls since I hadn't seen them around Redemption. None of them had collars, so they were Norms. Must be here to see the freak show.

The TV showed recaps of last week's *Saturday Night Showdown*. Mom didn't want me watching it since it showed Gifted dying for ratings. Most of the matches lasted until the "contestant" surrendered. When they announced a Gauntlet, a Gifted always died, but Gauntlets had only happened twice in my lifetime.

Firework Farley had been on last week. His name derived from his ability to project bursts of lights from his hands. As Gifts went, he had pretty lame one. He fought against a robot enforcer. Farley ran around, blinding the robot's sensors while trying to knock it down with the steel bat they gave him. It was over in the blink of an eye; the robot punched him once and down he fell.

I pulled my new paperback out and began to read. I felt a tap on my shoulder. One of the girls from the lunch counter stood there. I glanced over and saw all her friends staring at us. The first things I noticed were her huge brown eyes; they glimmered in the fluorescent light. Long brown hair, pushed behind her ears. I flushed a bit when I noticed how her V-necked sweater displayed her...

"Mind if I sit with you?" she asked. My head jerked up, face flaring in embarrassment. She smiled at me, but I could tell she was nervous. Her friends must have dared her to talk to me.

"I'm kind of busy," I said, putting my nose back into my book.

"Please, I just want to talk to you."

Against all better judgment, my hormones won out, and I heard myself say, "Sure."

She sat down across from me. "My name is Mandy. I go to Great Falls High. Are you new here?"

"No, I live in Redemption." Her eyes went wide, but instead of bolting, she gasped, clapping her hands together.

"O-M-G, you must tell me all about it. You must be really powerful to be in Redemption," she squealed in delight. "Is it true the high school is a prison? Are you worried they'll gas you the way the Eastern Asia Block did? My school doesn't have any Dissidents at it, but it would be cool if it did."

I frowned at her, letting pass the fact she'd just casually mentioned wiping out all the students in Redemption. The gas attack was an urban myth; Marcel had checked. "I thought most people hated Dissidents." Maybe I had misjudged Mandy, the way most people misjudged me.

She smiled sweetly at me. "My parents do, but my friends and I think they are really cool." I could see her friends watching us, with lots of whispering and giggling.

"So why did you come here, Mandy?" Pretty Gifted girls don't talk to me, double for Norm girls, to the point that the odds of the Protectorate freeing the Gifted were better than a beautiful Norm speaking to me.

A pretty blush lit her cheeks. "Well, honestly, I came on a dare."

"A dare?"

"Yes, I told my girlfriends it's wrong for people to be treated so badly, and they said I didn't know anything since I had never met a Mutt." She blurted out, before her hand covered her mouth. "O-M-G, I am like so sorry. I meant Gifted."

"And?" I snapped, a bit harsher than I should have.

"Well, then they dared me to come down here and kiss a Gifted." The blush intensified, staring down at her hands instead of me. "I don't want you to think I go around asking boys to kiss me, but I wanted to prove a point to my friends. They thought I would have to kiss one of those toughs or the tattoo freaks, but then you walked in. I thought if I kissed someone, he should be cute like you."

"So you want me to kiss you? Here?" These things didn't happen to me.

"Oh, no." She gasped. "I would die of embarrassment, kissing someone in public. I thought we could go behind the building."

"I don't know. I promised my..." *Okay, pretty girl asking to kiss me, and I'm about to tell her my mommy doesn't let me leave the building.*

I firmly pushed Mom from my mind, excitement rising at the thought of kissing Mandy. "Ummm, I can't be gone long."

She clapped. "Excellent, I'll be right back."

She ran over to her friends, and the giggling increased. She came back, wearing a long navy-blue coat, and grabbed my hand. "Let's go." Excitement radiated from her.

"Okay." *Ever the witty conversationalist.* I grabbed my jacket as I stood.

As we passed through the lobby, Blaze called from his usual perch at the front desk, "Tommy, what's up?"

"I'll be right back, just going out for a second," I said, quickening my pace, putting my coat on so I could get out the front door before he could stop me.

We walked around the black-painted brickwork of The Secret Lair and into a gravel parking lot behind it. A couple of cars sat unattended in the freshly plowed lot, probably the staff's. Mandy led me back to where the fire escape came down from the roof. She pulled me under the overhang.

"So you just want me to kiss you now?" I whispered, my voice quivering a bit more than I would have liked. I really didn't want to admit that at sixteen my mom was the only girl I had kissed.

Mandy laughed. "Like I would ever kiss a Mutt." Her face twisted into an ugly sneer. I looked over, and her girlfriends were watching from the corner of the building. Three big guys wearing varsity jackets turned the corner, strutted toward us.

"What's going on, Mandy?" I asked, but I knew. This kind of thing happened to me all the time.

The front guy, blond-haired and as pretty as Mandy, pulled her away from me. "Are you okay, babe?" he asked her.

Fear rose from the pit of my stomach like water from a backed-up toilet. My eyes darted around searching for an escape. I'd been ambushed by the kids in Redemption, but they weren't out to kill you.

"Chaz, I told you I could get one of them out here," she said, a cruel smile on her face. "I guess they are as stupid as they are lame."

Chaz barked out a harsh laugh. "I never doubted you, beautiful." His two behemoth friends moved around to make sure I couldn't run. I tried anyway but got thrown into the wall for my troubles. Mandy's girlfriends moved closer to watch.

"Look, I don't want any trouble. I'll just go back inside." I knew it was hopeless when I said it, but I had to try.

"After Mandy had to talk to you to get you out here? It'll take her a week to get the Mutt stench off her. My friends and I wanted to see how tough you mongrels really are." The other two laughed as each grabbed an arm to hold me still. *Chaz must not be able to hit a moving target.* He pulled back and punched me square in the stomach. The breath whooshed out of my lungs.

Mandy and her friends laughed, cheering on Chaz. *Big man, he can only beat up a guy with his arms held.* "Is that the best you can do?" I spat. They might beat me senseless, but I wasn't giving them the satisfaction of making me whine. "Maybe the girls should hold my feet for you."

"I don't need them to hold your feet, Mutt!" Two more punches to my stomach paid me for my smart mouth. I could taste vomit he had hit me so hard.

A stern voice came from behind the gang. "I think that's enough."

Chaz spun to confront the intruder. There stood mild-mannered Blaze, his arms crossed across his chest. "Go away, old man. This ain't none of your concern."

Blaze's tone sounded pleasant, like he spoke with an old acquaintance. "The boy was left in my care. Which makes it my concern."

The tough holding my left arm loosened his grip. "Maybe we should just go."

"No, Sal, we came here to have some fun. Ain't no old man gonna stop me when I'm having it," Chaz said as he turned back to Blaze. "You want him. You go through me, old man."

Chaz pulled his arm back to throw a punch. I swear Blaze didn't move, but the next second Chaz's head snapped back, and he landed on the ground. Blood flowed from his nose and down his chin. Droplets splattered his varsity jacket.

Blaze cracked his knuckles. "Young man, do yourself a favor and leave, now. I would hate for you to get hurt."

Chaz climbed to his feet, his nose still dripping blood. The girls all had looks of horror on their faces. Without an audience, Chaz might have left, but his pride was on the line.

Chaz circled Blaze, fist up, ready to fight. "Sal, Joey, get him."

Blaze stood so still you would have thought him a statue. Joey moved to the right, while Chaz moved to the left. Sal let out a yell similar to a charging elephant, which he could be confused for from behind, and ran straight at Blaze.

It amazed me to watch, though if you blinked, you'd have missed it. Blaze sidestepped Sal, kicked his feet out from under him, causing him to crash face first into the gravel. With a swift kick, he crushed Joey's left knee, sending him to the ground screaming in agony. Sal started to rise, only to catch a kick to the head, which knocked him out cold. Chaz, all sense having fled his pea brain, swung at Blaze, who caught his arm, reversed his grip, and promptly broke his arm. A swift kick in the ass sent Chaz straight into the unconscious Sal.

"You broke my throwing arm," Chaz wailed.

Blaze stood over his fallen opponent, grabbed his chin in a firm grip, and stared into his eyes. "I'm walking in to call an ambulance. You will tell them a gang jumped you. The girls will back you up." He looked at

Mandy. She nodded like a bobblehead doll in agreement. "If you tell them anything different, it will not end well for you. Do we understand each other?"

Chaz cradled his broken arm as he sobbed. He stared up at Blaze, fear written across his face. "Yes, sir." Mandy's girlfriends all bolted for an old station wagon, leaving her stranded with the injured boys.

Blaze pointed at me. "You, come with me."

I gulped. I knew I was in deep trouble. When my mother found out, I'd be dead, if Blaze didn't kill me first.

Even with death imminent, or because of it, I stopped as I reached Mandy. "Still want that kiss?" I asked sarcastically. She turned and ran, crying. I thought not, but it was worth a shot.

3
_____

Blaze jerked me by the arm, around the building, through the front door and straight to his office. I would have grabbed my arm away but for two things: first, I'm not strong, and second, he had me in a wrist hold that if I even hesitated, hurt so bad I thought I would pass out. So, as dignified as I could, I kept up the best I could.

He threw the office door open, shoved me in, and slammed the door behind him. He looked as calm as a massing thunderhead. Okay, I would have been happy with a thunderhead. After watching him dismantle Chaz and his goon friends, I was a bit scared.

"What do you think you were doing?" I could see the anger flashing in his eyes.

"Well." *As you can tell, I have a way with words.*

"Trying to get yourself killed, perhaps? Your mother asked me to watch out for you and you go and run off with some chick you just met. Let me ask, are you brain damaged or just plain stupid?"

"Ahhh, I guess...stupid?" Witty banter was my specialty. I wanted to curl up under a large rock and die.

"That would be my guess."

"Wait, did you say my mother asked you? You know my mother?" I blurted out. I am oh-so-observant sometimes.

"Yes, as a matter of fact I do."

The intercom on the desk chirped. "Blaze, we got Reclaimers coming down the street," Max from the front desk said. "Might be a random sweep, but given the trouble..."

Blaze uttered a couple of words my mother would not approve of. He flipped a switch and the four monitors on the wall lit up and the street outside sprang into view, as did the sides, the back, and the roof of The Secret Lair. Three toughs in Reclaimer patrol uniforms headed toward the shop. I saw them the last time I'd been here when they checked collars. The collars couldn't be removed outside The Block. Marcel's theory, and he had theories about everything, consisted of the collar had micro hooks which affixed to your skin to keep it in place. Still, any convenient excuse to hassle Gifted.

"Okay, Tommy. Those Reclaimers mean business. You've got to disappear." He hit the talk button on the video intercom. "Max, stall them. I've got to take out the trash."

Max winked at the camera. "Will do, boss. We can't let anything happen to Tommy."

"Where can I go? My mom won't be here for a couple of hours." I sounded a bit shrill, but if the Reclaimers thought I did something to Chaz, they could take me away, permanently.

"Quiet," Blaze said. He pulled out a keyboard and started typing. A second later, a panel in the wall slid open. He sprang up and led me to the opening. "You go down and stay down until I come get you. Understand?"

"Where am I going?"

"To The Secret Lair. Didn't you read the sign?"

The door slid shut, a light overhead flickered on, and the elevator sped downward. After a couple of seconds and a gentle stop, my stomach returned to its rightful place. If Alice had gone down a cyberpunk rabbit hole, this is where she would have come out in. Marcel would have died and thought he'd gone to heaven.

Before me lay a cavernous expanse, filled with technology and space-aged furniture. To the right stood an enormous concrete table circled by twelve Carbinium chairs with blue and silver padding. One of the chairs could have fit our couch, with room to spare. To the left stood a kitchen the likes I'd never seen. Huge refrigerators, four stoves and a wall of ovens. Mom would have been in her glory in a place like this.

I crept across to where a thirty-foot arch opened on to a room; a wall

19

of TVs with a semi-circle of padded armchairs A solid piece of stone rested before an enormous couch, which had been centered before the video wall. The main screen must have been a two-hundred-inch model surrounded by smaller screens. Our TV would have been laughed off the wall.

My head rotated like it was on a swivel, swinging left to right in a futile attempt to see everything. Another doorway stood on the right wall. After the first ride, my stomach wouldn't be pleased to enter it. I perched on the edge of the couch, next to a remote control. If I moved all the way back, my feet wouldn't reach the floor.

The main TV bloomed to life as I did, splitting into quadrants, each showing part of The Secret Lair upstairs. An adjacent set showed the outside views and feeds from what could only be local sources, both Reclaimer and Protectorate.

I focused on the view of Blaze at the front desk. "...disturbance out back earlier today. You know what happened?" The officer appeared a bit out of shape for the Reclaimers, must be why he pulled walking a beat in Great Falls instead of duty in Redemption or the Block.

"Just what I told dispatch when I called for the ambulance, officer," Blaze said. "I heard a noise out back and saw the three injured boys."

I cringed. What if Chaz told the Reclaimers what really happened? Not only would they be looking for me, they would shut Blaze down and maybe arrest him, too. I needed to get as far from here as possible. I ran to the elevator that had let me off, but I couldn't find the center seam for the door to the elevator, let alone a button to call it.

Get a grip, Tommy. I took a deep breath and went back into the room to sit back on the couch.

The officer stared at Blaze; obviously, he didn't believe him. "The boys told us a gang of kids jumped them, but gangs usually rob them after they beat them."

"Well, good," Blaze said with a smile. "It doesn't seem any of their injuries are life-threatening."

"No, they aren't, but it doesn't add up, Mr. Thomas."

"Those boys looked pretty tough to me. Maybe they scared their attackers off?"

Max stepped on camera and tapped Blaze on the shoulder. "Here's the surveillance clip the officer asked for." He immediately left, and he reappeared somewhere else, but I remained riveted on the scene with Blaze.

"Thanks, Max," Blaze muttered to empty air before handing the chip to the officer. The officer pulled a viewer out from his utility belt and snapped in the chip. He watched for a minute, sighed, and put the viewer away.

"Well, the video appears pretty conclusive. Thank you for your time, Mr. Thomas." The officer turned to leave and motioned for the other two to follow.

I decided it was a good time to breathe. I'd been sure Chaz would squeal to the Reclaimers. Blaze's warning must have penetrated Chaz's thick skull, so he kept to the story. They were beyond scared. Even mentioning a Gifted had started the fight would have been enough for me to be arrested. I can't believe how stupid I could be. I wanted to bang my head on the wall. Mom told me not to leave, Blaze tried to stop me, but Captain Stupidity went for a stroll with the pretty girl. If it had happened to someone else, I would have laughed at him for being an idiot.

Blaze didn't make a sound as he entered the room. Self-loathing must make you deaf. I just about wet my pants when he laid his hand on my shoulder.

"Sorry, Tommy." He walked over and took the seat next to me, laying the backpack I'd left upstairs at my feet. "I take it you saw my conversation with the Reclaimers?"

"Yeah, the displayed turned on when I sat down." Another screw-up to add to the list. I should have stayed in bed. "How did you have footage of a gang attack?"

"Dude, you aren't the first Gifted to screw up here. Lucky for us, Max is a wiz with digital images." The surfer personality, which hadn't been around while dealing with Chaz, snapped back into place. I liked it a lot more than the angry look from earlier.

"That's cool."

"True, but you have to understand though nowhere is safe for you, dude."

"I'm really sorry, Blaze," I stammered a bit trying to get it out. "She seemed so nice, and I figured if they came here, she couldn't be bad." I realized my face flushed with embarrassment.

"Tommy, I was sixteen once, a long, long time ago." He chuckled.

"She's a babe, and I'm sure all the Norms ignore you. It's tough enough being a teenager without the burden of having a Gift."

"Some Gift. More like a curse."

The smile vanished. "Tommy, your abilities, whatever they might be, are a Gift. It's the Reclaimers who don't see it them for what they are." I felt like his eyes would bore through my head the way he glared at me. "I would give anything to have your Gift."

"I wish I could give it to you."

Blaze rubbed his forehead. "Let me tell you a story, Tommy." He walked over and grabbed a silver picture frame from a shelf near the TV. "When I was a bit older than you, I worked with a team called Stryke Force. We fought criminals, both Gifted and not."

"I thought only the Gifted had teams?"

"No, there are a lot of people who fought crime, but the government only sponsored the Gifted teams. We did a lot of security work to pay the bills."

"I didn't know that."

"Before you were born." His voice had a softer tone than usual. "Raychel Downs, Pepper Spray was her alias, and we fell in love." He paused to show me the picture. Pepper Spray had neon orange hair cut super short and a mischievous grin on her face like she had a secret. I could see why Blaze liked her.

"As a kid, she had been struck by a car. She lost a leg and suffered a lot of damage. In college, she volunteered for a project to replace her missing parts with robotics, effectively making her a cyborg. After getting her Electrical Engineering degree, she built enhancements so she could fight crime." He took the picture back, cradling it in his hands as if it would break from touching it.

"The five of us, Pepper, Alyx the Summoner, Gladiator, Death Adder, and I went on a mission. It should have been a quick bit of intel gathering and home." He carried the photo back to the case, his back to me. "We walked right into an ambush. Alyx fell, a blast took off both legs under the knee. Pepper was cut down in cold blood by a psychopath." He stopped, staring intently at the picture. I could almost feel him reliving that day. "If it hadn't been for Jack Taylor and his team, we'd have all been killed."

"You mean Mr. Taylor?" I asked astonished.

"One and the same. Hero didn't come close to describing Jack. After all he did for me, I'd never work for the Protectorate."

I'd never known Mr. Taylor had been on a powered team.

Blaze coughed. "You see, Tommy, I don't have a Gift. If I had, I might have been able to get to her before she died."

I saw the anguish in his face as he held the frame in his hands. I knew the feeling; I'd be able to fight back if I had access to my Gift.

"Sorry." He held the photo for a minute or so. He placed the frame back on the shelf. When he turned around the old Blaze came back, big smile forced on to his face.

I pushed the fear and worry away. I couldn't get dragged down into self-pity now. "So what is this place?"

"Dude, it's The Secret Lair." He laughed. "Everyone assumes that what's the upstairs is, and we let them."

"But why have it? There aren't any more crime-fighting groups." I fidgeted, adrenaline still coursed through my veins.

"Ahh, but there are. Just because you don't have powers, doesn't mean you can't fight crime, but that's not what you meant, I'm sure. Your father built this place a long time ago, so I keep it safe."

I jumped off the sofa. "You've met my father!" My mother would never discuss the subject. She said it was too dangerous for me to know.

Blaze stopped, concern flashed across his face. "Your mother hasn't told you?"

"No, I haven't." Mom's voice shot from behind us.

I am so dead. I turned, realizing we hadn't noticed the hiss of the elevator doors opening. There stood five feet six inches of blond fury in high heels. Her face flushed red, and I swear she shook with rage.

"Susan, you have to tell the boy," Blaze started.

"No, Eugene, I don't. I am his mother, and I'll be damned if you'll tell me what is best for my son."

"But—" I'll give him this: it took a brave man to keep going.

"Eugene, shut it. I told you before this is none of your business."

"But it is mine, Mom, and I want to know," I blurted out. *Oh man, I'm dead now. Why does my mouth always run before the brain kicks in?*

She paused. Some of the red left, and her eyes didn't appear as crazy as before. "Tommy, your father is a wonderful man, but he is very dangerous. You have to trust me, honey. I will tell you, but not until you are older."

"I am not a baby, Mom!" My voice wavered, which kind of ruined the effect I wanted, but I was pissed off. "You can't control me forever. I deserve to know."

I grabbed my backpack and stormed across the room, fully intending to leave. Only problem here, I still couldn't figure out how to open the damn elevator. I just stood there, bag in hand, staring at a blank wall, my face getting hot with embarrassment.

I heard the click of Mom's heels as she came up behind me. "Tommy, why are you down here and not upstairs?"

Damn. Max must have told her what happened. I hung my head. *I'm toast.*

"No reason." Truly a lame response, but I couldn't come up with anything better under the circumstances.

"Really?" Is there a class moms go to teaching them how to pack all that sarcasm into one word? I will never understand how one word can say "I know you did something you weren't supposed to and think I'm too stupid to figure out you did it, but I know exactly what you did, and you better tell me or it will be far worse for you, mister."

"We had a misunderstanding with one of the girls upstairs today," Blaze said.

"So your definition of a 'misunderstanding' is you had to stop an assault on my son before the juvenile delinquents murdered him? Am I mistaken?"

I glanced at Blaze. He shrugged his shoulders in defeat. Sometimes you have to realize when the battle is lost, I guess.

"That doesn't mean I shouldn't know who my father is!" A bit louder than I intended, but I was right.

"Tommy, I told you to stay inside while I went into work, didn't I?" She used the lawyer voice on me now. The "I-am-totally-reasonable-and-you-are-a-liar" tone sprang into full force.

"Yes, ma'am, but—"

"Did you stay inside?"

I'm so screwed. "No, ma'am."

"Well, your father is a million times more dangerous than outside. If you slip, you could be killed. Do you understand?"

My gaze wandered around the room in search of anything that could help me. The Carbinium chairs, the three-foot-thick walls, the state of the art kitchen. This place could withstand almost anything. Why would you need a hidden base if you were a hero?

Because the villains would kill you whenever they could. *Oh crap.*

"But you told Blaze," I whined halfheartedly.

"Eugene? Can you please tell Tommy why you know without any details, please?"

I waited as Blaze sat rubbing his chin. He didn't look pleased, but he did what Mom asked.

"Your dad told me so I could protect you." The normal cheer had left his voice. "He figured your mom would need someone she could trust while he was imprisoned."

Mom glanced at me. I could tell she was upset, but I had the right to know who I am. "Your father made sure no one found out about his secret identity. A lot of the Gifted 'heroes' got big heads and talked about who was important in their lives, attended events without protecting their identities. When the Reclamation War started, they had nowhere to go, and their families paid for it, a lot of times with their lives." She reached out and rubbed my back. "When you get older, I promise I will tell you everything, and if anything happens to me, Eugene has permission to tell you. Deal?" She held out her hand for me to shake.

I wanted to refuse, but I took her hand. "Deal." It would be the best deal I'd get from counsel.

In all fairness to the kids, mothers shouldn't be allowed to be lawyers.

4

Monday morning came, as always, and I went off to school, though Mom took me there before continuing on to file some paperwork at the courthouse. After Saturday's fiasco, I think she worried about me taking the bus.

Marcel stepped off the second of the Institute's buses, so we walked in together. The majority of the Gifted kids lived at the Institute. Parents handed their kids over to the Reclaimers rather than move here as required. Montana wasn't exactly a hotbed of activity. Leaving your whole life behind for a Gifted didn't hold much appeal for Norms. Once Gifted reached eighteen, they had the option to move to Great Falls where a job would be provided for them or they could work at The Block. The rumors suggested Gifted being drafted into the military, but as far as I knew, the Reclaimers never trusted Gifted regardless that they couldn't use their powers. The collars of Gifted are only removed in two instances: refitting and death.

"Did you see Wendi yet?" Marcel asked. The Stevens twins lived at the Institute with him, so he always got to see her, the pearl in the rotten oyster of The Institute.

"No, Mom dropped me off. She's a bit paranoid after the weekend." I filled him in on the girl at The Secret Lair and the fight. I left out the rest, per Mom's orders. She would say request, but the tone in her voice brooked no deviation from her instructions, and after breaking her rule on Saturday, I wouldn't be breaking another.

Mr. Taylor stood inside the front door with a new student, a tall girl who had dark hair on one side, fire engine red on the other. Half Goth, half punk, miracles never cease in Redemption.

"Marcel, Thomas." He nodded to each of us in turn. "This is Abby Thompson, a new member of our school. She will be on the same track as you both. Could you please show her around the school and explain the rules to her?"

"Sure thing, Mr. T," Marcel said, pushing up his glasses and trying to stand straighter. His 'fro made him look taller than his six feet, but Abby had about half an inch on him if his hair was matted down. "It's a pleasure to meet you, Abby."

I tilted my head toward Marcel, a puzzled expression on my face. *My uber-geeky friend has been replaced by an alien, I'm sure of it. Pleasure to meet you?*

"Yeah, right," she replied. Her attitude screamed, "Don't mess with me." She wore her black leather jacket like armor. It made her silver collar gleam even more. As I got closer, I could see faint bruises poking out from under her Goth makeup.

"Come on, Marcel." After the weekend, I wasn't much in the mood to deal with girls with attitude. As Marcel and I headed down the hall toward class, I glanced back. Abby stood with Mr. Taylor, who appeared dumbfounded. "You coming?" I asked impatiently.

She glared at me, threw her backpack over a shoulder, and shoved past me.

I stared at Mr. Taylor. "Really? Why me?"

"She came from a bad situation, Tommy. She's scared and could use a friend. You been in her shoes before, you know."

"Great, just what I need." I wished Marcel's alien overlords would appear to save me, but no such luck. But Mr. Taylor had it right. I did know how it felt to be alone and scared. Saturday had reinforced that lesson quite a bit. I turned and entered school, another fun-filled day in the pen.

It was a quiet morning before second bell, for the most part. I almost spoke to Wendi, but my voice gave out when I tried. Our hands did touch when I handed her the folder she dropped as we passed in the hall on the way to history. *It's official, I am a loser.* I froze every time I saw her. She was elegant like a dancer; every movement flowing like mercury sliding across a mirror, her collar a symbol of royalty, not a shackle. The Norm boys treated her differently than the rest of us. There weren't jokes and insults; they stared at her and drooled. Norms don't touch Gifted, even if they are the most beautiful girl they've ever seen.

Abby was a different story. I tried to speak to her a few times on the way to class, receiving grunts and glares for my trouble. Her hair hung straight, black as night, making the red side even more jarring. Her being taller than me and somewhat muscular made me feel even skinnier than when it's just me and Marcel. She stomped down the halls, pushing past people as she went. A couple of girls made comments, and we had to keep her going. Attention is not healthy for Gifted.

Unfortunately, Mr. Powell's history class would start our day. Powell the war "hero" who had taken down the Cyclone Ranger of Omega Squad, one of the toughest Gifted around. Powell lost his whole team and displayed the scars and a pronounced limp from the lightning Cyclone Ranger used.

We sat down before Powell entered the room. The bell rang and still no Powell. I was beginning to think I might have one class of peace and quiet without Powell but no such luck. Powell, in his perfectly pressed Reclaimers uniform as always, strode through the door a manila folder under his arm. He set his hat on his desk, pulled the folder from under his arm, and turned to face the class, tapping the folder on his bad hand. Powell's grin told me he had something up his sleeve, and that it wouldn't be pleasant.

"Today, class, we will be discussing the penalties associated with the harboring of fugitives from the Reclaimers."

I'm sure the last thing a fish sees before the shark eats him sums up the way Powell stared at Abby.

"Wendell, what is the punishment for stealing a car?" he asked, strolling around the class, like he had all the time in the world. Under the circumstances, forty-five minutes was an eternity in hell.

Wendell scratched at his nose. "Prison, sir."

"Correct." Powell grinned. "How about, oh…say, murder?"

Wendell's hand flew up, but Powell ignored him. Instead, he looked at me.

"Mr. Ward?"

"Prison, possibly the death penalty." I waited for him to pounce. He only ever called on me to humiliate me in front of the class.

"So, we have varying degrees of punishment for different crimes," he said as he walked up and stood behind Marcel's desk. "So, what determines the degree of punishment? Mr. Quinn?"

Marcel actually flinched. Marcel feared Powell the way a claustrophobic does enclosed spaces. "I guess that would be the degree to which the legal system deems the behavior is unacceptable, sir."

"Correct, Mr. Quinn." He clapped his hand on Marcel's shoulder, beaming at his answer. This stank more than the locker room after wrestling practice.

"So, we've established the more heinous the crime, the worse the punishment." He stopped pacing and slapped the heel of his hand to his forehead. "Class, I have been irresponsible today." He strode across the room and stood in front of Abby's desk. I could see the tab on the folder now, it read Abigail Thompson.

"Class, this is Miss Abigail Thompson. She joins us from far-away Argentina, but she hails from Boston."

A few snickers and catcalls of Slag, Mutt, and bitch floated around the room. Abby's head was bowed, studying the clenched fists in her lap. Anger flared around Abby; her body shook with the effort to control it.

"So, Miss Thompson, do you happen to know the penalty for people who harbor fugitives?"

Abby's head shot up. Her eyes blazed with pure hatred for Powell, a snarl any predator would have been proud of escaping her lips.

"Mr. Powell," I said in my best dumb but innocent voice. "Did you ever serve in Argentina during the Reclamation Wars?"

He ignored me. "Miss Thompson, answer the question."

Abby shook, her fists unclenched to grip her thighs as she fought to control herself. If she struck Powell, she'd be in The Block before the end of the day, never to return. She took a deep breath and locked eyes with Powell, submitting defiantly. "They are executed."

"Why, yes, they are, aren't they? And to answer your question, Mr. Ward." He gave me his best "I won, you lost" look. "I fought on the east coast. I wanted to protect the country I love from a menace that almost destroyed it." He turned and walked back to the board, tossing Abby's file on his desk.

"Thanks," Abby whispered, her hands still gripping her thighs.

I nodded. Powell started into the history of the sub-continental destruction, but I didn't listen. I watched Abby out of the corner of my eye. On the outside she's tough as nails, but I wondered why Powell got to her so bad.

Marcel, who sat behind me, tapped me on the back. I leaned back in my chair so I could hear him better.

"Bruh, Powell's lucky she didn't fatality his ass," he whispered.

I kept my eyes straight ahead, no reason to piss off Powell anymore today. When calm and rational, he was at his worst. I wondered if Cyclone Ranger messed up more than his face.

"Bruh, if she'd hit him, it would've been all over." I could sense him shaking his head in disbelief. "What are we going to do? Mr. T asked us to watch out for her."

I didn't know any more than Marcel did. I wouldn't wish being sent to The Block on my worst enemy. Well, that isn't true. Brunner, I would make an exception for. And Powell, I would make an exception for him as well.

The bell rang. I grabbed my bag and moved to intercept Abby. We needed to have a talk about how things worked here before anything got out of hand. Marcel had the same idea as we escorted her from the room.

"Oh, Miss Thompson," Powell said from the front of the room. "One week's detention for not answering my question. You are dismissed."

"Welcome to the club." *It's going to be a long day.*

5

—————————————

It had been a week since the fiasco at The Lair, and I still checked over my shoulder for Reclaimer soldiers. Having Marcel over for the weekend would have helped, but most weekends they "lost" the paperwork or closed the office early or a litany of other reasons. Every third weekend they delivered, having figured out that after three, there would be legal hassles.

To make matters worse, it was the first Monday of the month, known as "field trip" day for the Gifted kids. Now I'm all for a day off school, but these weren't fun excursions to museums or to see a play. No, we got to go to The Block. Each of us has our collars tested, and refitted if necessary, all to ensure the public's safety. A Norm camera crew from some place in Texas followed us once to document the Reclaimers making the world safe for humanity. Overall, I think I would have rather been in school.

All of the Gifted teachers accompanied us, but this month, Waxenby escorted our particular group. According to the rumors, he had been a fighter called Commander Gravity back in the day. He didn't look heroic. He had a slight build with thinning sandy brown hair and a cheesy mustache. The only reason I gave any credence to the rumors is he walks with a pronounced limp. The kids are always making up names for him behind his back. Wonder Wimp and The Limp Avenger are the kinder versions I'd heard floating down the hall behind him.

After homeroom, they loaded us all on the specially manufacture Gifted Transport unit; we called it The Chain. Any resemblance to a school bus was strictly accidental. Two rows of seats faced toward the center aisle.

A guard from The Block searched me, finding nothing, as always. You learned early, anything on you ended up in the trash. In elementary school, the young kids would try to bring stuffed animals or blankets only to have them torn from them. The sound of sobbing surrounded the process of loading the bus the first few months every year as newly collared elementary kids were sent here.

The guards escorted me to my seat to buckle me in. This isn't your mom's seatbelt. Take a race car driving harness, add enough Carbinium to stop a rhinoceros, mix in a generous helping of damping circuits and you have the super seatbelt, guaranteed to stop even the worst offender dead in their tracks.

The guards strapped me in quickly and efficiently, they didn't get rough unless they felt you resisting. Abby made the mistake of pulling her arm away from one of the escorting guards, a woman who'd we nick-named Helga, with a long blond braid down her back and a unibrow. She grabbed the shock stick from the holster and jabbed it into Abby's back. She screamed as the energy surge hit her and crumbled like a used paper bag. A broken stream of obscenities flowed out of her mouth as she convulsed on the floor.

The two guards scooped her up and dumped her into the seat across from me. She drooled a bit while they belted her in. The guard checked her harness and moved on to bringing in Marcel. They restrained him without incident in the seat to my immediate right. We could talk, though the restraints made it a difficult task.

"What happened to her?" Marcel asked, watching the now twitching Abby.

I shook my head. "She pulled away from the Helga."

Marcel whistled. "Is she crazy or suicidal?"

"Got me, buddy." Luckily the guards handled things professionally, unlike the Reclaimers who patrolled Redemption. Every once in a while you got a mean one. They could hurt you, and you couldn't do anything to stop them.

The rest of the ride went by uneventfully. Marcel told me about the new tablet he wanted to get later this year. It made the day go by faster when we could sit near each other, even when I could only understand half the words he said. With six buses full of kids and teachers, you didn't always get to sit with your friends.

After a fifteen-minute drive, I could see the top of The Block in the distance. I felt my heart pounding against my chest and sweat dripped off my finger, pooling on the floor.

Get ahold of yourself, I yelled in my head. Every month the same panic attack, the rational brain fighting for control over the caged animal.

Half a day and we'd be out, riding back to Redemption. Mom would have meatloaf for dinner. But what if they decided to detain me? What if I never saw my mom again? My brain ran wild with dark thoughts as we moved closer to our version of hell.

The bus halted. I fought back a wave of nausea forcing its way up my throat. I gagged on the taste of bile but swallowed it down. The door's pneumatic pump hissed as it opened. The guard approached me. He pulled out a scanner and verified my name and collar ID. I kept my eyes down, barely breathing. Then the guard left. I chewed my lip waiting to hear something confirming things had gone wrong, but nothing happened. The all-clear shout came, and we moved into The Block. I tried to see outside, just in case it turned out to be the last time.

We drove into the terminal and stopped. The guards ushered us off the bus, with Abby dumped unceremoniously at our feet. Helga glared at both of us but didn't say anything. Everything ran smoothly. We had been doing this since kindergarten when we arrived in Redemption, having failed the Gifted testing. No one knew what those Gifts might be, but the machine indicated we had them, so the collar went on and our freedom ended.

Mom told me she guessed I'd be Gifted but decided I'd be safer collared than hunted for the rest of my life. Marcel's parents, and a lot of other families, weren't so lucky. A school official and two Reclamation soldiers in full combat gear brought him home. I can't imagine opening the door to see your kindergarten son collared and soldiers with automatic weapons at the ready to kill any troublemakers. It had to be the worst day of their lives, especially since Marcel had two younger sisters, the stress of waiting for years, knowing their other children could be ripped away like Marcel had been. In the end, his father signed the papers as his mother sobbed uncontrollably. Marcel told me his mother had packed his teddy bear so he wouldn't be scared. He had also told me he'd thrown it out, but I saw it in the back of his locker at the Institute. I didn't mention it. He had been through enough the way I saw it. I guess if your best friend can't cut you some slack, who will?

The Block's guards hoisted Abby, carrying her into the facility. Her shoes dragged on the polished concrete floor, smudging the perfectly shining surface. Hospitals could take cues from The Block. Everything was perfectly maintained; the white walls glistened. But if you knew what to look for, you could see the truth: you had no say in what happened here. The massive doors had Carbinium plating on the outside; the halls ran long and straight. Even where the hallways turned, the rounded corners kept you from being able to get a grip on the wall. They didn't take any chances in this place. It made me even more impressed the Grim Reaper had found a way out.

Marcel and I helped Abby into one of the chairs; her hands were zip-tied. Everything in the waiting room sat anchored into the concrete of the floor. The ceilings must be twenty feet high with turrets mounted at fixed intervals. If it took more than a couple seconds to kill the hundred plus people, I'd be surprised.

Every few minutes, the door would buzz, and the guards would come out and get the next person in line. They carried shock sticks, but nothing that could be taken or used against the facility. Cameras tracked the guards' every step. If anything went wrong, the operator sounded the alarm and all hell broke loose.

Once you passed inspection, they took you to the Holding Tank, a mirror image of this room. No one could return to school until everyone had been checked. The Air-Lock didn't hold a candle to The Block's facilities. Of course, none of us knew our powers or how to use them if we did. Still, no one had ever escaped from the Redemption School system.

The guards stopped in front of Marcel. He winked at me as they took him for his collar calibration. The Block had my nerves dancing like water on a hot skillet, but if Marcel worried about it, he never showed it.

I looked over at Abby. She studied the room with a critical eye, her arms straining against the restraints. "Relax before you get yourself hurt. You're lucky the guards didn't do more than shock you."

She grunted, but her arms relaxed. The lights dimmed to the point of darkness, then popped on again. I'd never seen it before, but it had been one of those days.

The guards retrieved me, taking my arms as I stood to go. Their grips were firm, but not painful. In a way, I admired the guards. Unlike some people, they tended not to be mean, just very serious about doing their job. As long as you didn't give them trouble, you didn't get any.

We set off down the hallway to the room we referred to as "The Freezer." This is the only room you are allowed to have your collar off. The door depressurized, swinging open without a sound. I always felt like I should be on the Death Star headed to the holding cells. No Luke Skywalker would be coming to save the day. I dropped into the chair, waiting while the guards set the wrist and ankle cuffs. Once they double-checked the restraints, they left and sealed the door.

"Good morning, Thomas," Dr. Sampson said from where he sat across the room. The ever-present drone of the dampeners filled The Freezer. Like everything else in The Block, nothing could be moved, and embedded lights filled the room with a blueish glow.

"Good morning, Dr. Sampson."

He picked up a tablet from the silver table he stood next to. He swiped a couple of times before addressing at me. "How is school going?"

Of all the people in Redemption, Dr. Sampson is my favorite Norm, a quick smile, always pleasant, and really cared about us. If you saw him in town, he would stop and talk to you. He played pro-basketball before the war and stood taller than any man I knew. His bald head was always a bit damp with sweat, which made it remind me of a piece of polished onyx I had seen in earth science.

"Okay." I shrugged. He tapped his tablet a couple of times, and the wrist restraints popped open, though the ankle ones still held me firm.

"Please take off your shirt, Thomas." I tried to tell him not to bother, but he held up his hand to stop me. "We are sitting here until you do."

I groaned. I pulled up my shirt to reveal the purple and black bruises left over from the last beating Brunner had given to me.

"Who did this to you?" Anger flared across his features. We had been through this before. The last time he had filed a complaint, Ms.

Robinson asked a couple pointed questions and I got my butt kicked after school.

"A guy at school, but you can't snitch. The vice principal tells the guys who are reported, and we get it worse."

"Thomas, it isn't right. You have the right to a safe education, regardless of your status."

"I know, but it only makes it worse."

He shook his head. I'm sure it killed him not to do something, but since the war, Gifted people were considered the enemy.

"Okay, I won't say anything. It appears your collar has gotten a bit small. I'm going to replace it."

He tapped his tablet, and a tray rose from the floor. A metal cover opened when Dr. Sampson reached for it. He took a tool from the tray, consulted his tablet again. The tray retracted into the floor with a hiss.

The collars appear to be a solid piece of metal, but they aren't. A latch holds the ends together so tightly the seam is invisible. The only people who can remove them work for the Reclaimers. Dr. Sampson brought over a thin, black device the size of a screwdriver and placed it at the back of my neck. The silver tube slid down and landed in my lap, more like a dead snake than the device stopping me from using my powers. Would knowing my power make it easier or just be more painful? My power could be screwing up, I do it a lot.

Being free of the collar felt amazing. A blast of air from overhead tickled my skin. Years of collaring made the freedom from it that much sweeter. The lights pulsed three times as Dr. Sampson fit me with a new collar. It tightened until it didn't move, but it didn't pull my skin as the old one had. I had grown more than I thought. After about ten minutes of calibrating the collar, Dr. Sampson snapped the collar around my neck once more, a prisoner.

"Okay, Thomas. I'll see you next month."

"Sure thing, Dr. Sampson." I tried to return his smile. Being collared like a rabid dog did nothing to improve my outlook on things. Dr. Sampson pressed a blue button on the wall, and the guards stomped into the room, removed the restraints, and walked me to the end of the corridor and through the security doors.

Ah, the Holding Tank. The architect of this place must be the dullest person in the world. Beige covered every square inch of the place. Even blue chair cushions would help, but who knew if a Gifted with a power over fabric would emerge and smother the guards?

At least I had finished with the inspection. Once you finished, you could hang out and talk. No one talked in the waiting room, not even during elementary school. I took a seat next to Marcel, whose fingers twitched. No tablets, phones, or any other gadgets drove him nuts.

All residents of The Institute's dorms had a stipend each month. They could purchase clothes, technology, and anything else they desired. Most of the kids used the supplies and toiletries the Protectorate provided, but having a non-Protectorate issued backpack or jacket at least gave the illusion of choice. Guilt-ridden parents could add to the stipend. Marcel's parents constantly added to his account, which supported his gadget habit.

Abby still wasn't out. I guess they shocked her a bit harder than we thought.

"Is that a new collar?" Marcel asked as I sat down.

"Yeah, how did you know?"

"The marking on the new ones is a tetrakaidecagon, where the old ones are dodecagon. The sheen is a bit different as well, probably a higher ratio of titanium to carbon fibers in the Carbinium-making process."

"Huh?" When Marcel talked tech, my brain sort of short circuited.

"Well, you see..." Marcel stopped mid-sentence. I followed his gaze to see Abby being brought from The Freezer. She limped along with a guard in tow, head lowered as if she silently prayed. She, somehow, looked different. Her black leather jacket hung; the hem of her jeans scraped along the floor. I dashed over to get her. Mr. Taylor had asked me to keep an eye on her, so at least she could sit with Marcel and me.

"You okay?"

"Fine," she grumbled.

The guard turned her around to face him. He stood a good half a foot taller than either of us, but he appeared a bit freaked out. "Are we going to have any more problems with you?"

I noticed Abby flinched when he put his hands on her. I didn't know her well, but something must have happened in there.

She smiled at him, the type of smile you see right before somebody does something supremely stupid. The guard took half a step back and put his hand on his shock stick. The guard had a pretty good bruise developing on his left eye.

"Why? You want another go?" Her tone sounded sugary sweet like she was flirting with him.

The guard started to pull out the shock stick. Somehow, I stood between them, my hand on the guard's. *It is official. I'm gonna die.*

"Officer, she won't cause any problems out here," I blurted a bit quicker than I would have liked. The nervousness in my voice didn't help either. "I'll take her to sit down. Her blood sugar is probably low from not eating breakfast."

The guard looked at my hand as it gripped his wrist. I removed it quickly. At that moment, I would have rather been in history class.

"Just make sure she doesn't, or I'm holding you personally responsible, Sport." The sport part he emphasized with a finger to my chest. *Great, another bruise for the collection.* The guard snapped his half-drawn stick back in place and left the Holding Tank.

Abby glared at me when I turned around.

"What?"

She punched me in the chest. "I don't need you fighting my battles." *What is it with hitting me in the chest today?*

"That's the point. There aren't any battles, especially here. You start something, and everyone else here pays for it."

"Whatever. You're blind to the fact you are doing their work for them. When you stop fighting, you become the sheep, and they keep you in line." She pushed past me, going to sit with Marcel. Abby definitely had issues, and stupid me jumped into the middle of them.

Someone touched me on the shoulder. Wendi stood there. My brain went numb while my mouth tried to work on its own. "Hi."

"Hey, Tommy." Her slight Iowan accent was music to my ears. "It was sweet of you to help out Abby."

"Alert, alert, this is not a drill. I repeat not a drill," blasted through my brain, while I stood there gaping like a brain-damaged idiot. I needed to say something, anything.

"I freaked out a bit." Except that.

She smiled and touched my arm. "Now, don't get modest on me. It took bravery to stand up for her."

"Thanks."

"I'll see you later, Tommy."

She spun on her heel and returned to her friends. Wendi Stevens thought I was brave. I could have busted out in dance, but didn't. A guy has to maintain his cool.

Marcel grinned ear to ear when I got back. "Wow, Bruh, Wendi talked to you."

"Not a big deal." I tried to sound cool about it. Plus, Abby didn't look in too good of shape. Her eyes, red ringed, looked like she had been crying.

"Thanks." Abby stared at the floor. "Marcel told me you took a huge risk. I didn't know they could lock you up for touching a guard."

"It's okay," I lied. "Plus, you'd have done the same for me."

Her eyes bored into me, searching for something. "You aren't mad?"

I was, or at least I should be. Wendi had kind of distracted me from being angry. "No, I'm not, but you have to listen to what we are telling you." Daily we had told her since Mr. T assigned us as caretakers last week, and she refused to listen. Maybe now it would sink in that we were serious, deadly serious.

"I will," Abby said, a bit sullen, but she sounded sincere.

"Do you want to tell us what happened?" I sat down on the floor in front of them.

"I woke up in the doctor's office. They hadn't restrained me, but the guard who brought me out stood there talking to the doctor." She peered around, probably to make sure we couldn't be overheard.

She lowered her voice and continued. "A power surge or something caused the dampening field to drop. Next thing I know, the guard's laid on the floor."

I hadn't seen the guard who had taken her in, but he must be new. Only the newbs would break regulation by allowing you to be in The Freezer unrestrained.

"A bunch of guards came in and forced me into the chair so I couldn't move. The doctor did something to my collar." She shuddered at the thought. "It felt like they tore something out of me."

I was at a loss for words. Even with the new collar, it had never hurt. Marcel looked puzzled as well. I hadn't ever heard of the collar causing pain. I'd have to ask Blaze next time I saw him. He'd been around more Gifted than any of us had.

39

"I'm sorry, but arguing with the guards isn't your best option. Keep your eyes down and your mouth shut. I don't know about Argentina, but bad things happen to troublemakers in Redemption."

"I didn't mean to cause any trouble for you guys." A stray tear rolled down her cheek. "You are the only ones who have been nice to me."

I nodded. I understood how she felt. The more friends you had, the more likely one would be taken away and sent to The Block. After a couple of friends disappeared, you got wary of making new friends.

"I wonder what's for lunch today," Marcel said, a grin crossing his face. "I hope it's tacos."

We laughed. Sometimes it's the little things that get you through the day. Your best friend or a friend you never thought you would have. You had to laugh in order to get by. The best way was being called brave by the coolest girl at school.

And Wendi called me brave.

6

I thought the weekend would never get here, but now all that stood between me and two days away from school was "detention." I walked in through the doors into a kicked hive of activity. The news reported another Gifted woman's body from Great Falls had been found mutilated in a grove of trees outside of Redemption. She'd been the fourth one over the last six months, all with their collars cut off.

The police chief spoke like people were jaywalking, not being murdered. If the victim had been a Norm, there would be a manhunt. They spent more time finding lost dogs than looking for the killer. This surprised no one, but it didn't make it right. Waxenby sat at the front desk, working on grading papers. I dropped my backpack and removed a pad of paper to doodle on, waiting for Abby and Marcel.

"Bruh, it's Friday!"

I fist-bumped Marcel as he flopped into his seat. Abby strode over and flopped in the desk across from me. She'd been in Redemption for almost two months—it didn't seem possible. Her bag hit the floor with a pronounced thud. "This thing gets heavier every day, I swear."

I laughed. "Long week."

Marcel took out the box containing the newest of the new tablets. "Man, the site glitched fierce. I got this for ten cred. Can you believe it?"

I shook my head. "Why didn't you order three?"

Abby reached over and gently tapped his forehead. "Marcel, you've got the brains, maybe you should use them."

He stammered as he answered. "Too excited, I bought it before they figured it out. It's been a weird week."

Abby agreed. "Yesterday, all the restraints disengaged on the ride back to the Institute. The guards stood ready to shoot."

I shook my head, thinking things like that don't happen in Redemption. The Reclaimers kept everything under control. Surprises got people killed.

Marcel charged into setting up his new tablet, muttering to himself about passwords, hack-proof, and assorted other tech-speak only he understood. Abby pulled out a deck of worn cards to help pass the time.

In the middle of our third game of gin rummy, which I was winning, the lights above flashed. Waxenby stood holding his hands up to calm the kids. "It's a drill, I think. Settle down and it will be over in a few minutes."

The noise lowered, but the buzz of frantic conversation continued. The lights dimmed, and a noise intruded into the room. A loud rushing sound emitted from the vents as they clacked open and hazy air blew into the room.

"Oh my God, they are gassing us!" someone yelled. Desks hit the floor as kids ran toward the Air-Lock doors. Waxenby yelled, "Get to the floor, stay as low as possible." What good would it do if they pumped in toxic gas, I didn't know, but I dove to the floor as instructed.

Screams and crying filled the room. Waxenby called for calm but to no avail. Some of the kids stood pounding on the Air-Lock door. They'd pound their hands bloody before anyone outside would hear them.

The loudspeaker crackled before a strong, clear voice announced. "Attention, students and faculty. The facility engineers reported the air handlers overloaded and purged the system, resulting in the vents expelling large amounts of dust and debris. The situation is under control. Please resume your normal activities."

Waxenby stood. "Please take your seats. Given the circumstances, I commend you all on your behavior during this mishap. I'm very proud of you all."

He stooped to retrieve the papers that had fallen off his desk. Marcel stood, offering Abby a hand. She must be in shock because she took it, and he helped her up. Then she punched him in the shoulder more out of ritual than anger. He laughed as they picked up their stuff from the floor. I pulled myself to my feet and grabbed my cards.

Abby smiled. "Misdeal!"

I threw the cards on the desk. "Of course, I was finally winning."

After losing four more games, we packed up as the final bell sounded. My stomach unknotted as the door swung open. I hadn't realized how tense I had been until it left. I noticed Abby's demeanor shifted out of high gear fight mode to her normal "I'll punch the crap out of anyone who pisses me off." Even Marcel heaved a sigh of relief as we hurried to get out of the Air-Lock.

Abby led the way. I wouldn't say we ran, but the room emptied much faster than usual. The teachers led us down to the bus lot where Abby and Marcel would be loaded on The Chain back to the Institute. It was a beautiful spring day, most of the snow had melted, and it was warm, well warm for Montana. We turned the corner, and Mom stood by the bus. Seeing us, she waved and then walked over to Vice Principal Robinson. Mom passed something to her. Robinson opened the piece of paper, shook her head, and said something to Mom I couldn't hear. Mom hands folded in front of her, a stern expression settling on her face when she replied.

Robinson looked to the sky as if asking God to intervene, but nothing happened. She pushed the paper back to Mom and strode off.

A smirk firmly affixed to her face approached us. My friends both muttered hello before angling off to be put on the bus. "Excuse me," Mom said in mock offense. "I thought you might enjoy staying over tonight, but I guess not."

Marcel stopped dead in his tracks. "Excellent!"

I whooped, the weekend pass finally come through.

Abby shot Marcel a disappointed glance as she continued toward the bus.

"That means you as well, Miss Thompson." Leave it to Mom to pull off double weekend passes. I wish I could have seen the administrator's smug grin wiped off her face when Mom got approval for those.

Abby paused, froze, then turned around slowly. "Are you serious? A sleepover with boys? We aren't five." Although her tone was cold, the gleam of hope sparkled in her eyes.

43

Mom laughed. "I'm sure if they do anything inappropriate, you'll box their ears."

Abby smiled as she strode back to us. "Damn straight I will." She winked at my mom.

Mom threw her arm around Abby's waist and moved toward the car. "We'll stop and get your clothes then grab pizza on the way home."

Marcel and I fist bumped. Marcel licked his lips. "Real pizza, yum. Can we get pineapple?"

I groaned. "Pineapple isn't a pizza topping. I can't believe you eat that crap."

"Crap? You eat tuna fish with skittles. That, my friend, is gross." Marcel pushed his afro back off his forehead, trying in vain to control the wildness of his hair. Abby being around made him stranger than normal.

"Skittles are fruit. I'm just getting my vitamin C with my sandwich."

"Are you serious? Skittles aren't fruit."

My witty response would have to wait. Abby and Mom sat in the car. Not wanting to be left behind, I tapped Marcel. "We'd better get going."

We ran to the car laughing the whole way. Things were back to normal, for now.

We ended up with three pizzas. I got pepperoni, Marcel ham and pineapple, and Abby all meat. None of them survived dinner. Mom had a salad. We set up a folding table in the living room so we could study for our English final. Mr. Taylor was my favorite teacher, always sticking up for us, and we didn't want to let him down.

We had unpacked our book bags when Mom stuck her head around the corner. "Abby, can I talk to you for a minute?"

She appeared surprised but answered. "Sure thing, Mrs. Ward."

Mom smiled at her. "Marcel calls me Mom, and when you are comfortable, you can as well."

"Okay." I could tell Abby didn't know how to take it.

"But for now," Mom said, "we have something to discuss away from these uncouth boys."

Abby laughed as she went with Mom.

I yelled after them. "The school nurse told you I didn't have any couths. She checked my scalp. Mom was there."

The laughter increased. Marcel put his head in his hands. "Couth is manners, not cooties, which are lice."

"Oh."

Marcel and I got our books and notes situated, grabbed Mountain Dews from the fridge for the three of us, sat down, and pulled up a video on Marcel's tablet while we waited for Abby.

After a bit of time, Mom appeared in the doorway. "Gentlemen, may I present Ms. Abby Thompson." She waved Abby in.

Abby stepped into the living room. At least I think it was her. Gone were the ill-fitting ripped jeans, t-shirt, and leather jacket, her punk-Goth uniform replaced with a black and white top and a below-the-knee black skirt. Black and silver shoes had taken the place of her combat boots, and her hair was pulled up into a ponytail. I almost fell out of my seat; she had makeup on.

I heard Marcel gasp, and I understood why. Abby had gone from tomboy to a girl. I wouldn't cross her for anything, but she was pretty.

Abby flushed. "Just say it, I look stupid."

"No, you are beautiful," Marcel proclaimed in awe.

"Seriously, all I can say is WOW," I chimed in.

She gave us a penetrating stare to see if we mocked her. "Really?"

We both nodded. "Seriously, you look fantastic," Marcel blurted out. I swear his glasses had fogged over.

"Oh."

Mom put her arm around her. "See, honey, I told you. You are still tough, right boys?"

We both nodded a bit more rapidly than was wise. I think I gave myself a concussion.

"I know you won't wear it to school, but I always wanted a girl, and you're so pretty, it's a shame to hide it. Plus, every woman needs a nice outfit for special occasions."

"Studying for English is a special occasion?" I said sarcastically.

Mom gave me her best "I'm an idiot" look. "Honey, anytime you study is a special occasion."

"Man, it must be a huge celebration if you actually got over a C then." Marcel grinned.

45

I put my head on the table with an audible thump. Some days it doesn't pay to get out of bed.

Abby excused herself to go change. She came back with her new clothes on hangers, dressed in her normal clothes. Her hair and makeup remained though. Marcel dropped his textbook, then kicked it across the floor when he bent to pick it up. With a nervous giggle, he scampered over and retrieved the book. His eyes never left Abby.

Mom hovered. I'm sure she wanted Abby to feel at home and make sure we behaved with a young lady in the house. "Abby do you need anything?" Mom asked for the tenth time.

"No, Mrs. Ward," Abby murmured. "Thank you so much for having me over. It's been a long time since I've felt..." She trailed off.

Mom wasted no time crossing over to kneel by Abby and hug her. Abby's face was a jumble of conflicting emotions. The tough chick warred with the little girl who needed a mommy. She melted into my mom, wrapping her arms around her. Marcel and I headed to the kitchen so they could be alone. While we were there, we got snacks and soda, might as well accomplish something while we waited. We returned to the two of the talking quietly on the couch.

Mom glanced over. "Alright, I've got work to do. Abby if need anything, honey, just ask. You are part of the family now."

Abby had tears standing in her eyes. "Thanks, Mrs. Ward...err...Mom." I swear I heard a gulp at the end of it.

Mom winked at her. "You two had better be nice to Abby, or else."

A chorus of "yes, ma'am" followed her from the room.

Abby turned to us. "Tommy, your mom is awesome. I wonder what happened to you?"

"What! I am the crowning achievement of her life," I exclaimed indignantly. "I'm the best thing ever."

"You mean besides being a lawyer," Abby said in a snarky tone.

"And passing the bar at twenty-two," Marcel added.

"She's beautiful."

"And buys me pizza."

"Alright!" I yelled. "I get it. Are we studying for our English test or what?"

They both laughed.

"You forgot a great cook," Mom yelled from the office.

The laughter returned. I don't know why I bother.

We studied for a couple of hours before taking down the table and getting sleeping bags out and popcorn for movie night. Mom came in, ready for bed. "Abby, you sure you wouldn't be more comfortable in Tommy's room?"

She shook her head, her ponytail flipping back and forth. "I'd rather hang here with Tweedle Dee and Tweedle Dum."

Marcel looked at me. "You're Dum by the way."

I chose not to drop to his level; plus, I had a mouth full of popcorn.

"Okay," Mom said. "I'll be in my room with the door open."

Abby grinned at her. "Mom, you have absolutely nothing to worry about."

"Hmmm. Good night."

A chorus of "good night, Mom" followed her out.

I had never had siblings, but it felt good not to be an only child for a little while.

7

School went a bit better after a couple of tough months assimilating Abby. Wendi said hello when she passed me in study hall. School would be ending for the summer this week, so three months away from Powell. Things looked up a bit. Who would have guessed I'm an optimist?

Mr. Taylor had asked me to stay after to help him get his room packed up for the summer. Since the rain continued and Mom would be at work for hours, I decided to stay after detention to help Mr. Taylor pack his room. With only a handful of Gifted teachers at the school, the kids fared far better with them. They broke up fights, offered advice, and you could actually get better than a C in their classes. Mr. Taylor brought the stories we read to life, doing voices, pulling out little-known facts about the author. While I wasn't a great student, I enjoyed learning about places and people I'd never get to see.

About five-thirty, I headed for the front of the school. Mom should be there to pick me up on her way home.

"Stop it, Chuck."

It sounded like Wendi's voice, and only one Chuck went to the school. I heard laughing coming from the science wing.

Brunner leered. "You want me, baby." The school was empty, so his voice carried farther than he thought. "You Slag girls always want it, right Ryder?"

"You know it, Chuck."

"She thinks she's better than us," Clint said. "You teach her good."

If Brunner and his gang of misfits hurt Wendi, I would kill them. I turned the corner at a dead run.

"Let me go!" Wendi screamed.

"You ain't goin' nowhere until I get me some," Brunner leered. I heard fabric tear and Wendi's frightened sobs.

Ryder and Clint stood off to the side. Ryder stood well over six feet, but he was stick thin, whereas Clint was short and dumpy. He wore heeled cowboy boots to make him appear taller, but it didn't help. He still only came up to my shoulder, even if he did outweigh me by forty pounds.

Ryder leaned on the locker, laughing. He resembled a depraved old man, rubbing his hands together and a gleeful smirk on his acne-pitted face. Clint, in his plaid shirt and camo baseball hat, had fallen straight off the turnip truck. Both egged Brunner on.

They finally noticed the sound of me running down the hall. Clint and Ryder blocked me, shoving me back. I wasn't heavy enough to bull past them. They laughed like lunatics, spit flying from Clint's braces the whole time.

"Look, your boyfriend wants to watch, Princess." Brunner stepped behind Wendi, so I could see her.

"Let her go, Brunner," My teeth clenched as I strained to thrust past Brunner's crew.

"Why should I?" he asked. "Nuthins gonna happen to me. Who'd listen to a Slag anyway?"

"Chuck." If I could just get to Brunner, I would pound him. I wasn't about to stand by and let him hurt Wendi. I never fought back, but that ended today. "Think about it. Fights in school are one thing, but this is a crime. The police will have to investigate it."

Brunner laughed. "You Slags are so stupid."

Wendi tried to pull away, but he had her around the waist. He tried to kiss her, but her head twisted away.

"Ya see, Slag." He sneered at me like I was a dumb puppy needing to be taught a lesson. "Powell says the day's comin' when we can do anything we want to you Mutts."

Ryder hissed. "Chuck, man, we ain't supposed to talk about that none."

The look of realization of what he had told me dawned over the glacier of Brunner's mind. He laughed a nervous laugh, glancing around to see if anyone else heard. "Don't matter. They won't be tellin' nobody. Will ya, Tommy?"

"You let Wendi go, and I'll keep the whole thing to myself."

"Nah, gonna have some fun with her first." He pulled her by her hair and kissed her full on the mouth.

I know it sounds cliché, but everything went red. I kicked Clint in the knee. He howled in pain, and I ducked under Ryder's attempt to subdue me. I slammed into Brunner's side, forcing him to let go of Wendi so as not to fall. Wendi bolted, but Ryder snagged her as she tried to run by.

Brunner was furious. He punched me in the mouth, a few times in the gut, and finished off with a kick to the groin for good measure. I fell like the prices at the bargain mart the day after Christmas.

Brunner stood over me. He had lost it. His face flushed, the veins standing out on his forehead. "I'm gonna kill you! Nobody hits me!" His shriek would have made any schoolgirl proud.

A calm voice floated down the hallway. "That's enough, Mr. Brunner."

I looked up to see Mr. Taylor standing a few feet away. He had his arms crossed and an implacable expression. There was a note of authority in his voice that I had never heard before.

Brunner's head snapped around toward the sound. "What?" If foam had erupted from his mouth like a rabid dog, I wouldn't have been surprised. "Taylor, this ain't none of your business. Get lost before I call the squad on you."

"Mr. Brunner, step away from Tommy. Mr. Hempt, please release Ms. Stevens."

Ryder's hands dropped along with his jaw. Mr. Taylor was always timid, but not now. Confidence and power resounded in his tone.

Clint put his hand roughly on Brunner's shoulder. "Chuck, we need to be leavin'."

Brunner stood up, straightened his shirt. He strode over to Mr. Taylor and spit in his face. "You'll get yours, but good, Slag."

Brunner cocked his head, and the twits followed him down the hall.

Once they were out of sight, I tried to get up, only to be engulfed by Wendi.

"Thank you so much, Tommy." She hugged me so tight all the bruises ached at the same time, though it was totally worth it.

"I couldn't let them hurt you."

Mr. Taylor came over. "We need to get you out of here." He handed me a white handkerchief. When I looked puzzled, he tapped his lips. I wiped my mouth and found Brunner had split my lip. "We do not speak about this to anyone."

I protested, but Mr. Taylor cut me off. "If it gets around what happened, Mr. Brunner will feel he needs to finish what he started."

"Okay, Mr. Taylor."

"I'll take Wendi to The Institute, and you go out front. Your mom is waiting for you."

Mr. Taylor gently pried Wendi's arms from around my neck and led her toward his classroom. I watched her go. Limping as I followed them, I cursed Brunner for the kick to the nuts. A low blow, even for Brunner. I hoped he hadn't damaged anything.

My backpack laid where I had dropped it at the entrance to the science wing. I slung it over my shoulder and move gingerly to where Mom waited to pick me up.

I ran through the rain to the car, hiding how much running hurt, popped the door, and dropped in the front seat. I pushed my backpack between the seats while trying to keep my head down. Maybe in the dark, Mom wouldn't see the fat lip I now owned.

Being the fierce lioness protecting her cub, she spotted it right away. She turned my face to her, flipping on the inside light to get a better look. "That's it," she said. The car sat in park as she reached to undo her seatbelt. I'm not sure who she thought she would talk to since, other than a couple teachers and the janitors, the school stood empty. I grabbed her hand before the belt unclasped.

"Mom, let me explain what happened." I heard the panic in my voice and tried to calm myself. I could see she was upset, but I didn't need a rampaging mom. "I need to invoke attorney-client privilege."

She didn't move. I had never used that before, and she knew how serious it had to be for me to ask for it. Her hand left the seatbelt buckle. "Okay, I'm listening." I told her everything, not leaving out any detail. I told her how upset Wendi was, how I couldn't let them hurt her. I told her how humiliated I felt that Brunner's thugs manhandled me so easily, how I wouldn't have been able to protect Wendi if Mr. Taylor hadn't come along. By the end, I cried my eyes out while my mom rubbed my back.

When I finally calmed down, I told her Mr. Taylor told me to keep quiet about it. She didn't love it, but she agreed. After a long time, we drove home. Mom took us for Fat Boy burgers on the way. I guess being a failed hero has some rewards.

We talked about everything but what happened during school over dinner. Chewing wasn't a lot of fun with a split lip and the inside of my mouth being cut. The ketchup on my burger was probably a mistake, one I'd remember not to make again.

A troubled expression flashed across Mom's face, but it disappeared an instant later. Her food sat growing cold, barely touched. The doorbell rang as I finished off my second burger having scraped off most of the acidic ketchup. Mom excused herself, setting her fries in front of me as she passed. Salt hurt almost as bad as ketchup, but I had worked up an appetite.

The bell rang again as I heard the door locks clank and the screen door squeak. Mom spoke to someone, but the rain made it hard to make out the details. I had started to get up when Mom and Mr. Taylor turned the corner.

I wish I could say I wasn't surprised, but I can't. In fact, I just about leapt out of my seat, something I only do when I forgot to put out the trash and Mom pulls in the driveway.

"I'm sorry to bother you, Susan, but I wanted to talk to you and Tommy." His short brown hair dripped on the shoulders of his soaked coat. Rain poured down outside, though it should stop in a while.

"Jack, you are welcome anytime. Let me take your coat. Let's talk in the living room."

He handed her his coat and took a seat on the edge of the couch. I carefully settled myself on the floor. Mom came in, sitting in the armchair by the window. "So what brings you here on a dark and stormy night?"

Mr. Taylor looked nervous. He wrung his hands in front of him. "Susan, I'm not sure if Tommy told you what happened after school?"

"He did."

"I took Wendi back to her room. She was a bit shaken, but she wasn't hurt." I realized he had a piece of paper in his hands. "She gave me this." He handed the paper to my mother.

She took it, unfolded it, and read the contents. Her face went pale.

I peered at the paper, attempting in vain to read it. "What is that?"

"Tommy didn't write this. It isn't his handwriting."

"What didn't I write?"

Mr. Taylor let out a huge breath, relaxing a bit. "Susan, I am so relieved to hear that. I didn't think it resembled his handwriting, but I had to ask."

"Will someone tell me what the hell is going on?" I guess my Gift is invisibility because no one knew I sat in the same room.

I got a full dose of the mom stare. You know the one, like when you fart in church or ask someone how old they are. I quickly closed my mouth.

Mom handed me the sheet of slightly crumpled paper. It read.

Wendi,

I really need to talk to you. Can you meet me in the science wing at five? Please, don't tell anyone, but it is very important.

Tommy

"I didn't write this."

Okay, there are times in your life you just need to repeat the obvious. If it hadn't been such a serious subject, I think they would have laughed at me. But instead I got.

"Dear, we have already established this didn't come from you."

"I guess Mr. Brunner slipped it to Wendi. He lured her to where no one would be."

"But, why from me? Wendi barely knows I'm alive."

Mr. Taylor's jaw actually dropped. "Tommy, I think you might want to ask Wendi about that at some point."

I swear I didn't mean to blush. It just happened on its own. Dating and my mom don't mix, especially in my house. Time to change the subject. "Mr. Taylor, how much did you hear?"

"Not much. I spoke up as soon as I saw the fight. Why?"

"Brunner mentioned something about Powell telling him he could do what he wanted." The whole thing was a bit fuzzy due to the repeated punching, but I knew he mentioned something along those lines.

Mom's face flushed. "Powell shouldn't be allowed to teach after what happened to him."

"You mean how he was injured taking down Cyclone Ranger?"

Mom and Mr. Taylor both laughed. "Tommy, is that what he told you?" Mom said.

"Yeah, he tells it all the time."

Mr. Taylor raised his eyebrows. "I guess it is a unique way to remember it. Not highly accurate, but certainly unique."

"What do you mean?" Had Powell been lying to us the whole time?

Mom held up her hand. "The real story you do not need to listen to tonight." She shot Mr. Taylor a stern look.

"But, Mom." It came out a more of a whine than anything.

"Tommy, it is time for bed. I'm sure Mr. Taylor probably wants to go while it's not raining."

Mr. Taylor reached over and put his hand on my shoulder. "Tommy, what you did took a lot of guts. Things would have gone badly if not for you."

Things had gone badly, and Mr. Taylor had stopped it. It wasn't brave, just stupid. "Thanks, Mr. Taylor. Good night."

I tried to listen through my bedroom, but I couldn't pick out their muffled voices. Can't blame a guy for trying. The fact Powell wasn't telling the truth about his glorious military past made me want to laugh. I couldn't wait to discover the real story, well, if anyone would ever share it with me.

I got ready for bed, but sleep didn't want to come. It was easy for Mr. Taylor to tell me I had been brave, but they ran away from him, not me. Face it, who would be scared of me, a hundred and twenty pounds of wimp? Okay, a hundred and thirty pounds of wimp—I've finally started growing. My mother always called me her string bean, and fussy toddlers were afraid of them.

I listened to the house getting quiet. The prospect of school in the morning made me feel like climbing a snow-covered mountain. One wrong step and you would plunge to your death. The good part was Wendi wouldn't be retelling the story about how Brunner's goons held me down without effort. I felt ashamed she had witnessed my humiliation.

I wished I could be more like Mr. Taylor. He had been a hero, used his

Gifts to protect people. He stood tall and strong, his collar a source of pride. Mine shouted to the world what a loser I was.

Every ounce of me wanted to make Brunner pay, but I couldn't handle him alone. The police turned a blind eye to crimes against Gifted people, but cause a problem and they'd cart you off to The Block before you could blink. Once imprisoned, you didn't come back out. It wasn't fair, but who said life was fair?

Sleep finally came but filled by nightmares of Brunner hitting me while Wendi laughed. By the time the alarm sounded, I figured the worst had to be over.

I would never be more wrong again in my life, not by a long shot.

8

T he next morning, the rain had stopped, but the fog had rolled in. It fit my mood. After a night of little sleep and less peace, I didn't want to go to school. We left earlier than usual since Mom had an early meeting. So, backpack in one hand and a Wild Berry Pop-Tart the other, we proceeded to school.

"Tommy, are you okay?"

"Yeah, Mom. I'm fine."

"It's the last week of school." I could tell she worried. "You could just stay home with me."

I thought about it. Walking the halls after yesterday would be tough. I wondered what I could expect from Brunner and his crew. Worse, I didn't know what Wendi would be like. "No, I think putting it off wouldn't make it any better. I can't let Brunner think he got to me."

"Okay, I understand, but I don't like it."

"Me neither, but you have always told me to play the cards you're dealt."

She smiled. I hoped she knew I could handle it.

The rest of the ride passed in silence. I watched Redemption flicker by as the fog billowed around the car. I imagined it was like flying would be, skipping amongst the clouds, playing hide and seek with the birds. Such a peaceful landscape, the fog blotted out all the ugliness Redemption held.

Hidden from view, Brunner couldn't hit me, Powell's nasty remarks went unheard, and the acid glares of the people who made their living off keeping the world safe from Gifted kids vanished. I wished I could just fly away and never come back.

The fog flickered up ahead as we approached the school. As we came closer, the red and blue flashing lights took on a weird life as they played against the fog. The shape turned into a Redemption Police cruiser parked near the entrance of the school. Probably a broken-down car or maybe a fender bender.

More police cars, all with flashing lights, emerged from the fog as Mom drove toward the parking lot. An ambulance and firetruck stood by the main entry doors. "It's early for disaster drills," I said absently.

Mom nodded. "Something isn't right." A uniformed officer waved us into the bus lot.

My stomach tightened, and a cold sweat broke out across my forehead. This many of Redemption's finest couldn't be good news. I forced my jaw to unclench as I peered into the gloom.

Mom parked the car, quickly exiting the vehicle. I grabbed my backpack and followed her. Stickley, the police chief, stood by the firetruck speaking with two uniformed officers. Mom marched toward the chief at a brisk pace.

I saw a car under the overhang that covered the main doors. Drunk driver. Maybe a school prank? I wondered why so many police would be here for a drunk driver. I should have stayed in the car, but Mom hadn't mandated it, which, in my mind, equated to permission. My path happened to take me on the far side of a cruiser from where Mom and the chief spoke. I saw her head whip around toward our parked car.

I increased my pace, wanting to see whose car it was, but then I realized something, or more specifically, someone, hung over the car. I ran. I ran as fast as my legs would carry me across the parking lot. I must have dropped my backpack at some point, but I didn't care. I recognized Mr. Taylor's jacket—he'd been wearing it last night. An atomic bomb burst in my head, destroying all rational thought in its wake.

"No!" I screamed. Mr. Taylor hung from the overhang of the school. I could smell blood, gasoline, and shit as I stood there, tears streaming down my face. His head flopped on his shoulder in a horrible parody of the way he looked over my shoulder when I didn't understand something we read. I shouldn't have been able to recognize him as his face had been destroyed. Blood clung to his clothes, his shoes, and dripped down onto the car under him. The fire department had a ladder up removing his lifeless body, a gruesome piñata at some horror Halloween party.

Mr. Taylor's car hadn't fared any better than its owner. The windows smashed, the car burnt in places. Slag and other, darker, words spray painted all over the car.

Mom appeared before me, but my brain couldn't process that she stood there. She tried to lead me away, but I pulled free and stayed in my front row seat to the horror show. She put her arm around my waist and held me tight. I don't know how long we stood there for. A forensic guy circled the scene, a human vulture, picking it clean of every detail with his camera. Every flash illuminated the murk, showing more of the grisly scene. They dumped him on a gurney, more flashes. A missing shoe, his foot hanging at an unnatural angle, his torn-up hands. Finally, they secured Mr. Taylor in a black body bag and wheeled him to the ambulance. The police chief came over to talk to my mom. While not in the government, being the only lawyer in Redemption, she carried a lot of influence. I didn't hear what they talked about.

I didn't care to listen.

"Tommy, let's go home." She led me back to the car, either in shock or numb to the point of oblivion. One of the few teachers who ever stood up for me had been murdered. Besides being a great teacher, he'd been a friend and role model. And now he was gone, butchered by people who had nothing to fear from him. The image of his swollen tongue hanging from the same mouth that Shakespeare had flown so effortlessly burned in my brain.

Why did they kill him?

We drove in silence, both lost in our own thoughts. Mom led me into the house, sat me on the couch, and headed to the kitchen to make coffee while I turned on the TV news. The red-bannered breaking news flashed across the top and bottom of the screen. Steve Nelson, the *Action Nine* reporter, stood outside the school. He had a serious look on his face all reporters get when covering a crime scene.

"We've spoken to Police Chief Stickley about the incident. Let's roll the footage."

Chief Stickley's large round face and beady eyes filled the screen.

Sweat rolled down his meaty cheeks to be lost in the numerous double chins. "Well, the perpetrator arrived at the school without his dampening device. He attacked multiple God-fearing people with his evil powers. Luckily, I was on hand to stop him. I tried to subdue him but ended up having to resort to deadly force."

Mom froze in front of the TV, her mouth hanging open. "The only thing he's ever stopped is a pizza delivery guy."

The scene switched back to the reporter. "Things could have been much worse if not for the heroic deeds of Police Chief Stickley. And now back to the news desk and Daphne Newsome."

"We've always known Discordants were dangerous. Thank God we've got dedicated Protectorate personnel here to keep us safe. We'll be back with the weather and more details on the Rampaging Discordant after a quick break."

Mom just about threw her coffee cup at the screen. She paced back and forth across the living room. "Lies, all lies. And that pig Stickley is setting himself up for a medal and a commendation."

"Mom, has anyone ever broken out of a collar before?"

She shook her head. "Those collars are indestructible. Without the tool they keep at The Block, you'd have to cut off the skin it was attached to."

I thought back to the women who had been murdered. All of them had had their collars cut off their necks. I shuddered, my hand involuntarily going to my neck.

The doorbell rang. I ran over and opened the door to find Officer McHale standing there. He was one of the officers assigned to the school as a public safety officer. Police should be the protectors of the public, but in Redemption, you didn't rate protection if you wore a collar. It made me sick to think how many Gifted lived in misery without even the basic protection the police offered.

"Hello, Tommy. Can I speak with you and your mom?"

I stepped aside to let him in. He took his cap off as he entered the living room.

"Mrs. Ward," he said, nodding to Mom.

"What can we do for you, Officer?" I wanted to put on a jacket to shelter me from the cold of her tone.

McHale actually had the decency to look a bit ashamed. "Chief wanted me to come talk to you and Tommy about what happened this morning."

"Talk then." My mother, the toughest defense lawyer in Montana, stood very still. I know other states in the Protectorate think that's like being the toughest kid in daycare, but she took cases no one else would touch. I have seen her stare down murderers and opposing attorneys. People went out of their way not to offend her. McHale must have drawn the short straw if he had come here.

He gulped. I actually heard him gulp. Under different circumstances I would have laughed, but laughing didn't seem appropriate today.

"I was instructed to ask if you were planning on filing a report on the Taylor incident."

"Incident!" It stunned me that he would actually walk in here and call Mr. Taylor's murder an incident. "Incident, he—"

"Tommy!" Something in her voice stopped me dead in my tracks. "Officer McHale, why would either of us want to do that?"

McHale shifted his weight back and forth. He looked like a wind-up toy as he swayed. "Ma'am, you were at the school." The tone in his voice tentative, making sure he didn't fall off the tightrope into the seething pit of lava he stood above. "Chief told me I should take a statement if you wanted to."

Mom just stared at him for a moment. "Do you need more witnesses? Are the police officers' statements not enough?"

McHale's mouth hung open. He had the same expression I got when Marcel went on about quantum physics. He drowned in water way over his head, and we all knew it.

"No, ma'am."

"Then why would you need our statement? Did something occur other than what the reports have?"

He glanced at me for help. Not getting it here, officer douchebag.

"No, ma'am." He spoke slowly, as he weighed each word before he spoke. "I'm sorry about Mr. Taylor. He was a nice man."

"Yes, he was."

McHale turned to leave. "Oh, Chief is requesting you join a meeting they are having this afternoon at the school to discuss funeral arrangements. Meeting starts at four in the conference room. Since you were close to Mr. Taylor and you being a lawyer and all, they thought it would be good if you could attend."

"Goodbye, Officer McHale." She opened the door and held it, waiting for him to leave. McHale slunk out like a whipped dog.

She stood watching until his car pulled away from the house. She shut the door, a bit harder than normal.

"Just what were you thinking?"

I jumped. "What?"

"Do you understand what would happen if you told McHale that Taylor was murdered? Did you not watch the news?"

"I did. They lied, he—"

"I realize he was murdered. So does everyone in town. The investigation is already closed." She resumed pacing across the living room. She did the same thing on the phone with her clients. "McHale came here to see if we were going to cause trouble."

The lights came on and guess what? Nobody's home. Ashamed, I ducked my head. Once again, my big mouth fired before my brain even knew it.

"Sorry."

"Tommy, there is no sorry. Look around. The people of this world hate Gifted individuals. There is no justice for you, you are collared, you are trouble. Period."

"I'll try harder, I swear." I wiped the tears from my eyes. "They killed him, and no one is doing anything about it."

"I know, honey." She pulled me into her arms, and we cried. I cried for Mr. Taylor, but I got the sense Mom cried for me.

That afternoon Mom and I headed to the school for the meeting. Mom insisted I accompany her, so I did, but not without protest. As usual, I lost. Having an attorney for a mom sucks sometimes.

We walked into the room Principal Wilson used for council meetings. A large conference table dominated the room, chairs arranged so they faced out. Three rows of folding chairs stood facing the table. The Norm residents of Redemption would fill these when the board met to discuss business. Today they were empty. Wilson, the acting mayor of Redemption, occupied the largest chair in the middle. He always dressed the same. Conservative blue suit, check. Thick retro glasses, check. Bad comb-over, check.

Vice Principal Robinson sat to his left. Her dark skin set off her blood-red nails; they always reminded me of claws they were so long. She spoke quietly to Police Chief Stickley. The name Stickley mocked his appearance. His protruding gut had its own zip code.

At the far right of the table hulked Powell, in full military uniform, buttons gleaming against the navy blue of his coat. His eyes bored into me as soon as I entered the room. The consummate military man in full dress uniform, but scum is still scum no matter how you dress it up.

I dropped into a chair in the back row, trying to not draw attention to myself. Mom strode down, sitting with her back toward me. The supplicant before the all-powerful Redemption board.

"Susan, thank you for coming," Principal Wilson said. "We wanted to include you in the discussion about Mr. Taylor's arrangements."

"Thank you for inviting me." She nodded to Principal Wilson.

Wilson cleared his throat. "Well, Chief Stickley asked that we do not have a public ceremony for Mr. Taylor. I will give him the floor to tell us why."

The chief stood. "While the police force regrets the necessity for extreme force in the subduing of Mr. Taylor." His eyes everywhere but at my mom. The man sucked at lying. "Having a public gathering sends the wrong message and opens things up for civil disobedience."

He sat down, and I swear I heard the chair groan. The idea of civil disobedience made me want to laugh. Most of the Gifted people in Redemption attended school here. Protests by Gifted had never happened since most times it resulted in a one-way trip to The Block. You didn't get to be an adult by causing trouble.

Mom stood up. "Jack Taylor was a respected teacher at this school." She turned to face Chief Stickley. "The way his life ended is a shame, but the students are hurt and need a chance to say goodbye."

"But what about protests or riots?" Chief Stickley whined.

"Chief, we have never had a riot or a protest in the fifteen years Redemption has been here. I see no reason for there to be one now." Her voice could have cut solid Carbinium.

Principal Wilson stroked his chin, trying for the all-knowing look is my guess. "I am inclined to agree with the chief in this matter, unless anyone else has an objection."

Stickley, a smug grin plastered on his face stood. "Well, I—"

"Let them have the funeral," Powell commanded. Every head in the room snapped around to gape at him.

"But why?" Stickley gasped, all the color draining from his face.

"So they can see what can happen to them when they get out of line." Powell stared right at me when he said it.

I swallowed hard thinking how this is how the rabbit feels when the hawk is coming for him.

9

M ost times when school got canceled, I was happy. Snowstorms usually caused school closings. Wednesdays were hot dogs for lunch and gym class, but today wouldn't be a normal day. The committee had taken Powell's "suggestion." No wake, but the funeral would be held. The kids from the school who wanted to took the bus to the church so they could pay their final respects. It made me proud that all of them came.

The morning turned out to be beautiful. The rain had passed, leaving behind a warm summer day. It would have been the perfect day if we weren't going to a funeral for my favorite teacher. The police held a perimeter around the church, dressed head-to-toe in riot gear.

Stickley was an idiot.

The deacon ushered everyone inside for the service. The church didn't have air conditioning, becoming borderline hot with everyone packed into the pews. I could hear people crying and barely held off joining in.

The deacon sauntered up the center aisle as everyone took their seats. He stepped behind the pulpit and opened a Bible, pausing to kiss it before he began. He spoke about how Mr. Taylor had been a shepherd to his flock. How he had guided us through the perils of being teenagers in a difficult time. The deacon spoke without a trace of sarcasm or scorn through the sermon. When he bent his head for a prayer, I discovered why. He wore the same collar as the rest of us. The silver reflected the light for just an instant, before being covered up again.

That flash made me think how it paralleled my time with Mr. Taylor. I saw a glimpse of him, and then they lowered him into the darkness. I wished Mr. Taylor could be like the good guys in the movies, always finding a way back from the dead. Wishful thinking was a whole lot of nothing. Dead is dead.

You ever get the sensation someone is staring at you? It feels like invisible rays are boring into the back of your head. I glanced around and found the shooter. A guy, a few years older than me, glared at me. A sobbing woman's head rested on his shoulder, her hair covering part of his collar. Based on the hair color and the slightly hooked nose, I thought mom and son. She must have been close with Mr. Taylor to be so upset. When I caught his eye, he resumed listening to the deacon.

We sang a couple of hymns, Mom off-key as always. She held my hand the same as she had since I was little. Mom always there, always solid. Marcel sat to my right. I felt for him, living at the Institute, his parents not wanting him, banishing him for being what they created. It sucked. The fact he was so awesome proved even jerks can have good kids.

He smiled a sad smile at me. Abby sat next to him, tears running down her face, her shoulder pressed firmly against Marcel. Mr. Taylor had been the one to ask us to watch over Abby. At the school, he'd been the only one to actually help Abby.

The funeral ended. I walked to the front with Jon, Marcel, a junior, and a couple seniors. As we lifted the coffin, it was heavier than I thought it would be. We carried Mr. Taylor's remains down the center aisle and loaded him in the hearse. Marcel, Abby, and I rode with Mom as we followed the hearse to the cemetery.

After parking, Marcel and I stood by the hearse while Mom and Abby left for the burial site. A few minutes later, the staff had the coffin in place, and we joined Mom and Abby at the graveside. The deacon said a few more words. Mom had arranged for flowers to be there.

The Institute kids didn't have dress clothes. The government stipend they got every month barely paid for clothes and toiletries. They looked more like a concert line than a funeral procession as each took a flower, stopped at the open grave. After a bit, they would drop the rose on the lowered casket and head back to the waiting bus.

The guy from the service strode up to me, and his mom attempted to stop him, but he tore his arm free. He stood a couple inches taller than me, but at five-nine, almost all the guys did. His greasy shoulder-length hair hung straight in the breeze. If fire shot out of his eyes, it wouldn't have surprised me.

"You, Ward?"

"Yeah, I'm Ward."

"This is all your fault—"

"Shut your mouth." Wendi interrupted him as she pushed between us. I had never heard Wendi angry before.

"But this jerk—"

"I said shut your mouth. You have no idea what you're talking about." He just stood there for a minute, a bit taken aback by Wendi's venomous attack. The lady he was with grabbed his arm and pulled him away. He pointed at me then turned in a huff and left.

Wendi stood there, her back to me as she burst into tears. Mom to the rescue, swooped in with a shoulder and an understanding ear. They moved off a short distance to talk.

I'm not sure which of us she'd surprised more. Bright and cheerful described Wendi. I hadn't ever seen her get mad, much less barge between two guys. I glanced over, their blond heads still close together talking quietly.

The line kept moving, kids dropping roses on the grave. Eventually, I saw Wendi enter the line to say her goodbyes. She clutched Mom's arm, her personal life preserver. Wendi looked as sturdy as the shaking rose she held in her hand.

Wendi stopped in front of me when she was done. "Thank you, Tommy." Suddenly, her arms wrapped around my neck. And she started crying again. Being a sixteen-year-old boy, I really had no idea how to comfort her. I patted her on the back, unsure what else I could do. I wanted to say something, anything, to make things better, but nothing would come out.

She let go after a while. She gave me a brave smile and headed to the bus with Jon. He nodded to me and mouthed, "Thank you." He gently led her away. I'm sure her week had been far worse than mine.

My turn came, the last one to go. Someone handed me a flower. I held it, staring at it, noticing how it shook. I should have done better.

Suddenly, I realized the open pit filled by a lonely box gaped at my feet. "Mr. Taylor, thank you for everything you did. I hope I can grow up to be as amazing you." I dropped the flower in.

Walking back to the car, I noticed Powell standing under a tree. The shade fell across his face, but I could still see the smile as he watched us. I knew he was behind this somehow, I just knew it.

The day proceeded, but honestly, the shock dulled me to the point of oblivion. I drifted room to room in our house. Nothing held my attention, and I couldn't sit down. Around ten, I gave up and climbed into bed, hoping sleep would help restore my scattered brain.

I couldn't sleep, but in the dark, I spent a lot of time thinking. Don't get me wrong, thinking isn't one of my strong suits. Marcel is around for that. Usually, it's lights off, and I'm out cold in two seconds. Tonight, sleep was the Roadrunner, and I was Willie E. Coyote.

I gave up the bed and went to sit at my chair by the window but didn't bother with the lights. Emotions warred inside of me. I wanted to cry, lash out, and make Brunner pay, or climb under a rock and hide. Mr. Taylor had left us. I had to face the facts. My head knew it, but a part of me refused to believe it. I had to deal with it, but tonight wasn't the time. The wound hadn't healed yet.

Morning crashed on me like my mood going into history class. I had fallen asleep at some point during the night. My neck cramped from falling asleep in the chair. I heard a soft knock on the door. When I didn't answer, Mom stuck her head in the door.

"I need to talk to you." She crossed to sit on the bed. "Did you get any sleep?"

"Some."

"I didn't sleep much either." I noticed the red-rimmed, puffy eyes and the rawness around her nose. I moved to sit next to her, putting my arm around her. It never dawned on me she had lost a friend she had known for years.

"I'm sorry, Mom. Are you okay?"

She tried to smile at me, but it came off as a grimace. "Honey, we need to talk."

Oh, man. Other than your girlfriend, the last person you want to hear that from is your mom. This was not going to be a good conversation.

"I had been thinking about this summer for a while. You are sixteen, and you should do more than lay on the couch watching TV."

"Come on, Mom." It came out sounding more spoiled five year old than I intended, but it wasn't fair. "Who is going to hire me in Redemption? I guess I can pick up trash for the summer."

She smirked. Under normal circumstances, it would have been a playful little smile, but those were gone, at least for now. "Did I say anything about Redemption?"

Let me tell you, having a mother who is an attorney is just plain wrong. She can twist words until they sit up and beg before fetching the newspaper. I'm not dumb, but I certainly acted that way sometimes.

"No, you didn't, Counselor," I teased. I didn't feel much like playing, but I needed to find a way to put Mr. Taylor's death behind me, even if it was only for a short time.

She turned serious on me. "I spoke with Eugene. After this week, I thought it would be best for you to not be here for the summer."

"Okay, so you are sending me away?" I tried to keep the hurt from my voice. I'm not sure it worked.

"Eugene has a job for you at The Secret Lair for the summer."

"What?" Actually, I think I shouted a bit. "Awesome."

"I thought you might enjoy that," she murmured. Sometimes I am stupid. Here I am, happy to go hang with Blaze for the summer, and Mom will be all alone.

"You know it would be cool, but I think I should stay here for the summer."

She hugged me. Well, more like momma bear hugged me. I think she cracked a rib, but I could handle it. "No, I'll be fine. I'm going to work in Great Falls for the summer, so I'll be close by."

Part of me wanted to be offended she would be in Great Falls, but in reality, it made me feel better. I don't know what I would do without her.

"But what about Marcel and Abby?" Marcel had stayed with us every summer since he moved here in kindergarten. We'd been best friends since the day we met. Abby hadn't been here long, but we had clicked. She was already more sister than friend to me, an annoying sister capable of maiming me, but still a sister.

She gave me the "You think I didn't already think of that" look. "Eugene has a job for him, too. Abby has been hired on by a hotshot attorney in Great Falls as an assistant for the summer. She'll be living there as well. I've had the paperwork in for over two weeks."

"Cool. You rock." My mom could work miracles. After we moved here, the Institute wouldn't release any kids to outsiders. Mom sued, stating the Abandoned Child Act, which passed after the Dark Brigade attack, allowed for children to be fostered by non-family members. She argued, and won, that Gifted children were covered and should be granted the same rights. The court agreed, but only on a limited basis, when no other authority had clear *in loco parentis* comparable to the Institute during the school year. Otherwise, Marcel would have lived with us full time, which still pisses her off to this day. Now the Institute has a process for visitation, which takes forever to get through. Mom is one of the few who use it in Redemption. Plus, the local officials are scared to death of her.

"They expedited the passes the day after Mr. Taylor died. One thing. You can't tell him about the underground," she said in her lawyer voice. "Now get packed, we leave in an hour."

M arcel and I arrived at The Secret Lair, bags in tow. Upstairs from the main store were two apartments. Blaze lived in the main apartment; Marcel and I set up in the smaller one. It was so different from our house in Redemption. Mom's style bordered on girly, but this rocked the minimalistic bachelor pad vibe. The bedroom had bunkbeds, where I claimed the top one. A small living room and a smaller kitchen worked fine for the two of us. The bathroom, immaculately clean, still smelled like the disinfectant that had been used to scrub it.

It turned out that Max had lived here, but a few weeks ago, he'd stopped showing up for work. Blaze said that Max did that sometimes and would show up with a story about a new girl he'd met and how it hadn't worked out. Blaze chalked it up to hormones.

Blaze saw we got settled, discussed the ground rules (only two—no leaving the store without permission and no one came upstairs but us), and told us training started at six a.m., so be downstairs on time. The best part about the set up was we had full access to the games and TV after ten p.m. when the store closed. We ended up going to bed way too late after playing *Soul Caliber*.

Six in the morning is never pleasant, especially on no sleep. We snagged a couple Pop-Tarts and Mountain Dews and headed down for our first day on the job. Frankly, my head was numbed by lack of sleep, but I wasn't worried. How hard could serving hot dogs and checking out games be?

We lumbered down the stairs, the lack of caffeine dragging us down. At the bottom of the stairs stood the office entry. It still amazed me The Lair fronted for such a technological wonder. I wanted to tell Marcel, knowing he would be in heaven down there, but the last time I hadn't listened to Mom, I paid the price for it.

The hallway ended with a door leading out into the café. I made sure the door closed and locked behind us; nobody wanted random people upstairs. The lights in the café were still off, but Blaze was talking in the game room. We made our way around the tables, drifting into the lit room.

Blaze was dressed in a martial arts outfit, and a group of people knelt before him in the same garb. The tables had been pushed against the walls to provide space for a weird martial arts arena. Way too early to process this amount of strange.

Blaze turned as we entered. "You're late."

"Oh, sorry we…"

Blaze frowned. "No excuses. We will be training every day at six and again after closing since you are only here for the summer. Nobody ever said Gifted couldn't learn to protect themselves with their fists." He handed us each a set of clothes: red shirt, black pants. "Go put these on and hurry."

We both bolted for the bathroom located between the café and the game room. I pulled on the uniform and headed back. A crash froze me in my tracks as Marcel fell, his pants half on. The door's latch popped when he slammed into it. "Uh, sorry, Bruh."

I laughed and went out to class. I stepped into the line Blaze had the students in, as he demonstrated the stretching routine, more for my benefit than the other students who already would know it. Marcel ran in a minute later, breathing hard. *Marcel, welcome to a bad time.*

The front door chime sounded as we moved through Needle at the Bottom of the Sea. A tall guy ran in and stopped midstride. I glanced over and almost fell—it was the jerk from Mr. Taylor's funeral.

He screamed and ran at me full tilt. Blaze stepped between us, restraining the ass-hat. "Enough, Turk." His tone held a steely note. "Go to the far end, and we'll pick up where we left off. You and I will discuss this later."

Turk bowed. "Yes, Shīfu." He straightened, shooting daggers at me. I got away from Brunner and got stuck with Turk. Life is so not fair.

For the next couple of weeks, we worked for Blaze at The Secret Lair. We got up at six to train with the class, worked in the store during the day, and then trained for another hour and a half after the store closed.

Marcel still floundered, even with all the practice. He couldn't get the rhythm of the moves, see how one step led into the next as a choreographed dance.

Me? I loved it. This dance would let me kick the crap out of Brunner.

It turns out funeral boy's name was Matthew West, but everyone called him Turk. Nobody I asked knew how he got that nickname. Personally, I think it is short for turkey, but I'm not completely sure of it. He was the student leader of the dojo, patient and relaxed with the class, well at least with everyone else. While I still worked to figure out the Push the Mountain, Move the Sea, Turk threw people across the room.

I still didn't get why he hated me so much. The first time I had ever seen him had been at Mr. Taylor's funeral. Turns out, I ended up being his favorite punching bag. Any chance Turk got, he hit me, hard.

Other than the Turk, working at The Secret Lair definitely ranked above of school. Marcel and I manned the kitchen over lunch and dinner. The rest of the time we cleaned, took out trash, and attended the front desk. It felt good to be appreciated for my efforts. As much as Mom would have loved for me to go to law school, college was out of bounds for me. Gifted could be employed in Great Falls, but the jobs were menial since no one wanted Gifted around. And we kids weren't allowed to learn to drive, so even those jobs didn't come up often. Still, I found myself enjoying the working at The Secret Lair.

Saturdays, we got out of work at six so we could see Mom and Abby. They would come get us, and we would all go out to eat something other than hot dogs and fries, then spend the night at Mom's apartment. I hadn't realized how much I missed them until the first visit. Abby loved to come into The Lair. She and Mimi, the waitress, became fast friends and excelled at giving me shit on a regular basis. Mimi had the mouth of a drunk Marine and used it a lot, Abby laughing the whole time. Marcel swooned like he would pass out whenever Mimi went on a tear.

After hours, Marcel and I worked with Blaze, though the extra lessons didn't help Marcel one bit. Marcel and I would grab a couple Mountain Dews, assorted junk food, and an XBOX and play until early in the morning. Even with Turk around, it was still the best summer of my life.

The low point came toward the middle of the summer. We were getting ready to close for the evening. Usually, we would practice with Blaze after, but he had gone upstairs sick. Turk sat by himself at a table, watching TV. Marcel asked him to leave so we could lock up.

"Hey, Ward," Turk said, his words slurring a bit. "Why don't you make me leave?"

Turk sounded drunk, and Blaze wasn't here to intervene as he did during class. I couldn't run upstairs and get him, so I would have to handle it myself.

"Turk, go home."

"Make me, Ward." He got up, lurched a bit, heading for me.

"What is your problem, Turk?"

"My problem is you, asshole." He got right up in my face. I could smell the beer on his breath, see the red of his bloodshot eyes.

My body tensed, but I forced it to relax in the way Blaze had taught me. The energy rushed through my body. I waited, seeing everything without watching anything.

"Go home, Turk. You're drunk."

"It's all your fault, your fault."

"What is—"

Turk's stance shifted just a bit. He slipped into Flashing Wings, his fist striking straight at me. I blocked and stepped back.

"Turk, stop now."

Marcel stood off to the side, paralyzed.

"It's your fault." He charged in, Gathering of Snakes led to Glancing Lance to Reversing Circles to something I hadn't learned yet and me

72

slamming into the concrete wall. Pain flared hot, a sudden fire through my head as something tore in my shoulder.

Turk stood over me, his face red with anger. "It's your fault he's dead. If he hadn't helped you, he'd be alive."

"What?"

"My Uncle Jack, you killed him."

He pulled back his arm, fully intending to hit me again. A chair smashed into his back, dropping him to the floor. A stunned Marcel held the chair in front of him, like he was taming a lion. Turk lay out cold on the floor.

"Well, I think Bowing to Buddha would have worked nicely, but the chair did a fine job, Marcel," Blaze said from the doorway.

1 0

Turk sprawled out cold on the floor, Marcel held the chair over
him, and I clutched my shoulder in pain. To be fair, Blaze
looked about as bad as I felt. It was the first time I'd never seen
him with his hair down. He resembled a grumpy yeti.

A loud clang made me jump, launching a new jolt of pain. Marcel had
dropped the chair. He could have been a kid who had broken the cookie
jar, his face a mixture of fear and embarrassment.

"Blaze, I'm sorry, but he—" Marcel started, but Blaze cut him off.

"Dude, I saw the whole thing." He held up the keys for the front
door. "I forgot to leave these for you to lock up. Worked out for
the best."

Blaze knelt down and checked Turk, who was coming around. He
groaned a bit, shaking his head as if to clear it. I'm sure the chair left a few
bruises. Blaze mumbled something I couldn't make out and helped Turk
over to a beanbag chair.

"Marcel, go to the front desk. Under the phone, you'll find a number
for a Nurse Irene. Please call her and see if she could assist us." He
grinned at what had to be a private joke. "Tell her we had a training
accident."

While Marcel hustled off to make the call, Blaze checked my shoulder.
From the tsk-ing noise and the concern on his face, it wasn't good. "My

74

guess is a broken collarbone. Dude, what were you thinking? Turk has years more experience than you do."

"Turk accused me of killing his uncle." It still didn't make any sense. He must be related to Mr. Taylor, but other than the authorities, only Mom and I knew the truth. Well, us and whoever murdered Mr. Taylor.

"Man, this is a mess," Blaze said. "I didn't know Turk was related to Jack."

"No one did. I asked around to see why he hated me so much."

"Tommy, I thought I'd been on some weird rides before, but you take the cake."

After what felt like hours, but actually was thirty minutes, Nurse Irene rapped on the front door. Marcel let her in and escorted her back to the trauma center. No white dress and nurse's cap, she looked more professional athlete than Florence Nightingale. Her long light brown hair was pulled back in a ponytail. She wore a loose fitting red and white top and spandex pants and carried a medical bag. She moved with the grace of a dancer.

"You boys are certainly a rambunctious lot. Couldn't you break each other during normal business hours?" Irene said, kneeling next to Turk. She smiled at me over his prone form. The combination of drunk and chair had kept him down for the half hour.

Nurse Irene checked Turk out. She flashed a light in his eyes and asked him some questions he groggily answered.

She shook her head. "Probable concussion. I'll take him to the ER just to be safe. Head injuries can be tricky."

Irene moved briskly over to me, poked around for a minute, and decided my collarbone was indeed broken but nothing needing to be set, only immobilized. I ended up with my left arm in a sling and a little depressed thinking about how I would be on the sidelines for any more training. At least it wasn't my right arm—that would have really sucked. I wondered if I would be able to beat Marcel at video games one-handed. I should be healed in time for me to go back to school. She gave me some ibuprofen for the pain and told me to go to bed.

I thought I was done training for the summer, but I couldn't have been more wrong. After three days, Blaze decided if I could work, I could train. No throws or sparring, but hours of balance and working on the wooden dummy. Blaze explained you had to train as if your life hung in the balance because when you needed it the most, it would be. Sometimes a fight went to hell, you'd get injured and one good arm is all you had.

After a week, Turk returned to the dojo. No sparring for him until he had a doctor's clearance. I ignored him, but I could feel his glare from across the room.

As I watched Blaze teach the class, I noticed something. He became a completely different person when he taught. During working hours, he strolled around total California hippie. The hippie vanished when Blaze walked into the "dojo." He still looked relaxed, but aware. Nothing escaped his sight: he picked out minor imperfections in a student's stance, the fact a hip twisted too far, or a minor misstep. He spoke in a warm, but stern voice. The most shocking was absence, no "dude" in his vocabulary. It made me wonder which version of Blaze I would want around more. Blaze reminded me of a puzzle, no doubt about it.

Class ended. Turk and I moved to leave as everyone turned the dojo back into the game room, but we weren't fast enough.

"Gentlemen, please join me."

Turk groaned. I knew how he felt. I doubted we'd be getting a "dude" type talk. And it would happen in front of the other students.

"Turk, tell me what happened."

Turk tried to look anywhere but at Blaze. It didn't work. Blaze held him in the vice grip of his gaze. "I was drunk," he muttered under his breath.

"Hmmm. And this gives you the right to strike another student?"

"No, sir."

"Then why did you do it?"

Turk tensed up, his face flushed. "It's personal, Shīfu."

Blaze considered him for a long time. "Personal is it? I would say it became public when you attacked Mr. Ward. Out with it." His voice cracked sharper than a whip.

Turk spoke through his clenched teeth. "He killed my uncle Jack."

"And why would you think that?" Blaze spoke to Turk like you would talk down a roof jumper, calm and reassuring.

Turk wiped a tear from his face. "Somebody called my house the day before the funeral. They instructed me to look on the porch." He paused for a moment as he tried to pull himself together. "An envelope lay on the steps. I opened it and there...there were pictures of Uncle Jack..." Sobs wracked his body as he let go.

Blaze guided him over and sat him in the café. I went over, grabbed a pitcher of ice water, and made a huge mess pouring as the glass slid on the counter since I couldn't hold it still with my left hand. Marcel ran over and cleaned up the spilled water. I mouthed "thank you" to him as I turned to bring the glass to Turk. I knew those photos were horrible, having seen the event in person. I had been devastated, and he wasn't my uncle.

I held out the glass of water to Turk. He slapped my hand away. The glass flipped over, smashing on the floor, glass and water flying in every direction.

Turk leapt to his feet, but Blaze restrained him. I still moved away from him.

"The note said Uncle Jack was killed because of you, Ward. It's all your fault he's dead."

Blaze nodded toward the door. I took the hint and fled. I rushed up the stairs with the words "You killed him, Ward," echoing up behind me.

I sulked in the living room, bouncing the unusable game controller in my hand. Blaze came in. He dropped down next to me on the beat-up brown and orange couch. I wanted to go home.

"You okay?" he asked after a minute of silence.

"Fine."

"Tommy, I know it is hard. Turk is blaming you, but it's not your fault."

"Wasn't it?" I said with a bit more heat than I meant, but it was my fault. "If I could have taken down Brunner, none of this would have happened. Mr. Taylor would still be alive if I had."

Blaze slowly shook his head. "You remind me of your dad." He laughed a small laugh. "He had the weight of the world on his shoulders. Always about what he could have done, should have done. In the end, it cost him."

"Cost him?" I knew better than to ask questions about my dad. Blaze had been sworn to secrecy, and his vow stood ironclad.

"His freedom, his family, everything." He shrugged. "When the Reclaimers attacked him, he wouldn't fight back. He said they didn't have Gifts, so he wouldn't fight back."

I sighed. "Great, being a coward must run in the family." All this hiding who my dad is for my "protection" and he's a chicken.

"Were you a coward last week?" I could feel his eyes on me, like he searched my soul. "You didn't attack Turk. You blocked everything he threw at you. Well, until you missed the last one."

"He was drunk. What kind of person beats up a drunk guy?"

"Exactly." A smug grin on his face. "While unable to defend himself, you didn't attack him. The same argument I had with your dad. Sometimes it is braver to not fight, Tommy."

Damn, I fell right into his trap. I hate it when people do that to me.

"Fine, he wasn't a coward, but he could have gotten away."

"The Reclaimers set a trap for him, and he ended up killing a lot of men. He knew they would never stop hunting him. He gave himself up so you and your mom could be safe. He was a hero."

"Thanks." I felt better. Not physically, my shoulder still hurt, and I had a lump on the back of my head, but I felt better.

"I'll handle Turk. He needs time to get his perspective back. Hate does bad things to some people, but underneath it, he's pretty tubular. Let's get the store open."

***

For the rest of the summer, I trained at becoming the best one-handed cook and busboy Great Falls had ever seen. My training moved from balance drills, to blocking, to one-handed weapons. Once my collarbone had healed enough, I started back punching and using the Bo sticks and other weapons. I could hold my own against most of the students, and I got a touch on Blaze once. He could teach a greased pig a thing or two.

Before we knew it, we had packed and cleaned up our apartment. Mom and Abby would be here in an hour, and while school sucked, I missed seeing Mom every day.

We headed downstairs, throwing our luggage in the store room behind the front desk. We kept the video games and lounge supplies in there. I went back to the kitchen to help Mimi out while I waited for Mom to arrive.

I thought I heard someone yell my name from the front of the store. I walked out into the café as Blaze hollered for me. *Mom must be here. They're early!* I turned the corner and stopped. Mandy patiently stood by the front desk.

"Hello, Tommy." The last time I saw her, she was surrounded by her friends, setting me up so her boyfriend could pulverize me. Now she had her arms around herself, small and alone, as if she had retreated into herself.

I did what any self-respecting sixteen-year-old boy would do in this situation: I turned and left. I made it all the way to the kitchen before Blaze caught up to me.

"What the hell is she doing here?" I grabbed the salt container and returned to filling the shakers for Mimi. Unfortunately, I was filling pepper shakers when I left, but I wasn't paying much attention.

"Blaze, I'll handle this, if you don't mind?" Mimi shooed Blaze out the kitchen door. Blaze nodded to her and left. Nobody crossed Mimi, especially in the kitchen.

"Salt goes in the salt shakers, Sport." She took the salt out of my hand.

"Sorry."

"Tommy, have you ever made a mistake?" She jumped up, sitting on the stainless steel island dividing the kitchen. She swung her legs, striped knee socks covering most of the tattoos she had up and down her legs.

I didn't need to think about it very hard. They were too numerous to count. I looked down, embarrassed I had come in the kitchen screaming.

"Me too." Mimi had a devilish grin on her face. Unlike most people, she liked making mistakes. "What if you made a terrible mistake that really hurt Marcel? Would you want him to forgive you?"

"Of course, I would."

"What would you do first?"

"Apologize." Damn, not again. I need to think before I talk.

"My guess is that is what Mandy is doing. Don't you think you can let her apologize?"

"Maybe. Okay."

Mimi jumped down and hugged me. She smelled of lilacs and motor oil, probably from her biker boyfriend. "Get out there, Tiger."

Mandy stood where I left her. Mom and Abby talked to Blaze at the front desk. Marcel stood, slack-jawed; beautiful didn't begin to describe Mandy. Today she wore faded jeans and a plaid button-down shirt,

79

instead of the tight-fitting sweater she had worn to lure me out. I thought it made her all the more beautiful.

She walked over, glancing back at the front desk. Blaze nodded once. She got closer so we could talk. "Tommy, I want to apologize. I know nothing I could ever say will make up for what I did."

I didn't say anything. I had nothing to say to her.

"I can't blame you for hating me, but I wanted you to understand how sorry I am. Chaz is an idiot, and I've dumped him. How stupid..."

I heard a voice say, "I don't hate you." I surprised myself realizing those words had come out of my mouth.

"Really?" she asked.

She looked me in the eye for the first time. Mimi was right. If I had hurt Marcel, I would want him to forgive me.

"Yeah, had I been smarter, I would have stayed inside."

"Thanks, Tommy. You don't know how much it means to me that you don't hate me."

I tried to say something that would make me sound smart or cool or something. Mandy leaned in and kissed me on the lips. You could have knocked me over with a feather.

She smiled at me. "I promised you a kiss, and I always keep my promises." She turned and left.

When I started breathing again, I noticed the audience I had forgotten about. Mom had one eyebrow arched, Abby and Blaze laughed, and Marcel looked like he would pass out in shock, his afro bobbing.

A loud whistle erupted from behind me. "Way to go, Tiger," Mimi shouted.

You see, I knew she really wanted a kiss.

The drive back to Redemption went by in a flash. The four of us laughed and joked as the miles sped by. Mom had her Rush CD in, and Abby joined in singing. It shocked me at how well she sang. Before we knew it, Mom signed Marcel and Abby back into the Institute and we headed home.

"Wow," she said with calculated deliberateness. "What a kiss."

I swear we didn't need headlights to light our way I blushed so bad. It's one thing to get your first kiss, but it is completely different to have your mom watching it.

"Can we talk about something else, please?"

"Sure." The mischievous tone in her voice had me on edge. I knew she was up to something. The left turn signal clacked in the background. "I saw you hug Mimi in the kitchen. You guys dating?"

"What!" It came out a bit shriller than I'd have liked.

Mom laughed. "Seriously, honey, the way you treated Mandy speaks highly of you."

"The same way Dad would have done it?"

"Blaze has a big mouth, but yes, that is exactly the way he would have done it." The laughter was gone, replaced by an icy silence. I shouldn't have brought it up, but it hurt. I promised myself in December when I turned seventeen, I'd demand to know everything.

"I thought Marcel might have a heart attack," I said, trying to lighten the mood.

"She's a very pretty girl." She laughed. "Marcel needs to get out more."

The uncomfortable silence fled, but I could still feel the underlying, unspoken pain we both felt.

Sunday flew by in a parade of new clothes, shoes, and school gear. I'd put on muscle and stood just shy of six feet, so we dropped off old clothes at Goodwill and spent the evening doing laundry and talking about everything and nothing.

Monday we returned to the school routine. We had chemistry instead of earth science and trig instead of geometry, but Powell's world history class was mandatory for all students. On a good note, being the last week of August, no Block trip for a week.

Marcel, Abby, and I were in all the same classes. I saw Wendi and Jon at lunch and last period study hall/detention in the Air-Lock. Wendi started sitting with me. Something had changed about her. The bubbly girl I had admired from afar had fled, replaced by quiet and moody. Jon hovered around her, a safety net should she fall.

In addition to math, Waxenby took over English class, but there I could sense the void left behind by Mr. Taylor's death. Brunner was worse than ever. None of the Gifted teachers would get involved. They turned the other way or hurried back into their classrooms. Who could blame them? No one wanted to die because they broke up a fight.

We sat in English in late September when the alert sirens wailed across the school. Another preparedness drill, which meant the Gifted kids should be prepared to be bored. Teachers moved the regular kids into the gym, the Gifted into the Air-Lock. The school guards, rifles in hand, stood outside the door.

The claxon ceased its blaring. All the teachers, except Waxenby, left to go to the lock-down review. The day was effectively over for us, stuck in the Air-Lock. The regular kids had a pep rally; we ate stale bag lunches and did busy work.

Marcel finished his worksheet in about ten minutes. He pulled his newest tablet out, tapped a few times, and jumped online. Waxenby peered over his shoulder laughing at whatever vid they watched.

Abby set her work aside. Her eyes flickered around the room like a caged animal set on escaping a trap. I could tell she had been pushed to the edge and worried what would happen next.

"Ms. Thompson, please resume your assignment." He barely glanced up from the vid.

"Why?"

With anyone but Waxenby, there would be trouble. To give him credit, he smiled his sad little smile. "Ms. Thompson, please do it."

She sneered. "I tell you what. I'll do my work when you tell us why you sold out."

The group collectively inhaled, and silence filled the room. Waxenby was a marshmallow; however, even he had limits. I put my hand on her arm, but she pulled away from my grip.

He stood up, pushed his sleeves up, and walked to the front of the room. "Well, Ms. Thompson, what would do you want to know?"

"Why you sold out. Why did you stop fighting and give up?" I think Waxenby caught her off guard by the change in her tone of voice.

He thought about it for a moment. "Hmm, sold out is it?" He pointed at Marcel, who frowned for a moment, rapidly tapping on the screen. He gave the thumbs up.

"Okay, while Wilson is busy with the pep rally, they won't notice the audio is out. Let's explain a few things about selling out to you, Ms. Thompson." He paced a bit, leaning heavily on his good leg, collecting his thoughts. "The war raged, and, frankly, the Gifted had lost. It was like the ants taking down a water buffalo."

"How could we lose?" I said. The idea baffled me. How could people with Gifts lose to the type of people who lived in Redemption?

"First of all, about selling out, by the time the Reclaimers had launched their holy war against the Dissidents," the word "Dissidents" was heavily laden with scorn, "I had retired." His pacing returned him to behind the teacher's desk.

"Retired?" Abby asked. "How do you retired from being Gifted?"

Waxenby gave a sad smile. "You never retire from being Gifted, but what you do with that Gift is up to you."

He walked from behind the desk, leveraging himself up to sit on the wooden behemoth. "I moved to DC when I turned eighteen with my Gift and a burning desire to fight on the side of good. I thought I would be able to join a team and fight against the criminals."

Abby cracked her knuckles. "Did you fight?"

Waxenby shook his head. "I did, but not in the way I had envisioned." He paused as if he were headed back in time. "In Alabama, people considered me strong, but in the big leagues, I barely rated."

Marcel raised his hand. "What can you do with your Gift?" he blurted out. His face got red enough to show through his dark skin, and he stuttered as he tried to cover his social gaffe. "If you don't mind telling us."

Waxenby laughed. "I have never understood the social niceties over asking about a person's Gift, other than embarrassing people whose Gifts did weird things like turning their pee neon green."

Everyone laughed, except Abby. Thoughts of Firework Farley on *Saturday Night Showdown* flashed before my eyes. Some of the Gifted on the show had abilities that could hardly be classified as Gifts. Mannequin Mark's ability of being able to turn his skin to plastic might be useful, if he could do anything while he was transformed. Songbird's high-pitched squeals could mess up people, but only if they didn't have earplugs. And yet they were still in The Block as hardened criminals.

"My abilities ran along the lines of being able to form objects out of condensed energy. A professor at MIT postulated I actually pulled gravity out of the earth to form the objects I made."

"Wow," I said truly impressed. Waxenby had a lovable loser persona to him. His thinning hair and cheesy, drab brown mustache gave him a safe appearance. His shoulders slumped. His pants were too short, showing off his mismatched socks poking out of his scuffed-up loafers. I had a hard time imagining him being anything other than a teacher.

Waxenby nodded to Abby. "So, to answer Miss Thompson's question, I lived in DC, working as slush editor at a magazine during the day. At night I had a cheap combat suit I would don and fight crime."

I sat slightly stunned. I had never been told about the pre-Protectorate days from someone who had been there. Sure, we got lots of it from Powell, but the Protectorate approved all his material. We never got the truth from someone who'd lived it.

"So, my last night as a freelance crime fighter started out as most nights did. I wore my gear, listening to a police scanner for any crimes I could stop. I figured if I made a name for myself, I might be able to get some work with one of the Gifted teams around the country." He twisted the ends of his mustache while he prepared for the next part of the story.

"An all-hands went out. The White House was under attack."

"White house?" I asked. "What's the big deal about a white house?" Why would someone attack a house because of the color?

"No, Tommy," he explained patiently. "Not a white house, The White House. The President of the United States lived there before devastating attacks on December twelfth, 2012. A Gifted by the name of Hypnos launched an attack to capture President Obama. He had a small army of robots similar to the ones on SNS."

"Oh, sorry." My cheeks felt a bit red. I'm sure Marcel knew what the White House was.

"No problem. Mr. Powell doesn't teach pre-Protectorate history much does he?" He smiled at me. "So, I got to the White House to find Pennsylvania Avenue a combat zone. As I approached, a League of Patriots member by the name of Titan was crushing robots with a city bus. Unfortunately for the passengers on the bus, he hadn't waited for them to exit. He left the remains of the bus on the street along with fifteen or so dead people whose only crime being they took the night bus to tour DC."

Abby quivered with pent up fury. "Wait! This guy, Titan, was a good guy?"

Waxenby dipped his chin. "Technically. The government funded teams to combat other nations and Gifted who went rogue, using their abilities to commit crimes rather than protect people. Some of the teams cut corners to get results. League of Patriots didn't care about the Norm body count as long as they stopped the threat. The government hushed it up and paid the victims' families."

"How could they not care?" Abby said on the verge of shouting. "Those were innocent people they killed."

"I know, not all of the teams ignored collateral damage, but with huge amounts of money in contracts on the line, a lot of teams didn't care who got hurt. Those teams were more mercenaries than heroes. The Reclaimers were a small group back then working to get the governments of the world to regulate the teams, but big money got its way."

"What a bunch of sick bastards." Abby crossed her arms and sat back in her chair. Anger radiated off her like heat off an old stove.

"I agree, but you wanted to know why I quit. That was part of it. So, I ran into the fight, attempting to take down robots. The military couldn't pierce the armor plating, but they fought. A friend of mine, G.I. Girl took a shot to her chest plate, knocking her out of the fight. I dragged her to safety, and the whole time she complained about how many shifts at McDonalds it would take to replace her armor."

He chuckled to himself. No one uttered a word so we could hear the rest of the story before they called for the Institute's buses to be loaded.

"I fought a few more robots near a group of Gifted but got separated. I had a shield over me as they unleashed a barrage of shots. The shield held but barely. I really thought I would die, but Cyclone Ranger landed next to me. He stood over me coalescing the air around us into a tornado. The robots shredded to pieces."

He cleared his throat, then shifted around on the desk before continuing. "After he finished, he asked my name. I told him, and he said, 'Oliver, go home. You almost died. Your Gift isn't strong enough for this. Go find a nice girl and have kids and watch them grow up. Please, do it for me before you make a mistake and end up in the same condition as the guy over there.' I followed his gaze then threw up. Dynamic Dirk lay in pieces on the ground."

Waxenby wiped his eyes. He looked like it had happened yesterday, not over twenty years ago.

His posture straightened, and a gleam returned to his eyes. For a moment, mild-mannered teacher Oliver Waxenby was gone, replaced by Commander Gravity. "I left the battle. As I passed the ruined bus, I heard a tiny cry coming from inside. I hunted around and found a baby still in its carrier. I cradled her and ran for the hospital. The nurses checked her over, giving her the A-OK, so I left her in their care. I went back to my apartment, packed up my stuff, and moved back to Alabama a couple of days later. I left my combat suit in the closet for the next wannabe who took the apartment. After the devastation of December twelfth, the big teams fought, but most of us laid low, figuring it would blow over. It probably would have if the Protectorate hadn't come up with the testing machine, but by then, the teams were gone and there was no one left to fight."

We all sat in stunned silence. It was so quiet you could hear the digital clock change. No one talked about what happened before the war. Most everything having to do with Gifted heroes had been erased. The Protector had made the world safe for everyone, the way the regulars looked at it. So what if huge parts of history vanished into thin air?

Waxenby lowered himself back behind his desk. "So you see, Miss Thompson, I didn't just quit."

"No, Cyclone Ranger told you to quit, and you ran off with your tail between your legs." Abby's face flushed with anger as if Waxenby had done something to her.

Waxenby was normally a meek and mild kind of guy, but that vanished. "It is easy to sit there and criticize me when you've never been on a battlefield, never smelled the cooking flesh of your friends, and never watched people die trying to defend others from ruthless, evil creatures."

"You have no idea of what I've seen, Waxenby. You quit. If it weren't for cowards like you, we wouldn't be caged." Her voice was low, but harsh. I could see tears welling up in her eyes as she studied her hands.

"Oh, wait, I forgot," he said, putting his hands up in mock surrender. "When you were collared at five, you fought until they subdued you."

"I didn't get collared at five. If I had been, my parents would still be alive," she mumbled, tears flowing down her bright red cheeks.

Marcel tilted his head as if examining Abby. "Everyone is collared at five. It's the law. No one is exempt from testing."

Waxenby stopped cold. Embarrassment crossed his face as the realization dawned he had mocked Abby. He stepped over and squatted in front of her desk. "I want to apologize, Abby. I shouldn't have lost my temper."

Abby shook her bowed head, her long hair hiding her face. Tears pattered like raindrops on her desk. "I shouldn't have yelled at you, Mr. Waxenby. It's this place, the Air-Lock, Redemption, I'm a trapped animal waiting to be put down."

Abby stood, surveying the room, but there was no place to go. Wendi appeared at her elbow, put her arm around Abby, and led her off. They moved to the back of the room together, talking. Waxenby watched them go. After a long minute, he stood and returned to his seat behind the desk. I got up to check on Abby, but Wendi caught my eye and gave a little shake of her head. Wendi had it under control.

I approached Waxenby, who was still visibly shaken. I stood in front of the desk. Waxenby didn't glance up from the paper he pretended to grade. "Yes, Tommy?"

"Thank you for telling us. I don't know about anyone else, but to me, you're still a hero."

His head came up, a mildly suspicious look on his face as if I was pranking him. "Thank you, Tommy. Ms. Thompson is right though, if more of us had fought, maybe things would have been different."

I shook my head. "I think there'd been a lot more dead Gifted, and where would the kids in Redemption be without teachers like you and Mr. Taylor? You help keep us safe on a daily basis. Isn't that what heroes do?"

He considered this for a moment. "You always surprise me, Tommy. From what I've heard, you've done your fair share of saving yourself. Thank you for the kind words. Why don't you see if you can get your homework finished?"

I turned to leave, but I needed to ask. "Do you know what happened to the baby?"

"Last time I checked she was doing well. She'd been adopted by a family in Texas."

"See? You are a hero." I walked back to my desk.

Marcel's head came up, raising one eyebrow. "Everything solid, Bruh?"

"As good as it can be." I thought about the story Waxenby had told and Abby's dead parents. One thing is for sure, the Reclaimers play for keeps.

I opened the door, which squealed, announcing I had gotten home. I really need to get a can of WD-40. Even though the TV blared and Mom sat in the kitchen, she appeared as if summoned. She held an old, beat-up towel covered in grease.

"Disposal on the fritz again?"

She smiled until I got a bit closer to her. She tilted her head up, examining me like a bird would a worm it considered. "What's wrong?"

"Nothing." I tried to move past her.

Why she doesn't get when I say, "nothing," it means I don't want to talk about it, I'll never know. Her arm barred my path. Now, I'm a couple inches taller and thirty pounds heavier than before the summer started, but attempting to move the arm would be foolish. With no dad to speak of, Mom had wrestled and roughhoused with me my whole life. She would have me in a Double Nelson before I got to the stairs. It didn't matter what Blaze taught me over the summer; I would let her win, and I wasn't sure how much "let" would be involved.

"What happened?"

I sighed and told her.

"Well, Oliver shouldn't have yelled at her, but I'm sure he didn't realize her parents had been killed." Her words didn't match up with her mama bear protecting her cub scowl.

"Did you know Mr. Waxenby used to be a vigilante?"

Mom folder her arms and gave me the mom stare. You know the one where you want to crawl under the nearest object. "Tommy, when Oliver and the rest fought criminals of every shape and size imaginable, they weren't vigilantes. Sit down." She pushed the mute on the TV remote before setting it on the coffee table.

I sat in the chair by the TV screen as she sat on the couch. I hated the chair since I couldn't see the screen, but I didn't want to be distracted.

"You have to understand. Things have changed since the Protector took over. Back then Gifted and non-Gifted criminals alike were too powerful for law enforcement to handle." She paused for a moment before continuing. "Oliver fought crime. He risked life and limb to protect people who couldn't protect themselves."

"It didn't sound like he had a very strong power." I still worried about Abby. She wouldn't talk to any of us before the Air-Lock unlocked.

"Not the way he tells it," she said. "I think that was the point of the story. Every collared kid thinks they would be powerful, that their Gift would save the day. When, in fact, the majority of those kids would be the same as Waxenby or the Fireworks guy on the TV."

I laughed. I could see Waxenby in his Commander Gravity get-up running around banging on robots like they were garbage cans.

"It sounds funny, but he's right."

I had never stopped to think about it before. I always thought I would be able to fly or throw buses the way Titan did, but what if all I got was a force stick to hit things with?

"Mom, could it happen to me?"

"It could, but I guess we won't ever know." I must have looked heart-broken because she clapped her hands together to get my attention. "You don't want to hear it, but I'm glad you are safe."

"Safe?" I sat thunderstruck. I got picked on, ridiculed, and beaten up on a regular basis. Even though I could defend myself, I couldn't unless my life was in jeopardy. "You think what I go through is being safe?"

She shook her head. "Tommy, people died in the war. They were torn apart, burned, stabbed, left for dead, by the very people they swore to protect. I hate how you are treated, but you are alive. Bruises heal; dead doesn't."

Great. My mother is happy having me collared like a stray mutt. I could be out helping people, saving Gifted kids from Redemption, but my mommy wants me shackled so I can't go anywhere. I had enough.

"Mom, I can't believe…"

She gasped. Her hands went to her mouth. I thought she was having a heart attack or something. All the color had drained from her face, and she shook. Her eyes were glued to the TV screen.

"No," she groaned.

I looked as a new commercial for *Saturday Night Showdown* filled the screen. Desmond Roberts, the host, announced a new death match. The only people who died in death matches were Gifted.

I jumped for the remote and turned up the volume. "We know you've been waiting, you've been hoping for it, and after nine long years, we've got it for you." Stan was part used car salesman, part jackal feeding off the Gifted people in The Blocks around the world.

"No, not him." Mom had tears standing un-cried in the corners of her eyes, her hands clenched together like she struggled to hold on to something.

"Mom, they must have captured the Grim Reaper," I said, moving over to sit next to her. She scared me. I had never seen her this way before.

"The Protector has heard you. So I am pleased to announce next Saturday, we will put this Dissident in the ring for the first time. I give you..." He paused for dramatic effect. It had to be the Reaper—he was the biggest name they had.

"The last member of the infamous Omega Squad, I present Cyclone Ranger!" They cut away from Stan to show footage of him in action: lighting arcing out from his hands, destroying Redeemer troops, whirl-winds tearing down buildings.

Have you ever seen a person completely melt down? I hadn't until that moment. My mother, the rock my life had been built on, the woman who made judges nervous, exploded. She screamed, crying, pulling me into her arms. Her hands gripped my back so hard I thought my lungs would shoot out my mouth like a cannon.

"Mom, it's okay," I said in between gasping breaths. "He's powerful, he'll last for a long time."

She pushed me back, holding me at arm's length. "Tommy, Cyclone Ranger is your dad."

There is a point when you are on a roller coaster where you have no weight. You are in free fall. Your stomach is in your throat until gravity catches up. That's about how I felt. I had asked about my dad over the years. I never got much for asking. Mom told me it was dangerous. Now I knew why.

"Huh?" My wit knows no boundaries.

Mom sobbed uncontrollably. "I never meant for you to find out this way. This is a terrible way to find out about your dad. I should have told you, I should have..." She slid to the floor.

I wondered how this could be any worse. Maybe being hung over a great white shark while dripping blood would be worse, but not by much. I find out my dad is one of the most powerful Gifted heroes of all time the same moment he is handed a death sentence. I felt like a guy who bought a mansion, and a sinkhole destroyed it the next day.

The TV screen blazed with lightning bolts and explosions. Images of his days with Omega Squad flickered by. Traitor, Murderer, Criminal flashed over the top of his exploits. The last segment was the worst: the mighty Cyclone Ranger being perp walked in. People threw things, spit on the man who had fought to keep them safe. Mom cried soundlessly next to me; I lay on the floor beside her. At the very end, he looked up into the camera. He had what Mom always called "a strong chin." I had the same piercing blue eyes, but wasn't nearly as handsome. I could see parts of him in me, but I saw more of Mom. I wondered if my Gift would be as strong as his.

Stan came back, screaming about the death match, and I tuned him out. They had a flashing red X over Cyclone Ranger's face. I had waited my whole life to meet him, and now I wouldn't ever get the chance.

Mom sat up, her crying coming under her control. I ran for a box of tissues. She nodded her mute appreciation and took a tissue, wiping her eyes and nose. "I'm sorry, honey. I should have told you before now. I was so scared you would slip and say something."

"Why would it matter?" Dad had been in The Block for almost fifteen years. He was still famous, or more likely, infamous, but harmless.

Mom only said one word, and I knew she was right. "Powell."

13

The next day at school, paranoia set in fast. Every kid who looked at me, the way the teachers spoke all confirmed they knew Cyclone Ranger, Powell's most hated Gifted, was my dad.

I floated through my morning routine, avoided Brunner, and survived math and English. I dreaded going to history class. Powell had brought up my dad, though the way Mom told me last night, Dad surrendered rather than "have the blood of any more innocents on his hands." I didn't quite get it. If guys with guns are trying to kill you, how they are innocent?

Mom told me how Blaze had spoken to him at length, but he wouldn't be swayed. If the world didn't want or need his protection anymore, he wouldn't fight it. So, he gave himself up, and they locked him in The Block. Of course, at the time, they hadn't invented *Saturday Night Showdown* and weren't killing the most powerful Gifted on the planet for ratings.

I went into history and took my seat. Powell talked to Brunner, Clint, and Ryder. The Redemption version of Neanderthals. Brunner might be the chieftain, but they worshiped Powell.

"So I popped up and hit Dominion with a burst before she could recover," Powell said, mimicking the action of firing his weapon.

"Was she as hot as they say, Mr. Powell?" Ryder asked, barely retaining the drool from running down his weak chin. His nose by far too large for his head and long, greasy blondish-brown hair stuck out at all angles. Thin as a whip like me, but nasty as a rabid ferret.

Powell grinned his best lecherous grin. "Oh yeah, she had a rack out to here." The story pumped him up, he made hand gestures and everything, while students both Norm and Gifted came in. "And what an ass. I wish they had shown her off before they ended her, I tell ya."

"Man, you should have nailed her right there, Mr. P.," Clint said. The polar opposite of Ryder in just about every way, except the nastiness. Short with rolls of fat poking over his belt, even more so than last year, and escaping the hand-me-down shirt complete with a couple missing buttons. His face covered with angry, red welts from acne and eczema.

"Wish I could have, Clint, but I had to face down Cyclone Ranger. He had already fried my whole team; I had a duty to avenge them." Powell resumed his position with his imaginary gun in hand. "I took a shot, but he moved faster than I'd believe possible. I rolled left, and the car I leapt behind exploded, raining shrapnel in every direction."

"Wow," they all said simultaneously. Powell had told this story a hundred times to these guys, but with Cyclone Ranger in the gauntlet, Powell became a minor celebrity in Redemption.

"I threw a stun grenade at him, but a wind gust knocked it out of range." He circled the crew, hands out, ready to pounce. "None of my weapons could touch him, so I waded in for hand-to-hand combat."

"Didn't he scare you?" Clint asked, only to be punched in the shoulder by Brunner.

"Powell ain't scared of any dumb Slag." Brunner's eyes gleamed with the imagined glory of the fight.

"I didn't have time to be scared." Powell threw a series of imaginary punches. "I dove at him, and we traded blows. The Dissidents all wore body armor, so I had to make my shots count. He swung for my head, but I ducked his blow." He ducked low, then pretended to uppercut Brunner, who fell like he'd been poleaxed. "And hit him square in the jaw, knocking him out. For all his powers, he couldn't fight worth a shit."

I kept my head down, but a laugh escaped my lips before I could catch myself. Having heard the real story, Powell became so much more lame.

"You got something to say, Mr. Ward?" Powell said, the light of victory dying in his eyes, replaced by the normal angry look he reserved for us "Slags."

"No, sir." I fought to keep a straight face. "I sneezed."

"Sounded more like a laugh," Powell said, as he moved to stand over my desk. "You think taking down Cyclone Ranger single-handed is funny?"

Single-handed my ass. What a liar, stuck as the history teacher/babysitter for a bunch of Gifted kids who didn't even know what powers they possessed. I never cared for Powell before, but now I realized how pathetic he really was.

"Not at all, sir. You got awards for it and everything, right?"

From the scowl he gave me, I'm sure I am lucky to be alive. Obviously, I hit a nerve with that one. His face flushed beet red, veins popping out along his neck. I thought he might stroke out.

"Yes, I did." He pivoted and walked to the front of the room as Abby and Marcel slid into their seats on either side of me.

"Get ready for class," Powell yelled at his fan club. "Didn't you hear the bell ring?"

All three practically ran to their seats.

"What was that all about?" Abby whispered, her face hidden behind her open textbook.

"A lesson in revisionist history."

The rest of the day drifted by. The final bell rang, and most of the kids went home while we all moved to the Air-Lock for "detention." Since most lived in the Institute's dormitory, there wouldn't be much of a difference. For the ten or so of us who still lived with our parents, it was a drag since we had homes to go to. The Air-Lock was the one safe spot in the school though, and the only place where we could kick back and relax on school grounds.

The other bad part of the Air-Lock, my phone didn't get a signal. Marcel had some super antenna he used so he could surf the web during lockdowns, but the rest of us suffered. As I left the building to catch a ride home with Mrs. Hannah and her son Steve, I received a text from my mom.

"Be a bit late," it said. "Company for dinner, please straighten up."

I shot back a quick "Okay" and climbed into the car to go home. The house was always slightly messy with Mom working so much. I picked up folders and piles of paperwork and set them in the dining room/office. I placed the dishes in the dishwasher and cleaned off the kitchen table. The last company we had was Mr. Taylor the night he died. I hoped tonight went better.

Twenty minutes later, a car pulled into the gravel driveway. I walked into the living room since company always came through the front door and not the messy mudroom. The door opened, and the smell of pizza filled the air. I smiled. Must be important for pizza.

Mom came in carrying a Gino's pizza. No wonder she was late. Gino's was in the next town over; we drive by it in the bus on the way to our monthly Block visits. Behind her, Wendi held the storm door. My jaw dropped. Wendi Stevens eating dinner at our house. I would have believed The Protector had freed all the Gifted and taken us to Disney World before I ever thought Wendi would be in my house.

"Honey, can you take this?" Mom said, more to stop me from gawking than from any need for assistance. "I invited Wendi to have dinner with us. I thought she might enjoy a night away from the dorms."

Wendi closed the door behind her. "Thank you, Mrs. Ward. It is really nice of you to invite me over. Hey, Tommy."

"Hi, Wendi." I wondered if maybe I hit my head and lay unconscious some place.

"Wendi, you are always welcome here. Let's go eat before the pizza is cold."

My mom has to be the coolest mom in the universe. Usually Marcel and Abby would spend the weekend—the permit issuers finally surrendered in their "lost" paperwork war against Mom now that we're juniors—but this was on a whole new level. I took the pizza out to the kitchen.

Over dinner, we talked about school and the stupid things our friends did. We laughed, drank way too much Pepsi, and the evening slipped away. We moved into the living room and continued to talk until the phone rang. Mom excused herself to take it in the office.

"Your mom is really nice Tommy," Wendi said after Mom left the room.

"Yeah, she is pretty great."

Wendi stared down at her hands in her lap. "Jon and I were born on a farm in Iowa. Our parents brought us here after we failed the testing. Mom wanted to stay and have a farm here, but Dad refused."

"I'm sorry." I didn't know what to say.

"It's okay. At least I have Jon, and my mother sends care packages and visits every chance she gets. Mom is good people but didn't have any idea what to do when we failed the test."

I reached over and took her hand. "We have a Gift, which makes us special. The Protector made it into something bad."

She looked into my eyes. I could tell she wanted to believe me, but it was hard when you spent your life being called a Slag or a Dissident because you'd been born a certain way.

"Do you really believe that?"

"I do. Before the war, most of the Gifted lived normal lives. The most powerful ones set out to protect all people," I said. Knowing my dad had been one of them made me feel a pride I had never felt before. He had risked his life and lost his freedom to protect people. "There used to be ones who used their Gifts to do harm, but the majority used their Gifts to do good."

"But all those people died when the Dark Brigade destroyed all those cities." Her tone indicated she wanted to believe but wasn't there yet.

"Yeah, and Omega Squad brought him to justice."

"I never thought of it that way."

"Mom never let me forget about it." I smiled. "And you know, you always should listen to your lawyer."

She laughed. We sat holding hands on the couch for a while, watching some Food Network show. It was really nice to be together.

"Tommy, I have something to ask you," Wendi said, shifting so she faced me. "I'm wondering if you would be my boyfriend?"

If a safe had fallen out of the ceiling and landed on my head, I couldn't have been more shocked. My brain screamed say yes, but all that came out was, "Umm."

Wendi pulled back, her cheeks flaming red with embarrassment. "I'm sorry, I shouldn't have asked you, but you are so nice to me, and I have liked you for a long time, but I couldn't bring myself to talk to you." She stood up and looked for an exit.

I leapt to my feet behind her. "NO!" I yelled, not meaning to. "No, I mean yes, I will be your boyfriend. I was shocked is all."

She turned to face me. "Why were you shocked?"

I turned red as a beet. "I didn't think you liked me."

"Everybody knows I like you." She smiled at me. "That's why Brunner knew to use a note from you to get me alone."

I must have scowled. I wanted to kill the bastard.

"I shouldn't have brought it up," Wendi said, taking my hands in hers. She pulled me close and kissed me.

Mom stood in the office doorway. "So, I leave the room for a minute, and you two are kissing. Tommy, this seems to be becoming a habit."

I love my mother more than anything, but I could have killed her at the moment.

Wendi giggled. "Sorry, Mrs. Ward," she said with a wicked grin. "I had to give my boyfriend a quick kiss."

Mom sagely nodded. "Boyfriend, is it? Well, I have to get Wendi back before curfew, so finish up you two."

We both laughed, though I think it sounded a bit forced. The second kiss more than made up for it. Imagine that. I was dating Wendi Stevens.

The gods of fate had blessed me for a change.

14

Over the next couple of weeks, Wendi and I spent as much time together as we could. She ate lunch with me and hung out in the Air-Lock after school. It should have been the best time of my life, but the tension of knowing the Gauntlet approached had me freaked out.

Mom was worse. She jumped at every sound, snapped at every little thing. I would find her sitting, sobbing or staring out the window like a mannequin at a department store. She was losing Dad all over again.

I walked in the house after school. The Norms at school were excited. Kids my age had been too young to watch Dominion's match. It had been nine years since the last Gauntlet. I felt ashamed I had ever watched the show, but the thrill of seeing Gifted using their powers made me watch.

Mom sat in the office watching the leaves fall. "Mom, why don't you get an injunction to stop the show?" I said, hoping a good legal fight would snap her out of it. "You could file an injunction against it and make a judge rule on it."

She didn't respond. Time to try again.

"Mom, you are the most feared lawyer in Montana. If anyone can save Dad, it's you," I said. Mom never backed down from a lost cause. The great defender of those who couldn't defend themselves.

Nothing. Tears streamed down her cheeks in a silent goodbye to her husband and the father I never knew.

"We can't just sit here and let them kill him." It came out a bit louder than I should.

Her icy gaze swiveled from the window to me. Okay, maybe the last part went a bit over the top, but she needed to stop feeling sorry for herself and fight.

She stood up, her face never betraying any hint of emotion. It was bad. "You don't think I haven't thought of that?" Her stone-cold voice scared me more than the fires burning in her eyes. "You think I want to sit here and watch my husband be torn apart? The robot pulled Dominion's arms out of her sockets and paraded them around the arena while she bled out on the floor."

"Oh." According to Blaze, the Gauntlet had started out as a yearly event, but after they had killed off the most powerful Gifted, it became a special event. Nobody wanted to see a death match with Fireworks Farley. He'd be dead before the intro finished.

"I watched as they mauled a beautiful woman because of her Gift. I would do anything to save your father."

"Then let's do it!" Now we were getting somewhere.

"I can't."

"Why not? You are the best..."

Something behind her eyes broke, and the cold shattered. "Because of you, Tommy," she screamed. "If I try to fight it, they could figure out you're his son, and I can't chance it. I can't save him because of you." She gasped, her hand going to her mouth, tears streaming down her face

I turned and ran out the front door.

"Tommy, come back, I didn't mean it," chased me down the street.

I ran as fast as I could, but I couldn't outrun the words. My father would die, and it was my fault.

I ended up checking into the Institute dorm a few hours later. Spare rooms were set aside for visiting parents, Reclaimer brass, and the like. If your parents traveled outside the safe zone, the kids stayed here. Mom had fought to have Marcel and me released to go to Connecticut with her for a deposition one summer when we were too young to be left alone, but it was shot down faster than tequila in a frat house.

I checked my phone: ten voice mails and even more texts. I deleted them all. I spent the night talking to Wendi, Marcel, and Abby, but had to lie about the subject of the fight. Even Marcel had to be kept in the dark.

School came and went on Friday. Gradually, the calls and the texts stopped. I read the last one, and all it said was, "I'm sorry. Come home when you are ready."

I couldn't face her yet. I stayed another night at the dorms, but when I woke on Saturday, I had to go home. At eight o'clock, the show came on, and I couldn't let Mom watch it alone.

After lunch, I walked home. Even in September, Montana ran toward cold, or maybe my nerves made it feel that way. Either way, I wished I had a jacket with me. I rehearsed all the things I wanted to say. I thought over how my dad's life meant more than my safety. I thought I was ready.

I opened the door. The loud squeak announced my arrival. I barely got the door closed when I was tackled by a hundred and twenty pounds of mom. She grabbed me and hugged me hard. I should have pushed her away, told her how hurt I was, how she had no right to blame me, but all I could do was hug her back and cry.

"I'm so sorry, honey," she said over and over. She meant it to her core, but I still hurt. We spent the afternoon talking, and she kept apologizing until I finally had to tell her to stop. Things would get better, but it would take a while. I didn't know how long it would be.

They dedicated the hour pre-show to showing clips from Omega Squad's greatest crimes. We skipped the pre-show since it lied. Omega Squad being portrayed as villains didn't sit well with either of us. The Protectors wanted to justify their murder of my father to the masses, and the TV did that.

We sat talking, waiting for eight o'clock to arrive. I fidgeted in my seat; Mom kept pacing to the kitchen for no apparent reason. The time dragged like slogging through molasses with concrete shoes on. It was its own special kind of torture.

The clock showed 8:00, and I turned on the TV. "Welcome to *Saturday Night Showdown*," Desmond Roberts's voice boomed through the speakers. Reclaimer enforcers wished to be built in his image, with a pencil thin mustache and a gleaming bald scalp. His dark skin glowed on the screen, making him larger than life.

"Ladies and Gentlemen," he said, strolling across the stage, which stood twenty feet above the arena floor, the protection barrier flickering a ghostly blue below his feet. "You've seen the footage. You know this man to be a Dissident." He paused, allowing the crowd to work itself into a frenzy. "In fact, he is one of the most heinous war criminals we've ever captured, and tonight he enters the Gauntlet!" he screamed into the microphone.

The crowd thundered their approval as Roberts strutted across the stage, basking in their adulation. Showing their hatred and ignorance they beat on the seat backs; those armed with signs waved them.

"Let's go over the Gauntlet rules." His tone was charged and powerful. He stroked his mustache and launched into it. "Each week our contestant will have a new challenge to face. Each week the challenges become increasingly difficult. Normally, if a contestant yields, the match is over, but not in the Gauntlet! All fights are to the death!"

The crowd burst forth with another wave of noise, invigorating Roberts. Old carnival barkers had nothing on him.

"Let's go to the arena!" Roberts said as the lights dimmed over the audience and flared over the killing floor.

His voiceover continued as a camera panned the area. "If a contestant reaches ten victories, they win, and we will never see them in the arena again, but that has never happened. Justice may be blind, but she can sure kick some ass!"

I squeezed Mom's hand. "Mom, you don't need to watch this. No one has ever lost the first challenge."

She smiled a weak smile at me but didn't move. "I have to watch. Has anyone made it to ten matches?"

"Supreme Samurai made it to the eighth match, but his sword broke." Since we found out about Dad, I had watched every episode from all the previous Gauntlets. I needed to know what he'd be up against. "Dad doesn't have equipment to break. He's the strongest Gifted around. He'll make ten."

She held my hand a bit tighter, but she didn't smile. "I hope so, but they really can't let him win."

"Bring out Cyclone Ranger!" Roberts said, his deep voice resounded through our living room.

Five heavily armed guards ringed a lone figure dressed in a black combat suit with blue lightning bolts detailed up each leg. His hands were fastened behind his back with silver handcuffs. Even in The Gauntlet, they feared him. One of the guards who'd escorted him out carried his helmet. He surveyed the arena, the Reclaimers' worse nightmare. Dad stood ramrod straight; his strong jaw and dark hair with a touch of gray at the temples would have marked him a star in earlier times. I now knew where I got the dark hair from.

The five guards went out, one guard tossing his helmet to land by Dad's feet, leaving him by himself. Once the guards had exited the arena, the handcuffs holding his hands behind his back dropped to the floor. He moved his arms to his side, standing at full attention, helmet laying on the ground next to his feet. The arena was the size of a football field, with various barricades and obstacles scattered around for cover or to cross trapped areas.

"Cyclone Ranger, are you ready?"

He didn't nod or make any other gesture; he stood still and waited. The crowd booed and flung curses, which crashed against the rock of his determination.

"Go!"

He didn't move. He stood like a statue on the starting line. The top-down view showed where the basher bots sat waiting. The slowest of all the bots and easiest to defeat, possessing little armor, swung an iron club up and down. An easy test, more to show off his powers than to be of any real challenge.

Roberts's voice came on again. "Folks, I think there may be technical difficulties. Cyclone Ranger, the match has started. Can you hear me?"

"I can hear you." His deep voice held a steel to it that I'd never master. The microphones stationed at the top of the ring picked it up perfectly.

"Then go, man," Roberts said in a frustrated tone. "You've got to reach the finish line to win."

"I will not fight for your amusement."

"What?" Mom and I both said in concert with Roberts and most of the viewing public.

"I swore to only use my Gifts in defense of life, to protect the weak and innocent, not as a part of your sideshow," Dad said. "I swore an oath I will not break."

The TV went black, and a commercial promptly took its place. We sat in stunned silence, unable to process what had just happened.

"What happens now?" Mom said, concern heavy in her voice.

I shook my head. "I don't know. They always fight."

She gasped. "They won't kill him?"

This had never happened before. Usually *Saturday Night Showdown* was minor-league Gifted running around trying to beat the course like one of the crazy Japanese game shows. No one had ever stood on a matter of principle before.

The beer and fast food commercials finished, and Desmond Roberts returned. "We are back and ready to begin." A faint sheen of sweat covered his bald head. This obviously was not going as planned.

The camera panned back to Dad, who now had his helmet on.

"Go!" Roberts said, a lot less forceful than the first time.

Cyclone Ranger walked across the start line.

"Hello folks, this is Chip Calloway, here at what should be an exciting match-up. The powerful and deadly Cyclone Ranger, last of the outlaw Omega Squad, versus the Bash Bots. There are six bots on the field, waiting for their chance to end the menace of Cyclone Ranger once and for all." Chip's bold voice had a smarmy tone that made you want to wash after hearing it.

Dad paused before he stepped between a series of yellow and black striped concrete pillars. The camera switched over to what the robot saw, always a great shot for Gifted with energy attacks. As he entered the robot's field of view, the club came down. He sidestepped the club and vanished to the side. The robot turned to track his prey but could not find him. The shot changed to one of the arena wall cameras. Cyclone Ranger had leapt on the back of the robot, his hands hidden by the robot's head.

"What in the world is he doing?" Chip cried out. "I expected a shot of lighting to remove the bash bot, but I never would have believed this."

After a minute, the robot stopped spinning and started walking through the pillars, Dad still attached to his barrel-shaped back. The next obstacle had two bash bots standing behind iron grating. In theory, the grating would protect them from the lighting, but it didn't do anything to slow down the steel club the bash bots wielded. Since the bash bots were programmed to attack Dad, and he couldn't be seen, the captured bash bot simply destroyed the two unmoving targets.

"That can't be fair," Chip Calloway said, echoing the views of the crowd. They came to see the infamous Cyclone Ranger's mass destruction, not watch a life-size version of *Robot Wars*.

The last obstacle was a twenty-foot steel wall with three doors. Each door had an attack bot inside ready to stop the player from reaching the exit and the red button that ended the match. They had flexible legs and could swing their clubs in many directions. If you passed one, the other two would attack as well. Using his lightning, it would have been an easy victory. Using a bash bot, who knew what would happen.

The bash bot veered to the far left door then turned the face the audience. Dad reached over and kicked the door, so it opened. The attack bot charged through the door seconds later, only to be met by a steel club crashing down on its head. He did the same thing twice more to eliminate the final two bots.

"What an ingenious method, folks," Chip Calloway called out. "I checked with the referees, and there is nothing that says you can't use the bots in your battle. Well played, Cyclone Ranger."

With all the bots finished, Dad deactivated his ride and walked through and pushed the red button. Confetti flew down, and a door appeared in the wall, which he used. Chip Calloway kept going on about what a unique solution to the challenge, but a rules change had to happen.

Mom turned off the TV. "Well, he's safe for another week," she said, a tight-lipped smile on her face. "Only nine more until it's done."

I nodded. Tonight's was easy, but Mom was right. They couldn't let him win and would kill him sooner or later, no matter the cost.

15

_____

M om declared Sunday picnic day. She refused to waste such a beautiful September day in the house, worried about things neither of us could change. So she packed up enough food to feed a small army and headed to the Institute's dorm. We picked up Wendi, Marcel, Jon, and Abby, the permit officials didn't even try, and drove to the river.

The public park was always full of Norms, but Mom knew a secluded spot on the Milk River. A hole in the old service fence let us access a great parking spot behind a grove of trees for the Mom-mobile. No sense announcing to anyone driving by that we were back there. We divided up the gear and off we went, marching like a line of army ants through the scrub trees and clumps of grass. After ten minutes, we emerged from the tree line into a clearing complete with log "benches" and a ring of rocks for a fire. It was our special place for when we wanted to get away.

Marcel was an old hand, having been here many times over the years. He gathered kindling, placed it in the rock circle, setting the larger twigs on top. To the side, he had collected a good number of larger branches. Before long, we'd be ready to cook hot dogs and s'mores over the open fire. I filled the old red plastic bucket we left to put out the fire when we were done, or if the fire got out of hand, again. Who knew a hollow log could explode and set the campsite on fire?

Mom, Wendi, and I prepared the food together while Marcel and Abby collected more branches for the fire. A half an hour later, we had everything ready and sticks for hot dogs and marshmallows. Jon sat off to the side while everyone else worked. His manner screamed he would rather be anywhere but with us.

"Jon," Mom said not looking up from the cooler. "Could you give me a hand and get the extra bag of ice from the van?"

"Yes, ma'am," he said in a sullen tone. He headed back toward the van.

When he was out of earshot, Mom turned to Wendi. "Is everything okay with Jon?"

Wendi flushed a bit. "I'm sorry, Mrs. Ward." She hesitated as if to gather her thoughts. "Jon didn't want to come today. He thought you only invited him because of me. He thinks he's in the way, a fifth wheel."

Mom nodded. "He doesn't seem to be having a good time." She folded her arms across her chest. "I wanted him to come along so I could get to know him."

Wendi bit her lip, a sure sign she was frustrated by the situation. "He isn't happy I'm dating Tommy," she blurted out. She quickly turned to me, her eyes pleading for me to understand. "Not that he doesn't like you, because he does, but he thinks Brunner has been bothering me to get at you, and he's very protective."

I stood there, stunned. We had been together for a lot less time than Brunner had been an issue. I could understand where he was coming from, but Brunner had attacked Wendi before we'd become friends. I said as much, earning a withering stare from my mom.

"Well, being a protective mother, I can understand how he feels. Wendi, he's your brother. How should we handle it? I want him to be able to be around all of us."

"I'll talk to him." Wendi ran off to talk to her brother. I still didn't know how to take what she had told us. I wouldn't want her in the middle between Brunner and me, not that I had much choice in the matter. He hated all Gifted, but he had it out for me.

"Okay, we just do what we are going to do when they get back," Mom told the three of us as we grabbed some snacks. "Hopefully, Jon gets more comfortable as the day goes on."

By the time we jumped in the river, Jon splashed and played around with the rest of us. Mom stayed in a folding chair with her Kindle pretending to relax. For as much as she tried to take our minds off Dad, I could tell it was still gnawing away at her.

"Kids, let's get ready to eat." Mom folded up her chair, grabbed her tote bag, and walked back to the site. Wendi dunked Jon one more time for good measure. Her quickness got past Jon's strength advantage every time. Seeing them together in a relaxed environment let me glimpse how much they loved each other. I hated to admit I felt a slight twinge of jealousy.

Mom bustled around camp. Jon snapped his towel at Marcel, who definitely didn't appreciate it. Abby, however, jumped right in, and the two of them chased each other around, flicking towels at each other. I decided not to join since things had gone so well up until now. I dried off, hung my towel in the sun, and jumped on getting the fire started.

Wendi knelt down next to me. "I've never built a fire before. Can you show me how?" She winked at me. I smiled back, and she nudged me, saying. "Stick to the fire lesson."

Jon sat on one of the log seats we used—okay, Mom brought a folding chair, but Marcel and I used them. Mom moved around the camp, setting out picnic food for dinner.

I picked up the newspaper and twigs to start with. "We use kindling and paper to get a small fire started. Then we gradually increase the size of the wood until it's large enough to cook on."

I handed Wendi the lighter, and she got the fire going. Before long, we had a growing fire, fed by a constant flow of small branches that we broke up and tossed in. The fire reflected in her eyes distracting me to the point that I burnt my fingers, twice.

Mom came over to check on the progress. Jon cleared his throat. "Mrs. Ward, thank you for inviting me. I know you didn't have to." He sounded sincere, and I felt a bit bad for some of my earlier mental comments.

Mom straightened, regarding Jon for a moment. "Jon, you are always welcome. All the kids call me 'Mom,' and you can as well if you are comfortable with it."

Jon blushed. "Um, I'll try. Can I ask you a question?"

Mom laughed. "You just did, but go ahead."

He smirked, clearly uncomfortable. "Wendi said you are a lawyer, but what kind of law do you practice?"

Oh no! Work talk, the never-ending topic.

Mom brightened. "I practice family and civil law, mostly around rights for Gifted. If you're interested, I'm happy to answer any questions."

"Well," Jon said. "I wondered about the cases you've handled for other Gifted."

This would be a long talk, I could tell. Mom launched into the cases she's handled, including the permit battle for Marcel's living with us. Anything about law just excited her.

As I listened, I still thought it worth the risk to use the courts to stop the matches. She could launch tons of legal attacks to buy Dad time. She worried about me being found out, but she had told me no one had discovered his real name, so we couldn't be connected, and to stand by and watch him die without trying galled me. I fought down the urge to say something, but I knew it would just lead to more hurt feelings, and this was difficult enough already. Honestly, I still felt wounded, and the thought of tearing off the scab was more than I could handle.

Wendi and I held hands as the sun set, and the fire crackled and popped. Mom handed out sticks and hot dogs once the fire was fully engaged. Wendi and Jon had never been to a picnic, so Abby made snarky, but ultimately helpful, suggestions to Jon, while Marcel and I hung with Wendi. After the hot dogs, potato salad, and the rest, Mom brought out the s'mores. Abby squealed in delight when she saw them. Puzzled looks flew between Jon and Wendi as they assembled and ate the messy goodness. Wendi ended up with it on her nose. Jon had three, and you could barely see his face through the mess. Wendi teased him mercilessly about needing a bib, but nothing could ruin Jon's mood, at least tonight.

We all helped clean up, packed the car, and drove back to the Institute's dorm to sign everyone back in. At least for a short time, I had fun with my friends as a "normal" teenager. Monday it was back to the drudgery of high school and Brunner's abuse.

Monday started the same way as every other Monday morning. I overslept, rushed to get dressed, and grabbed a couple of Pop-Tarts as I ran out the door so Mom could drive me to school. I ate as rapidly as possible because I still tensed whenever we pulled into the school's driveway. Part of me expected to see another body hanging there each day. I wondered if I'd ever get the vision of Mr. Taylor swaying from the end of a rope out of my head.

I jumped out of the van, having gotten the ritualistic morning kiss on the cheek, and caught up to Marcel in the hall as he walked into home-room. Brunner cracked a couple of lame jokes as we took our seats, and the day was off to another in the endless litany of bad days.

School trickled by like a grease-filled drain, but I was looking forward to seeing Wendi in the Air-Lock before going home. It sort of made the day bearable.

The last bell of the day rang, so I stopped at my locker, dropped my books, and strolled toward the Air-Lock. As I crossed over the science hall, dodging kids running for their lockers, a huge weight struck me, hurtling me to the ground.

"What a Slag," Brunner proclaimed, standing over me, the conquering gladiator. I looked through his legs to see Clint and Ryder, but also a bunch of other kids. The prospect of a fight always drew a crowd. It was a bit unusual for the end of the day when the Norms got to go home or to their part-time jobs. "So, what do you think the Slag Princess sees in this toad?"

Laughter boomed from the crowd. Brunner stood on stage now, the Desmond Roberts on his own *Saturday Night Showdown*. He strutted back and forth, working himself up. "I think I'll have to show her what a real man is." He waved his arms pumping up the crowd.

The crowd let fly encouragement. "You show that Slag" and the "slut deserves it" rang out, boosting Brunner all the more. He kicked me hard in the side, flipping me onto my back like a turtle. More laughter and catcalls rained down on me.

Brunner leaned down so his mouth was near my ear. "I'm going to take your girlfriend and make her scream, and there ain't nothin' you can do 'bout it."

All the pent-up fury from the last time Brunner attacked Wendi burst through the dam of reason. I stopped thinking, stopped hearing my mom telling me to not make myself a target, to be safe. I had enough.

The hours of training at The Secret Lair with Blaze kicked in. Brunner's balance shifted as he perched over me. Before he could react, I gripped the front of his shirt, rolled away from him, and threw him head first into the nearby wall. While he lay there stunned, I got out from under him and on my feet.

Clint and Ryder moved in to hold me, but Brunner screamed, "Leave him! The Slag is mine!"

Like a lumbering giant, Brunner got to his feet. He'd never leave Wendi alone until I made him stop. The time had come to stand up to this bully and end this once and for all.

"I'm going to kill you!" Brunner raged as he charged. I quickly side-stepped, my leg snaking out to hook his and send him to the floor again face first. It was the same move Blaze had used in the parking lot.

Clint and Ryder helped him up. Blood flowed from his nose from where he hit the floor. Since bull rushing me didn't work the first time, in Brunner's mind it would work better the second time. Brunner flew at me, arms thrown wide to crush me in a bear hug where his size would give him the advantage. I ducked under his arm and let him run into the wall without any assist. An "ooooh" emanated from the crowd from the audible crash. Brunner considered himself the toughest guy in the school, and I was making a fool of him.

He wheeled around, his face red with rage. He ran toward me throwing wild punches, hoping his greater reach and strength would be enough. It didn't work.

I blocked his left fist, returning a solid punch to his sternum, knocking the wind out of him. I stepped back unleashing a roundhouse kick to Brunner's exposed head. My foot caught him cleanly in the eye and mashed his nose as it flew by. He dropped like a sack of turnips off a truck.

Clint and Ryder stood, mouths hanging open. The cheering crowd quickly dispersed. The familiar clack of Vice Principal Robinson's heels coming down the hall gave me all the warning I'd get. I knew I was done for.

"Mr. Ward." Her voice shrill with anger. "What is the meaning of this?" She pointed her finger at me, the blood red nail looking all the more vivid against her dark skin.

"He tripped," I said, suddenly wishing I hadn't. This was going to be painful.

"Tripped. Tripped!" Her voice went up an octave with the second one.

Any higher and the dogs would be the only ones to hear her. "You seriously believe I will buy that he tripped?"

I really didn't care what she thought since I'd be expelled and possibly sent to The Block. Maybe I could share a cell with my dad before people like Roberts cheered his death all in the name of ratings.

Two hands settled on my shoulders from behind, startling me in the process. "Vice Principal Robinson, I saw the whole thing, and Tommy wasn't a part of it," a familiar voice said behind me. "Ryder and Clint fought with Chuck, and they got the better of him. All three should be expelled for the week."

"What?"

"You heard me."

"Fine." She stamped a foot to emphasize the word. "I'll prepare the paperwork for the principal's signature while you take care of this mess. Good day, Mr. Powell."

I watched as she turned and left. Most drill teams would kill to be able to execute that precise of a turn, especially in six-inch red stiletto heels.

The grip on my shoulders tightened to a point where it became painful. I couldn't see his face, but his eyes would be filled with hatred. He hated Gifted as it was, but I had made a fool of his pet. The only thing that would make it worse would be to tell him Cyclone Ranger was my dad.

"Tommy, this isn't over, not by a long shot." The edge in his voice sliced the air like a scalpel of controlled fury. "Justice will be served."

He pushed me away, so I stumbled. I should have gone to the Air-Lock, but I didn't. I ran home. My mom was going to kill me, and I didn't think I would mind if she did.

I sat alone in the living room as the day drew to a close and the sky darkened. The headlights flashed through the windows when Mom pulled into the driveway. The screen door squeaked its song as it opened. Mom walked in, closed, and locked the door. She tossed her keys and briefcase in the office on her way to the kitchen. She glanced my way and stopped abruptly as she saw me sitting in the darkening room. "Tommy, are you alright, honey?"

I drew a deep breath and let it out, like Blaze had taught us. It should have helped calm my nerves, but no such luck. "Mom, I need to tell you what happened."

She flipped the light switch on and took a seat across from me. "Go ahead."

After another try at calming myself, I let it all out. The words were jumbled, events half explained as my mind crashed through the events of the day. As I finished, I could tell she was worried.

"Well?" I asked hesitantly.

She rubbed her chin. "You are okay? Brunner didn't hurt you?"

"No, I'm fine," I lied.

She didn't say anything for a while. "I'm glad you weren't hurt. I really need to think about things. I'm going to go lay down for a bit. I love you."

"I love you, too, Mom."

I don't know how long I sat there thinking about what I could have done different or how this would play out. Mom didn't emerge from her room, so I went in to bed. Sleep was a long time coming.

16

As Mom drove me to school, the silence stretched between us. She was worried at the ramifications of hitting Brunner, but I couldn't stand by and watch Brunner continually humiliate and hurt people I cared about. He had it coming for a long time, but I doubt Mom fully understood considering how much of Brunner's bullying I'd hidden.

The car pulled off into the parking lot for the Redemption post office. School was a mile down the street; this must be serious.

"Look, Mom..." I couldn't tell how she felt, but I guessed not happy summed it up. "I am really sorry about yesterday. I..."

She started to cry. Not big waterworks, more of a slow leak. "Tommy, I knew one day you would have to fight back."

"What?"

She tried to smile, but it came off as a sickly, weak attempt. "You are too much like your dad." Her voice barely audible over the car engine. "He never could let anyone be hurt, always standing up for the underdog. He would be very proud of you."

I stood dumbfounded. I thought she would cut into me for fighting, not this. "You were the one who always told me we protect the people who can't protect themselves."

She nodded as she put her hand on my cheek, caressing it softly like

114

she would do when I was a kid. It actually made me feel better. I hoped no one from school saw.

"You have to listen to me. Today is critical for you." She locked her eyes on to mine so I would really hear her, ashamed she had to force me to listen. "You keep your head down. Do not challenge Brunner. If he starts a fight, let him win."

"First, you tell me how proud Dad would be. Then you tell me to let Brunner kick the crap out of me?"

The tears continued to well in the corner of her eyes. "A few bruises and your hurt pride is a small price to pay. I am going to Great Falls today, and Brunner will be gone by the end of the week, but you can't be a threat or Powell will have you sent to The Block."

The Block. The name crashed over me like a tidal wave of ice water. I nodded. All of this was my fault. I should have gotten a teacher instead of confronting Brunner. I should have run when he cornered me, took a few punches to soothe his ego. What a mess I had made of things.

"I'll be back by eight tonight. We can talk more then. Promise me."

I felt like the world's biggest ass having put her through this. I needed to do better so she didn't have to worry. "I promise." I realized I truly meant it.

She leaned over and kissed my cheek.

"Just because I agree with you doesn't mean you get to be all kissy." Fake indignation was strong in my voice.

She laughed. "My big boy. Too big for Mom's kisses?"

She pulled out of the post office and a couple minutes later dropped me off at the school with a quick "love you" and off she went. I turned to face the torment waiting in the halls of Redemption High.

I assumed the best hang dog expression I could muster and shuffled into the building with all the other car riders. I cringed as I expected for Brunner's booming voice to call me out. I headed to my locker by way of the cafeteria. He hung out there with his crew most days, but he wasn't there. I got to my locker and to my first class without so much as anyone pushing me or calling me a Slag. I could get used to this.

The morning sped by. I kept my head hung and out of trouble. Powell's history class would be the true test. I slunk in, sliding quietly into my seat. Powell stood by his desk, more prison guard than history teacher. He glared at me while I sat head bowed dreading the impending bell.

I felt the pounding of his boots approach my desk. Lewis C. Powell, Officer of the Reclaimer's Army, would wear fatigues to school if they allowed him to. That didn't stop him from wearing his combat boots instead of normal shoes the rest of the teachers wore.

"Mr. Ward." I'd heard friendlier snarls from a wolverine. "I wanted to inform you Mr. Brunner, Mr. Whit, and Mr. Hempt are all on suspension for a week after yesterday's incident."

I glanced around. This is Redemption High, and this is Mr. Powell. Maybe I hit my head a lot harder than I thought the other day. In the school's history, a Norm had never been suspended for messing with a Gifted. Marcel checked it out once during detention to win an argument. We didn't rate protection, short of being permanently damaged.

"Um, I'm sorry about that, sir," I mumbled a bit more than I would have due the sheer enormity of the statement.

"Why?"

"Err, I know they are your favorite students, sir." *Okay, enough with the "sir" crap already.* This guy is as bad, if not worse, than Brunner, and I was bowing and scraping like some peasant. See, I did listen to Powell's lectures sometimes.

"Nonsense." His voice reverberated around the room in true drill sergeant style. The kids turned in their seats to see what was going on since he normally belittled me or encouraged the class to do it for him. "Those boys were flat out wrong. Their behavior is not suited for the school grounds."

I suspected an impending aneurysm or psychotic breakdown. I now knew how Alice felt when she fell down the rabbit hole. Powell had stood over me many times while Brunner worked me over and never said a thing. Something was seriously wrong.

He nodded and returned to his desk to start class. Abby and Marcel had arrived during the exchange. They both looked as baffled as I did.

"What was that all about?" Marcel whispered from behind me.

"Brunner has been suspended for the fight I told you about at lunch." I kept my voice low.

"Something is going on," Abby whispered as she leaned down to tie her shoe, which didn't need tying.

"I know." I wondered if it had something to do with why Mom had gone to Great Falls this morning. Maybe she would put an end to the Brunner situation once and for all. I leaned back, pondering what a Brunner-free life would be like.

The day ended as Marcel, Abby, and I headed to the Air-Lock. An amazing day with no Brunner and everyone leaving me alone. I couldn't wait to see Wendi and tell her what had happened. I entered through the massive double-layered door that gave the Air-Lock its name. We went over to where we normally sat. A Sudoku puzzle sat before Waxenby, brow furrowed in concentration, as people drifted in.

Wendi and Jon hadn't shown up, which was odd since they had the closest lockers. The final bell rang, clubs and activities for Norms and the Air-Lock for the Gifted. The door boomed shut announcing detention had officially begun. Something was wrong. The guard outside didn't seal the doors until we were all accounted for. I had seen Wendi before homeroom.

I approached Waxenby's desk. He glanced up from the puzzle, a smear of graphite across his nose where he'd been rubbing it. "Mr. Waxenby, Wendi isn't here, but the guard sealed the door."

"Wendi?" He rubbed his chin while he thought, leaving a matching smear across his chin. He shuffled some papers on the desk. "Oh, here it is. Mr. Powell signed her and Jon out for a disciplinary board hearing."

I panicked a bit. "Why? Are they in trouble?" I tried and failed to keep my voice level. I concentrated on keeping my wits. Pissing off Waxenby wasn't going to help.

"No, Tommy," he said reassuringly. "The disciplinary board was convened to discuss Mr. Brunner's behavioral issues. Miss Stephens was asked to testify, and her brother escorted her is all."

"Really?" I said before I could stop myself. The words tumbled out of my mouth like clowns from a car. "Mr. W., there has never been a teacher who would stop Brunner or anyone else from beating on any of us. Why now?"

"Tommy, I honestly don't know, but I am optimistic this will be a good thing for us. It has been fifteen years since the attack. Maybe things are changing for the better."

"Do you really believe that?"

"I have to Tommy, otherwise why bother?" His gaze dropped back to his puzzle, and I returned to my seat.

Why bother indeed.

The door hissed as it opened. We emerged into a beautiful fall day that made the Montana winters feel so much worse. The Norms all screamed and ran around, not a care in the world. The Gifted kids stood silently in a line as the guards loaded them into The Institute's buses. It never failed to drive home how different we were treated. If I ran across the bus lot, I'd be dropped by a stun stick.

We passed the edge of the school. I heard "Hey, Tommy" from the bushes. Marcel and Abby stopped as I walked over. Two hands grabbed and dragged me in.

Jon's face was bloody and swollen from what must have been a major fight. Most of the Norms at school stayed away from him due to his size, unlike me.

"Jon, what the hell happened?"

He slammed me into the side of the school. My head banged against the red bricks, dazing me for a moment. I figured my future held a lot of mental impairment from all the concussions.

Marcel and Abby made their entrance stage left and late. Abby shoved Jon away from me. Not for the first time did I think not to piss Abby off. She stood an inch shorter than Jon, and I'd guess as strong, if not stronger.

"What do you think you're doing?" She kept her voice down so the teachers herding the kids to the bus didn't overhear us and come to investigate.

"I told her to stay away from you," Jon said. You could start a fire with the heat coming off him he was so mad. "I told her you'd get her hurt."

"What are you talking about?" Abby stepped between the two of us. I pitied Jon if he swung on Abby. She would have no problem with knocking him on his ass.

Jon slumped to the ground, drawing his knees to his chest. He was in pretty bad shape. Marcel sat next to him.

"Jon, you have to tell us what happened," Marcel said in a calm voice. How he did it, I'll never know. The sharp pain from the bouncing off the wall subsided to a low thrum.

"Powell told us there was a disciplinary meeting over Brunner attacking Wendi. He told me to come along." He stopped and gathered himself. "We went to the teacher's parking lot to meet him, and Brunner and his guys jumped us and pushed us into Brunner's truck."

Oh my God. Brunner wasn't about to leave Wendi alone. Brunner was a sadistic prick, and I knew he'd hurt Wendi to make me pay. I wasn't about to let that happen.

"They told me they would kill her if I didn't bring you with me. They beat me up to prove they meant it, then they pitched me and took Wendi."

My brain began to boil with rage. This had gone too far. I couldn't let him hurt Wendi. Mom would have to understand.

"Jon, where did they take her?"

"They are at the fishing camp over on the Milk River. They said if you didn't come tonight, they would kill her and dump her."

I steadied myself. "I'm going to go get her."

"Not without us." Abby cracked her knuckles, ready for the fight. Marcel looked like he would wet himself, but he held firm.

"You don't go anywhere without me," Jon said. "She's my sister, and I owe Brunner some payback."

"Okay, let's go."

17

O ur first order of business was to sneak away from the building. The four of us hiding behind the bushes were bound to be noticed sooner or later. Abby helped Jon up so we could move away from the bus lot. We stood at the bottom of the loading dock. It wasn't great, but since it sloped downward, it got us out of view for the moment.

Marcel, always good with thinking on his feet, spoofed Powell's phone and emailed the guard station he would be returning Abby and Marcel to the dorm directly. Otherwise, when they noticed them missing from the bus, the guards would sound the escape alarm. That would buy us some time. Plus, it would implicate Powell if something happened to them.

"Okay, so now what?" I said. The blank looks on my friends' faces told me we were all in the same boat.

Jon's words were a bit muffled by his swollen mouth. "You got her into this, Ward. We have to get Wendi back before he hurts her."

"We do, and I will get her back." I tried to keep my anger under control. Mom had warned me about this, but there was nothing I could do to stop it. "How we get all the way out there is the problem."

"How do we get where?" A voice came from behind us making us all jump. Waxenby stood at the top of the loading ramp, arms folded and waiting on an answer.

"We want to go see the new *Blade Runner* this weekend," Marcel said quickly, filling the void in the conversation. "Tommy's mom won't take us, so we were figuring out how to get there."

Waxenby nodded as he approached us. "So, let me guess. You beat the tar out of Mr. Stevens here so you could have the ambulance take you to the theater?"

"So you aren't going to buy he fell from the loading dock, and we'd come to help him up?" I hoped he would take the hint and go away.

"No, I will take the truth, unless you would rather discuss it with the principal."

I glanced around; shrugs and nods answered me. So I told him. He listened, his eyes getting wider as the story unfolded. I told him about Brunner, how we thought they'd been involved with Mr. Taylor's death, and the kidnapping of Wendi.

"We have to get the police," he stated as he turned to go. I held his arm, drawing a stern look, but he didn't say anything.

"We can't," I said rushing on before he could interrupt. "Powell is the Protectorate representative in Redemption, and he protects Brunner."

I understood, now, idiot that I am, the suspension had just been to get Brunner out of school so he could get even with me out of the public eye. "Who do you think the police will believe? Us or him? They won't even listen to you because of the collar."

He stood stone still for a few moments, digesting the information. Waxenby had been an adult when collared, but he knew how things worked.

"Alright, we go get in my car, and we'll drive to the camp," he said, patting his sweater vest like it was combat armor. Thankfully the Protectorate hadn't stopped adult Gifted from driving. "We get Wendi, and then we come back."

"You have to let me do this alone." I held up my hand when he started to object. "If all Brunner wants is to kick my ass, then he will, and I'll bring Jon and Wendi out, but if you go with me, they won't and this will continue."

He nodded his agreement, a "boys will be boys" look on his face. Once Brunner was the top dog again, Wendi should be safe from him. At least I hoped so.

Waxenby took the lead, marching across the parking lot and out of sight of the bus guards. We climbed into his lime green Ford Fiesta. Well, mostly green, except for the gray patches from his last "accident." Gifted cars tended to be easy targets for Norms who were cowards. Teaching didn't pay well, and a Gifted teacher made even less. It was better than walking the twenty miles to where Brunner waited for us, but not by much.

W axenby put his hand on my arm as I exited the car. "Look, I don't like this." Worry covered his face.

"It's my ass getting kicked, so I'm not too pleased either." I tried to keep the smile on my face.

"Thirty minutes and then we are coming for you both," he said, scanning back and forth between us. "Good luck."

He let go of my arm. I closed the door, and they drove off, leaving Jon and me a good ten-minute walk through the trees to where the camp was situated.

I turned to Jon. "I'm sorry." I didn't know what else to say. I never meant to put Wendi in harm's way; I wanted her to be my girlfriend. No wonder Dad had kept us away from the public view. Norms such as Brunner and his crew would hurt anyone who got in their way.

Jon frowned, but grudgingly nodded. "Tommy, I told Wendi to stay away from you, but for all of that, you're a good guy. I appreciate you sticking with me."

I wish I felt brave. Actually, I swung between throwing up and wetting my pants. This wouldn't be a Mom-approved course of action, but how could I chance he would really hurt Wendi? My dad would have waded in to stop Brunner, and I wasn't going to let him down. Not for the first time, I wished he were here to help.

"Okay, I guess we'll be twins in a few minutes." Nothing like gallows humor to brighten the day.

The forest crept toward darkness as we walked. The sun receded as the day wore on; shadows lengthening as we moved closer to our target. The trail leading to the camp became harder to make out. Tripping became more of an issue as roots grabbed my ankles.

As the forest thinned, I heard a shriek from ahead. Without thinking, I dashed into the clearing. Wendi was tied to a post in the center of camp. Brunner's knife flashed in the late day sun. I screamed something incoherent and charged, all thought of a peaceful, placating entry thrown to the wind.

I didn't make it past the last row of trees. Something snatched my legs from under me. I face planted like a skateboarder on a bad halfpipe run. Blows rained down on me when I tried to get to my feet. I managed to get to my hands and knees before a blow to the back of the head turned off the lights.

T he constant throb of my head was what I noticed first. Next was that my shoulders burned from holding the weight of my body. I counted myself lucky my healing collarbone hadn't cracked under the stress. The rope cut into the flesh on both wrists, my arms extended to either side. My head hung forward from being out, so I just left it there.

I wanted to look around, but my eyes wouldn't cooperate at the moment. I thought back to my lessons with Blaze, but he hadn't taught me how to get out of this one.

"Brunner, you got what you want." I heard Jon's voice from in front of me. "I brought Ward. You promised me Wendi in return. She didn't do anything to you."

"Listen, Slag." Brunner would be having a fit because Jon stood a good three inches taller than him. He liked his victims smaller than he was. "I don't owe you nuthin'. Get out of here before I lose my temper."

"Ward for Wendi is what we agreed to," Jon said, his voice rising in anger. "I kept my..."

A sharp crack resounded through the clearing. I got one eye open to see Clint standing over Jon's prone form. Clint had a shocked look, holding the baseball bat like it was a snake. "Chuck, I think I killed 'im."

"We're gonna kill 'em both, so you got a head start is all," Brunner said with a caustic laugh. "By tomorra these two will be dead, and I got me a new girl."

Ryder laughed from the stump he lounged on. Brunner's beat-up truck was parked by the water. They must have come in from a different direction. Without moving my head, I pushed through the daze to get a read on the situation.

Wendi stood twenty feet across from me, still tied to the post, and her face had a good size bruise. Her blouse had been torn about halfway down her chest, the fabric ragged from the violent attempt to remove it. I fought to keep still and silently vowed to kill Brunner.

A fire pit made of old concrete blocks and part of an oil drum sat between us. I must have lost focus for a moment because suddenly Clint stood on the left, the bat on the ground. He stared at Jon as Ryder dragged him to another tree and chained him to it. Jon groaned as he slumped against the tree. At least he wasn't dead.

A surge of hope flooded through my addled brain. Waxenby should be coming anytime. Once he got here, this would all be over.

I kept my head down, playing possum, waiting out the half an hour until the cavalry would emerge from the trees and save the day. Eventually, I heard a branch break from the direction of the path. Brunner jumped to his feet, his face going beet red. I resisted the urge to laugh; he would get his.

"Just how inept are you three?"

I flinched. It wasn't Waxenby; that was Powell's voice. I didn't dare move and let them know I was awake. Abby and Marcel moved into view, their hands bound with zip ties behind them. A moment later, Powell entered my view, Waxenby's body over one shoulder.

"I didn't realize Waxenby here had any fight left in him," Powell said sounding mildly impressed. Waxenby landed with a thump like last week's garbage on the ground by the fire pit. Powell's left eye was swollen and starting to turn color. *Way to go, Commander Gravity.*

"See boys, that's why these Slags are so dangerous." He spat on Waxenby. "Even the meek ones can catch you off guard."

Ryder shoved Marcel over to the tree next to Jon and tied him in place, jamming a burlap bag over his head. Jon still didn't look so hot, his head hung forward, blood dripping into his lap. He needed a doctor yesterday.

Clint didn't have it so easy. He went to push Abby, and she kicked him square in the crotch. Squealing in pain, Clint grabbed himself as he fell to the ground in a fetal position. He vomited on the ground, crying the whole time.

Brunner jumped at the chance to hit her, backhanding Abby across the face. Instead of stopping her, she blasted him with a vicious head butt. Blood gushed from his already bruised nose. His hands flew to his ruined nose, cursing loudly. He wasn't getting any better looking with all the damage his face had been taking.

Abby turned to run, but Powell stood in her way, his pistol pointed at her. His arm solid as a rock, not showing the slightest tremor. "You move, and I'll put it through your head, Slag."

Abby stopped, standing absolutely still. Ryder dragged her over and tied her in place. Even from a distance, I could feel the rage seething inside her.

Brunner stomped over and kicked her in the face. Her head bounced off the tree, blood flowed down her face, a gory mask concealing her. "See how you like it, Slag," he screamed at her unmoving body.

Powell stood in the center of the clearing, the victorious general overlooking the battlefield. He stared straight at me. "Now that the children are put to bed, the guest of honor is awake. You ready for the main event, Tommy?"

I lifted my head and looked him in the eye. "Bring it on."

18

P owell laughed a long, hearty laugh. "Boy, you have no idea how much I've been waiting to do this." He motioned at Waxenby lying on the ground. "Brunner, take care of the trash. We'll be having a bigger audience than I thought."

Brunner dragged Waxenby by the feet past Jon and Marcel. He secured Waxenby to the same tree as the unconscious Abby. He pulled on the ropes to make sure he wasn't going anywhere. He kicked Abby in the head again, blood spraying from her already bleeding mouth, before returning to where Powell stood in front of me.

"As soon as it gets dark, the fun begins." Powell barked a harsh laugh.

"When do I get Wendi?" Brunner whined. "You promised me I could have her."

Powell turned on Brunner. "Soldier, you'll follow orders."

"I ain't one of your Reclamation soldiers, Powell." Brunner acted like a child who couldn't get a candy bar at the grocery store. "You promised I'd get to kill people, and any girls were mine."

A disgusted look crossed Powell's face. "I told you, Mr. Brunner, when I give the go-ahead, you can do as you please."

"We got to kill Taylor," Brunner complained. "All this time and we only got to off one Slag."

"Enough," Powell roared. "You'll follow orders without complaint." He paused to emphasize his words as he did when he was discussing a particular point he wanted to stick in history class. "After sunset, we will make an example of these Slags."

"Example of what?" Who knew I was so brave? I guess knowing you'd be dead soon kept you from caring what your mouth did.

"The Reclaimers wanted all you Slags eliminated, but the Protector collared you instead." Powell paced back and forth. "The public couldn't stomach mass executions, so here we are. Slags either imprisoned or collared and kept close at hand."

"What threat are we to you?" Blaze's voice echoed in my head about how uncontrolled anger would lose you the fight before the first blow. I tamped the rage down as I spoke. "We are collared before we can even use our Gifts."

"Gifts? GIFTS!" His voice edged toward the upper registers. He stormed over to stand before me. "This is what your Gifts do, Ward. That bastard killed twenty of my men and left me looking this way."

The damage was much worse than I had ever noticed. Cracks and scabs still remained in his scalp. His ear withered like a flower in the hot desert sun. No one dared stare, so this was the first time I got to see the results of my dad's attack up close. Mom told me Dominion had taken control of him at the time, but I wasn't overly proud at the moment.

"You see, don't you?" He regained his normal stern composure. "Once we kill enough of you, the Slags hiding in the wastelands of our nation's greatest cities will come forward, and then we will destroy them once and for all."

Powell walked toward the river, back straight, head held high. As he stood outlined by the setting sun, I saw the proud warrior who had defended the United States instead of the broken man who would kill me to start a war because he never left the last one. He strolled down the riverbank away from camp as if there wasn't a care in the world.

Once the sun set, Ryder and Clint built the fire higher. I saw Clint rubbing his crotch where Abby had kicked him. They made multiple trips to the wood pile just beyond the clearing. Meanwhile, Brunner perched on a stump watching Wendi, a hungry look in his eyes and toilet paper stuffed up his nose to stop the bleeding. He reminded me of a dog waiting for scraps to fall off the table. Absently, he pulled the knife out of the stump and juggled it between his hands while staring. Powell lurked somewhere close by.

I pulled again at the ropes, my arms straight out like the Michelangelo anatomy picture the science teacher had in her classroom. I couldn't really feel them any more since they had been there for at least three hours. Mom would be getting home soon to find an empty house. I guessed she'd understand what happened since our bodies were the trophies of Powell's sick game. He would be sure to share them to get his war. I wondered if he would put them outside the school.

I tried to flex my shoulders again—any sense of feeling would be a welcome change, even if pain was all I got for my trouble. A noise to my left caught my attention. Clint stood behind the pole my left arm had been tied to. He chewed his nails, his eyes darting around the fire lit clearing.

"Tommy, I'm sorry. I didn't know Chuck would take it this far. I thought we was messin' with ya to get even fer the other day."

"It's okay, Clint," I said as softly as I could. "Can you loosen the ropes? My arms are going to fall off soon."

His shoulders slumped as he looked at his shoes. "He'd kill me if I'd did. I'm sorry though."

He fled, leaving me to my fate. I couldn't blame him; crossing Powell and Brunner would be suicidal. I felt my last chance slide away.

My team laid in ruins. Jon barely conscious. Marcel huddled in a ball, crying softly inside the burlap bag. Abby, still unconscious, with blood covering her face from her busted nose. Waxenby caught my eye, but there was nothing he could do; even Commander Gravity had his limits, especially without his Gift.

Wendi was still tied to the post across from me. Four cedar posts and the crossbeams remained from the old picnic shelter, which had stood here before a storm destroyed it. I tried to catch her eye, give her some hope, but I felt lost myself.

Focused, Brunner rose from the stump, still carrying his knife. He kissed Wendi, and the hand not holding the knife pawed at her breast. She gave no reaction and stared off into space. I tasted the bitterness of failure rising my throat.

His eyes flickered around the clearing, searching intently. The knife leapt back and forth between his hands, as he muttered to himself until he made up his mind. Leaping from the stump, he quickly cut Wendi's ropes. She slumped forward into Brunner. Shoving her against the post with one hand holding her neck, he slid the knife under her shirt, cutting through the fabric.

Wendi screamed an awful, soul-rending scream of terror. She tried to fight back, but Brunner put the knife to her throat and she stopped.

"Brunner, I swear to God, I'm going to kill you." My voice burst out as loud and harsh as I could make it.

He spun around, putting her in front of him, the knife still to her throat. Tears streamed down her face, mixing with the dried blood, which dripped off her chin. Her eyes pleaded for me to help, but I was helpless, tied like a piñata waiting to be beaten until all the stuffing came out.

"Ward, you wanna watch while I do your girl?" He sneered from behind her. The firelight flickered across his face giving him a demonic appearance, which was right on the money. "At least she'll have a real man before she dies."

I surged against the ropes, but they held, shooting waves of pain up my arms. Brunner laughed. I tried again, but the only things giving way were my shoulder sockets.

Powell decided to make his appearance, the Caesar entering his Coliseum. He surveyed the mayhem that had ensued in his absence. He shook his head, disappointment clearly written on his face.

"Powell, I got tired of waiting. She's mine."

"Mr. Powell, please," Wendi pleaded, her voice barely above a whisper.

Powell rubbed his eyes. "Fine." Annoyance thick in his voice. "You won't follow orders, get it over with, but for God's sake, drag her over there and kill her when you're done." He pointed off into the tree line while he walked across to my post.

Brunner's face lit up like a dog with a new toy. Wendi shrieked hysterically, the sound bouncing around the clearing and off the water, pulling with all her might against his hold as he took his prize to the appointed area. Clint and Ryder followed, not wanting to miss the show.

My brain exploded with a mixture of rage and grief. I had to stop all this. "Powell, my dad should have burned your freaking head off when he had the chance. He would save us all a lot of trouble," I declared in the area where only the two of us could hear what was said.

Powell laughed closing the final distance, his face inches from mine.

"Nice try, Ward. Trying to save your girlfriend is admirable, but you'll listen to her scream before I kill you."

"My father is Cyclone Ranger," I hissed, the words burning my mouth as I broke my promise to my mom, but this was my last-ditch effort to save Wendi. "He carried you to the aid station and let them think you had captured him. All the stories about taking down him down were all lies. Did you tell your buddies you wet your pants he scared you so bad?"

"Stop!" he screamed.

"How proud your family must be," I kept on like a matador taunting the bull. "The mighty Lewis C. Powell, pants wetter! If he'd been on target, it'd have blown your head clear off."

Powell molted red, his burnt scars leaving white patches in the crimson. He turned toward the wood screaming, "Brunner, you can have playtime later!"

Brunner started to protest but paled when he realized Powell's pistol was leveled at him. He stopped trying to saw off her jeans and returned Wendi to the post, holding her while Clint and Ryder retied her.

"Get the truck. We're going to see how Mr. Ward likes being burnt." His eyes crackled with insane energy. I'd just pushed the big, red button in Powell's brain.

Brunner ran, throwing the knife into the stump as he went. Headlights illuminated the clearing when he drove up in front of us. Powell banged on the hood, and the latch popped with a hollow thud.

"Clint, get the jumper cables from the back." Powell opened the hood, propping it open with the metal arm. Clint tossed the cables to him. The madman smiled over his shoulder at me as he hooked up the cables and made a show of touching the clamps together producing a shower of sparks.

Powell got inches from my face, quietly spitting words back at me the same way I had done to him. "Two people in the world know that story, and Cyclone Ranger is the other, so I know you're telling the truth. I'm gonna make you beg for me to end you. When I'm done, I'm going to pay a visit to your beautiful mother and make sure she suffers just the way my wife did when Titan smashed her and my baby girl to death."

Oh my God! I never thought that by telling Powell I would put her in danger. Tears rolled down my face as I realized what I'd done. Powell would kill us all anyway, and my big mouth now cost the only person who loved me her life as well.

"Ryder, get a bucket of water," Powell said over his shoulder. "Not so mouthy now are you?"

I shook. I had never been so scared in my life. "Please, don't hurt my mom. She didn't realize who he was when they got married," I lied.

"Too bad. I'll take pictures so Cyclone Ranger knows who killed his family before he dies in the arena. Then, Tommy boy, we'll be even for what he's done to me."

Ryder returned with the water in a beat-up orange bucket. It sloshed mightily as he ran.

Powell dumped the cold river water over my head. I spluttered as it hit me, making the cool night much worse. "We need a good connection, so you really feel it."

He tore my shirt open and jabbed me with the live ends of the cable. Pain coursed through my body. I think I pissed myself, but I was soaking wet, so I couldn't tell. He let me hang for a second before he touched me again. This time, he left them on longer. The pain was incredible. I tried to scream, but only a hoarse, animal sound came out.

I could hear my friends screaming for him to stop, but the pain kept on. I writhed like a puppet on a string, dancing to some lunatic's commands.

The pain stopped abruptly. I panted, trying to catch my breath. I could taste blood in my mouth from where I had bitten my tongue. Another bucket of water washed over me. The pain flared at the cold touch, but afterward, it numbed my skin to the pain.

"Not so tough now?" Powell mocked me as I limply hung from the ropes. "I'm going to finish with your face, same way your daddy did to me, so they'll see the burns on your body. You want to beg for your life?"

Powell floated before my unfocused eyes. He smiled at me, waiting for me to beg. He leaned closer, so I spit blood in his face. "Go to hell," I croaked out through my torn lips and swollen tongue.

"It's a shame you're a Slag. You would have made a fine soldier, Ward."

A clamp attached to my right ear. I could smell the ozone coming off the clamp as he waved it in front of my face. Without warning, the second clamp was pushed into my cheek.

The world went completely white for me. The pain faded away. The energy balled itself up in my chest, growing stronger as the electricity pumped into me. It kept growing, threatening to blow me apart.

"Why isn't he burning?" I heard Powell yell. "Give it more gas."

The engine revved, and the power flowed into me faster, coiling around me, twining around me, a living thing, searching for a way out. I screamed, a mixture of agony and ecstasy as the power coursed through me. Just when I couldn't hold anymore, my collar shattered, glistening shards of silver tinkling to the ground around me.

The power unleashed a super-nova. The truck exploded in the back-lash, shredding the engine. A pulse of pure energy erupted from me, a shockwave tearing across the clearing. It knocked Powell and everyone standing to the ground.

The ropes burned away. The power still flared within me. Ryder and Clint bolted for the trees. I couldn't let them go; they would bring the Reclaimers. This ended tonight. The raging torrent coalesced at my command into twin arcs of lightning. They streaked from my hand, incinerating them before they reached the edge of the clearing. My animal brain snarled its approval as I destroyed the threats to my pack. Powell got to his feet, pistol in his hand. I pushed at him with two hands, the jet of lightning launched him out of the clearing, toward the river.

Brunner staggered away from the burning wreckage of his truck. He stopped as I approached him. Energy crackled from every pore of my body. I held up my hand, watching the ribbons of energy leaping from finger to finger.

"Tommy, please," Brunner stuttered. Then he gasped and fell to the ground, his knife sticking out of the center of his back.

Wendi stood over his limp body, glaring down at him. "See what please gets you?"

19

Wendi sagged to the ground crying. I wanted to comfort her, but arcs of electricity skittered around me like fireworks on Reclamation Day.

Marcel and Abby helped Jon over to where we were. He already looked better than earlier though still worse for wear.

Waxenby sprang into action. "Marcel, find me a cell phone that isn't one of ours. Jon sit down on the stump there. I'll check your wounds in a minute." He motioned for Abby to join us. "Abby, can you tend to Wendi? She's been through an ordeal today. I…" He paused, his voice becoming less firm, less confident. "I don't think she can handle a male near her right now."

Abby nodded. She glanced over to where Wendi sat staring at Brunner's corpse. "I'll see what I can do." Wendi flinched when Abby placed her hand on her shoulder. She gently led Wendi to the other side of the fire. I could barely hear Wendi's sobs as she clung to Abby.

Marcel arrived with a phone in hand. "It's a bit scorched, but it still works. Could you use mine? It has much better signal strength out here."

"No, we don't want any calls traced out here," Waxenby said as he started to make a call. "Collect everyone's cell phones. We need to destroy them." He tossed his own phone to Marcel, who promptly dropped it.

"What?" Marcel said, shock and outrage on his face. Even after being captured and almost killed, the geek in Marcel still shined through. "I just got a Droid Universe. I saved three months of stipend to get it."

Waxenby paused dialing, sighing. "Marcel, they have GPS devices in them. If the Reclaimers track the signal, they'll be able to tell where we are. Do you want to answer for the deaths of Powell and three Norms?"

The color drained out of Marcel's face. "I'll get the phones."

Waxenby finished making his call, moving away from me. I guess all charged up I was causing interference. "Mr. Wizard, I need a book."

I could hear a voice from the phone, but not enough to tell who it could be.

"This is Bean, and there's been a problem. I've got to get a book from the library."

After a pause, he listened to whoever spoke on the other end. "Oberon?" After another pause, he said, "Okay, you'll need to grab Miss America. She's not safe." He ended the call and turned off the phone, sticking it in his pocket.

"What was that all about?" I asked.

Waxenby peered around the clearing. "Getting orders. We aren't safe here. I'm taking you to a hideaway, so to speak."

"What the hell is Oberon? I want to go home," I blurted out.

He chuckled. "No, Oberon is the code name for the safe house. We need to find Powell's body and destroy the evidence."

The side effect of crackling with energy is you glow. In essence, I became a human flashlight. We scoured the riverbanks, but after a half an hour, the only thing we found was Powell's Black Chevy Yukon parked on the utility road down by the river.

Waxenby pulled a heavy-duty flashlight out of the SUV, and we continued the search. With the steady light, we found small parts of Powell. Waxenby pitched them into the river with a flicker of gravity. At last, we found one of Powell's arms with the shoulder still attached. It smelled of burnt meat. I threw up as Waxenby encased it in the bubble floating behind us like a goldfish in a bag from the fair.

Waxenby continued to survey the area, but there weren't any other large chunks to see. "We'd probably find more during the day, but we've taken too long already. The rest of him must have landed in the river. Let's get back."

The floating piece of Powell followed us to the SUV. The navy blue uniform sleeve still held the Reclaimers insignia on his wrist. It gleamed in the orb's glow. The blue bubble, a space-age luggage carrier sitting on the roof as we drove, proved Waxenby's ability to multitask. I doubt Salvador Dali could come up with a more surreal portrait.

We loaded Powell's remains, Brunner's dead body, and our phones into the truck. Waxenby took the rest to Powell's SUV. With everyone gone, the only sound was the crackle of the fire. I still couldn't believe I'd broken free of the collar that had marked me for most of my life, but there was a cost. I'd killed three people in the process.

"Tommy," Waxenby said from beside me. "You've got to burn the truck and the bodies. We can't leave any evidence."

I held up my hands, and the energy still flickered, but I could feel it receding. "What do you want me to do?"

"Start the energy flowing into the truck." He flexed his arms as he talked. I guess he was still sore from being tied up. "Go until I tell you to stop."

The power surged down my arms, out my hands, and into the truck. My hands felt burnt from the raw energy leaving my skin. The ecstasy offset the pain, which amplified as I pumped more through my hands. I caught a whiff of burning flesh. Brunner's last chance to bother me would be the stench he left behind.

The truck burned, the energy feeding its devouring destruction, erasing all signs we had been here. I noticed a blue dome form over the truck, so it appeared to be encased in glass. I saw Waxenby out of the corner of my eye, hands outstretched toward the flames, sweat beading on his brow. He used his Gift to contain the fire.

"Keep going," he said through gritted teeth.

I pressed as hard as I could. The truck and its contents melted into the soil, compressed by the blue globe. Unbearable pain curled my hands into fists.

"Stop!" Waxenby shouted. I let go of the power. I felt totally drained and in need of a nap. The spot where the truck and its grisly contents has stood showed a scorched patch of earth. A good rain and all the evidence would be gone.

I sat down on the stump we all had been using, panting from the exertion, hands throbbing and burnt. Waxenby smiled the same way Marcel did when he got new geek gear. "Gift. How?" I said, too tired to care if I sounded like a Neanderthal.

Waxenby gingerly picked up my hands and examined them. I could see some of the skin had blistered from the electricity flowing out of me. "Let's get your hands in some water, then we'll talk."

He grabbed the bucket that an hour ago was a part of my torture and led me to the riverbank. He drew water and placed my hands into it. I swear they hissed with relief.

"During the fight, a burst of energy erupted from you. The closest thing I can say was it reminded me of an eruption." He rubbed his chin. "It must have shorted out the collars because they all popped open, and my Gift returned. Abby had snapped her ropes, so I made a force knife and freed Marcel. We had to carry Jon until he regained consciousness. Wendi stood too close to the fight for us to chance it. An amazing display of pyrotechnics to be sure."

I just nodded. I was too tired and a bit overwhelmed by the whole thing. After a few minutes, Waxenby took me to the SUV and put me and the bucket in the rear hatch where I promptly fell asleep. Who says the Gifted don't know how to party?

I don't know how long I slept, but when I woke, it was in a cot, not the trunk of the SUV. My head let loose a low-grade roar as I sat up. I dropped my legs over the side of the cot, forced myself to stand, and stumbled a bit toward the light coming from under the door.

I opened the door a crack to let my eyes adjust to the light as much as to figure out where I was. I saw the back of Marcel's head sitting at a cafeteria-style foldout table. I opened the door wider, cringing as my eyes screamed in protest at the light flooding in.

"Why, good morning, Princess," Blaze's voice came from across the room. Everyone turned to stare at me as I tottered into the room. Marcel jumped up and helped me into a chair. One of the many reasons he's my best friend.

"Where are we?"

"Let's just say we are at a friend's house." Waxenby set his coffee cup down. "Or if it makes you feel better, this is Oberon."

The room could have fallen out of the 1970s. A green stove and beat-up fridge were situated on the far side, flanked by orange counter tops and bright yellow cabinets. I seriously wished I had colorblindness at the moment.

"Well, it's better than the alternative," Marcel said.

I shot him a quick smile. Jon appeared surly as always, hunched over the table. I started a bit when I realized the girls weren't here.

The click of another door opening caught my attention.

"I thought I heard you were up." Mom came at me faster than was necessary, but I grabbed her in a hug anyway. As uncool as it is to admit, sometimes a guy just needs his mom.

"I'm sorry," I whispered.

She pushed me back, locking my eyes. "Tommy, this isn't your fault." I could see her fury, but not at me. "Powell's a psycho. He could have killed all of you."

I nodded. Words wouldn't come out. I saw Abby and Wendi by the door. I went to hug Wendi, but she pulled away, tears streaming down her face. She fled back into the room and slammed the door.

"What did I do?"

"Nothing," Abby growled. "She had a really bad time yesterday." She opened the door and closed it quietly behind her.

Mom slid her arm around my waist. "Wendi's going to need some time, Tommy. You're going to have to be patient."

Then I remembered Waxenby's words from the clearing and felt like a moron. Mom had represented some Gifted women after they had lived through some bad stuff back when I was thirteen, and she had explained a bit, what I could handle at the time. I was going to need another conversation.

Jon's eyes stabbed into me with accusations. Rage contorted his features. "This is all your fault, Ward. I told you to stay away from Wendi."

"You would be dead if not for Tommy," Marcel said. "He even got rid of your collar, and all he gets is crap from you?"

Waxenby stood. "Enough. Jon, we've talked about it. Brunner hassled Wendi long before she spent any time with Tommy. You told me so yourself."

Jon stared at the floor, unwilling to meet Waxenby's eyes. "Sorry,

Tommy." His words were almost too soft to hear. "I could never forgive myself if anything ever happened to her."

"Me too."

"Okay, if everybody is cool, we need to discuss the plan." Blaze turned to Mom. "Susan, I know the score, but we need the girls. Everyone has to be on the same page."

She excused herself. A few minutes later, the three sat at the end of the table. I tried to keep from staring at Wendi, but I couldn't help myself. She appeared as fragile as a china doll, a stark contrast to her killing Brunner with his own knife. She caught my eye for a second, but I couldn't decipher what it meant.

"Okay, dudes. We already covered your tracks, the best we could in such a short time. It's been twenty-four hours since school ended yesterday. Officials are searching for Powell, his three pets, and the four of you. Good work on hacking Powell's email, Marcel."

Marcel smiled like a happy puppy. "Just thought it was best."

"It saved us," Blaze remarked. "Susan called Tommy in to the police as a missing child, and Oliver is AWOL."

"I'm a rebel," Waxenby chuckled.

Blaze snorted a laugh. "Once again, Marcel has been a great help. When the Reclaimers went to Powell's this morning, there were emails back and forth between him and Brunner about killing the six of you and dumping your bodies. Marcel, you are a handy dude to know."

"No problem, glad to help." Marcel beamed with pride.

"Susan is heading back to Redemption to do her legal thing as a frightened mother."

She glanced at me from the corner of her eye. "Don't need to be an actress to pull that one off."

"Oliver is going to take the rest of you dudes to Dresden," Blaze said.

"Ohio?" Marcel blurted out.

"No, Dresden is an old League of Patriots safe house." He paused. "Well, more like a safe fortress, but you can lay low there. There is one more issue."

"What issue?" Abby asked. Her tone bordered on hostile, which in past experience meant she was upset, and, frankly, after the last twenty-four hours, who could blame her?

Blaze held up a thin silver strip. "I need to suppress your Gifts."
The room erupted in chaos.

20

Everyone was shouting, and to my surprise, so was I. We had just gotten out of the collars and Blaze wanted to put us back in. No way.

"Whoa, dudes," Blaze held up his hands, surrendering before the onslaught of teen angst. "They are bracelets, and you can take them off."

Somewhat mollified, we sat down so he could explain.

"Oliver is the only one who knows what and how to use their Gift," he said.

I heard Abby mumble, "I can use mine." Her low voice sounded disheartened by the fact. I didn't get a chance to ask before Jon butted in.

"Tommy can blow shit up," Jon said dismissively.

I grimaced. Another glorious screw-up by Tommy Ward. Mom was seriously going to kill me.

Waxenby shook his head slowly. "I'm not so sure, Jon. The way it happened could have something to do with how his Gift manifested itself."

"Regardless," Blaze continued, dragging the conversation back on track. "None of you know what your Gift is yet. Dresden will help you discover your powers, but until you are safely hidden, we don't need anyone bursting into flame or sneezing acid all over the place."

"But what if we need to fight?" Abby asked.

"Then pull the bracelet off and hope your Gift kicks in before they take you down."

"They wouldn't stand a chance." Abby's look of playful malice played across her features. She scared me.

We quickly packed what little we had and headed for our escape vehicle. I'd been asleep when we arrived in the dark. Turns out Oberon is part of a trucking company near Great Falls. I doubt the Norms who work there had any idea they doubled as a front for a Gifted safe house.

We waited until after hours to load the van to make the thirteen-hour trip to Dresden. Mom stood near the Mom-mobile as the others climbed into the Midville Driving Academy van.

"Tommy, I wanted to talk to you for a minute before you go," she said.

I hung my head. "I'm sorry, Mom. I shouldn't have gone after Wendi myself."

"Tommy, if you hadn't, Wendi and most likely all of you would be dead. I am proud of you. You put yourself in harm's way to protect Wendi."

I couldn't bring myself to tell her I panicked. I wasn't the brave guy who stood up to evil and didn't flinch. I'd peed myself when they touched me with the cables.

"As much as I hate to admit it, your father would have done the same. He always put other people's safety ahead of his own, except for us."

"He thought he kept us safe."

"I know you think that, but he deserted us." The bitter tone crept into her voice. "I don't want you to make the same mistake. Your family comes first, and sometimes it means running with them. Do you understand?"

I did all too well. In her lawyer way, she spoke what I knew. The five of us were like family now, and we had to protect each other.

"Gotcha." I hugged her. "Mom, Powell said he would do terrible things to you. Shouldn't you come with us, to be on the safe side?"

"I have to go back." The corners of her mouth curled down. "If I'm not there screaming about you being taken by Powell, the Protectorate will get suspicious. Plus, Oliver told me you hit the bastard with so much juice he's probably on his way to the moon."

I smiled at her. I still had Wendi with me. No more Brunner or Powell. The Earth was a better place already. I guess I'm the scumbag remover. I

141

tried not to think about the others I had vaporized; Clint had only just found his conscience an hour before he died.

I hugged her once more, said goodbye, and drove off into the night to start my new life.

The sun peeked above the South Dakota horizon as we drove into what could only be described as a concrete cave. Waxenby steered the van off the paved road onto a gravel road into an abandoned railway tunnel. We pulled into the dark recess, the headlights flickering over assorted debris.

After a couple hundred feet, we came to a collapsed part of the tunnel. Waxenby hopped out of the van, flashlight in hand, as he looked for something. He stopped at a panel in the wall before returning to the van.

"Everybody ready?" he asked, his face covered by a big cheesy grin.

"Ready for what? We're in a collapsed tunnel," Abby said.

He held up a control of some sort. "For this." He pushed the button. A wall slid down behind the van, reflecting the taillights off the metallic surface. The van shook a bit as we descended into the ground.

Marcel shook with excitement. His head needed to be on a pivot so he could see everything at once. "How cool is this?"

"You haven't seen anything yet," Waxenby said. "I've heard stories of Dresden, but this is my first time here."

We stopped descending; a metal freight door slid open before us. We left the van in what looked to be a small parking area. There was room for ten cars, though only a motorcycle and a blue sedan were present, with a door reminding me of the Air-Lock back at school.

The door opened, leading into a hallway that ended in a door that mirrored the first. Waxenby entered a code, and his palm scanned to confirm his identity.

"Why wasn't the lock on the first door?" Marcel said, a bit bewildered. "That's not good security design."

The lock clicked, and the door swung open. Waxenby motioned for everyone to go in. "If I wasn't authorized, the far door locks and nothing good happens after that."

Marcel gulped, quickly exiting the hall. I guess sometimes it's better not to know. I followed him into a room that should have been on a high-end real estate show instead of underground in the middle of South Dakota. The hardwood floors gleamed, reflecting the sunlight coming in from the windows. I took a double take. The windows overlooked the ocean; a white sand beach stretched off into the distance.

"Um. That can't be real, can it?" Abby said.

Waxenby laughed. "From what I understand, it's a prismatic display that cycles with the time and season. Underground it is really tough to keep your circadian rhythms in sync."

"What is this place?" I asked, wonder thick in my voice. I fell through rabbit hole and ended up in tech heaven. Wendi had the same reaction as me—there was too much to see all at once.

Waxenby took a seat at the slate gray oval table dominating the right side of the room. Twenty industrial chairs surrounded the table. The chandelier alone was worth more than my house. Abby leaned against the wall near the table; her eyes scanned the room. I noticed she spun her watch while she stood there.

"Around the country, there are safe houses for the various Gifted teams. This one," he said sweeping his arm to indicate the room, "was owned by The League of Patriots. Old missile silos make great hideouts. Everything is state of the art, or it was before the war."

"This is amazing," Marcel whispered as he studied the prismatic display, walking around to see it from different angles. "We don't have this technology now."

"The Gifted teams had a lot of tech the general public had no idea about. Gifted engineers fabricated devices for the major teams, such as the bracelets you wear now."

"Or the collars we used to wear," Jon growled perching on another chair close to where Abby stood.

Wendi sighed. "Jon, stop it. We should be thankful Waxenby knew places to get us away from Redemption." I could hear the irritation in her voice. She moved over to stand between Jon and me.

Waxenby nodded. "We don't know where the collars came from. The bracelets you are wearing dampen your abilities, but they don't inhibit them. There would have been no need for the space station prison if we had the collars."

"For being a math teacher, you are certainly well informed," Jon said.

Waxenby shrugged. "Before I was collared, a few of us with lesser Gifts were given information from the teams since they were all being hunted then killed or interned. They wanted us to form a resistance to free the Gifted from the Protectorate."

"And you did an awesome job at that, I guess," Jon sneered. Abby stepped over and punched him in the shoulder. To his credit, he didn't flinch, much.

"Knock it off, Jon." The attitude was wearing on my nerves. "The only reason we got out of Redemption was because of Waxenby."

"I can't believe this is real," Marcel said, awe heavy in his voice standing in front of something else made of metal and blinking lights of unknown use, at least to me.

A voice came from across the room. "*Dios mío*! What are you *niños* doing here?"

All heads snapped around at the sound, both Jon and I stepping between Wendi and the intruder. The owner of the gravelly voice had a wispy black beard, long, straight hair, and a neck tattoo. Faded fatigues and combat boots stood in sharp contrast to the black dress shirt with red piping and a turquoise bolo tie. *Is cowboy guerilla a fashion trend?*

Marcel's jaw dropped. "W.T.F. That's the Grim Reaper."

With a roar, Abby pulled her bracelet off, threw it aside, and charged. Her hair trailed behind her as she closed the thirty feet, the red side of her hair flowing like the fire out of a jet engine.

Grim Reaper, caught unaware, moved just as fast. Abby was a whirl-wind of punches. He blocked the first few, then Abby connected with a vicious uppercut throwing him ten feet into the wall. He came off the wall, seething mad, scythe at the ready.

Both charged but bounced harmlessly off the shield Waxenby placed between them. Abby tried again, but the blue energy wrapped around her, pinning her arms and legs.

"That is quite enough from you two," Waxenby said. "Jose, you know better than to startle unsuspecting people."

The scythe winked out of existence, and the mood lightened margin-ally. "Sorry, Ollie. *Abuela* warns me about sneaking up on people." He rubbed his jaw. "I expected no one to be here."

"What's he doing here?" Jon said, still standing in front of Wendi. She was crouched on the ground, her hands over her head.

I knelt next to her. "Everything is okay now. It's under control." I reached out to help her up, but she flinched away from me. I heard Mom's voice in my head: "Take it slow." I waited until she put her hand on my arm, and I helped her up.

Marcel picked up Abby's bracelet from the floor, tossing it to me as Waxenby lowered the shields. She snatched it out of my hand. A curt nod was all I got as her eyes never left the Grim Reaper.

"I ask the same of you, boy." He matched the nastiness in Jon's question. "I'm hiding out from the Protectorate after breaking out of The Block. So, you on the run or a school fieldtrip?"

"How did you know about this place?" Waxenby asked.

"I got to talkin' with Siren back in The Block." His Latino accent had kicked in more now as he relaxed. "She told me where and how to get in. Same as you, I'm guessin'."

"Something like that," Waxenby said noncommittally. "Well, we'll take the silo since there is more of us."

"We're all on the same side now, Ollie. Let me help you train up these ones." He smirked. "Girlie there is one tough *cerda*. She could be a great fighter."

"I'll think about it, Jose. For now, we are going to catch some z's."

We followed Waxenby out of the room and down the switchback stairs leading to the silo. *"Buenas noches*, Ollie," echoed down the stairs with us.

Waxenby punched the wall, a blue glove covering his hand. "I should have stuffed a shield in his mouth."

21

The next morning, we made the decision to take off the dampening bracelets and let our Gifts manifest. Before the war, kids would begin to exhibit their Gifts around ten to twelve. Being older, Waxenby thought we would change faster.

We dropped into a routine as the days wore on. Start the day at seven a.m., run the track, hit the weights, wash up, and eat breakfast. After a couple of hours off, the afternoon was all testing to see if our Gifts were manifesting. Marcel and I cooked dinner most nights, and Abby helped where she could. The summer at The Secret Lair made the transition easier since we'd been working in the kitchen. Jon and Wendi cleaned up after, making jokes none of us understood. Seeing them work together displayed how effortlessly they revolved around each other. After, we watched old movies or hung out talking about training. Nobody mentioned school; I think all of us understood we'd never return for senior year.

Jose, the Grim Reaper, was our workout coach and sparring partner. He taught us combat techniques, dirty fighting, and generally thumped us pretty good. He also taught us to use the knife always strapped to his hip, but on the training dummies. It turns out Gifted have better reflexes, heal faster, and have a much higher pain tolerance than Norms if we aren't collared. Morning bruises were gone by dinner, which would've come in handy when I was Brunner's punching bag.

Waxenby let Jose help after we all agreed to keep to first names and we didn't talk about anything but training with him. Jose was a murderer and assassin, but he knew how to fight.

A couple of weeks into training, I sat on a bench outside the boxing ring, watching Jon get his ass handed to him. The ring was padded to help soften the landings, but they still hurt. Jose's faded denim shirt and knife belt hung over the turnbuckle. Jose's knife had become an extension of him, his weapon of choice. None of us could be seen as a threat, so why bother carrying it? I watched Jose goad him into losing his temper, and after that, it was all over but the bleeding.

"Can I sit here?" Wendi said. I was so focused on the training I didn't hear her approach, a habit I needed to break before it broke me, or so I've been told by Jose.

"Sure thing."

"Jon's so angry. I don't know how to reach him. He's never been a hothead." She shook her head.

And the award for understatement of the year goes to... "Jose is good at getting to him," I said instead. *And getting to me*, I admitted to myself without it coming out of my mouth, for once. I let the silence lengthen like the shadows as the sun set.

Breaking the silence, she brought the light back to help the healing. "Tommy, I'm sorry I've been avoiding you." She put her hand up when I started to protest. "Brunner hurt me. I still have nightmares about it. The funny part is the whole time I knew you would save me somehow. Not Jon, you."

She looked up, but the match went on. Relief flooded her face. "He'd never forgive me if he heard me say that," she blurted. "Afterward, I was scared and ashamed at what had happened and I couldn't face you."

I reached for her hand but stopped short. She slowly took my hand in hers. Her skin felt warm and soft, like the sun after a rainy day. I smiled at her, probably way goofier than I ever intended.

"I understand, or at least I think I understand, but either way it's okay. I'm worried about you." It had been hard to not be with her, but now maybe things could start to go back to normal. "I didn't want to fail you. I'm glad you are safe."

147

She leaned over and kissed me. I could feel her trembling. It was like our first kiss all over again.

"Ward, what the hell are you doing?" Jon yelled from the ring we trained in. His face turned purple as the anger took over, again. "I told you to stay away from my sister."

"*Hombre*, chill," Jose said, holding his hands up, ending the match.

He pushed past Jose, a sneer plastered across his face. "Why don't you come up here, and I'll wipe that stupid smirk from your face."

Wendi stood up, hands on her hips and cold as stone. "Jon, Tommy is my boyfriend, and it is none of your business."

"Wendi, this is between Tommy and me."

I glanced at Wendi. She nodded slightly, so I knew it was okay. This had to end, and if it took a beating to end it, so be it. I just didn't know who would be on the receiving end.

Given we healed faster, nobody wore boxing gear since in combat your opponent wouldn't be. I climbed between the ropes, pushed the hair back from my eyes, and got ready. Jon being six three, I gave up five inches and thirty pounds of muscle, but Blaze had taught me well.

"Come on," I said. Jon ran at me like a rampaging rhino. I sidestepped him, letting him bounce off the turnbuckle. He spun, sweat flying off him in a wide arc. He moved in low, circling me, looking for an opening. I cleared my mind and blocked the punches as they came. I didn't throw any; I hoped he would calm down.

"Fight me, dammit!" he screamed.

He came at me again, and I slid to the side and punched him in the side of the head. He shook off the blow then rapid fired punches at me, slamming one into my jaw, after which I stopped feeling the individual attacks, and it became one massive building bruise. Out of sheer reflex, I hit him with an uppercut, which drove him a good six feet in the air. He bounced off the mat, his body making a loud thud as he hit.

I wanted to check on him, but Jose waved me off. "Nice punch, Ward." Jose grinned at me. "I didn't think you had it in you."

Crap. No last names. Jon blew it for me. I needed to talk to Waxenby and see what he thought. Jon was on his feet. I turned to climb out of the ring so I could go find Waxenby. Jon and his big mouth.

"Tommy!" Wendi yelled. Jon snatched the combat knife from where it hung on the turnbuckle and charged at me. I flowed into my overhead block, but the knife was gone. Jon looked as stunned as I did. Wendi stood at the far wall, knife in hand. In the blink of an eye, she had gotten into the ring, taken the knife, and gotten out again.

Jose punched Jon square in the face, flattening him to the floor. The psychic scythe was out, its ominous green glow a few inches from his face. The blade trembled as if he couldn't decide if he should use it.

"Jose, it's okay, man," I said as calm as I could. "He lost his temper. No harm done."

"Wheres I come from a guy pulls shiv on ya, you put him down like a dog," Jose growled, staring down at Jon, his accent flipping from Latino thug to New York mobster. I swear you could feel the ice flowing through his veins. "You ever do that again, punk, 'n I cut you. *Capisce?*"

Jon nodded rapidly. The blade winked out of existence. Jose gaped at me as if he saw me for the first time. "Watch ya back with that one." He ducked through the ropes, grabbing his shirt and sheath, got the knife from Wendi, and left.

Jon glared at Wendi. I couldn't tell if he was pissed or relieved she'd taken the knife. He shot her a disgusted sneer and left the ring.

I turned to Wendi. "Thanks. I guess we're even," I said, managing a weak smile, even though her twin brother had tried to stab me.

"Did you see how fast I ran?" she squealed in delight.

"As a matter of fact, I didn't, Speedy Gonzales."

F rustration built in me as the days wore on. I couldn't do anything with my Gift. I wondered if the night I killed Powell had burned me out. Marcel dove into the tech left behind at Dresden. The way he lovingly spoke about it made me think they were dating. Maybe they were…the AI was pretty advanced.

Waxenby called us all together in the "living room." This place amazed me. The eight chairs, arranged in a circle around a round coffee table, molded to your body, reclined in zero-G position, had massage and heat features. While you were in them, you could access news feeds, watch TV, listen to music, or anything else. The best part is you were the only one who could see or hear it. Marcel explain it transmitted data directly into your sub-neurological cranial bio-something-or-other. I didn't care how it worked, as long as it did.

Wendi and I linked our sessions so we could talk while we watched movies together. Usually old romantic comedies that she liked so much. The chairs allowed us to bond and talk without the physical contact that set her on edge.

Jose, face drawn in a frown, had taken "old blue" to get some supplies. My guess is Jose had been voluntold to go away for a while. He grumbled as he stormed out to the parking area we had originally entered through.

I studied my friends. All of us had changed since the day the collars came off nearly three weeks before. I'd grown and filled out, as had the others. I wasn't sure if exercise or being Gifted had brought the changes, but we all could have been professional athletes. Abby showed the greatest change. At six four, she stood taller than Jon and bordered on being more muscular. Little things set her off now more than ever.

"Good morning, class," Waxenby said with a laugh. "I wanted to discuss some of the changes you've been going through."

We glanced at each other, hoping this wasn't a sex talk. We all squirmed in our seats, not sure where he was headed.

"Most Gifted go through manifestation slowly. They grow faster than their peer group, being more athletic or, like Marcel, learn at an acceler-ated pace. You've all compressed that into a few weeks. As with most things, there are good parts and bad parts. You know the things your Gifts allow you to do, but there is a price for using those Gifts."

"A price?" Wendi asked, her voice shaking a bit.

Waxenby nodded. "Yes, a price. The price is dependent on your partic-ular Gift, and the degree is tied to how strong it is."

"How do you gauge how strong you are?" Marcel said.

"There isn't a measurement, and what we are talking about is never discussed amongst the Gifted. If you know the drawbacks to someone's Gift, you could find a way to exploit it."

"Like with the Grim Reaper?" Abby said as she peeked over her shoulder toward the door as if she expected him to appear.

"Exactly," Waxenby nodded. "I will take each of you aside and explain what I know about your Gift and the drawbacks, if I know any."

He signaled Marcel, who had a box sitting next to his feet. He stood up and gave us each a silver watch. Marcel didn't have one on, so I wondered why he gave us each one.

"The watches Marcel built will act the same way the collars used to. If you wear them long enough, the changes you have seen will recede." Waxenby glanced at Abby, who, in turn, gave him a slight nod as she fastened the watch to her wrist. She shot a smile at Waxenby.

Marcel jumped into the silence surrounding the announcement. "I put a switch on the side to dampen your Gift like the bracelets Blaze gave us. You can still access your Gift if needed."

"Thank you, Marcel," Waxenby said. "If you inhibit your Gift, it will take some time to restore it after the watch has been removed. Any questions?"

We all shook our heads. Since I still didn't know what my Gift was, I shoved the watch in my pocket.

"When you're ready, find me, and I'll tell you what I know and answer any other questions."

I noticed Wendi walked off with Waxenby. Abby stared at the watch on her arm. I wondered why she so readily put it on. Some things were better left unasked. I returned to watching anime.

I woke with a start, having drifted off in the recliner in the zero-G position.

"What the hell did you tell her?" Jon yelled, bearing down on Waxenby, who stood by the coffee table. *A front row seat for Jon's big mouth, wonderful.* "She left in the middle of the night. I found this note on her bed."

"I told her the truth, Jon," he said in a calm voice. If there was ever a time for a shield in the mouth, now would be a great time. "She needed to understand the powers and liabilities of her Gift."

Jon paced back and forth like a caged animal, the note crumbled in his hand. "She's fragile. We were fine until we got mixed up with you freaks. What exactly did you tell her?"

"A person's Gift is private." He sat down on the table. "If she had wanted to tell you, she would have."

"She's aging," Marcel said from the hallway door. "The price for speed is aging. Every time she uses her Gift, she will age around five times as fast. Most speeders die in their twenties. Not a big deal if you use it for five minutes, but it adds up."

Jon turned on him. "And just how do you know that, Geek?"

151

Marcel adjusted his glasses; he had a smirk on his face. Geek was a compliment to him. "Hers is the one Gift that has been studied due to the negative effect being overtly visible. The computer library is full of data on it. You would have realized that if you could read."

"Well, I'm going after her." Jon threw the note on the floor, heading for the door.

A blue shield sprang up in front of him. "Let her cool off and see if she comes back. We can't chance a lot of people coming and going if everyone else is going to stay safe."

Jon stared daggers at Waxenby. I thought it would get ugly, but Jon huffed and backed down. Waxenby dropped the shield.

I started to chime in that I wanted to go as well, but given Jon's feelings about me, it might make it worse.

Waxenby stepped closer to where Jon stood. "Jose will be back soon, and we'll discuss it. Once it's dark, we'll decide on the best course of action. I promise."

"Fine," Jon snapped. He turned to leave. "I let you stop me for now. Once it's dark, I'm going, and no one is stopping me. Understood?"

Waxenby nodded. Jon stomped off.

"Well, that was exciting," Marcel quipped.

I laughed a bit nervously. "You've got a strange sense of what's fun."

"If you thought that was fun, wait until we tell him he can't go," Waxenby said with a grimace.

Oh joy, just what I always wanted, to be locked with a raving lunatic. It was going to be a long day.

22

The day dragged. I packed my backpack three times trying to keep my mind off things. A tap on the door frame roused me from my organizational obsession. Abby stood there, a crumpled piece of paper in her hand.

"Sorry to interrupt, but can I come in?"

"Sure thing." I stepped to the side to let her in. We all stayed in the "recruit" wing according to Marcel. The rooms were fairly Spartan in comparison with the rest of the place, but the bed was large and comfortable with a dresser and desk. The bathroom was self-cleaning, and the shower had about ten spray heads. There were League of Patriot rooms on the lower levels of the silo, but they were coded shut, and Waxenby forbid Marcel from cracking them open.

Abby took a seat on the bed. She cocked her head to the side, bent over, and picked up an envelope off the floor. "You should read this since it's addressed to you." She twisted her watch around her wrist, something obviously bothering her.

I took the envelope, but the expression on her face caught my attention. Her eyes were red-rimmed and puffy. Something bothered her, and I doubted it was Wendi leaving.

"You okay?"

She stared down at her hands, not looking at me. "Can I talk to you?" she said, her voice small.

"Of course."

She sat there for a few minutes, and I flopped down next her and waited. I could almost hear the struggle in her head over what she needed to talk about.

"I guess you are wondering about why I put the watch on yesterday," she said.

I had wondered but had been so caught up in being left out I hadn't even given a second thought about why she would give up her Gift after just getting it. "I didn't want to pry," I said.

She sighed. "I should have told you and Marcel about this before, but I was afraid you wouldn't want to be my friend if you knew."

I punched her softly in the shoulder since I wasn't sure how to handle Abby not being Abby. "We'll always be friends."

She smiled a sad smile. "You should probably hear my story before you say that."

I sat back against the headboard to listen.

She shifted uncomfortably before she spoke. "I was born in Boston to Norm parents, but we had quite a few Gifted in our family. After the war, when the Protectorate started testing people for Gifts, my parents left the US for Argentina. They told me if I wasn't Gifted, we would move back someday."

I nodded. Her voice trembled a bit, but she kept going.

"We lived in a small town so we could duck the soldiers when they came to test. There were a lot of Gifted in the area, so we expected to be safe. The townspeople treated us like family, and they hid us while the soldiers tested people," she said, a look of longing in her eyes.

"Just after my twelfth birthday, I changed. I grew taller and stronger, but I had a hard time controlling myself. I would be gone for days on end. I hunted in the jungle, killing to eat. I became an animal. Slowly, I got control of myself, but the people were freaked out. There were rumors I'd become a werewolf or some sort of demon. We moved around, but the rumors followed us. Finally, my parents gave up."

She glanced over at me. I'm sure she expected to see a mask of horror on my face, but all I felt was bad for her.

She continued. "I had been home for a week. I had things under control, so we went to town to get supplies. As we entered the town square, the soldiers came out, rifles pointed at me. I tried to fight, dropping a couple of soldiers in the process, but they got the collar on me. My strength was gone. I pleaded with my parents to help me, but they wouldn't even look at me. Two of the soldiers pulled me to my feet and moved me away from my parents."

"They betrayed you?" I blurted out. I couldn't imagine a parent turning their own child in.

She shook her head slightly. "No, not exactly. The captain approached my parents, who were smiling at him. My father extended his hand, but the captain slapped his face instead. His men moved up and pushed to their knees in front of the store we were going to shop in. Other soldiers lined up, readying their rifles.

"'We brought her here for you,' my father begged. My mother sobbed uncontrollably next to him, clutching his arm. 'You promised us that you could help her.'

"'The harboring of a Dissident is a capital offense. You are both guilty under the Protectorate and I, a duly appointed enforcement officer, am carrying out the sentence.'

"'Abby, I'm sorry,' my mother wailed. 'We love you.'"

I gasped. No wonder Powell had brought up the penalty for harboring a Gifted her first day at school.

"Anything else they would have said ended with the sounds of gunfire. Their bodies jerked as the bullets slammed them against the stone wall, blood smearing down the wall as they slid, lifeless to the ground. The soldiers dragged me away. I tried to run to my parents to say goodbye, but they put me in a truck and sent me to Redemption."

Tears were sliding down her cheeks as she finished her story. "So now you know. You are friends with a monster."

"If there is a monster in your story, it's the Protectorate, Abby." Anger and grief mixed in my brain. These are the same people who took my dad from me, who shackled me and let Brunner and Powell almost kill me. I needed to hit something. "They lied to your parents about helping you, then killed them."

She gaped at me. "Did you not listen to my story? I lived in the jungle, killing animals. I became a savage."

I shook my head. "If the Protectorate hadn't forced you into hiding, you would have had help. Abby, none of this was your fault."

She cried. I moved next to her, and she hugged me. I think she broke a couple of ribs in the process.

"Like I told you before, we are always friends," I said between gasps for air. "Unless you crush me to death."

Abby left to talk to Marcel, buoyed by my taking her side. Though she never skipped, I saw a spring to her step. I noticed she didn't spin the watch either. It must be a huge relief to not be carrying around such a secret, as I knew from personal experience.

I closed the bedroom door and flopped on the bed. I opened up the crumbled note, trying to smooth out the wrinkles the best I could. I had already read it twice, maybe third time was a charm.

Tommy,

I'm sorry to have left without saying goodbye. After talking with Mr. Waxenby, I need some time to think. My Gift gives me great speed, but the price is more than I might be willing to pay. I know I should use Marcel's watch to stop the effects, but I'd feel dead now that I know what having my Gift feels like. I need to be away from everyone and think. I'll be back when I know what to do.

I love you,

Wendi

I laid there, thoughts rampaging through my head. Thanks to Marcel, I knew she'd aged due to her Gift. I wondered if she would live longer since she was fifteen when her powers kicked in. I couldn't bear to think of my beautiful Wendi dying as an old lady at twenty.

I paced my room for a long time. Wendi needed time to think. Hadn't I run away from Mom to do the same? Who was I to drag her back here? She had the watch. She could live out her life away from us and the need to use her Gifts. I decided I'd put my backpack in the ready room until I figured out what the plan was. At least I'd stop repacking it.

"Where are you going, Tommy?"

"Putting my backpack in the ready room. Figure if we go to get Wendi, I'll be prepared."

Jon stood, stepping in front of the door. "You should go back to your room. Nothing you can do." His eyes flickered to one area of the room.

I followed his glance. Jose sat in the corner where Jon had looked. Something was going on, and I'm not sure I liked it. Just what I needed, more bonding time with a pissed-off jerk. "You aren't going anywhere without me," I said.

Jose chuckled. *"Hombre,* I told you he'd not be left."

"Fine." Jon gave an exasperated sigh.

"We'd better get going if we want to find her. She couldn't have gotten far."

Jon laughed. The sound had all the warmth of being plunged into ice water while holding a block of ice. "We can't get there by morning on foot."

"It's only been about twelve hours," I said, doing the math in my head. "She couldn't have gone more than twenty miles if she walked all day."

Jon shook his head. "Man, you are stupid. She can run faster than a car. We are less than three hours from our farm. She's been there all day."

"How do you know that?"

"She left a note on her bed." He pulled out a sheet similar to the one I had read earlier. "She went home, wanting to talk to our mom. She probably thinks she'll treat her like your mom treats her."

The bitterness lacing his last sentence was an open window into Jon. He seethed, not just at me, but at what his parents had done to him. How they had left him and Wendi at the Institute instead of staying with them. I felt for him; I had seen the same thing with Marcel over the years. Not for the first time, I was extremely thankful for my mom.

"Well, I guess we have a long walk then," I said, trying to be a bit friendlier. "We should get started."

"You boys not going on foot." Jose stood, tossing his car keys in the air as he came toward us. "Since you boys aren't allowed to drive, I'll take you to get the *señorita.* It'll be fun."

I followed them out. Me, a psychopathic killer, and a hot head. What could possibly go wrong?

23

The drive took a little over three hours, listening to thrash metal the whole time. Who knew screaming could be considered music? We broke once for food at a burrito joint Jose liked. I don't think the health inspector had ever seen this place, or maybe he didn't make it out again. After eating, we filled up the car and headed out. Around ten, Jose slowed the car to pull off the road into some trees near the entrance of the Sleepy S Ranch.

We were in the country, and the crickets and whip-poor-will night songs sounded like a mix by a crazed DJ, but better than the trash metal. The scent of cow pies carried on the breeze, definitely letting you appreciate that cattle were around somewhere. Lights shone through the trees from the farmhouse.

Jon moved to the split-rail fence that ran across the front of the property. A tall, white farmhouse stood at the end of the gravel drive. Jose and I stumbled along behind him. A SUV sat parked next to the house, but other than that, it could have been the frontier days in Iowa.

The three of us quietly got out of the car, shouldered our bags, and crept to the fence for a better look. Jon set down his backpack, fishing around in it. Finally, he produced a large knife with a tie-on sheath. He strapped it to his thigh.

"What the heck is that for?" Last I knew we were getting Wendi, not launching an attack on a fortified position.

"You never know when you'll need a good knife." Jose nodded his approval.

Jon hopped over the fence, leading the way to the house. Jose and I had to actually climb over the rails, Jose swearing in Spanish the whole time. A few scrapes and minor injuries to my pride later, I was over the fence crouched between Jon and Jose.

"Well, she's here," Jon said.

"How do you know?"

"I can smell her perfume."

Wendi wore a lavender perfume, but as hard as I tried, I couldn't smell it. A look of disbelief affixed itself to my face. It was pitch black, so I figured I was safe.

"Don't look at me like that. I can smell her perfume," Jon remarked somewhat absent-mindedly. "Let's get a bit closer. I think she is in the kitchen."

Following the best we could, we stumbled through the trees toward the side of the farmhouse. "If you two didn't make so much noise, I think I could hear what they are talking about," Jon said, moving a bit toward the house.

We waited. I tried not to breathe so as to not make too much noise. I felt as if we were stalking prey instead of going in to get my girlfriend.

"They are arguing over Wendi showing up." Jon sounded pissed. "Let's go. We should get this over with."

"Why?" slipped out of my mouth before I could stop it.

"He hates Slags."

Great, I had to ask.

We spent what seemed like hours of tripping over rocks, sliding into divots, and generally making a mess of our stealth entry, but we made it to the house. Jon paused at the bottom of the stairs, took a deep breath, squared his shoulders, and went into the kitchen, Jose and me in tow.

We slipped in through the door into a mud room. The far wall held coat hooks and a bench with a lot of work boots scattered around it. Jon moved to the left and into the kitchen. It wasn't what I expected, more palatial palace than rural farmhouse. Our kitchen would have curled up

159

and died of embarrassment. I could lay down on the granite island and still not reach the sides.

The same could be said about Wendi's mother. Her appearance had nothing in common with the stereotypical farmer's wife. Long, frosted-tip blond hair drawn back in a ponytail showed off her dangling earrings. The red jacket and form-fitting black capris belonged in a big city, not in the middle of nowhere Iowa. Her face distorted with anger as we stepped into view. "And what in the name of all that is holy are you doing here, Jon?" she said, throwing her hands into the air.

"Nice to see you too, Mom. I came to get Wendi. She isn't safe," Jon's tone could have frozen lava, "here."

She sighed loudly. "Finally, someone is thinking." She turned back to Wendi. "Honey, I know you are scared, and your Gift does extract a heavy toll. Wear the watch and save yourself."

I stepped off to the side of the kitchen near the massive dining room table. Being in the middle of a family fight wasn't my idea of a fun time. A photo on the refrigerator of Wendi's parents told a story. Both Jon and Wendi got their appearance from their mother. Their father wore a Reclaimer's unit hat over his cropped brown hair. With my luck, he had served under Powell. Mrs. Stevens was the cheetah to his rhino.

"Mom, I told you. I just need a few days to think about things," Wendi said. "I'll stay away from Dad. He'll never be able to tell I'm here."

Jon reached out and grabbed Wendi's arm. "You heard her. We aren't welcome here."

Wendi tried to tug her arm free, but Jon wouldn't let go. She reared back, and suddenly she stood next to me. Jon stared at his hand, a look of disbelief on his face. He recovered quickly, heading toward us. I moved to intercept him. I wasn't about to let him hurt Wendi because he was angry.

"Out of my way, Tommy."

I put my hand against his shoulder. "Jon, we will work this out. Just back off and let's talk about it."

He slapped my hand off his shoulder. "You can all talk about it. I'll be outside."

Jon stormed out the door, slamming it with a resounding crash. I was surprised the glass didn't shatter.

"Well, that went well," Mrs. Steven said. "Anyone want a drink? I need one."

Jose grinned. "*Si!*"

Mrs. Stevens stepped over to the built-in liquor cabinet on the far wall of the kitchen and poured two glasses out of a Jack Daniels bottle. She handed one to Jose and then took a sip of hers before moving to the end of the granite island.

"Thanks," Wendi whispered in my ear. She gave me a quick kiss on the cheek and returned to her seat at the kitchen island. I stayed by the door, my nerves dancing like they were at a rave.

Wendi's mom considered me. "So, you must be the Tommy I've heard so much about."

"Yes, Mrs. Stevens." I tried to keep the shakiness out of my voice. No such luck.

"I won't bite, Tommy." She paused to take a drink, though her eyes never left me. "Please, call me Tracy."

"Okay, Tracy," I said, proud I didn't fumble over the words.

"Mom, I'll stay down in the cabin so no one sees me." A small pout appeared on her face.

Mrs. Stevens took a larger drink from her glass. "Wendi, it isn't that I don't want you here."

Wendi cut her off. "Forget it, Mom. Jon has been right the whole time. You dropped us as fast as you could. You never wanted us, and now you certainly don't want us back. I guess the care packages and the visits were just to soothe your guilty conscience."

"That's not fair," Mrs. Stevens implored, setting her glass on the island. "The reason I want you to leave is it isn't safe for you here."

Jose smacked his lips loudly, having finished off his drink. "*Cariño*, listen to your mama, she knows what she speaks of. She has the right of it." He set his empty glass down with a sigh.

"Please, help yourself to another." His face lit up as if seeing an old friend after years apart. He walked to the cabinet and refilled his glass, much higher than the original. Nothing better than having our driver drunk.

"I get it." Wendi looked to be torn between crying and punching someone. "I'll go back to Redemption, where it's safe." Her voice cracked as her pitch rose into the higher registers. "I was almost raped there, and you want me to go back?"

She burst into tears. Mrs. Stevens moved around the island and caught her in a hug. They were both crying. She stroked Wendi's hair, speaking in the low, soothing tones moms have.

Lifting the side door window's curtain, I looked out, wondering where Jon had gone to. His temper was the worst I had ever dealt with. He snapped at the drop of a hat. I had a clue on what some of his powers were, but not all. I needed to have Marcel research it when we got back to Dresden.

The sounds of crying had stopped, so I let the curtain fall back into place and turned around. Wendi, her face still blotchy and red from crying, cleaned up the tears with a napkin. Jose leaned against the wall by the dining room, clearly enjoying his drink. There wasn't any liquor at Dresden.

"Tommy, do you have a safe place to take my kids?" Mrs. Stevens asked, her look a silent appeal for help. "It really isn't safe for any of you here."

"Yes, ma'am."

"I'll make sure they get there, Tracy," Jose said, sliding his glass across the island toward her. He nudged me on his way out. "I'll be at the car. Don't be too long."

I nodded to him. "I'll bring her when she's ready."

She smiled at me and resumed talking to Wendi in a low voice. I examined the pictures hanging on the refrigerator and in frames on the walls. They were all of her husband, an avid hunter and fisherman based on the photos. The crunching gravel announced Jose pulling the car into the driveway, faster than I expected after the walk in, but maybe the moon had come out since we arrived. I stood for another minute so the girls would notice, but they were still talking. Jose and Jon would be pissed if they had to wait.

"I think we should be going." I heard a faint click behind me and tried to turn, but the feel of cold metal against the back of my neck changed my mind.

Someone was behind me with what felt like a double-barreled shotgun. "You aren't going anywhere boy," the iron hard voice said. "Look, my daughter the Mongrel is back, and I'm not letting you go again."

Daddy's home!

24

I slowly raised my hands. From all the pictures, Mr. Stevens knew how to use the gun he held.

Wendi screamed.

"Hank, put the gun down," Mrs. Stevens said, jumping in front of Wendi.

"He'll lower the gun, or I'll gut him like a pig," I heard Jon say from behind us both.

The pressure eased from the back of my head. I backed away from the awkward family reunion. Jon's combat knife pressed against the side of his father's neck. Hank Stevens stood rock still, the shotgun pointing at the ground.

"I didn't even hear you come up on me." Even with a knife at his throat, the man's admiration stood out on his face. "I'd never suspected you'd have it in you."

"I can do a lot of things I didn't use to." Jon grabbed the shotgun and shoved his father into the kitchen.

Hank caught himself on the island from the overly aggressive blow Jon delivered. He moved with an easy grace to stand straight and face the four of us.

He smiled. "I'll be turning the bunch of you into the Reclaimers. Tracy, you should have called as soon as they showed up."

Jon raised the shotgun, aiming for Hank's head. "I'm not going back to Redemption, even if I have to kill you to do it."

"Boy, you aren't going back to school." He barked a harsh laugh. "You'll be going to The Block and maybe even be center stage for *Saturday Night Showdown* after they give Cyclone Ranger what he deserves. They've not killed him yet, but they will."

The hammers click back into place. Mrs. Stevens stepped between them, putting her hand on the gun barrel. "Jon, I'll take care of this."

"No, Mom." Jon's voice cracked with intensity like I had never experienced before. He sounded excited. "He's a Reclaimer and an abuser, and it ends here."

"No, put down the gun," Mrs. Stevens said forcefully.

Amazingly, the gun lowered. She reached over and took it out of Jon's limp hands. She turned to face her husband, who reached for the gun.

"Good job, Trace. I'll cover them while you call…"

"Hank, listen to me." Her tone held the same forcefulness she used on Jon. "You will forget anyone was here. We had a fight, and you hit me. You will go to the Brass Spittoon and tell your damn war stories for the rest of the night. Go home with Marlene, and don't come back until Sunday. Do you understand?"

"Yes, I understand." Mr. Stevens looked like a zombie, slack-jawed and unfocused.

"Go get in the truck and drive."

"Get in truck." He shambled to the door, opened it, and left. The truck started up in the driveway and pulled out.

"How did you do that?" Wendi said in awe.

"You aren't the only Gifted in the family, dear. Jon, close the door. We need to talk."

Jon hesitated. "Should we get Jose?"

"No, I slipped a sleeping agent into his drink. He should have made it to the car before falling asleep."

"I should leave." Having drugged Jose, she obviously didn't want spectators for the family meeting.

"No, Tommy. You need to hear what I have to say, so please sit down."

I dropped onto the stool. Wendi sat on the stool next to me. Jon closed the door, went to the dining room, and moved a chair in front of the window overlooking the driveway. He had the knife back in the sheath, but I noticed it wasn't snapped in.

Mrs. Stevens took a large slug from her glass. She sighed heavily. "Sorry, using my Gift drains me."

We sat at the island quietly while she gathered herself. The stools probably cost more than our house. Wendi's hand slid into my mine. I gave it a quick squeeze and her a reassuring smile.

Jon decided to break the silence. "So how are you Gifted and not living with us in Redemption?" He paused then added, "Mom."

She rubbed her forehead. "The test they use doesn't work on mental powers from what I can tell. I passed the initial test while I was pregnant with both of you. When you were tested, you both failed, but I couldn't admit I was Gifted."

"Why not?" Jon asked, his voice harsh. He squatted on the chair, the predator waiting to pounce.

She shook her head. "You weren't there. If I admitted to being Gifted, they would have killed me as well as knowing they had missed Gifted in their testing." Her hands shook as she picked up the empty glass, considering it. "Not all of us were crime fighters or working for the government. Before the tests, people would accuse their neighbors of being Gifted. Someone accused a friend, Heather Wilkins, of being Gifted. A group of 'concerned citizens' dragged her and her entire family out into the street, beat them to death, and then burnt their bodies. I found the charred remains of a pacifier the next day." She crossed the room, filled her glass again, taking a large swallow before returning.

Wendi gasped. "Couldn't you have used your Gift to stop them?"

Her laugh sounded cruel, self-mocking. "Gifts have limits. An angry mob isn't listening. I would have been killed as well, being a sympathizer and all."

Jon snorted from where he was. "So instead you just hid?"

"Where better to hide than with the Reclaimer's chief enforcer? He paraded me around like a trophy, the status of purity. Meanwhile he was killing innocent people who didn't even have Gifts." Another long pull from her drink. I wondered if self-medication helped deal with the memories.

"But that wouldn't stop you from staying in Redemption with us," Wendi said. "We were alone, we needed you."

Tears chased each other down Mrs. Stevens's cheeks. "I know." Her voice was barely audible. "I tried to shield you from the test, but I failed. Your father doesn't even realize I visit. I am so sorry. I love you both, but I didn't have a choice. If I did anything, they would have killed me."

Wendi stood up and walked past Jon to the door. "Well, I guess we'll be dead to you now, won't we? I'd rather die than abandon people I love." She left the house, slamming the door on the way out.

Jon didn't say a word; he just followed her out the door. I sat, unsure what to do. "I'm sorry."

"Tommy, please, when she calms down, tell her I still love her, but," she stared down at her drink, "I'm a coward." Glancing up, Mrs. Stevens shattered eyes implored, begged forgiveness. "Please."

I left the house, the answer unspoken.

I slept until mid-afternoon after our trip back from the Stevens's farm. My worldview had been turned upside down. Hidden Gifted still lived outside The Blocks. Freed of the collar, you could have a normal life, especially if you lived off the beaten track.

The pre-show for *Saturday Night Showdown* came on, and I promptly hit the mute button. I dropped into one of the video chairs across from the ones Abby and Marcel sat in. It was bad enough listening during the live show. From the looks of it, Dad hadn't had to use his lightning yet, relying on brains and wind to see him through. The network must be fuming.

I thought back to how Mom had said he deserted us. I wondered if he rated a coward as Tracy Stevens thought herself or heroic for turning himself in and not letting us be caught. Until the test had come around, even suspected Gifted were killed. Would my dad have stood out, drawn attention to his wife and infant son? Could we have hid until the worst had passed, ducking the Reclaimers as they purified the country? I wish I had an answer, but every question just brought more questions, never answers.

Wendi slid in beside me. Close, but not touching. It was a big step forward, but I still had to restrain myself from reaching out. When she felt ready, she would let me know. Like at her parents, when she put her hand in mine. I noticed the watch strapped to her wrist. No early death. I knew the price she'd paid, though both roads had their costs. More and more questions.

"Why are you watching this?" Wendi said. "I would think under the circumstances this would be the last show you would want to watch."

I hesitated. I longed to tell her, but I couldn't bring myself to break the last promise I made to my mom. Wendi and Marcel, maybe Abby, were safe, but not Jon and never Jose. Reformed or not, the Grim Reaper's history did not lend itself to sharing secrets. "I wish Cyclone Ranger could make it through the Gauntlet. He's the strongest of the Gifted; it would give us hope."

"Hope is for losers," Jon said as he strolled across the room to the chair he preferred. "The game is rigged, they'll off him in the last episode regardless to keep us in our place."

"If anyone can beat the game, it is Cyclone Ranger," Marcel said as he pulled open a bag of chips he passed to Abby. "I've found some files in the database. He could pump out more megawatts than some power plants."

"As long as he kicks some ass this time," Abby said, dumping some chips into a bowl and returning the bag to Marcel. She shoved a handful in her mouth while trying to complete her thought. "Hrmph hrumph hurmp."

"Was that English?" Marcel asked, a big smile on his face.

She finished chewing. "I'm tired of him running."

I grinned. "Oh, I thought you said Marcel looked cute tonight." That got a good laugh from everyone but Marcel.

"Hey, some girls find my geek skills quite charming."

Abby winked at him. "Only if they're nerds."

I hit the unmute button to break up where this one was headed. Desmond Roberts's voice boomed into the room. "Folks, we've got a special treat for you tonight." The camera zoomed in on him. He held a coil of metallic rope in his hands. "Tonight, we at *Saturday Night Showdown* are unveiling a twist to the Gauntlet. This will add excitement to the game. We are calling it the Lightning Rod."

The crowd cheered, mindless in their anticipation of a better match than the previous five weeks.

"Here's how it works." Desmond uncoiled the rope as he spoke. "At twenty feet long, one end will be fastened around the waist of Cyclone

Ranger, and the other will be fastened to another Dissident. The goal of the game is for Cyclone Ranger to keep his partner alive through three rounds."

"Wow," Marcel said. "The tether stops him from flying and reduces his mobility. He's in trouble."

It did indeed, but more importantly, it kept Dad from refusing to fight again. Now he was responsible for another's safety.

"And here is our dynamic duo for this match," Desmond shouted, and the crowd booed and screamed as they entered the arena. "Cyclone Ranger and..."

"Fireworks Farley!" we all said in unison.

"That's right! One of our favorites, Fireworks Farley!" Desmond practically sang out his name. "He's been on the show many times, and he's back to face the Gauntlet with Cyclone Ranger."

I groaned. It would have been one thing to be paired with Steamroller or Major Chaos, Gifted who could actually fight, but Farley was a waste they used to fill in between real matches, more court jester than a Gifted warrior.

Farley ran out to stand next to Dad. They couldn't have been more opposite if they tried. Where Cyclone Ranger stood tall, muscular, and dressed in a black combat suit with electric blue lightning bolts up his legs, Farley was short and chunky. He wore a purple and gold combat suit with a mask over his face, where Dad wore a helmet, his face hidden by the dark faceplate.

"Folks, this is a show you will not want to miss," Desmond said in his best used car salesman voice. "And we've got a lot more twists coming up in the second half of the Gauntlet. Don't make plans for the next few weeks. These will be shows you'll tell your grandkids about."

The Protectorate couldn't let Dad win—it would expose the lie of living past the end of the Gauntlet. The Reclaimers couldn't let him win, or it would show they could be beaten. If there was ever going to be a chance for the Gifted of the world to live free, Cyclone Ranger had to escape. I knew what I had to do.

"Guys, we are going to rescue Cyclone Ranger."

2 5

"What? Are you nuts?" The chorus of voices chimed in after my grand announcement.

"I know it sounds crazy, but they would never expect it, and it would let the Gifted see there is hope," I said, glancing around at my friends. "Look, we can't just sit by while they murder the most powerful Gifted. We have our Gifts now; we can use them for good."

Jon snorted. "It's a suicide mission, but you have fun, Tommy." He balanced on the back of the armchair, his normal roost.

Marcel punched up the remote display, and all the chairs rotated toward the main TV. The sound boomed through the room as the mute came off. "Don't get all triggered. If he don't fight better, there's no use getting salty." Abby leaned forward with an intensity that scared me a bit, devouring chips at an alarming rate.

Marcel had it right. Three turrets slid up from the floor, firing a stream of bullets, the casings clattering to the floor like rain on a tin roof. The guns centered on concrete pillars supported by metal poles, allowing them to swivel. Farley dived behind a concrete wall. Dad tried to use his wind Gift to force the guns to shoot at each other. Without warning, the walls dropped into the floor as new ones rose. They were out in the open, Farley still rolled in a ball on the floor, his arms covering his head.

Cyclone Ranger couldn't move Farley to cover. He threw his arms out in front of him, flickers of electricity dancing up and down them as he took aim. With a blinding flash, a bolt of blue lightning arced across the room. The closest turret exploded, scattering shards of burning metal around the combat floor. In quick succession, two more bolts found their mark, leaving smoking pieces of metal scattered across the floor.

"Welcome to the party, Cyclone Ranger!" Chip Calloway's voice announced the play-by-play. "I guess we are finally gonna see what the Ranger has left after all these years."

"Wow!" Marcel shouted. He jumped up, arms raised above his head in victory. "Awesome!"

The second wave slid into position. Four chrome-plated robots, shaped like crabs with metallic whips for tails and circular buzz saws instead of claws, moved into the arena from concealed doors in the walls.

They were low to the ground and surprisingly fast. A metal skirt protected the legs from damage. The deafening whine of the spinning blades drowned out the screaming of the crowd.

Dad pulled Farley to his feet, forcing him to stand. Farley shook but stayed up this time. The crabs advanced as the barrier walls dropped. Other than the three concrete podiums and remains of the guns, there was nothing to hide behind.

Dad blasted the closest crab, but other than knocking it back, it was unaffected.

"Dang, they grounded the crabs." Marcel flopped back on the couch. I swear Abby bounced next to him. "Now that's not fair."

I wondered if Dad had thought the same thing. He grabbed Farley by the arm as he ran to the center pylon. The crabs moved to attack from the sides. Dad pushed Farley up on the pedestal. Farley screamed something, but it was lost in the crowd noise, pointing toward the crab moving in quickly. The metallic tail whipped at Dad, scoring a solid hit on his face-plate, cracking the thick plastic shield.

"Cyclone Ranger now knows what eggs go through," Chip Calloway quipped.

"Bruh, that had to hurt."

"He needs to open up full on them crabs," Abby said. I noticed she kept punching her own leg like she fought alongside Dad. I'd chosen well to sit over here.

170

The crowd was going nuts. Nothing had even touched Dad until now, but they saw a crack in the armor and the scent of blood in the air.

The crab slashed with a saw. Dad dodged, causing the saw to hit the pillar. Farley and the burnt remains of the turret gun both shook from the shock. Farley hugged the top of the pillar like a drunk hugging the toilet.

Dad threw himself under the next swipe of the blade. The saw tangled with the cord that held the two Gifted together, sparks arcing as it made contact. Dad jumped on to the back of the first crab, caught the tail, and laid over the back.

"Welcome to the rodeo folks, Cyclone Ranger's on the bucking bronco now!" Chip Calloway said in a fake Texas drawl. "Head 'em up, move 'em out."

"He's covering the optic sensor array of the robot. Ingenious." Marcel's voice was tinged with awe.

The other three crabs converged for the kill. The first crab to arrive came head-on. Dad flipped the tether, freeing it from the wreckage as the other crab moved in. The crab's saw, now unrestrained, shot forward, striking the second crab squarely in the center of its carapace. The shell split in two, pieces and parts flying out of the rent. With an ear-splitting shriek, the saw sliced through, stopping the other crab dead in its tracks.

"Now that was a smart move," Jon said. "But he's still got three more out there."

The crab Dad rode spun back and forth trying to dislodge its unwanted rider. The tail would have been able to lash him, but it held fast under Cyclone Ranger. The saws couldn't reach its own back.

The next crab lashed out, striking Dad, leaving a wide cut across his legs. Blood dripped from the injuries. The lash flashed toward him a second time, but with much different results. As the tail approached, Dad rose up, grabbing the metallic whip. A flash of light, and he was on the move. He jumped off the crab and stood with his back to the pillar where a screaming Farley perched.

Dad looked up at Farley. He must have been saying something because Farley ceased screaming and nodded. The two crabs charged at him, blades sweeping toward him. At the last moment, he spun and ran behind past the pillar, Farley jumping down and running with him, the tether swinging between them. The crabs went to either side of the pylon and stopped. Their tails had been fused together when he caught them. Now

171

they were held by the pillar, neither one smart enough to back up and go around.

"Wow," Chip Calloway said. "They are stuck together after that maneuver. If Cyclone Ranger makes it through the Gauntlet, he could always work as a welder."

We all laughed. The sight of the two floundering crabs set us off. It was either the stress had gotten to us, or it was extremely funny. I'm not sure which.

The two crabs sparked, out of commission, one left to deal with. Dad reached down and picked up a three-foot long piece of jagged pole from one of the guns. He turned, gesturing at the approaching crab, giving Farley instructions. The crab lashed out, trying to strike Dad again. He dodged, always barely out of reach, moving back from the whip-like tail.

The real threat never showed up on the crab's radar. Farley darted in and sprayed the crab's sensors with a barrage of fireworks. The robot's optics were fried by the high-intensity lights. With a swirl of winds, Dad flew. The pole, acting like a lance, stabbed through the controls and out the bottom of the crab.

He pulled the bar out and jumped off the corpse of the crab. He severed the blades, tossed them into the air. They began to spin faster and faster as they rose, held aloft by the wind he generated. They spun toward the protective energy barrier that covered the arena; the crowd screamed in panic. Instead of breaking through, the blades sped downward toward the two trapped crabs, slicing them neatly in two.

The crowd screamed in dismay as we rejoiced at the victory. Abby high-fived Marcel, knocking him over the arm of the chair he sat in. Wendi grabbed my hand, breaking contact too quickly when she realized what had happened. I felt Jon's stare burning into me, but I ignored it.

In the arena, Farley and Dad were shaking hands. The air horn blared, signaling the third round had begun. From the floor in front of the exit button rose a behemoth.

Chip Calloway's voice overlaid the crowd noise, dropping into a sinister register of a movie announcer. "And introducing the Enforcer."

The robot was ten feet of gray-green metal with four arms. The right arm ended in a wicked chainsaw; the left held a weighted net. The bottom arms ended with nasty hooks instead of hands. The head was squat, two antennas coming from where its ears should have been. A glowing red orb strobed back and forth like Kit from the old Knight Rider show Marcel loves.

"Will Cyclone Ranger reach the exit?" Chip Calloway's voice dropped. "Or will the Enforcer put an end to his villainous ways?"

I rolled my eyes. Dad had been in The Block for fifteen years—his "villainous ways" had been over since I was a baby.

Screams ricocheted around the arena from the frenzied audience. Silver chains flashed against the charged protective barrier. The crowd threw them out when they thought Gifted would die. The camera panned the crowd showing red faces distorted as they screamed for blood. Veins bulged, eyes bulged from exertion, the cream of the crop of humanity.

Dad and Farley moved behind the center pillar, heads close together. The Enforcer started its ponderous walk toward its victims. The roar of the chainsaw echoed through the TV speakers.

"Oh, they aren't happy to see the Enforcer from the way they are backing away from it," Chip Calloway squawked. "No, folks, they don't want anything to do with him. That chainsaw is as deadly as it is loud."

Dad and Farley backed behind the concrete pillars, leaping over the neatly sliced wreckage of a crab to do so. By all the hand gestures, they were formulating a plan. The Enforcer stomped across the intervening space, each step rattling the cameras.

"I think I'm going to be sick," Marcel groaned.

From behind the center pillar, Dad launched a blast of air into the Enforcer's chest. It didn't have any effect. In response, the chainsaw swept down, sheering off the pillar at the floor. Sparks erupted as the pillar flew across the arena, resting against the left-hand wall, shiny bullets scattered around it.

The Enforcer relentlessly marched forward, red orb sliding across its face. Dad dragged Farley to the left, headed to where the pillar laid on the floor. The Enforcer stopped, its head tracking its prey. The left arm came up, firing the net toward the running men. Dad rolled under the projectile, but it hit Farley, slamming him into the wall. The rope dragged Dad across the floor from the force of the net.

Dad sprang to his feet, launching himself behind the fallen pillar. He took the metal rod from the turret, using it as a pry bar on the concrete.

The Enforcer had made its turn, bearing down on Farley, immobile against the wall due to the net. The footage bounced with every ponderous step the Enforcer took. Farley panicked, his screams unintelligible over the TV feed, but the weighted net held him with no room to move.

The concrete broke apart, a metal box clattering out onto the floor. Dad snatched it and ran to Farley. He slid under a hooked arm as he reached his trapped partner. He tugged up the part of the net so Farley could break free. Dad grabbed him around the waist, and with a jet of wind, they flew across the arena as the chainsaw slammed down where they had been standing a second earlier.

"Oh my," Chip Calloway said. "That was as close as a photo finish at a horse race."

They crashed in a pile but quickly got to their feet. Dad handed over the box and gestured to where the Enforcer was moving toward them. The camera zoomed into Farley's face. Sweat ran out from under the jester's mask he always wore, his eyes wide with fear. He nodded at Dad, but he didn't look happy about it.

They moved apart, Dad holding the metallic rope that tethered them together. He started to spin in a circle, Farley running around him. As the Enforcer approached, Dad combined the momentum with a gust of wind, propelling Farley, who soared over the outstretched arms of the robot. A second later, Dad launched himself after Farley. A hooked claw scored a hit, spinning Dad to the side, but he still managed to get over the top.

"Whoa," Chip Calloway yelled through the TV speakers. "What a mighty hammer throw!"

Farley crashed with clang and a thud on the Enforcer's right shoulder. The metallic box he carried slid from his grip, but he caught it before it fell. He jammed it under the Enforcer's head, leaping clear as a bolt of lightning hit the box. The explosion was epic, the sound blasting through the speakers threatening to deafen us. Pieces blew in all directions forcing the two contestants to duck for cover. Sparks flew from the protection grid over the arena as the severed head struck it, cables trailing behind it. The headless robot toppled over with a boom after a blast of wind from Dad.

"This is amazing," Chip Calloway said. "Who would have thought to use the ammunition from the gun to take down the Enforcer? This is why Cyclone Ranger is a danger and must be stopped."

Now more than ever, I realized the Protectorate would kill Dad no matter what, and I was the only one who could save him. But how?

26

"Tommy, wake up," was how my day started. I looked at the clock by the bed to see numbers I have never seen that early in the morning peering back at me.

"Marcel, it is three-thirty." I pulled the pillow over my head.

He flipped on the lights. "I think I know what your Gift is, but I don't want to advertise it."

That woke me up faster than a bucket of cold water. It bothered me everyone else knew what their Gift was, but after weeks of trying, I still couldn't produce a spark. "How?"

"I found an encrypted record in the old mainframe system that sounds like what happened to you," he said, his voice barely above a whisper. "I want to test my theory. Meet me in the level seven gym." He left the room, quietly closing the door behind him.

Level seven wasn't the gym we normally used. I threw on my sweat suit and headed down the stairs, careful not to make any noise. Marcel's level of caution might be exaggerated, but I would be an idiot not to follow his lead. I carefully closed doors behind me as I went. The soft glow of embedded lights made it easy to traverse the space, but with no darkness to conceal us, speed would have to do.

The click of the stairway door sounded louder than an air-raid siren to me. I leaned against the stairway wall, sighing in relief. None of the others had the codes to open the doors to the lower levels. Marcel had pried them out of the Dresden systems. Frankly, it scared me at how easily he slipped into secure areas and retrieved classified data. The worst part, Marcel enjoyed it, maybe a little too much.

The spiral stairs descended over forty levels, but lucky number seven held Marcel and the key to my Gift. At least I hoped so. My heart raced at the thought of knowing what I could do. Marcel had told me level seven had belonged to Titan. Aside from picking up buses and throwing them, the database indicated he topped out at eight feet and weighed over four hundred pounds. I'd hate to make him mad.

I keyed the pad, and a ten-foot door slid into the wall. Beyond it lay Titan's personal space. The huge furniture was solid Carbinium, worth more than some countries. Pictures of Titan with politicians and Hollywood stars covered the walls alongside newspaper headlines touting The League of Patriots' victories.

I stopped when I saw the front page from *The Washington Post*. It showed The League of Patriots together after the attack on the White House. Titan stood in the back, in front of him stood, according to the caption, Golden Avenger, Slipstream, Jinx, and Dominion. Even in the grainy photo, Dominion dazzled in comparison to the rest. Her beauty might be the only thing Powell's story got right.

I continued around the floor, marveling at the artwork on the walls and the expensive fixtures that hung everywhere. I hadn't been on the private levels since Marcel had broken the security codes. Good thing it wasn't public knowledge or Jose would be loading his car for the nearest pawn shop. I wish it surprised me that Marcel had directly disobeyed Waxenby.

Following the lights that came from the right hallway, I entered into the Valhalla of workout warriors everywhere. Giant racks of weights gleamed in the overhead lights of the room, thick blue padding with golden paths covered the floors. Machines to do every conceivable exercise could be found here. The room had to have been fifty yards wide and deep. The cost just to excavate this room must have been incredible.

"Hey." Marcel was dressed in sweats, duffel bag by his feet. He bounced on the thick padding like a kid on a trampoline, though I doubted he'd be doing flips anytime soon.

"Okay, so what's up with the *Mission Impossible* set up?"

Marcel pulled out a small device, tapping on it quickly. The gym door shut, and the light over the door changed from green to red. "I want to keep these levels locked. There is a lot down here that would be bad if it fell into the Protectorate's hands, so better safe than sorry."

"Makes sense." Marcel always thought ten steps ahead. "But why couldn't we do this with the others?"

"Two reasons." He held up a finger. "First, telling everyone the exact nature of your Gift isn't the best thing to do. We don't know all of Jon's or Abby's or for that matter Jose's or Mr. W's." He put up another finger. "Second, I'm not sure it will work and don't really want people seeing what I have in mind."

Marcel sounded ominous to me. "What exactly do you have planned?" I could hear the worry in my voice. I trusted Marcel more than anyone, but this was getting weird fast.

"Just bear with me," Marcel said as he knelt to pull some things out of the duffel bag. He handed me a two-liter bottle of Tab. How Waxenby drank it, I would never understand. "Go set this on the bench by the wall."

"Okay."

A wooden bench stood against a section of empty wall. I set the bottle in the center and walked over to Marcel, who now stood by a huge punching bag.

"We need to have a control for me to know if my hypothesis works." Marcel pointed to the largest punching bag I have ever seen. "Punch it."

"What?"

"Look, Bruh," he said. "You are going to have to trust me. Some of the things may seem strange, but I have a theory on why you are able to generate electric potential."

"I'm blocked," I said disconsolately. "I guess my Gift can't work unless I'm stressed."

"Hit the bag."

I shrugged and hit the bag. The only damage done was to my hand. "Well, that didn't do…" I started to say when I was blown across the room by what felt like a freight train full of elephants. I hit the wall, bounced off, and landed flat on my back. I wiped my nose with the back of my hand, leaving a trail of blood on my hand in its wake.

"Sorry about that." Marcel's voice was a bit wobbly. He held a silver cylinder in his hand, which he quickly placed back in the bag.

I stood up slowly. "What the hell did you do?" I asked as I got to my feet.

"It is part of the test. I didn't want you to go all Boomshakalaka on me. Could you hit the bag, instead of me?"

Why bother? The bag hadn't moved the first time; it wasn't going to move the second. Marcel moved out of my way quickly as I stalked over. I pulled back and punched the bag as hard as I could. The bag didn't move. Neither did my arm, in a way.

"Wow! You punched through the bag," Marcel said, clapping excitedly. He kind of looked like a cheerleader. A geeky, nerd cheerleader. Still taller than me and his afro bounced.

"What happened?" I said as I removed my arm, unleashing a torrent of sand from the hole as the bag emptied on to the floor.

"One more experiment, and then I'll explain." He removed an orange industrial extension cord out of the bag. One of the plugs was cut off to expose a couple bare wires. He handed me the stripped end and ran to plug it in. "Hold one wire in each hand, and then I'll plug it in."

"Are you crazy? You'll electrocute me."

"Trust me, Bruh."

I sighed. I must be as dumb as Brunner always called me. I held the white wire in my right hand, black in the left.

"Ready?"

I nodded. This was going to hurt. Marcel plugged the cord in, and my body convulsed as the jolt of electricity hit me. Flashes of the night by the river flew through my mind. Thoughts of Powell standing over me threatening my mom. The physical pain drifted far away, but the emotions hit home hard.

The burning sensation ceased as suddenly as it had begun. Marcel ran over to check on me. I could feel the energy inside me, crackling along my arms, across my back, the power coursed through me.

"Shoot the bottle." Marcel could barely contain his excitement.

I knew what would happen. It was the same as when I burned Clint and Ryder to ash. I pointed, releasing the pent-up energy as a solid bolt of lightning. The bottle didn't even explode, it just ceased to exist in that moment. Nothing reached the floor.

"Whoa!" Marcel yelled. I hadn't realized I still pumped lightning into the charred concrete wall. I snapped my hand shut, and the flow snapped off like I had flipped a switch. I could still feel the energy swirling through my body, so I poked Marcel. The quick pop scared him half to death. I laughed.

"I guess I had that coming," he said with a smirk, though I did notice he rubbed his side. "I found an encrypted file on a server locked down so tight no one should have ever been able to get into it, but I did. It listed out abilities and the signs for how to detect them. Most were obvious, such as Wendi's speed, but one looked odd."

"Odd how?"

"Latent Gifted's powers present under differing circumstances, but most needed a trigger to transubstantiate." Marcel launched into instructor mode. "According to the archives, many Gifted didn't present their Gifts until a significant physical or emotional trauma. In your case, Powell touching the electrified jumper cables invoked your manifestation."

I thought about it for a minute. Marcel was right; Powell had triggered my Gift with the jumper cables. I didn't create the energy; instead, I used what was there. "So I act as a lightning rod, passing out the current I absorb?"

Marcel thought for a minute. "Not quite. Your absorption coefficient is off the charts. The amplification magnification has to be a factor of ten plus."

Which made a lot of sense. Jon beat the crap out of me, but when I hit him, it threw him into the air. I couldn't normally punch very hard. "So it isn't just electricity and being hit."

"Kinetic energy."

"Sorry, Professor. So, I can only absorb electricity and kinetic energy?"

"Well…" Marcel paused, stroking his chin while he thought. He really needed a beard, or better yet, a goatee to pull it off, but wispy chin hairs were all he could manage. "No, it should be any form of energy you're exposed to."

"So I can absorb lasers?" I had pictures of protecting innocents while the lasers bounced harmlessly off my chest. "I'd be the coolest."

"Painful is the word I would use." Marcel grabbed my hands and flipped them over. My palms bore blisters where the wires touched my skin. "Your body still takes damage when you absorb the energy. You can absorb the laser blast, but your clothes can't, and it will hurt, even though it appears the damage isn't permanent."

He was right. As we watched, the welts shrank. In an hour or so, they probably wouldn't be there at all. "So it is painful for a while. I can live with that."

The look on Marcel's face worried me. He was a terrible liar and even worse at hiding his feelings.

"Okay." I gave my best impression of Mom's lawyer's voice. "Out with it. What aren't you telling me?"

He hesitated, probably wondering if he should tell me or not. "Bruh, from what I saw in the files, there is a big downside to your Gift."

"And what would that be?"

"If you absorb more than your Gift can handle, it will kill you." Marcel's tone held an edge of worry. I could see he struggled with helping me and protecting me from myself. "The problem is no one knows how much is too much."

Dying was a definitely a downside, but now I could rescue my dad from The Gauntlet.

Armed with the knowledge my Gift wasn't blocked or useless, I did what any normal teenager would do.

I climbed back into bed.

Nobody is at their best at five-thirty a.m., especially me. After being bruised and electrocuted, sleep was my best friend.

I rolled out of bed at the crack of two, jumped in the shower, and got dressed. By the time I finished, my stomach's protests were loud and clear to anyone nearby. I left my room and headed into the kitchen area for breakfast. I poured Frosted Flakes and milk into a mixing bowl, grabbed what looked like a clean spoon, and flopped on the couch to join the pow-wow already in session.

Waxenby, his face red with anger, pushed a finger at Jose who stood, arms folded across the table from him. Marcel and Abby sat on the other couch eyes moving back and forth watching the verbal tennis match. Jon perched on the back of the chair, his feet on the cushion. A definite no-no with my mom.

"What's up, guys?" I said around a heaping mouthful of cereal. One thing about using your Gifts, it leaves you as hungry as working for three days without eating.

Wendi slid over to sit with me, an eyebrow raised at the amount of cereal in the huge metal bowl. She nudged me with her elbow as I shrugged at her.

Waxenby turned to face me. "Tommy, did you suggest rescuing Cyclone Ranger from The Block?" All eyes locked on me. My spoon dripped milk as it stopped dead halfway to my mouth.

"Um..." I am a sparkling conversationalist to be sure. "Yes?"

"And why would you suggest such a hare-brained scheme?"

I paused. I couldn't come right out and say because he's my dad. Waxenby would probably be okay, but Jose wasn't a safe bet. It's hard to trust someone that murdered twelve guards, and from the information Marcel found, that was the least of his crimes. "They are going to kill him. If we could break him free, Gifted all over the world would have hope."

"No one has ever been freed from The Block." Waxenby pushed his thinning hair back into place from where it had slid to cover part of his forehead. "Believe me, it has been tried many times. Plus, they moved a lot of Gifted to The Block in response to your breaking out."

"Jose broke out," I said spraying the floor with milk and soggy Frosted Flakes as I pointed to Jose with my spoon. "If he can get out, we can get back in the same way."

Jose nodded. "It would be tough, but it is doable."

Waxenby's eyes almost fell out of his head. "You and I have a much different definition of doable! You killed a lot of people breaking out."

"They didn't all die, Ollie." Jose's slow drawl floated across the room. "*Hombre*, they would never expect it. The kids are listed as dead, and with seven of us, we could get in, free the Cyclone Ranger, and maybe a lot more in the process. It would be a blow against the Protectorate they couldn't cover up."

Waxenby shook his head. "You know full well these kids were only listed as dead for the public. A car accident is hardly an original excuse. The Reclaimers have been searching the area for them. Not only would we be fighting through the guards and defenses of The Block, but there is a platoon of soldiers on maneuvers and another of engineers working on the levees."

Marcel cleared his throat. "We don't need to get him from The Block."

"And how do you figure that, *hombre*?"

"Cyclone Ranger will fight twice more at The Block's facilities, but then they are moving him to Las Vegas to fight the last three weeks in the Megadrome."

"And that helps us how?" Waxenby said, glaring at Marcel. "The Megadrome is just as bad as The Block, and there are always troops on hand for R&R."

Marcel, a sly smile on his face, said, "Who mentioned anything about attacking the Megadrome? We ambush the convoy as they move him."

Jose nodded as he sat down in the empty recliner. "That could work, but we would need more people."

That puzzled me. "Why more people?"

"We'll need a power team to take out the leads. Wendi speeds in to blow the hatches, and the rest of us take out the guards and get the Ranger."

Jon leaned forward. "Where do we get more Gifted?"

Jose smiled. "Washington D.C." The Latino accent had left again, replaced by a slightly nasal tone. "The Underground will want in on this. We can grab four or five high-powered guys who will gladly take down the lead cars and the followers. It will be a huge win for them."

"I'm in." I had to rescue Dad at any cost.

"You can't be serious?" Waxenby said. "Tommy, I told your mother I would watch out for you. Getting killed trying to rescue a political prisoner isn't my idea of protection."

I stood up looking him in the eye. "She'll understand."

Honestly, I didn't know if she would.

The rest of the day flew by as we packed up the Midville Driving School van for the trip to D.C. According to Waxenby, after the attack on D.C., the Protectorate had erected a barrier around the city rather than deal with the millions of dead bodies inhabiting the city. Rumors of malformed people and mutated rats roaming the city had kept all but the most hardcore looters out. The ones who went in were never heard from again. D.C. belonged to the dead.

Jose explained most of the destroyed cities around the world held cells of Gifted who had braved the horrendous conditions of the destroyed cities rather than surrender or be killed by the Reclaimers. The cell there consisted of fifty or so people, many of them Gifted. Jose was convinced they would help free Cyclone Ranger.

The next argument started over who was going. Waxenby wanted Jose to go and come back. Jose wanted everyone because if we ran into trouble, we would have more firepower. In the end, we decided Wendi, Marcel, and Waxenby would head to K'vothe, an Omega Squad safe house. Waxenby kept the location secret in case we were caught. Marcel walked us through how to contact him so he could get us to a rendezvous. Jon, Abby, Jose, and I were making the trip to D.C. to recruit help. We had two and a half weeks to make the trip and launch our attack.

I was placing the last of my clothes in my backpack when I heard a tap. I turned to find Wendi standing in the doorway, biting her lower lip. It had become a nervous habit with her while we'd been in Dresden.

"Hey, what's up?"

She stepped in and closed the door. "I want to talk to you before you go." She took a seat on the corner of the bed, one leg crossed under her other leg. "Do you think you could go to K'vothe with Marcel and me?"

I sat down next to her, reached for her hand tentatively, giving her time to pull away, then, when it didn't move, took her hand in mine. My stomach flipped as I raised my eyes to hers. "You know I have to go with Jose to get more help."

She frowned. "This is way more important to you than freeing a prisoner. What is really going on?"

I made the decision in an instant. "Cyclone Ranger is my dad."

She gasped in surprise.

"He left Mom and me when I was a baby to protect us from the Reclaimers. I can't sit here safe and let him die without trying to save him."

"I knew there had to be more to it." The grip on my hand tightened like she was worried I would slip away.

"You can't tell anyone," I said, wishing I hadn't as soon as it left my lips.

She let go of my hand. Her hurt shifted to anger. "Do you think I'm so stupid that I would betray your trust? Jon would never go along with the plan if he knew. I wish I understood why he was so against us."

It made me feel good for her to confirm what I had been concerned about Jon, but I wished I hadn't insulted her to do it. "I'm sorry, I haven't told anyone, even Marcel."

She grabbed my hand again. "Apology accepted. You should tell Marcel, but now isn't the time. So, you will be careful while you are gone?"

185

"Of course I will." It was nice to know she cared. I had wondered if Brunner had destroyed the Wendi I had fallen in love with, if she could ever care for me the same way I cared for her. Hearing the worry in her voice, the shifting of her weight back and forth as she spoke, told me things could get to a good place for us.

I noticed her lip quivered. "Promise me you won't do anything dangerous. I couldn't stand if anything happened to you."

I pulled her close. I could smell the lavender scent, the touch of her hair caressing my neck as we embraced. She slid back, and I kissed her softly, the warmth of her lips taking my breath away. "I love you," I said and froze. I felt it, but it wasn't the right time. It was too soon. *I am such an idiot.*

"I love you, too." She kissed me back.

The moment shattered as Jon pounded on the door, both of us jumping off the bed, guilty looks on our faces. We both laughed nervously as I grabbed my bag and headed toward the car.

I guess that worked out after all.

W e parked at a deserted warehouse on the waterfront. Two days of driving, sleeping in run-down motels, and a non-stop diet of fast food had left us all tired and irritable.

We climbed out of the van, stretching and examining our bleak surroundings. A wharf stuck out into the choppy, dirty water as a cold October wind blew in off the Chesapeake Bay. The defunct naval base sat dormant in the distance.

Trash swirled around the parking lot as we stood there. Old and faded graffiti covered the walls of the warehouse. Not many people lived this close to D.C. anymore, as the drive through Norfolk had confirmed. The main part of town continued to be active, but since the Protectorate closed all the naval bases, the waterfront stood deserted.

"Y'all wait here while I signal the Underground fo' to send us a Squid," Jose drawled as he strolled toward the warehouse.

"What's up with the sudden southern accent?" Jon asked with a head bob toward Jose's retreating back.

"I don't know, but he sounded like he was from Boston the other day," I said. "It's almost as if he's got multiple personalities."

Jon scoffed, sneering at me. "Imagine that, something you don't know. I'll never get what Wendi sees in a waste case like you."

"You need to stow it, Jon." Abby shoved Jon, driving him out of my face. "We are on the same team. It's getting old."

Jon's hand settled on the black hilt of the knife now constantly tied to his leg, his black trench pushed back so it was out of the way. If he claimed to be Wyatt Earp and threw on a cowboy hat, it wouldn't surprise me from the way he held himself.

"You touch me again, and you'll get back a stump," he said softly.

Abby growled and tensed to move. I grabbed her hand as she pulled at the dampening watch's clasp.

"Enough. Everyone is tired and sick of each other. We need to remember why we are here."

Jon rolled his eyes. "Oh, yes. The great plan to rescue Cyclone Ranger. You have the hots for the guy or what, Tommy?"

I sighed. Things would never change with Jon. Not for the first time, I wondered why he hadn't gone with Wendi rather than hound me. My guess is he couldn't stand to be left with the safe group. The other thought was he just loved to annoy me. Could be both for all I knew.

"Ignore him, Tommy," Abby said. She walked to the end of the wharf. Trash floated in the dirty water, adding an enticing smell to the stench of oil and decay.

A loud hiss erupted from near the dock, spraying the foul water all over us. Wonderful, as if I didn't smell bad enough after two days in a car. A jet-black hull of steel rose up, supported by thin metal legs. It looked like a walker from *War of the Worlds*.

"What the hell is that thing?" I asked.

"That would be our ride," Jose said behind us. "Welcome to the Squid."

A panel slid to the side, revealing a hatchway. Metal clanged as a ramp shot out to provide an entrance into the ship. Ship stretched the meaning of the word, it appeared more like a cross between a missile silo and an erector set.

Jose clapped me on the back and swore under his breath before wiping his hand on his jeans. "Oh well. *Hombres*, welcome to the Squid. This is how the Underground gets in and out of the city. The Reclaimers mined the bay, but the Squid can avoid them, so we can come and go."

He climbed up the ladder, stepping through the hatch. He looked out when no one else followed. "Either get on or we're leaving without you."

I glanced at Jon and Abby. They both shrugged, so I went in. I hoped the thing smelled better than the dock. I was sadly disappointed.

We took the ladder down into the faintly-lit Squid. Old fold-down seats and standing water on the floor greeted us. Jose pulled down a chair and buckled himself in with a four-strap harness. "We ride in style today."

Abby grunted and took a seat. Jon glanced at me and did the same. At least we weren't swimming.

The entrance hatch clanged shut above us as I fastened the belts across my chest and waist. Seatbelts in a submarine didn't do much to alleviate my dread at being underwater in a leaky old death trap. The engines roared to life behind us. Abby shouted something, but talking over the noise of the engines didn't work. I glanced over at Jose; the bastard wore earplugs.

The Squid lurched away from the dock, tipping to the left so hard I would have flown across the aisle onto Abby if not for the belt. Abby flattened against the seat, directly down from me as I hung from the straps. The engines belched, and then the Squid leveled itself out so we sat normally. Disneyland could learn a lot about rollercoasters from the Squid.

The loud noise, days of driving, and gentle rocking action sent me off to sleep. I don't know how long we traveled. Twice we made rolling turns that scared me to death. I thought sleep would be impossible after each, but my weary body took over.

I came awake as I felt the Squid slow. I reached for the clasps that would release me, but Jose shook his head. The engine cut back.

"What's going on?" I yelled over the subdued engine noise.

Jose took out an ear plug. "Not sure, *amigo*, but it's *no bueno*."

The engine fired up, and Jose quickly put back in the plug before the Squid jolted. A loud metallic clang could be heard from outside the ship, louder than the engines. The Squid rolled hard to the right as a low *thwump* sounded much closer than I was comfortable with. The ship slid sideways through the water. Another bang and *thwump* followed, causing the ship to roll like a fumbled football across the ground. The lights flicked as water hissed through two places in the hull. Abby and I were spared the soaking, but Jon wasn't as lucky.

The engines screamed as the pilot righted the ship. More dull thumps went off, but no more leaks developed, and the Squid sped off through the water.

Eventually, the engines slowed then stopped. The bulkhead door creaked as it opened. A young guy with long, greasy hair shoved under a knit hat popped his head out. "Everybody okay?" I guess you didn't get clean and polite pilots on the Squid.

Jose snarled. "*Qué coñot*. You try to get us killed?"

The pilot flipped him off. "Protectorate changed the mines or something. You can walk back if you'd like, *señor*."

I stifled a laugh. Not many people stood up to the Grim Reaper and lived. Of course, once back on dry land, he might not.

"We're past the minefield, and we didn't take too much damage.

Should be a quiet ride from here." The door slammed shut with a loud metallic clang. My gut tightened. It sounded a bit too much like the mines hitting the hull for my taste. The engines came back on, and we resumed our voyage.

Some change in the Squid announced we were almost there. We climbed steadily, tilting us toward the rear of the cabin. Vertigo swept over me as the world inclined as we rose to the surface. The Squid jumped as it broke free of the water, plunging back down to float to our final destination, dropping whatever was left of my stomach to my ankles.

Once we stopped moving, Jose unbuckled his harness. We followed him out of the hatch. The pilot stood on the dock, speaking to a man in overalls and a clipboard. Jon and Abby jumped down rather than use the ramp. I decided to walk down the far safer alternative, plus I'd promised Wendi I'd be careful.

Once all together, Jose led off. As we passed the pilot, Jose rabbit punched him in the back, dropping him to his knees. The pilot screamed in agony, and having been on the receiving end of Jose's punches, I knew why. Jose seized him by the hair and drove his fist into his face. Blood fountained out of the man's broken nose.

"Why…" the pilot stammered.

Jose got down in his face. "You'd better know who you dealin' with before you flip 'em off, *hombre*." Jose hooked the front of the pilot's coat and threw him in the bay. He turned on overalls man. "You got a problem?"

"No, no, sir, I don't." The man backed away, his hands raised in surrender.

Jose spat at his feet. With a jerk of his head, he indicated we should follow. These are the times I'm very happy we are on the same side. We passed through the derelict buildings, around dead cars, and through waist-high weeds. In the distance, a bridge swayed slightly on its remaining supports. All around stood devastation.

"What is this place?" Abby said. Her voice sounded loud in the absolute silence of deserted city.

"That was known as the tidal basin." Jose gestured back over his shoulder. "Up ahead is where the Underground has set up shop. We need to keep moving. If you see rats, run."

At a pace just short of running, we headed for the Underground's base.

Our heads were on a swivel as we followed along. We had all heard horror stories of rats the size of small dogs roaming the cities destroyed by the death ray. Everyone laughed them off as urban myth, but seeing the remains in person made me rethink my belief.

We moved across what once had been a series of concrete roads crossing over like the beginning of a braid, still packed with the crushed remains of traffic from the day Washington died. I looked both ways out of a lifetime of habit then chided myself as there was no possibility of any traffic on these roads.

A mass of blacked bricks next to a burnt stump of masonry stood before us. Some sort of building had been there, but the surrounding area sat empty except for the tumbled blocks and twisted, rusted metal sticking up out of the heap. Jose circled around the base, but I walked up, standing on the support stone. "What was this?" I asked him.

Jose paused, surveying the area. He joined me on the stones with Abby and Jon in tow. "This used to be the Washington Monument. George Washington founded the United States long before the Protectorate renamed us the North American Zone." He shook his head as he spoke, his face twisted in what I took to be disgust. I swear he sounded like Mr. Coe, our neighbor from Boston. "After the Protectorate took over, they destroyed the monument and the White House where the United States President lived so people would give up hope of things ever returning to normal."

"It must have been huge," Abby said.

"Yes, it was," Jose said. "It was beautiful and overlooked a reflecting pool. People would come from all over the world to see Washington. We had better get moving before it gets dark."

I stood for a minute imagining what it would have had been like. I couldn't. Sadness crept in, mourning for a marvelous place I'd never seen.

I ran to catch up with the others. We followed along the potholed road leading to the Underground. The street overflowed with wrecked cars and trucks as if an unruly toddler had flung his toys across the city. According to Powell, when the death ray hit, people disintegrated on the spot. These drivers died instantly, but their cars kept going, as evidenced by the wreckage we passed through.

The road led toward a gray five-story building. Most of the windows were covered with boards. The top of the building had once had a decorative edge, but the majority of the façade had fallen off. The remaining parts looked like jumpers standing on the edge before they leapt to join their brothers who had gone before them to their deaths.

I awoke from my reverie by a scraping sound coming from behind the rusted hulk of an old mini-van that stretched across the sidewalk. Jose froze, his hand up to tell us to stop. The sickly green glowing scythe popped into being, a beacon in the failing afternoon light. The scratching noise continued. Jose motioned for us to follow, his finger across his lips, as if we needed to be told to be quiet. Jon's eased his knife out of the scabbard as we crept past the dilapidated van. Abby pulled off her dampening bracelet. Without an energy source, I couldn't fight. Blaze's voice echoed in my head: "The only time you stop fighting is when you're dead." I wasn't sure if the moves Blaze had taught me worked on giant rats, but I'd go down swinging.

Two rats climbed over the remains of the rusted mini-van, noses high in the air, sniffing. I could see a third one's back, taller than the broken-out car window. The lead rat's thick corded tail lashed against the mini-van's roof, the sound echoing in the silence of the deserted street.

Jon reached down and snagged a chuck of concrete from the sidewalk. The rats charged, squealing as they ran toward us. Fresh meat must be rare in a city of the dead.

The lead rat dropped as the improvised projectile hit it right between the eyes. The second made the mistake of going after Jose. The scythe flashed, removing the rat's head in one move. Jose grabbed his skull, screaming in agony as he sunk to his knees.

The third rat launched itself at me. I tripped over a bumper off one of the cars, falling backward off the sidewalk into the weeds. The rat's teeth snapped where I would have been if I hadn't fallen. I kicked it in the face, but it barely noticed. I rolled to the side as the rat leapt, fully intending to land on me. Suddenly, it swung away from me, smashing into the remains of a truck. The metal gave way as the rat impacted the rusted chassis, leaving a dent the size of the entire car. Abby screamed as she reversed the rat's direction and threw it a good fifty feet into the weeds. She ran over to pull me up.

"It didn't bite you, did it?" She vigorously searched me for damage, and I'm surprised her checking didn't do any.

"No, I'm fine thanks to you," I said. "Abby, I owe you one."

Jon approached from behind us. He'd never gotten close enough to be in any danger. I guess using rocks had its advantages. "You are completely useless. Abby should have left you for rat food."

I reached up to put my hand on Abby's shoulder before we had a full-blown fight on our hands. I noticed Jon's knife was still out. Jon barked out a laugh. "Some Gifted you turned out to be."

Jose gained his feet, though he swayed dangerously. "We've got to get to the building. There are bound to be more of them close by."

Abby put her arm around his waist and helped him as we made our way to the safety of the building. We could hear the rats now climbing through the wreckage of the vehicles to get to us. The weeds on the other side of the road rustled, the noise growing stronger by the second.

"Over here," a man yelled, waving to us.

The doorway, flanked by the remains of two massive urns, stood twenty feet away. We charged for the ramp that ran up to the building's landing. A rusted steel fence surrounded the landing, an older man dressed in a blue jumpsuit held the gate open, screaming for us to get in. Others stood inside, rifles pushed through the chain link, ready to open fire.

Rats rampaged from all directions. Gunfire erupted, hitting the rats as they roared across the pavement. Abby threw Jose over her shoulder, and we ran for the door. One overly brave rat leapt at Jon. He flowed around the rodent, his knife slashing through its throat as he rolled passed the carcass. He didn't even break stride, still arriving at the barricade first. I ran in closely followed by Abby with Jose yelling to be put down.

The gate clanged shut. The men finished off the closest rats, which were promptly attacked by the others. Food was food when it came to rats.

The older man ushered our group into the foyer before locking up the doors behind them. The foyer with a massive marble staircase was bigger than our house. I spun to take it all in. A huge blue circle with an eagle inlaid inside it dominated the view. Department of Commerce ran along the top of the circle. This place must have been magnificent before the war. Now everything stood dirty and in disrepair. Chips in the floor, scratches in the woodwork. This was not the Taj Mahal.

"Never thought I'd see the mighty Grim Reaper carried in like a sack of rice," the man said as Jose was lowered to the ground. The men with the rifles lined the walls, on guard for another attack.

Jose rubbed his face with both hands. "Tenji, I don't know what happened. I killed the rat, and everything went *loco.*"

Tenji laughed. "Well, I doubt you ever killed an animal before. Must have knocked your socks off."

"At least that's all they did," I said. No one laughed. It had been one of those days.

Tenji shot me a puzzled look before addressing Jose. "So what brings you home again? I thought you would be out for a few more months?"

Jose shook his head. "Not now, Tenji, we can discuss business later."

"What is this place?" I said, still amazed at how big the foyer was. Some of the lights still worked, some flickered. A second story banister wrapped the upper floor. Bodies moved in the shadows up there, many of them at the rail. More joined them, strangely silent. I heard the scrape of metal on metal. I could sense people watching us.

Tenji stepped over to me. "This was once where the government made rules on how people could do business. It is all very grand to impress the people who came here as to how important they all were."

"So the Underground uses it for a headquarters now?"

"The Underground?" Tenji asked, obviously confused by my question. "Reaper, who are these people you have brought amongst us?"

Jose had gotten up while we talked, and he stood next to Tenji. "These, *mi amigo,* are most of the missing students from Redemption," he said, a smile creasing his face. "And they are going to make us *mucho dinero* when we sell them to the Reclaimers."

It took less than a second for all hell to break loose. Jon's knife whistled out of its sheath, hitting the man across from him in the throat. Abby punched the closest man to her, the sound of breaking bones audible over the commotion. Both were dropped by arcs of energy coming from the second-floor overlook.

I glanced up to see seven men with strange rifles pointing down. "Why?" I asked Jose. He smiled as Tenji leveled a chrome pistol at me. "It's just business, Tommy."

Tenji fired the Taser pistol at me. The shock knocked the breath out of me. I fell to the floor, to lay by my fallen friends.

Jose laughed. "Sweet dreams, *niños.*"

2 9

I hit the ground and lay still, feigning unconsciousness. I had absorbed the energy from the pistol shot, but they didn't realize it.

"Okay, Reaper," Tenji said. "What is going on? Why are these kids thinking we are the Underground? I thought they were new recruits the way they fought for you."

Jose's laugh was an ugly thing, I almost turned to see his expression. "I've been living with these brats since they broke their collars. The Protector is fuming mad they got away and is willing to pay through the nose to get them back."

"After he betrayed us, you are going to help him?" Tenji asked, his tone agitated. "We help him take down the do-gooders and then he imprisons us with the rest."

"Tenji, it's all good. He made a solid business decision. We were competition, and he wanted to run the show. He knows we are here but hasn't moved against us."

"But why turn these kids over to him?"

"Money," my former boxing coach said. I knew he had been a murderer and assassin, but he'd been more of a coach and mentor than any of those things to me. "Plain and simple. We bring him the kids, he gives us a lot of money and an island in the Pacific. We are out of sight, and he gets the rest of the world. Once he makes an example of these kids, no one will ever defy him again."

I stiffened. We were screwed, but Wendi and Marcel were safe. Jose didn't have a clue where they were. I needed to find a way out and quick. Once the Protectorate had us, we'd be publicly executed or thrown into the Gauntlet.

"I don't like it," Tenji said.

"You don't have to. I run the Syndicate now, and we do things my way. Got it?"

"Yes, Reaper. So are all three Gifted?"

"The one who killed Campbell has a hunter-type Gift." I heard a boot thump and a sickening crunch. "He can hit just about anything and is Olympic athlete level."

Tenji whistled in appreciation. I hadn't known Jon's Gift type, but that could be a useful piece of information for the future. If any of us had a future.

I opened my eyes just enough to look through the lashes since Jose and Tenji stood behind me. I faced the staircase, so if I dropped them, I could get to the door. This might be the best chance I had, but I couldn't leave Abby and Jon behind. I closed my eyes, thinking of an alternative plan.

"The girl reminds me of Titan. She grows when she fights, but she starts morphing. I haven't seen her let loose yet, so I'm still not sure."

"What about Mr. Twenty questions?"

Even unconscious, I'm getting dogged. I hoped they moved me soon before the smell made me sneeze. The door swung open to the heavy thud of boots on the wood floor.

"*Qué haces?*" Jose said sharply. "Leave them for rats."

"Sure thing, Boss." The door reopened and slammed shut. *What a prick! How could you leave your fallen to be eaten?*

"He is the one who broke them all loose. The kids said he let go with enough power he shorted their collars. He ended up evaporating two kids and killed Powell in the process."

"He killed Powell?" Tenji's voice held a note of awe.

I heard boots coming down the stairs, any chance of escape left with the reinforcements. I didn't have enough power to take down a whole group of people. Even if I built up more energy, I couldn't carry Abby and Jon. Plus the rats outside would have us for dinner, literally.

"Yeah, but I think he burned out his Gift in the process. Not a flicker of energy since. He's a warranty case, so he's safe." Jose flipped me onto my side. He yanked the watch out of my pocket, letting me roll face down.

"Too bad, I'd like to thank him for taking out Powell."

"Here," Jose said. "Put one on each of the two. Don't bother with Tommy. Take the third to the tech guys."

"What are they?"

"One of the other kids reprogrammed the chips from the collars to stop their Gifts temporarily. Put them in the zoo until we are ready to ship them out."

"Yes, Reaper. It shall be done."

Two guys picked me up and carried me through the building and down a few flights of stairs. I heard voices as we went, but not enough to make out what they were saying. We passed through a kitchen; I willed my stomach to not growl in hunger. Remaining limp, not opening my eyes, I tried to map the turns we made. If we did escape, knowing how to get back to the front would be helpful. Abby or Jon groaned as a metal door opened. They dropped me on the floor and left me alone. Jon and Abby were put in cells, a series of metallic clicks followed. Jon got a few more kicks from the guards before the metal door clanged shut with a loud bang.

Listening like my life depended on it, I waited until the guards left. I was on a stone floor, the surface rough and cold. I counted to one thousand before I cracked my eyes without moving too much. *Phew, no guards.*

I tilted my head slightly so I could see more, sure surveillance cameras would be watching. Bunkbeds stood along one wall, and an old metal picnic table dominating the center of the room. I heard noises from the far corner but couldn't see who made them.

Abby and Jon were each in a cell, shackled to the wall, with Marcel's reprogrammed watches affixed to their wrists. Both were still out cold. Abby appeared smaller than usual. I guess her Gift really did increase her size.

Assured the guards had left, I got to my feet. The pistol's energy churned inside me. I touched a metal bedpost, but I didn't shock it. The red blinking eye from the camera mounted in the corner of the room kept me from using my Gift. Them thinking I was burned out was a good thing under the circumstances.

I walked to the first door. I opened it and peered inside. There were toilet stalls, sinks, and showers. Well, at least I could use the bathroom when I needed to.

The next room was fronted with Plexiglas dotted with air holes.

"Welcome to the zoo," a voice said. I jumped, startled. At the back of the room sat a teenage girl. She had shoulder-length light brown hair and bright blue eyes. Her t-shirt read "Stay Calm and Kill Zombies."

I regained my composure. "Hi, I'm Tommy."

"You can call me Molecular Mollie." She grimaced. "How did you get so lucky to be added to the zoo?"

"The Grim Reaper brought us here." I sounded depressed even to my ears. I should have never trusted him. "He told us we were going to get help from the Underground to free Cyclone Ranger before they kill him. How about you?"

She sighed. "I am part of the Underground. Well, my parents are. I'm Gifted, but you can't be a member until you are eighteen, and I'm only fourteen. I decided to prove I was ready and got nabbed by the Syndicate."

"Why aren't you behind bars like the rest?" I asked. The air holes had a fine mesh over each one.

"Watch and you'll understand." A second later, she was replaced by a white rabbit, then a rather large cricket, then a turtle. She shimmered, and Mollie was back, knees pulled up to her chest, her arms wrap around her legs. "See?"

"So if you had bars, you could just morph into something small and get away."

"Got it in one, Genius." Her face lit up with a smile. "I'm hoping my parents can get me out of here. Usually they will trade us for supplies, but I'm never going to live this one down."

"I know the feeling. So, who else is in the zoo?"

"I haven't been here long, but I hear the guards talk." She moved closer to the barrier. She pointed to the far enclosure. "Over there in the corner is Puppeteer. He can take control of anyone he touches, so they keep him covered and blind so he can't get out. Feeding time is interesting to say the least."

"I can imagine. He must have a hard time with the bathroom."

Mollie laughed. "No doubt. The next one is a guy in a wheelchair when he's here. He sounds crazy, if you ask me. He's got a big Italian dude sleeping out there who takes care of him. He's up with the doctors again, but he's kept down here when he's not being treated."

Imprisoning handicapped guys was extreme even for The Grim Reaper. He ceased being Jose once he double-crossed us. The transition came too easily; I should have listened to my gut. "Reaper is running his own prison?"

"Yeah, it is a nasty business down here. Your friends are in the next two, and the rest are empty for now. Sometimes they bring down drunks or guys who got in fights."

"What is the Syndicate? I've never heard of them."

Mollie shrugged. "My folks say they were criminals before the attacks. Now they hide in all the destroyed cities. We think they leave to commit crimes. The real Underground can't get the resources to fight the Reclaimers since we are constantly fighting off the rats and these guys."

"That sucks."

"Well, it sure beats being locked up in The Block."

She had a point there.

I woke to incoherent screaming. I jumped off the bunk I had fallen asleep on. The wheelchair guy was behind the bars raving, pulling at his long blond hair, tears streaming through the stubble on his face. Both his legs were gone, leaving only the stumps where his knees should be.

"Alyx, I'm here," a deep voice said from behind me. I turned to see a short, muscular guy roll off the bottom bunk. They must have returned from the doctor while I was asleep. He moved to the door—really, he flowed with a gracefulness I'd never seen, even from Blaze.

"Come Alyx, things are good now, you are safe." The calmness and caring in his words juxtaposed his muscular exterior. Alyx continued to sob uncontrollably as the big man held him, gently patting his back as he spoke softly to him.

Alyx settled after a bit. The man came over to me, hand extended. I shook it. "Hello." I noticed a trace of an Italian accent. "I am Nico Desiderius, but you may call me Gladiator if you wish."

"I'm Tommy." I didn't shake my semi-crushed hand. The dude was even more impressive than I first thought. He could have been a professional bodybuilder, but not in a burly way. "My friends Abby and Jon are over there."

"My friend is Alyx." He jerked his head toward the wheelchair-bound man. "Would you come over and meet him?"

I hesitated for a moment before nodding.

"It is okay," Gladiator said, putting his hand on my shoulder. "The drugs they force on him cause him issues, but he is stable now."

Alyx's head lolled to one side, but at least he wasn't screaming. His dark eyes had a far-off vacant look to them. "Hello," he rasped.

"Hi, I'm Tommy." I wanted to add something, but words escaped me.

Gladiator smiled. "Where are you from, Tommy?"

"Redemption." I probably shouldn't have told him, but under the circumstances, I figured it couldn't hurt.

A frown creased Gladiator's face. "You aren't collared. Do you not have a Gift?"

I paused. If someone listened in, I didn't want to admit I hid it. "My friends and I were attacked by a man named Powell."

"Powell? General Powell of the Reclaimers?"

"Yes, but retired to teach at the Redemption High School. He planned to kill us, but I managed to kill him. My Gift burned out in the process."

Gladiator nodded, a look of admiration on his face. "He was a mighty warrior. You did well to kill him."

"Thanks, but it was self-defense. I didn't know what I was doing. It just happened."

"That is the way of battle," Gladiator said approvingly. "And with you not having any combat training. It is impressive."

"I had a little." I felt a bit self-conscious. From the number of scars crisscrossing his exposed skin, Gladiator had seen more than a few battles. "Blaze trained me in martial arts at The Secret Lair."

"Blaze!" Alyx shouted. "Blaze save me, don't let them do this. Please, not my legs. No!"

"I'm sorry," I said frantically, looking from Gladiator to Alyx.

Gladiator held Alyx's head, speaking to him in the calming voice he'd used before. It worked, as Alyx calmed down. Gladiator turned back to me.

"How is it you know, Eugene?" He emphasized Eugene. I understood I needed to use Blaze's real name. It must be safer.

"He's friends with my mom. I worked for him at The Secret Lair in Great Falls. He taught me some Kempo since I got bullied." I tried not to, but my eyes kept flicking to check on Alyx.

"Eugene was with us the day Alyx lost his legs." He watched Alyx out of the corner of his eye. "He tried to help but couldn't reach us."

"Then how did you get here?"

"The Syndicate wanted to use Alyx to open portals so they could come and go, but after he was compromised, his magic became unreliable. They keep him drugged so he can't escape while they try to figure out a way to force him to do their bidding."

"He can do magic?"

"Yes, he is extremely powerful." A wistful look crossed Gladiator's face. "He could move you around the world in a moment or collapse a building with his magic. But my friend is rarely lucid between the drugs and the guilt."

"Guilt?"

"Eugene fell in love with a member of our team."

"Pep..." Gladiator's hand covered my mouth in a second.

"Yes, her name was Raychel." He took his hand away, his piercing eyes imploring me to be careful. "Alyx loved her as well. Grim Reaper killed her to get even with Eugene. The same fight where Alyx was hurt. It drove him mad. We were captured by the Syndicate and brought here a short time later."

"How long have you been here?"

"Over ten years," he said simply. "We've been prisoners of the Syndicate for almost twenty. There is no way out of here. We've tried many times."

A new voice chimed in from the doorway. "Tommy, that is a lesson you should take heed of," Grim Reaper said. "The only way out of here for you is in a body bag."

I felt my heart sink into my stomach. If Gladiator and Alyx couldn't break out of here, what chance did I have?

3 0

Grim Reaper walked into the room, two armored guards flanking him. He jerked his head toward the back. They dragged barely conscious Abby and Jon from their cells. They quickly handcuffed them and dumped them on the other side of the table.

Gladiator sneered at Reaper. "What kind of man brokers children with the enemy?"

Reaper laughed. *"Hombre, the only thing that matters is the payola,"* he said. "These kids will get us out of this hellhole once and for all." He tossed a cell phone on the table in front of me.

"What's that for? Galactic Legions got a new game?"

He waved the guards out. When the door clanged shut, the Reaper began. "You are calling the dead drop and getting where the next safe house is."

"And just why would I do anything you asked?"

He removed a pistol from his belt and put it to the back of Abby's head. If she noticed, she didn't bring her head up from where it slumped on the table. "If you don't, I'll blow Abby's brains all over the table."

"Why do you want to know where the safe house is?"

He shrugged. "I'll be honest with you, we need Marcel." He pushed the gun more firmly against Abby's head. "With his Gift, we wouldn't need to commit crimes; he could provide for us. I'll even sweeten the deal and let everyone go if you call now."

I thought about it for a second. There was no way I was handing Marcel, Waxenby, and Wendi over to Reaper. We were all dead anyway.

"Maybe I should have picked Jon instead. No." A wicked grin settled on his face. "That might be doing you a favor."

It dawned on me he didn't know I had heard his plans to turn us over to the Reclaimers. "I'm not calling, Reaper. You can go to hell before I'll hand my friends over."

"Well, don't say I didn't warn you." He pulled the hammer back. "Pick up the phone and dial. At the count of three, she dies."

I locked eyes with him. I had enough stored power to knock him out. I would have to time it perfectly.

"One."

I gathered the energy. The hair on my arms stood on end.

"Two."

I set my arms on the table, ready to fire the energy into the man who had betrayed us. I was only getting one shot, so it had to be perfect.

"Th... Wait."

My arm shot out, but I stopped just before I released the strike against him. The gun was pointing at the ceiling. Something had changed.

"Gladiator, we've got to get you all out of here before the guards bring the Reclaimers down here. They will be landing on the roof in thirty minutes," Reaper said, but he sounded different. Yet another accent came out of his mouth.

Gladiator glared at Reaper. "Why should we believe a scum bag like you, Reaper? You have no honor."

"Because this is Pepper Spray, you big dolt."

"Pepper?" Alyx asked coming out of his stupor.

Reaper handed the gun to Gladiator before reaching out to cup the ravaged magician's cheek. "I'm so sorry, Alyx. I never meant for any of this to happen."

My mind balked at the Reaper stroking Alyx's face with the words of their long dead teammate coming from Reaper's lips. Where was Jerry Springer when you needed him? Reaper pulled a hypo and shot it into Alyx's arm. "That will counteract the drugs they've been giving him for a few minutes."

"Pepper," Alyx sobbed. "I tried to save you, but Reaper killed you, and Ruby Lash took my legs while I tried to get to you. Blaze tried to save us both, but he couldn't. We had no Gifts. If we had, you might have lived."

Tears were running down Reaper's face. "You did all you could, Alyx, but I dropped as soon as Reaper hit me. I saw through his eyes what they did to you both. I'm sorry, I couldn't stop him, but I can now if we hurry."

"How is this possible?" Gladiator said.

Yay! I'm not the only confused one.

Reaper unlocked Abby's handcuffs with a key from his pocket and tossed it to me. He slapped them around his wrists after looping it around one of the legs bolted into the cement. "When Reaper kills, the person is trapped within him. We all can experience what he does, just as he knows what is happening now."

All those people stuck in the cesspool of Reaper's head. Yuck! "So it is like he has multiple personalities." I reached across the table to unlock the handcuffs holding Jon.

"Right," Pepper said. "Alyx, listen to me now. I can't keep control of him for much longer. You have to find Jinx. She is in Charlotte. Marcel can get the address for you. Tell her Pepper Spray should be called snow spray. You have to go now."

Alyx's eyes lit up like a kid on Christmas morning. He began speaking in a language I didn't understand, but I could feel the power. I wondered idly what would happen if I tried to absorb the magic but thought better than to try. A slim bluish-red disc appeared about waist high, spinning with a crackling energy as it grew until it was large enough for Gladiator to shove Abby and Jon through.

Alyx yelled, "Tommy, I can't hold it open much longer. Run."

I heard Mollie pounding her fists against the Plexiglas, screaming. I pointed at the wall, and lightning arced from my fingers into metal frame, shattering it. A heartbeat later, a hawk flew past me to freedom. Gladiator hefted Alyx out of the chair, threw him over his shoulder, and ran to the portal.

"It is collapsing, we must go," Gladiator yelled to me. He jumped through.

I grabbed the cell phone as I vaulted over the table, landing in front of Pepper Spray/Reaper. I wanted to free Pepper, but how do you release a dead person out of someone else's mind?

"Tommy," Pepper shouted as I ran for the portal. "Tell Blaze I love him more than anything, but he has to let me go."

"I will, I promise." I dove from prison to a parking lot under Carolina blue sky. The portal winked out of existence. We were safe, for the time being at least.

I walked to the street seeing a sign labeled Mint Street. Across the road stood Bank of America Stadium. My mother would have been ecstatic, having grown up a huge Panthers fan. Good thing it wasn't Sunday, or this place would have been packed during a home game. A small seating area, complete with a globe suspended on flowing water rotating it, offered a good place to get oriented and figure out a plan.

We had escaped but had no car, no money, and a legless man without his wheelchair. The good part of our predicament being it was early on a Saturday morning, so when we appeared in the middle of an abandoned parking lot, the guy who noticed rubbed his eyes, swearing loudly about the effect of too much acid.

Mollie pounced on me, hugging me like there was no tomorrow. "Thank you, Tommy, for getting me out of the cell."

I grinned. It made me feel good for something nice to have occurred out of the debacle. "We'd love to have you on the team, Mollie, if you'd like."

She shook her head. "My parents are going to kill me as it is. They'll be worried sick. I've got to get back, but I hope to see you again." She pecked my cheek, morphed into a hawk, and flew off into the bright blue sky. I watched her go, marveling at her Gift.

Gladiator carried Alyx up and got him seated on a bench where they spoke together softly. Abby sat on the ground, still not completely recovered from what they knocked her out with. Jon sprawled on the other bench, working with a small knife he'd kept in his boot to get the watch off since the clasp had been fused shut. Once his Gift kicked in, he'd heal the broken nose, bruises, and any other damage he had sustained.

I checked the cell phone Reaper had kindly provided. I switched off the GPS; Marcel would be so proud. I dialed the dead drop we had agreed on and left the safe message. Five minutes later, the phone rang from a blocked number.

"The swan flies low over the pond." Marcel's voice came over the phone.

"Make sure to duck or you'll get goosed." Jon rolled his eyes, but no one would ever guess that passphrase.

I quickly caught Marcel up on what had happened. I told him Pepper had told us to seek out Jinx. I could hear his fingers flying over the keyboard as we spoke. The phone chirped in my ear.

"There's her address," he said. "Give me your cross streets."

I ran over to the street sign. "Mint and Stonewall."

The tapping continued for a minute. "Go across the street to the stadium and find the ATM."

I jogged across the deserted street. I passed the Panthers' ring of honor, the statues of John Kasey, Sam Mills, and Steve Smith watched as I searched the grounds. I turned a corner and there it was, the promised ATM.

"Okay, I'm here."

"Wait for it..."

The ATM beeped several times before it presented a pile of twenty-dollar bills. "The camera is off so hurry up before someone sees you."

I stuffed the money in my pocket. Having a whiz kid at home base was certainly handy.

"Thanks, man. You're the best!" I could tell Marcel had a smug grin on his face even over the phone.

"Throw that phone into a storm grate. Just because the GPS is off doesn't mean they can't find it."

"Will do," I said. "Tell Wendi I'll see her soon."

"You had better, Bruh." He let out a huge, exasperated sigh. "Her moping around is driving us nuts. Catch ya later."

I hung up. She was moping over me. Maybe today would be a good day.

I called a cab before dumping the phone and went to a low-price hotel nearby. The vending machine got raided. We hadn't eaten since before we'd boarded the Squid. With Abby and Jon needing to heal, food became a much greater concern. Healing minor injuries at Dresden emptied the refrigerator after sparing; Jon's injuries would take a grocery store. Everyone got cleaned up while Jon argued the entire time about needing to replace his knife. Gladiator assured him Jinx could provide a more than suitable replacement. Even after he quit bitching, the sulking continued.

When everyone had finished, we called, from the hotel phone, a cab from a different company. We stopped at a hospital supply store for a new wheelchair on the way to Jinx's house since Gladiator couldn't carry Alyx around without attracting notice.

The small suburban community we drove into was dotted with cars parked in driveways and kids on skateboards yelling and laughing. I watched them with envy. This was the life I had missed out on. Hanging with my friends, eating dinner with my parents. Instead, I had schizophrenic lunatics trying to sell my dad's and my murder being broadcast on TV.

The cab pulled up to a small white house with a huge maple tree in the front yard. The walkway was lined with shrubs, and a Carolina Panthers flag flew from the column of the porch. We got out of the mini-van taxi, and Gladiator helped Alyx into his new chair as I paid the driver and asked him to wait, just in case.

I went up and rang the doorbell while the others followed at a distance. The door opened, and a short, very dark, very angry woman stood in front of me. "I don't want any," she said in a huff. "You kids think I have nothing better to do than buy overpriced magazines or waxy chocolate bars so you can go on some band trip, well, forget it."

The door slammed in my face. So much for Plan A. Unfortunately, I didn't have a Plan B.

S o, Plan B turned out to be the same as Plan A. I rang the doorbell again and awaited the swirling mass of energy that was Jinx.

The door opened. Jinx stood there, arms crossed, her foot tapping impatiently. "Did you not understand me the first time?" she said, her voice rising in anger. She looked past me to see Alyx being wheeled around the corner. "Now you're bringing cripples to sell your crap? Well, if I haven't seen everything before now, I certainly have now. I can't believe the tactics you kids will go to so you can get away from your parents. I should call the cops on you."

"Pepper Spray should be called snow spray." I cut her off before she actually called the cops.

She stopped dead, the energy completely contained behind her eyes. "Come again?"

"Pepper Spray told me to tell you she should have been called snow spray." I realized I was more scared of her now than when she was ranting at me.

"Where did you hear that?"

Gladiator halted the wheelchair at the bottom of the stairs. "Jinx, Pepper told him."

"Gladiator?" she said, her hand over her mouth. "Oh my God, Alyx, what happened to you? Lord Almighty, get in here before one of my nosy ass neighbors sees you standin' out here."

Gladiator waved off the driver, who peeled out like the cops were on his tail. I cringed. So much for not attracting attention. We pushed-pulled Alyx up the trio of stairs and into the house. I understood now why people scream about handicap-enabled buildings, and we only went up three stairs. We shoved him over the raised door frame with a heavy thump. The foyer held a staircase and a couple plants with a Jesus Bless Our Home plaque hung over the entry into the living room in front of us.

Jinx turned to Gladiator. "Okay, I'm happy to see you boys, but what in the hell are you doing on my doorstep?"

Gladiator jerked his chin toward me. "Thomas can answer your questions far better than I can."

I gulped. I'd get one chance to talk her into helping us with my plan. "Miss Jinx," I started, only to be interrupted.

"My name is Alicia, or Mrs. Reynolds if you feel the need to remind me how old I am." Agitation was clear in her voice. "Jinx vanished a long time ago. Start with how a youngster like you knows Pepper Spray and a joke I haven't heard since the day she died."

"Sorry," I said slowly, trying to process everything since she spoke so fast. "It's kind of a long story."

"Honey, I've got all day, but we can at least sit down while you talk." She ushered us into the living room, indicating we should sit on the deep red couches as she settled on the edge of a recliner. Gladiator stood behind Alyx's wheelchair.

So, I told her about Reaper bringing us to Washington D.C. to meet the Underground. How he betrayed us and his plan to sell us to the Protectorate. I told her how Pepper Spray said she was trapped in Reaper and told me to find Jinx and tell her the joke and how we got to her house.

"Wow!" Clearly, we impressed her, and hearing it out loud, I felt a bit impressed too. Not bad for three kids from Redemption. Abby and Jon grinned as well. We had gotten away from a guy who had killed twelve guards escaping from The Block.

"You look parched." She left the room and returned shortly carrying a tray of filled glasses. I hopped up and held the tray while she passed the drinks out. I set the tray on the table and took mine back to my seat. It seemed like years since we'd had anything other than water to drink. I sipped my tea like normal before almost spitting it out. It contained enough sugar to kill an elephant.

Abby and Jon had similar reactions. Jinx laughed. "First time drinkin' sweet tea? Welcome to the South." She settled into the recliner, out of place with the stylish decor of the room, but what it lacked in style, it appeared to make up for in comfort.

Alicia took a sip of her iced tea. "So, the question is what are you going to do now?"

"Well, we went to D.C. to recruit help to free Cyclone Ranger," I said a bit hesitantly. I felt like a fool for having trusted Reaper, and the voice of self-doubt wormed its way into my brain. I could barely control my abilities, let alone take down the elite guards who would be all over Dad during the move. What if Marcel was wrong about the timetable of when they moved him to Vegas? Could we pull it off without help?

"And?"

"Well, I was hoping that you could help us."

She laughed a long loud laugh. "Now that's rich. And just why would I want to? Cyclone Ranger never did anything for me."

A loud crash sounded from around the corner, stopping me from answering her question. Alicia jumped up, running toward the sound. Gladiator jumped to his feet, standing protectively in front of Alyx.

"We have company, Harold." Alicia's voice came from the other room. "Yes, sweetheart, you can come meet them."

Alicia stepped back into the room, holding the arm of an older man, his salt and pepper hair thinning badly, but his beard grew wild, almost reaching his chest. He wore a slightly vacant expression as if he were seeing things hidden from the rest of us. His hand reached out to hold something in front of him like a small child showing an item to their parents.

"Mr. Fix-it?" Gladiator said, shock etched on his face. "We thought he was taken by the Protectorate."

Alicia huffed. "He's my husband, and it is very hard to keep things from me when I really want them," she said, the last portion accompanied with a glare that cut through me.

My wound from the glare didn't last long. I stood in the same room as a legend. Mr. Fix-it designed and built most of the gear and safe houses for all of the Gifted teams, as well as the enhanced teams like Stryke Force.

Harold returned from wherever he had been. "Gladiator? Alyx? Did the suits not work?" he said, his voice thick with grogginess as if he had been awakened from a deep sleep. "Oh, my. Alyx. What happened to your legs?"

Alyx didn't respond. He floated in a drug-induced, deep catatonic state, the shot given during the escape only a temporary reprieve.

"That wheelchair is awful," Harold continued, not realizing he hadn't been answered. "Let me go downstairs to the workshop. I have a proto- type you can try." He wandered off the way he had come.

A mixture embarrassment and grief warred across Alicia's face as she watched him shamble off. She turned back to face us, almost daring us to mention anything about Harold.

Gladiator cleared his throat. "Jinx, what has happened to Mr. Fix-it?"

Tears welled in her eyes but never left them. "This is what our 'Gifts' bring us." She pointed back to where Harold had left. "That man created some of the most amazing things this world has ever seen, and it has stolen his mind in the process. Nothing, and I mean nothing, comes without a price in this life. His abilities have consumed him to the point where he doesn't even recognize me anymore."

Gladiator hung his head, embarrassed. "I am truly sorry, Jinx. I suffer to think of the pain you must endure." He glanced over at the sleeping Alyx.

She turned to Abby, Jon, and me. "You kids think these abilities are great to have? You are stronger, faster, and smarter than all the Norms? Let me tell you, they are a curse. If I could give mine up, I would in a heartbeat."

"I'm sorry we've intruded," I started. A siren wailed outside the house, the sounds of screeching tires and men running could be heard from outside.

"Now look what you've done," she snarled. "Those are Reclaimers out there; we need to get you hidden."

Gladiator's hand strayed to his hip as if he wanted to pull a sword and wade into battle, but we hadn't gone to the sword shop on the way.

"Grab your glasses and follow me, quickly," she said. Gladiator flipped

Alyx over his shoulder and moved to obey. I folded the wheelchair while Jon and Abby grabbed up the glasses to follow. Jon even thought to wipe the table with his sleeve to get rid of the water marks.

"No evidence," he said with a smirk when he saw I had noticed.

"Smart."

Alicia held the door that led down to the basement. "Follow the stairs to the bottom and stay in the workshop until I come get you."

"Attention, the house!" a man's voice boomed through a megaphone. "Step out with your hands over your head now, or we will enter by force."

"Won't they take you to The Block?" I worried she would pay the price for us showing up on her doorstep.

She barked out a laugh. "Honey, machines don't work on me. A bit of Jinx Juice and they'll swear I'm as normal as any Reclaimer soldier."

I followed the rest down, the wheelchair held awkwardly in my arms. I heard a pneumatic hiss and saw a slab settle over the top landing sealing us in. The walls were sheets of steel, as were the stairs. Obviously, this wasn't the standard track home add-on.

I left the wheelchair at the bottom of the stairwell against the far wall. There in the center of the room sat a new wheelchair, computer panels welded to the back, wires running to the wheels, and control panels zip tied to the arms. Gladiator set the sleeping Alyx in the new chair, gently stroking his face as Alyx's head lulled to the side.

If Santa's workshop exploded, it would look like this. Wires, computer boards, and tools warred over the horizontal spaces that scarcely could be called tables. Some were disintegrating particleboard on old wooden sawhorses and others, I kid you not, things like Waxenby's force fields floating mid-air, and everything in between. This is the room where organization went to die. My mom would have hated it; I loved it. Chaos and magic reigned supreme here.

Harold stood facing an empty whiteboard. His mouth moved, but nothing audible could be heard. His hands clenched and unclenched as he stood there. Abby bumped a stack of computer cases. A piece rattled loudly when it fell to the ground. Harold turned toward us, his eyes glazed over. They slowly focused. "Gladiator? Alyx? Did the suits not work?"

"They worked fine, Mr. Fix-it," Gladiator replied smoothly. He made no mention he had already asked upstairs.

"Oh, good." He noticed Alyx in the new wheelchair. "Oh, I made a prototype wheelchair. I hope Alyx can use it."

"Thank you. I'm sure he will appreciate it greatly."

"Good." He turned back to his whiteboard again.

"What the hell are we going to do now?" Jon looked irritated. "This was a waste of time. We should have gone back to meet up with the others."

"We need help to free Cyclone Ranger," I reminded him.

Jon rolled his eyes. "We've got them. We have enough firepower to free one dude."

"What we need are weapons," Abby said. "Without an edge, it will be tough to do anything other than hide."

"It is too bad Mr. Fix-it is ill," Gladiator said as he shook his head, his rawhide bound ponytail swaying behind his head. "He would have been a great asset."

They were right. We needed to get an edge, and Marcel could work wonders with existing pieces but couldn't create from scratch the way Harold did. If we could get gear, even if it didn't work, Marcel should be able to get it running.

"Jon, do you still have your watch?"

"Yeah, but the clasp is wrecked."

"Give it to me and find some duct tape."

He practically threw the watch to me, the knife and rust-colored marks visible from where he had cut off the band. Abby and Jon scurried around looking for duct tape.

"Man, the world would fall apart without this stuff," Abby said, raising the gray roll over her head in triumph.

I shot her a smile. "Excellent." I caught the roll she had thrown to me.

Harold was oblivious to me as I approached with the watch and tape. Taking his left wrist, I placed the watch on it, taping it in place and activating it. I stepped back, waiting for his eyes to refocus as the watch suppressed his Gift. Without his abilities, he should return to being plain old Harold.

The minutes passed, but nothing happened. A hand settled on my shoulder. "Thomas, it was a valiant effort, but it may be Mr. Fix-it is really sick, and the watch can't cure that."

I nodded, but there were days when even your best isn't good enough.

Failure had become my sidekick, always there when I didn't need it. The day would come when they realized how useless I am and left me, assuming I didn't get them killed before then. Their blood would be on my hands.

ours passed, sitting idly in the workshop while who knows what had happened upstairs with the Reclaimers. Alicia said she would be fine, but as the day rolled into night, I wondered if it was true. A buzzer beeped at eleven, and Harold robotically walked to a control panel and pressed a button. A George Jettison bed slid out of the wall. He got in, pulled the covers up, and fell asleep, gently snoring within minutes.

All those hours and he'd not changed at all. I'd have to get the watch back in the morning. I should have done it once we knew it hadn't worked, but I didn't have the heart to admit defeat. One by one, everyone else found a semi-comfortable place and drifted off to sleep.

I couldn't sleep. My time to rescue Dad grew shorter with each passing day, and I was no closer than the day we left Dresden. We had three Gifted who could fight. Wendi's speed would come in handy, but not when the fighting broke out. Waxenby, by his own admission, was a lightweight. Gladiator would be helpful, but Alyx's magic fluctuated with his mental state. Now Jinx refused to help, and Mr. Fix-it drifted beyond reach. In the westerns, the cavalry always showed up to save the day. Where was Clint Eastwood when you needed him?

"In the holy name of God, what is that?" Alicia's voice woke me abruptly. From the shocked looks around the room, I wasn't the only one. I followed her pointing arm to Harold, the duct-taped watch visible from across the room. I groaned; I should have removed it last night.

Gladiator intervened on the rampaging Alicia. Even though she barely reached his shoulder, I'm not sure I would have gotten in her way. "Jinx, calm down."

"Don't Jinx, calm down me," she said trying to push past the mountain of muscle. "What the hell is on his wrist? I save your bacon, and you are down here messing with my helpless husband."

"It's my fault." My face was flaming red with embarrassment. "Marcel reprogrammed the chips from our collars so they suppressed our Gifts if we needed to. I thought it might help Mr. Reynolds to get better."

I don't think I had ever seen anyone as angry as she was. "No, what you thought is he could help you with your asinine plan to rescue Cyclone Ranger. You could have seriously hurt him by putting that thing on him. Get the hell out of my house."

I hung my head and moved to the stairs. Another in a long line of screw-ups. "I'm sorry."

"You keep going, Mister. I never want to see your face on my doorstep again!"

"Leecee, what are you screaming about?"

"Harold, you be quiet, I'm telling these kids how it is." Her eyes went wide with disbelief. Slowly she turned to stare at Harold, now scrubbing the sleep from his eyes. Tears welling in her eyes, and her voice caught in her throat. "Harold, you know who I am?"

"We've been married forever." He sat up and swung his legs over the edge of the bed. "How could I ever forget you?"

It's a good thing we were in a soundproof room because the decibel levels would have had the Reclaimers back if they hear the shriek of joy as Alicia flung herself across the room to tackle her husband. For his part, he appeared a bit confused.

He glanced at the watch, a shadow of doubt sliding across his face. "I slept a bit later than normal, but..." He stopped and scratched his head. "Where did I get this watch? I don't remember it."

He moved to pull the mass of duct tape off. A chorus of "stop!" rang around the room.

Harold paused, panning the room, for the first time seeing the five strangers arrayed around his workshop. "I am completely lost, and if I'm not far off, I've missed significant time."

Alicia pulled herself away as she wiped the tears from her face. "You've been here the whole time, but for the last ten years, you've been a zombie."

He nodded, still peering around. "I don't seem to have my drive to create new things. I actually feel like I did as a child." He stood up and walked over to Gladiator, who placed Alyx back in the new wheelchair before he greeted his old friend.

"It is good to have you back, Mr. Fix-it." Gladiator extended his hand.

Harold shook it. "Nico, it is good to see you as well, my friend." He smiled with a soft laugh. "You still haven't aged a bit. That witch did good work. I wish I could replicate it."

"She was a vile creature." Gladiator wanted to spit but wouldn't do it inside. "I have seen too much grief to think it a blessing, but I am glad to see you better."

"I'm not so sure I agree, but then again, I haven't been alive for over two millennia," Harold said. Alicia hovered around him, her hand constantly touching him as if to reassure her that he was real. "Is Alyx sick? What happened?"

Gladiator ran down the story of Alyx's injuries, being captured, and our arrival as Grim Reaper's prisoners. Abby, Jon, and I interjected portions where Gladiator didn't know things. We ended up with a tag-team telling of the trip to Charlotte and meeting with Alicia. She filled us in on the house being searched and held overnight while she was tested and questioned about the reported subversives who were at the house. *Wow, I've never been a subversive before.*

"Well, now," Harold said, noticing the condition of his clothes and the facial growth in dire need of grooming. "I think I'll take a shower and get a clean set of clothes while you all eat some breakfast. If you'll excuse me."

"I'll be down with breakfast in a bit." Alicia smiled, a lot. "They probably left bugs, so I can't let you upstairs."

Harold took his wife's hand, and they left the room. I heaved a sigh of relief. That could have gone badly. Alicia may have hung up the costume, but she was as fierce as anyone I'd ever met. I curled back up on the mat I slept on and dozed off while we waited for breakfast.

217

Abby shook my shoulder. "Tommy, breakfast. Well, really it is a late lunch, but who's counting?"

I rubbed the sand from my eyes, but my stomach was wide awake, grumbling at the smell of bacon. Time plays tricks on you when you are underground for extended periods of time. Without the sun, every hour is unchanging. Waxenby said the casinos in Vegas were the same way.

I wondered how Wendi was. I missed her more than anything. I wanted to hear her voice, touch her hair, smell her lavender perfume. Lifetimes had passed, but I could still hear her say I love you when I closed my eyes.

I got up and grabbed a plate. Bacon, scrambled eggs, and toast. I looked over to where Alyx ate slowly, his hands shaking. Gladiator sat next to him, his food untouched, watching him like a hawk.

I filled my plate and dropped next to Abby on the floor. Jon roosted on a table across from us. Alicia came down the stairs with a jug of orange juice and a coffee pot. Even with her hands filled, there was a bounce in her step. "Sorry it took so long. I had to run to the store. I only have enough for the two of us on hand, and I know how teenagers eat."

Alicia's eyes danced as Harold entered, fully shaved, dressed in a white lab coat and clean clothes. He kissed Alicia, who rubbed his bare face with oohs and ahhs.

"Thomas," he said as he pulled a chair out to sit in front of me. "Tell me about this watch and how it works."

I gulped down the last of my eggs, not wanting to talk with a full mouth. "Sir," I started.

Harold held up his hand. "Son, you saved, if not my life, then my sanity and returned me to my wife. You call me Harold, or Mr. Fix-it if you need to, but I'm not a sir."

"Yes, sir, err, Harold," I stumbled on. "My best friend, Marcel, took the remnants of the collars we all wore and reprogrammed the chips somehow so we could turn them on or off to stop our Gifts from working. It worked on us right away, but it was overnight before it helped you."

"I had been in that state for years according to Leecee," he said, grimacing. I'm sure the thought of all the lost years bothered him more than he let on. "It shut my abilities off, but it took my brain a while to fight through the effects is my guess."

"My girlfriend," which earned me a dark look from Jon, "wears one to stop hers."

Harold pursed his lips, twisting up his face as he thought. "Hmmm, what kind of Gift does she have?"

"She's a speedster." I thought I used the same term Marcel had told us.

"Yeah," he sighed. "I've seen many a youngster turn old before their time because of that particular Gift."

I nodded but couldn't add anything, so I took a bite of bacon instead.

"So Leecee says you are planning on rescuing Cyclone Ranger."

"That was why we went to D.C." The thought of Reaper screwing us over still made me see red. "I'm not sure if we can pull it off without help."

"Cyclone Ranger is a good man. I think I can help you out." A cup clattered to the ground. Alyx convulsed in his chair, head shaking, arms flailing about. Gladiator kneeled before him, making sure he didn't hurt himself. "I think I had better see to Alyx, then we'll see what Mr. Fix-it has in his goody bag for you kids."

I smiled as he left to treat Alyx. If anyone could help him, it was Harold. I grabbed more food and a big glass of juice. Alicia spoke quietly to Gladiator, whose eyes never left Alyx. It hurt to see the pain in the big man's eyes.

"You think he's going to be okay?" Abby said from next to me. I just about dropped my juice. For someone so muscular, she could move like a panther.

"Harold will have something." I wished I felt as sure as I sounded. "He's a miracle worker after all."

She chucked me in the arm. "Thanks for getting us out of there," she said, lowering her voice. "I was scared to death. If I ever get my hands on the Grim Reaper, I'm going to shove the scythe up his ass."

I chuckled. If anyone could, it was Abby. "I'll hold him for you while you do it."

Alicia walked over, Jon in tow. "You mind helping me carry the dishes upstairs?" We glanced over to where Harold spoke to Alyx. Light flashed on the control panel on the wheelchair. It appeared more like a cockpit of a plane all lit up.

"What about the bugs?" Abby asked.

"They are listening to the *Food Network* and assorted household sounds," she said with a smirk.

"Sure thing." I grabbed up plates and serving dishes. We trekked up the stairwell to help clean up. I did the dishes while Jon and Abby dried and Alicia put the things away.

An hour later, Gladiator pushed the wheelchair, which hovered a couple of inches over the floor, into the kitchen. Alyx's color was better than any time since we met them at the Zoo.

"Jon, Mr. Fix-it has requested your presence downstairs," Gladiator said.

A sopping hand towel landed over my face as he left for the workshop. I could only imagine what miracles were contained in the workshop, but I'd have to wait my turn.

Damn, I hate waiting.

33

Jon came up carrying a backpack and an old guitar case. Abby went down next, so I helped Alicia with some chores, more to pass the time than out of any true desire to be helpful. My heart pounded, and my palms sweated as I waited my turn. Finally, Abby emerged, green backpack in hand. She gestured for me to go down.

It took everything I had not to run down the metal staircase. I stepped into the workshop, my head on a swivel. Harold sat on a rolling stool, a pair of magnifying glasses propped up on his forehead. He pushed another stool over to me. I sat.

"Tommy," Harold said. "So, why save Cyclone Ranger?"

I paused. Harold smirked at me. He knew something but wasn't saying. "They are going to kill him on TV. It isn't right." I fought to keep my voice level.

Harold shook his head. "No, it isn't. Your father would have told me the same thing." My jaw dropped. Harold laughed. "Tommy, I am probably the only person alive who has seen the faces of the most powerful Gifted in the country. I built and fitted gear for almost every one of them. You're the spitting image of your dad when he was your age."

I smiled at the compliment. "I have to save him. I grew up without him, but I can't let him die without trying."

"Well, then," he said, slapping his knee, which caused his thinning hair to bounce up. "Let's see what I've got for you. Ordinarily, I would build something, but my Gift is off, thanks to this here watch. Let's start with the suit."

He walked me over to a contraption, a cross between a time machine and giant pill. Wires crisscrossed the outside, hooked to circuit boards and a series of colored buttons. He stepped aside so I could climb in. "Once the door shuts, place your clothes in the drawer that opens."

I got into the capsule, the door swung shut behind me, and a soft yellow light glowed from the walls. A hiss accompanied the appearance of the drawer. I kicked off my clothes, shoving them in. I guess I should have folded them, but I was distracted. I placed my feet on the blue footprints that were centered on the floor.

Harold's voice came over the tinny-sounding speaker from above my head. "Tommy, hold your arms straight out to your sides and close your eyes, please."

I did. I could see the red light through my eyelids as it ran up and down my body. A chime sounded, and the light turned off. "Go ahead and get dressed."

I did so as fast as possible. I pushed the door open and stepped out. A whirring sound came from beside the machine. My very own combat suit assembled before my eyes. The same midnight blue as my dad's.

"Now, it will take a bit to finish," Harold said from where he stood by an open cabinet. "So, Tommy, we need to discuss your Gift. You don't have to tell me anything, but the more you do, the better I can configure your gear to suit you."

In the old days, a person's Gift, as well as their identity, were highly guarded secrets. Everyone knew about Cyclone Ranger's lightning and wind, but he would have aspects of his Gift that would leave him vulnerable to attack. "I'm not sure how to explain it," I told him. So I described all the things I had gone through, Powell with the battery, Marcel's tests, and the shock pistol in D.C. Harold's mouth gaped more as the story went on.

"Tommy," he said softly as if I were a bubble that would burst if he spoke too loudly. "I've only seen one other person with your type Gift. You are an amplifier. You absorb energy and can expel it at a much greater level."

"Is that good?"

He scratched his head. "Are guns good? A gun can protect you or kill you. Same thing here." He paused as he thought. "The other person I've studied tried to absorb too much energy and exploded, taking down the greater part of a city block."

I whistled. A huge explosion, and it could be me. A surge of panic took me. *What the hell.* My Gift could turn me into a small warhead, just doing what I couldn't control.

"Now, from what I understand, this person tapped into a transformer at a power plant while trying to break into Fort Knox," he said, stopping to notice the confusion embedded on my face. "It was where the old government stored a lot of gold. So don't do anything stupid, and you should be okay, but never let on you have a limit, or it could be used against you."

I nodded, too spooked for words.

"The thing is, I don't have anything on hand that I think could help you," he said, his tone wrought with disappointment. "I could try taking off the watch and build you something..."

"No, Harold." He wouldn't lose any more of his life on my account. "You've done more for all of us than we had the right to ask for."

"Thank you, Tommy." A proud smile lit up his face. "I can see not only do you look like your father, but you have his strong character as well." He paused to walk to a small dark wood box, which lay near the bed he had slept in. He opened it, pushed a few things around, and pulled something out. "The one thing you would never guess about your father is he was always a bit of a practical joker." He held out a silver ring, a dark blue stone in the center.

I took the ring, noting the inscribed lightning bolts running around the band. The stone shone with a deep gleam. I ran my finger over it and almost dropped the ring. A shock hit my finger as soon as I touched the gem. The slight energy from that one instant started bouncing around in my chest, building.

Harold laughed. "Your father gave it to me. He would shock people with it when they weren't expecting it. Just never use it on a Norm; it could stop their heart. I'm sorry I don't have more for you."

I held the ring, a ring my dad had held, and felt closer to the man I had never met, the father I had never met. "You've given me more than you'll ever know."

I put the ring on as Harold pulled my combat suit out of the machine and packaged it up in a black backpack. He walked me through the controls in the helmet before adding it to the bag. He stopped to grab a silver duffel bag, and we went back up the stairs.

The upstairs was in chaos. The vans were back, Reclaimers setting up all around the house as I watched. "What happened? I thought the bugs were taken care of."

Harold tossed Gladiator the bag. "That is your armor and sword." He moved to look out the window. "They are raiding to see if you came back is my guess."

"So, what do we do?" Abby asked. She was dressed in a fitted combat suit, helmet under her arm.

"We shoot our way out is my vote," Jon said, dressed in a brown and green combat suit. He carried throwing knives on his wide belt and combat knives in the tops of his high boots. A quiver of arrows poked over his shoulder for easy access. Mr. Fix-it had even provided a composite bow, which was out and strung. "There are only twelve guys out there. Abby, Gladiator, and I take all of them down before they know what hit them."

"And what do you think happens to us after you bring the Reclaimers down on our heads?" Alicia commented, highly agitated. "You've destroyed our life here."

"Now, now, Leecee." Harold patted her hand. "We need a bit of misdirection. Alyx, can you open portal into the house next door?"

"Nico, roll me to the window." Alyx had dark circles under his eyes, but his eyes sparkled for the first time since I'd met him. Obviously, whatever Harold did for him worked. He started chanting, moving his arms in a strangely rhythmic pattern. A swirling mass of lights grew from the wall, expanding to show the beige and green living room of the next house over.

"Alicia, from the front window, short out the van's engine. Tommy, I want you to shoot through the bay window and hit the transformer. It will mess with their night vision," Harold said as he stepped over to Jon, pulling an arrow from his quiver. "Jon, fire this arrow into the truck pointed up the street. Throw the front door open and then get back here pronto. Any questions?"

We all looked at each other, wondering which of us would speak first. As usual, it was me. "And what exactly will that do?"

Harold, devious smile on his face, said, "Do it. You'll understand in a minute."

It amazed me how similar Harold's grin was to Marcel's when he knew something no one else did. I shrugged. Jon and Alicia hopped through the portal, followed by Abby. Harold put his hand on my shoulder before I could jump through. He walked over, unscrewed the light bulb from a nearby lamp, and switched it on. "You might want to charge your battery first."

A quick check to make sure Alyx and Gladiator weren't watching, then I clenched my jaw and stuck my finger into the open socket. Energy and pain shot through my system, combining and overpowering the ring's shock. The skin on my fingers crackled as the electricity poured into me. It stopped without warning. Harold held the plug up. "A little goes a long way with you, Tommy. Remember, you need to be careful."

I nodded my thanks since I was a bit buzzed from the energy. I jumped through the portal, landing in the middle of the neighbor's living room.

Jon and Alicia stood by the front door as I entered the foyer, almost tripping on the plant dominating the wall. The owners must have green thumbs.

"What took you so long?" Jon asked impatiently. "They are getting ready to move now that it's full night."

"Sorry, needed a snack," I quipped. I wasn't about to go into how my Gift worked with him.

"Well, get going." He bounced on the balls of his feet, itching for a fight. Alicia pointed into the dining room, which held a massive bay window. I stepped behind the circular glass table centered under a ceiling fan.

"Hurry it up." Jon held the doorknob, ready to move.

I pulled the power into a ball, centering it in my chest. I pushed out my arms and nothing happened. I did it again and still nothing.

"What are you doing?" Jon said, his voice just short of a shout. "They are moving on the house. If they kick down the door, we're hosed."

He was right, they were gathered up between the van and the truck.

The commander gestured toward the house, giving out assignments. I needed to act.

I tried to remember how I did it in D.C. I panicked and really didn't remember. I concentrated on the transformer sitting between the houses. The Reclaimers gathered near it. One hit would do the trick. If they caught us, my dad would die, and so would we. I couldn't let that happen. People depended on me.

I crushed the power into a tight ball, so much it felt like my heart would burst from containing all the raw power. I threw my arms forward. I saw the Reclaimers stand as they attacked the house. The energy arced up and down my arms as the bolt of swirling blue lightning erupted from my arms.

The bay window and a good portion of the front of the house ceased to exist. A plume of debris flew like a shot from a flechette gun, shards of glass acting as a million darts. The transformer turned into a geyser as it melted under the surge of electricity I threw at it.

Jon flipped open the door, aimed quickly, and fired his arrow through the open truck window. A second later, the doors opened and slammed shut, the engine revved, and the truck took off down the street.

I could see men rolling around on the ground screaming in pain from where they had been hit by the remnants of the house and transformer. A few lay still on the ground, lit by the fire burning across the yard and into the street. Someone cursed loudly that the van wouldn't start. Chaos reigned supreme.

We headed back through the portal. The night was just beginning, but hopefully the killing was over.

J on and Alicia high-fived once we were back and the portal closed. Alyx flushed, sweat beaded across his forehead, his hippie appearance ruined by the wicked gleam in his eyes. Gladiator hovered over him like a mother hen.

Harold had an iPad out, pecking at it rapidly. I peeked over his shoulder. He drove the truck down the street we had come in on. "How are you doing that?" Harold could give Marcel a run for his money in the tech department.

"There's an app for it." He chuckled to himself. "Leecee always left science shows on while she ran errands. Must have sunk in while I was absent."

"So what's the plan?" Abby asked as she reentered the room, from watching the diversion from the entryway window. "What's left of the Reclaimers won't be bothering us anytime soon."

Harold twisted the iPad, and the view shifted as he turned onto another road. "Well, they think you are getting away in their armored truck currently," he said his eyes twinkling with undisguised mirth. "Leecee spent the last twenty-four hours telling the Reclaimers she saw a car pull up next door, and the cab driver was wrong. You've just confirmed those facts."

Jon let out a whoop. "We sure did." He jerked his thumb at me. "I thought Tommy would blow it, but what he did was blow it up."

I wished I shared his enthusiasm. I wanted to free my dad more than anything, but killing people wasn't right. Jon rehashed the whole thing, going into the gory details of the Reclaimers after the bolt hit the transformer. I tuned him out, not wanting to know. A hand sat on my shoulder. Gladiator stood behind me. For such a big guy, he moved like a cat.

"Killing men should never be taken lightly, or we are no better than they," he said quietly. "I see it bothers you, which is good. You understand what it is to be a true warrior. The ones who rejoice in slaughter..." He paused to shoot a meaningful glare at Jon. "We are to be wary of, for they can become as bad as the monsters we fight."

"Thank you. Does it get any easier?"

He shook his head. "The day it does, fall on your sword before you become one of them."

"So the armored truck will be in the lake in a few minutes, minus the rogue Gifted who attacked the Reclaimers," Harold said. "We have to move quickly to get you out before backup arrives. Alyx, can you do one more portal?"

Alyx reluctantly nodded. "One more, I think, but where should we go?"

Gladiator shook his head. "He is weakened. You can't ask more of him."

"I know, Nico." Harold steered the truck as he spoke. "I would love to let him rest, but this place will be hot for you in under ten minutes."

"Will you come with us," I blurted out. "We could use your help to rescue Cyclone Ranger."

"No way, honey." Alicia crossed her arms and gave Harold a look, daring him to defy her. "Jinx is gone and I will not lose my husband again after I just got him back. Not for you, not for Cyclone Ranger, not for anything."

Harold grinned sheepishly. "I'm afraid I have to agree with Leecee. If we vanish now, they will assume we were in on it and we can't chance them finding the workshop." He hurriedly added. "And I just got my wife back."

She huffed at him, but the corners of her mouth turned up. "That's right and don't you go forgetting it mister."

I couldn't get over how sweet it was to see them together. How selfish could I be, asking them for more help. The fact two Gifted had gone for so long without being noticed made me realize if I could get Dad out we could vanish and be a family for the first time.

"Thank you for all you've done," I said. "Where should we go to next?"

Harold laughed. "Why the happiest place on earth, Disneyland!"

Alyx snorted. "One portal to Disneyland it is." He grew still, focusing on something only he could see. A cold chill ran up my spine as the portal appeared, the size of a grape, a couple feet from me. As it enlarged, so did the feeling of ice in my veins. I think I'll stand back further next time.

We said quick goodbyes and stepped through to the 1980s.

I stepped from Alicia's immaculate home to terracotta tiles and velour furniture. Mom would have had a fit. The far wall held pictures of Alyx surfing and a couple of surf boards leaning in the corner of the room.

"Are we supposed to stay here?" Jon asked, tone boarding on rude.

Gladiator tensed. "This is Alyx's home and you will be respectful. You have no idea what he's been through."

Jon opened his mouth, but Abby shut if for him. "We appreciate all you've done for us, Nico." She elbowed Jon. "Right?"

He winced, but agreed. I sighed with relief. A fight between Gladiator and Jon would be a disaster.

Alyx wheeled through last. The wheelchair Mr. Fix-it gave him hummed along under its own power. He looked like someone had just shot his best friend. Rolling across the room, he came to rest in front of the wall of photos, many showing his intact legs. He didn't move for a few moments. "Tommy, make the call, let's get out of here," he said, his eyes going from one photo to the next.

The phone actually had a cord and a glowing number pad with numbers big enough to see from Mars. I shook my head, wondering if there was a museum missing their artifacts. I dialed the number Marcel had drummed into my head. "Joe's Pizza." the recorded voice had a truly horrible Italian accent. "We be makin' the pizza so leave a message." I chuckled. Marcel could be so weird.

"Han, this is Luke, we need the Millennium Falcon now." I ignored the amused grin I was getting from Abby. Damn Marcel and his geeky crap. "Chewy and Leia are with me, and we have..." I paused to think up quick code names for Alyx and Gladiator. "Err, C3PO and R2-D2 with us for retrieval." I hung up the phone.

"I would have gone with Yoda and Boba Fett." Alyx said, turning to face us. His smile was warm, but his eyes appeared haunted.

Abby dropped on the couch. "What is this place?"

"This is the basement of my parent's house where I grew up." He gestured around. "They gave me the basement so I wouldn't mess up the upstairs. After I left, they kept it for when I need to crash. You'd be surprised how often you come home to raid the fridge when you can step from anywhere to home in under a minute."

"Do they still live here?" Abby asked.

"No," he said quietly. "They passed away a few years ago. They left me the house. Blaze set it up so the house is maintained and looks lived in. We have found it handy to have a place to lay low from time to time."

"Whose surf stuff is this," Jon blurted out.

I mentally face palmed. Leave it to Mr. Sensitivity to blunder into what was obviously a painful subject.

Alyx's face darkened. "Mine." His face flushed red as he stared daggers at Jon's back. Gladiator stepped over, laying his hand on his shoulder in an unspoken gesture of support.

At least Jon had the decency to be embarrassed if the flaming cheeks were any indication. "Oh, sorry," he mumbled.

The phone rang startling us all. I picked it up. "Your delivery will be at noon on October 25th to the foyer of the Railroad Museum in Ely, Nevada." The recording clicked off. I hung up the phone.

"We get to go play with the trains." I tried sounding enthused to break the black clouds gathering over our group. It was going to be a long trip.

The destruction from the Dark Brigade attack made travel a nightmare. There wasn't road maintenance in a lot of places, and the Reclaimers had constructed bases at critical junctures to monitor who and what was moving. Gladiator turned out to be an excellent driver and, with help from Marcel's intel, we made it without incident.

Two days and a lot of losing rummy games to Abby and Alyx later, we were back with Wendi, Marcel, and Waxenby in the safe house. Dresden and K'vothe had a lot in common. There were extensive training areas, but where Dresden had been a nuclear missile silo, K'vothe was converted from an old silver mine in Nevada's Grant Range. Instead of vertical with stairs everywhere and equal-sized room, K'vothe meandered and expanded randomly.

The best part was Wendi. She looked far more beautiful than I had remembered. Her arms wrapped around me as soon as I entered the main room. It felt great especially after how nervous she had been around me before I left. Jon starred daggers at me, but he could pound salt for all I cared.

We caught everyone up on the details of our trip: the betrayal by The Grim Reaper, the escape from the Syndicate, and the time with Jinx and Mr. Fix-it. Marcel rapid fired questions about Mr. Fix-it. They had similar talents. Though he didn't like the idea of his talent consuming him, he beamed at the thought he might get to meet Mr. Fix-it one day.

All I wanted to do was shower and sleep, not necessarily in that order. I owed it to Pepper Spray to follow through after she saved us all. Wendi followed me, but I asked for a few minutes, forcing myself to ignore the hurt in her eyes. I promised a full explanation later.

Marcel had encrypted cell phones for us to use. The boy was remarkable. I dialed the secure line to The Secret Lair. After a few rings, Blaze's familiar voice came on the line.

"Hello?"

"Hey Blaze, it's Tommy." I tried sounding casual, like we were scheduling a sparring match or something inconsequential.

"Dude, what's up? You shouldn't be calling here, it's not safe." He still picked up on my discomfort. "Are you okay?"

"I'm fine. Marcel encrypted the line so it can't be traced." I had to get this over with fast the way you did with tearing off a bandage. Quick and painful, but it would be done. "I found out something and I'm not good at this kind of thing so I'm going to tell you."

There was only silence at the other end for a moment, then the loud squeak of the office chair. Thank God he sat down. "Go ahead, Tommy."

So I told him about being imprisoned in the Zoo and how Pepper Spray took over Grim Reaper and what she had said about loving him, but he needed to let her go.

S oft sobs tore at my heart as I listened. The grief I'd glimpsed the first day in the Secret Lair exploded with the news. "I'm sorry, Blaze."

"Don't be sorry, Tommy." His voice thick with emotion. "Raychel was my universe. Every day I had with her was a blessing. Thank you for telling me."

"She saved us all. If she hadn't stopped Reaper, he would have killed Abby and I would be in Reclaimers' hands."

"She always helped people." He paused to cough. "No matter how much it cost her."

I didn't know what to say. He caught me up with what happened since we had left Redemption. I asked him to tell my mom I missed her and to not tell her about what had happened. No need to worry her. We said our goodbyes and I sat staring at the phone, wondering not for the first time if anything good ever came out of being Gifted.

35

The good part of being inside a mountain is the lack of sun to wake you up. The bad part is being there with people that hadn't stayed up talking with their girlfriend until 4:30. I seriously considered strangling whoever was pounding on the door.

I stumbled to the door, opened it, and glared my best drop-dead glare. Marcel stood there, inflamed nose and puffy eyes. Ever kicked a hurt puppy, yeah me neither.

"Hey." He sneezed into a tissue, his afro flopping down to cover his face. It took real talent to pick up a cold in a sealed environment, but then he went into locked rooms none of the rest of us could get into. "I found the convoy transporting your dad. The only time they are vulnerable is tonight, so we need to plan."

My sleep deprivation vanished, replaced by a surge of adrenaline. Great news to start the day. I clapped Marcel on the shoulder. "I'll be there in five, let me get dressed."

"We are in the war room." He closed the door as he left.

This was awesome. The Reclaimers would never be expecting an attack on the convoy. We should be able to swoop in, extract Dad, and be out of there before they knew what hit them.

I jogged down the hall, snatched a Mountain Dew from the fridge, and entered the war room. Six massive flat panels covered the front wall. An oak table with room for fifteen dominated the center of the room. The chairs were massive, meant to hold Gifted far bigger than the average Norm. Marcel stood before the group, clicker in one hand and a tissue in the other ready to start his presentation.

Everyone else was already seated, so I slid into the empty chair at the front. Marcel nodded to me, detailing the plan. A live feed of the convoy appeared on the screens. It looked life-sized with all the screens displaying it.

"This is what we are facing." He gestured at the screens. "Two Humvees, a truck with eight Reclaimers, and the tractor-trailer with Cyclone Ranger in the back. Each of the Humvees had M2 heavy machine guns mounted on top. The Reclaimers are armed with SIG556 rifles and a disruption launcher."

"Disruption launcher?" Abby asked around bites of the apple she was eating.

"They were used during the Reclamation. They fire a flexible mesh which wraps around its target and disrupts the use of your Gifts. It's the same technology they use in the collars."

Abby swallowed hard. "Oh, that's not good."

"No, it's not," Marcel continued, his voice rough and deep from his cold. "The good news is after all the times they've transferred prisoners between Redemption and the Megadrome they use rookies and older guys for guard duty during the transit. They should be easier to deal with than the guards at either end."

I certainly hope so. The guards at The Block were tough and well trained. I'd seen them drop a three hundred pound guy with a couple shots of their nightsticks. Gifts or not I didn't want to tangle with them if I could help it.

"So Marcel," Waxenby said into the quiet. "Do you have a plan?"

He shook his head. "I don't, but Jon does."

Jon's grim smile robbed the heat from the room. A shiver of excitement raced up my back. This would be epic.

The moon hung low in the sky. Cold air flowed under my faceplate of my combat suit, but the rest of the suit made me impervious to the elements. Mr. Fix-it knew how to build a top-notched suit. No wonder he provided for all the Gifted teams back in the day.

Everyone was in place, patched into Marcel who was monitoring from K'vothe. Jon and Waxenby crouched at the front, hidden from view by an abandoned gas station that provided cover for the mission. Wendi and I were in the back and Abby and Gladiator in the middle.

"Okay," Marcel's voice came over the coms. "The convoy will be passing you in two minutes. Good luck."

I closed my eyes and said a quick prayer. This had to go right, I had to get Dad before they could kill him. Wendi squeezed my shoulder. I smiled at her, not that she could tell through my faceplate.

The roar of the semi rumbled in the distance as the front Humvee's light crested the rise. My stomach tightened and my palms drenched in sweat, we would only get one shot at this. I tensed, ready to rise up and take out my target.

The front Humvee drove past, and all hell broke loose. Jon stepped out firing an arrow into the front passenger tire of the leader. At the same time, Waxenby pushed the rear panel with a force bolt. The utility vehicle careened, rolling onto its side, sliding along the pavement, throwing sparks into the night. Air brakes fired as the semi tried to avoid the wreck suddenly appearing before it. It failed. The semi jackknifed, swinging the trailer around until it struck the downed Humvee.

The back vehicles stopped in time to avoid the cascading wreck in front of them. With a defiant yell, I unleashed the pent up energy I have siphoned off the power outlet Marcel had rigged for me. It delivered the energy, but in a lower voltage so it wasn't as painful as raw current.

The arc of electricity set the night on fire. The full blast struck the side of the Humvee, knocking it over. Flames burst from the exposed under-carriage of the wrecked vehicle.

The transport had survived the wreck in one piece. Gladiator and Abby rushed in to take down the troops before they could bring the disruption launchers to bear. Gladiator threw open the tarp covering the opening, sword out ready for a fight.

"There's no one here," Abby said, her voice low and guttural. "Something is wrong."

Wendi streaked off, a cheetah to my lumbering bear. "The Humvees are empty," her voice came over the coms. "It's a trap!"

A loud bang sounded as the side of the semi fell open. Grim Reaper, Tenji, and two others stood in the opening. One was small, head to toe in black. His hair shimmered with hair gel that plastered it to his forehead. The other, an obese guy who looked more like a short-order cook than a member of the Syndicate. He wore a navy blue jumpsuit and sneakers.

"Time to party boys and girls," The Grim Reaper yelled from the trailer, hoisting a nasty machete. "A little payback is in order."

"What the hell is going on?" Marcel's shrill voice sounded in my ears. "I'll have Alyx open a portal. Abort the mission."

It was too late. Gladiator launched himself at Grim Reaper as Abby went after Tenji. After being captured by the Syndicate, we had a score to settle.

The small guy leapt from the back of the trailer. Sporting two foot long daggers he came straight at me. I fanned my fingers dispersing a wide arc of electricity. He slid, arching his back like a rubber limbo dancer, under the arc. He flipped up in the air and came down on me with both knives aimed for my head. I put my arms up to deflect the knives, knowing it wouldn't be enough.

I felt a whoosh of air and my assailant bounced off the pavement, one of the knives flying free of his grip. Wendi stood a few feet away. "That's one you owe me." She ran off again.

I pulled back my arm and let go a globe of energy. Dressed-in-black stood as the ball impacted his side. It blew him a good fifteen feet away. He lay on the ground smoldering, his gelled hair standing on end. He looked down for the count.

My friends were still fighting so I went to help. Gladiator kept on the defensive as Grim Reaper hacked and slashed at him. Knowing his scythe would absorb you was plenty of reason to be careful. A swift kick to the leg dropped Gladiator. Grim Reaper laughed as he stood over him. I gathered the energy to shoot, but Jon beat me to it. Three arrows stuck in rapid succession pinning him to the side of the trailer. Gladiator regained his footing, and the fight resumed.

Abby didn't fare any better. Tenji was small, but lightning fast. He shot a blast of fire at her as he dodged her attacks with ease. Wendi sped by, taking shots at Tenji, but they had little effect. I saw her blur racing toward the fight again, but Tenji did as well. He grabbed Abby's arm, pivoted, throwing Abby into Wendi's path. They collided at full speed.

Wendi looked like a pinball hit by a flipper. She flew back, skidding across the pavement and under the wrecked tractor-trailer.

"Wendi!" I yelled and ran toward her. If anything happened to her, I'd never forgive myself.

"You aren't going anywhere," A voice said from behind me. I felt sick, a cloying smell invading my helmet. "Viper's best weapon is not his fangs, but his poison."

I clawed at my helmet, I needed air. I choked. Hot vomit splashed on my faceplate as the poison did its work. My vision fogged. I pulled weakly at my helmet but to no avail. I was done.

A fist punched me in the center of my chest. Knocking me back. Fresh air flooded in. I opened the faceplate. I greedily gulped down a lungful of clean, crisp air. I saw the short-order cook guy, Viper as he called himself, as his scream cut off abruptly. The green cloud pressed in around Viper's head. He fought to break free, but Waxenby stood nearby holding a force bubble around his head, forcing Viper to breathe his own poison. Turnabout is fair play.

"Go check on Wendi," Waxenby said. I swear he was smiling. "I'll take care of snake boy."

I ducked under the trailer and found Wendi in the dirt off the side of the road. I helped her up. "You okay?"

"Just a few bumps and bruises." She winced as she straightened up. "I guess we need to practice more."

A shout went up from the fight. "Enough! Oblivion will put an end to this."

Oblivion? Who the hell was that?

"Oh my God! Run!" Waxenby came over the coms. "I'll try to hold him off."

"What is going on?" I yelled.

"Run, Tommy!" Gladiator roared, panic thick in his voice.

"Get to the rendezvous," I said to Wendi. "I'll meet you there."

"I won't leave you."

"Go, Alyx can get you out if things go bad. Marcel needs to be up on what happened."

"I love you," she said and disappeared.

"I love you too," I whispered to the empty space around me.

I ran as fast as I could. An enormous blast struck out in all directions. I was thrown from my feet, landing in the dirt on the side of the road. The tractor-trailer flipped over. The troop transport burst into flames. I rolled into a depression as the blast flashed over me.

I laid there, catching my breath. "Tommy," Grim Reaper's voice came over the comm. "I've got Ollie. You know what I want. Don't make me wait or Ollie will pay the price."

"You bastard," I screamed, rage flooding through me. "I'll get you if it's that last thing I do."

"You come up against me, hombre, and you end up *muerto*. Pepper no save you again."

An engine roared to life. They were getting away. I saw Waxenby thrown in the back of what looked like an armored half-track. I threw both hands straight out. Energy surged through my arms hitting the truck, pushing it across the road, but the motor was still intact. They revved the engine and took off.

Could today get any worse?

Floodlights illuminated the wreckage from our failed rescue attempt. "In the name of the Reclaimers, put your hands up and surrender peacefully or you will be detained by force."

Why yes, things could get worse.

36

I did what any teenage boy would do when confronted by an authority figure. I ran. I could see the remains of the abandoned gas station from the flames and the searchlights of the three helicopters hovering above the ground. I probably had enough juice left to take one down, but not three, assuming I could short out the engines. It hadn't worked on the truck, which worried me.

I dove under the trailer, slipping out of view of the helicopter behind me. The others were nowhere to be seen. I hoped they had made it behind the station. Nobody could have survived the blast.

"Tommy, hurry," Wendi's voice said in my ear. "The portal is open, but they are getting close."

"I'm almost there." I turned the corner of the gas station. I saw Wendi illuminated by the blue and red lights of the portal.

"Is Abby with you?" Gladiator said. "I lost her in the blast."

"No, I'll go look." I turned to search for her.

No rang in my ear. Wendi propelled me through the portal and I lost my last chance to find Abby.

"We have to go back," I shouted as I pulled my helmet off. "Waxenby's been captured, and now Abby is missing. We can't leave her out there."

The war room exploded into chaos as the portal winked out of existence. Gladiator bled from a number of machete cuts, and Alyx rolled over to check on him. Wendi fell to the floor in exhaustion, small wrinkles around her eyes from her aging during the fight. I could feel the energy swirling in me ready for one last blow. Marcel held his head in his hands at the front of the room where he'd laid out Jon's plan for the rescue a lifetime ago.

He whispered through the afro covering his face. "I'm sorry, Tommy, I'm sorry, it's too late."

"What do you mean, it's too late?" I asked, my tone much harsher than it should have been.

"I patched into the Reclaimers' helicopter radio." He blew his nose and wiped his eyes before he continued. "They found Abby unconscious and detained her. She's headed to a holding facility for questioning. I'm sorry."

I threw my helmet against the wall. This was supposed to be simple. Run in, knock out some guards, and escape with Dad. Jose screwed us again. "I'm going to kill Grim Reaper when I get my hands on him."

He pushed the hurt and embarrassment down before delving into the situation. Marcel was in professional mode and looked shamefaced. "It's my fault." He stammered a bit in the process. "He leaked the info to the Reclaimers, but I didn't find the information until just now."

"Great job," Jon said. "The brainiac screwed this one up for good."

"Shut up, Jon." I needed Jon's attitude like Viper needed another donut.

Jon rounded on me, his face red with rage. "Why don't you make me, Ward?"

I gathered the last of my energy to blow his damn head off, but Wendi was faster. She stood between us before I got to my feet. "Enough! We are all tired and worried about Abby."

"Ward, the only thing you're good at is losing. Abby would be here if you could fight worth a damn," Jon said, turning his back.

Before I could stop my big mouth from running on its own power, I blurted out, "Big man hiding behind the gas station shooting arrows. I'm sure you were the first one through the portal."

The whole room went silent. Jon twisted around slowly. His eyes bored into me, the rage replaced with an icy stillness that scared me more than I wanted to admit. "What did you say?"

I tried to apologize, but he launched himself at me before any words came out. He landed a right cross on my jaw. My head twisted to the side as stars flashed in front of my eyes. Say what you want, but he could throw a punch.

"Jon, stop," Wendi screamed, but he pushed past her, jamming a knee into my groin and an uppercut that put me on my back.

"ENOUGH!" Gladiator roared. "Oliver and Abby are in the hands of our enemies, and you two bicker like children."

Wendi shot Jon an angry glare before helping me to my feet. I shook my head to clear the cobwebs.

"Dude, I am sorry. I didn't mean it." I held my hand out to Jon as a peace offer. "I'm just upset things went so bad tonight."

Jon slapped my hand away. "Listen, Ward." His face hovered inches from mine. "The only reason I'm here is to keep Wendi safe. I'm not your friend. We aren't buddies. Don't forget it."

He stomped out of the room, pausing to kick a chair out of the way in the process.

"I'm sorry, Tommy," Wendi started.

I held up my hand. "It's fine, Wendi. I shouldn't have said anything. I don't want to come between you two."

"Thanks." She smiled at me. "I knew I picked you for a reason." She gave me a quick kiss and sat in a nearby chair.

Marcel sat, a wireless keyboard in his lap, running through some program. The code streamed by on one of the monitors of the war room. "Here we go, Las Vegas local station has breaking news."

A perky Asian anchor read the report, a mug shot of Abby in the upper right corner of the screen. "We have confirmation an escaped Dissident has been captured in Arizona just outside of Mesquite, Nevada. The details have not been released, but we are going to our own Diane Patterson, who is outside the Megadrome with her report. Diane." She sounded serious, but her smile never wavered.

"Thanks, Dion." Diane's long brown hair was perfectly styled, and her sweater set matched her eyes. The Megadrome and a group of Reclaimer guards loomed behind her. "We have confirmation the armored personnel transport has arrived carrying the Dissident the Reclaimers allege destroyed a set of school buses returning from a field trip in Provo, Utah."

The scene changed to the site of the attack on the kids, viewed from a helicopter circling the destruction. Two yellow school buses were off the side of the road, one burnt to the point of being unrecognizable. Emergency workers were moving among the fallen, offering aid to the wounded as Reclaimer soldiers stood guard as if another attack was forthcoming. A row of small body bags and a couple larger ones had been arranged in a line.

"As you can see the devastation, reports have the death toll at over twenty students and staff. The *News Three* copter is on site to bring you pictures from this terrible Dissident attack on a pair of school buses," Dion said in tandem with the footage. "As Diane reported earlier, one of the Dissidents has been captured and is being held. The search is on for the others who attacked defenseless students. We will be following this story and breaking into programming as new information becomes available."

"Are they faking the footage, Marcel?" I couldn't believe the Reclaimers would go as far as killing innocents to get to us.

"I wish they were." Marcel looked a bit green, his voice shaking as he spoke. "They killed over thirty kids for no reason."

"There is a reason," Gladiator said. "Any time the Gifted commit vile acts, it makes the people afraid. Scared people do not complain or rise up against their oppressors. The Protectorate needs the Gifted to maintain power. That is why Cyclone Ranger must fight and die, as a reminder of how dangerous the Gifted can be and how benevolent the Protectorate is."

"But what happens when all the Gifted are gone?" Wendi said. "What will they do then?"

Gladiator shook his head slowly. "As you can see from the television, they don't need Gifted to have people afraid. They just make up their own."

Gladiator left the room. The silence lingered—even *Wheel of Fortune* was muted on the screen. The happy faces and celebrations at guessing a phrase mocked the tragedy being laid at our feet. The soft clicking of the keys emanated from where Marcel sat with his laptop as he wreaked havoc on the Reclaimers' systems between sneezes and coughs, trying to find out what was happening to Abby.

I'd screwed everything up. From trusting the Reaper to the idiotic plan to rescue a man who'd surrendered and refused to fight until forced.

Maybe I should be happy we'd escaped, get Mom, and move on with our lives. We could get Mom and disappear, blend in with the Norms in another part of the world, join the Resistance, or live in the remains of the fallen cities. Alyx had been all over the world, he could open a portal, and we could be somewhere else and start over. I could take Wendi to the movies, hang out with friends, have a normal life. Was that too much to ask for?

"Tommy, the news is on," Wendi said, gently shaking my shoulder to wake me up. I had fallen asleep on the couch.

Marcel yawned. "They waited for the early morning news to make their announcement. Must have missed the prime-time slot of the news cycle."

Wendi turned up the volume on the TV. "I'm certain we annoyed them with our bad timing."

A gray-haired, hooked-nose man in uniform stepped in behind a podium emblazoned with the Protectorate insignia. The caption at the bottom read General Mahady, Reclaimer Dissident Special Ops. "I have a short statement and then will introduce a survivor of the massacre and Captain Jenkins, who led the rescue. Please be seated."

The rustling noise of the journalists could be heard from off-camera. The general adjusted his notes and looked up. "On Wednesday night while returning from a trip to Provo, the students of Eldorado High School were attacked without warning. There are thirty-two dead, fourteen more critically injured and may not survive. One of the perpetrators was captured by Captain Jenkins's team. We are aware of at least two more Dissidents were involved, one pyro and one exothermal, who killed the fleeing students and faculty."

We all sat up. "They think Abby is part of the Syndicate," I said. "They don't know who was there." Luckily, Waxenby had been taken by Reaper, so they didn't have him. Though I'm not sure if you could call that lucky.

"Shhh." Wendi nudged me in the ribs.

"There may be others. This is the most brazen Dissident attack we've seen in years. The perpetrator we did capture has been uncooperative in revealing the cell's location or providing any motive behind this unprovoked attack. The Protector will be announcing further measures to ensure the safety of the people. We will not rest until these criminals have been brought to justice. Miss Stacy Whiden will now recount the event of that night. Please no questions. She has suffered enough without being badgered."

A small dark-haired girl was wheeled out and parked next to the podium. Four slashes crossed the left side of her face, destroying what must have been a beautiful girl. It made me sick to think the Protectorate had ruined this girl's life on purpose, though most of her classmates paid a much higher cost. She looked up at the general, who nodded at her. The camera zoomed in to get a better view of the cuts on her face.

"I was riding on the bus back from Provo, when the bus ahead of us swerved and stopped in front of us. Our bus struck the side, but most of us were okay." She paused, calming down in the process. A tear ran down her face. "We started getting out of the bus, just like the drills we always do, when the first bus exploded. People panicked. I started to run, but this thing with claws attacked me." She quietly wept. After a moment, she continued. "She would have killed me if Mr. Bradley hadn't tackled her, but she had already done this to me." The cry of anguish erupting from her broke my heart. The nurse ran out and rolled her off stage.

"Now, Captain Jenkins." The general moved to stand at the side as the captain took the podium. "We had a call from a concerned citizen who saw people milling around an abandoned gas station on Route 15. Local law enforcement was sent to investigate, but when they failed to report in, we were dispatched as backup. We had four helicopters with special op soldiers. When we arrived on the scene, a large explosion occurred. It threw both buses like they were toys, killing a large number of civilians in the process. We observed multiple suspects fleeing the scene. Teams were deployed to neutralize the Dissidents: one was taken down, the rest escaped." He paused, looking grim. "Local first responders were called in while our field medic treated the most serious injuries."

The general stepped back in and shook the captain's hand, posing for the photo op. Then he resumed his place at the podium to answer questions.

I jumped as the TV turned off. Jon stood behind us, remote in his hand. Wendi braced to stand, but he held up his hand. "I shouldn't have blown up earlier. Gladiator is right. They took Abby and Waxenby, and we have to get them back."

I nodded. "Thanks, Jon."

"Tommy, we have scores to settle with these bastards. When you go after them, I want in."

Given my track record, I'm not sure if us being on the same side was a good thing or not.

37

The next two days were spent in the war room attempting to find a way to free both Abby and my dad. Waxenby would have to wait since there were only two episodes left. Every plan fell apart. We wanted Alyx to get us in the Megadrome, but unless he scouted it first, he couldn't. It's not like the Reclaimers gave tours of one of their most protected sites.

Marcel scoured the blueprints he had retrieved, searching for a hole in the defenses. Nothing. Frustrations rose, as did voices, and feelings were hurt. Luckily, feelings mend and no one resorted to fists.

We spent most of Saturday apart, thinking, looking for anything that could give us an edge. Alyx and Nico snuck out to scout possible portal locales, just in case. After all the time at the Zoo, being confined didn't sit well with them. I can't say I blamed them.

At eight, we settled in front of the TV to watch Dad's second to last match. Part of me wished he would lose so I could get away from the insanity of planning to break him out. The rest of me wanted to know my dad so bad that I would do anything to get him out. No wonder I had a headache—a war was being fought in my brain.

We muted the commentators as they recapped the previous eight weeks of matches, a proverbial greatest hits of the Gauntlet until this point. The crowd, much larger in the Megadrome, lacked the energy of previous weeks' smaller Block audiences. No one really expected it to end tonight with the ultimate spectacular scheduled for next week. We turned on the sound as they panned down to Desmond Roberts standing on the stage at the end of the arena. The red strobe of the finish button gave him a decidedly devilish appearance. It fit him well.

"Good evening, ladies and gentlemen," he said sweeping his arm across the assembled audience. They cheered their response. "We have the penultimate match for the Gauntlet tonight. Cyclone Ranger has bested eight of the hardest courses we've ever seen in *Saturday Night Showdown* History."

Boos and catcalls erupted from the crowd. Brief blue flashes sparkled from vaporizing trash thrown against the Megadrome's protective shield, keeping the spectators safe from stray shots and escaping Gifted.

"But tonight will go down as a first in the annuls of *Saturday Night Showdown*," he said, a knowing smirk playing across his face. "Tonight, the Protector himself has requested we punish one of the vilest criminals in recent memory."

"I really hope they captured Grim Reaper," Marcel said.

Jon shook his head. "This is going to be bad."

Wendi gripped my hand harder. I patted hers, hoping against hope it wasn't what I thought it was.

"We have The Butcher of Bus 219. The one who's responsible for thirty-three deaths and rising. Introducing Cyclone Ranger's partner for the rest of the Gauntlet, The Butcher!"

"Oh my God, no!" Wendi said. "They can't do this."

"Sis, these bastards killed all those kids just to frame Abby, so there are no limits." Jon turned to me. "We are getting her out no matter what, Ward."

I nodded unable to speak. Fire burned away all my doubts. By the end of the week, they would be free.

On the screen Abby and Dad walked out of the entrance. Abby still wore the combat suit Harold had made for her, a bit dirty but no visible damage. She didn't have her helmet. The crowd went nuts shrieking for blood and vengeance. I couldn't really blame them. I would be furious if I thought she had killed all those kids.

"We are going to Chip Calloway, the voice of *Saturday Night Showdown* for the call," Desmond said as the camera zoomed in on Abby's tear-streaked face.

"Thank you, Desmond. And good evening to all the fans out there." The camera backed out to show the arena for the opening shot. "This will be a historic fight. For the first time ever, we will have a double Gauntlet. The Butcher of Provo will fight for her life. If they win out the next two matches, they will be detained in The Block to live out their lives. If they lose, well, we all know what that means, don't we? And I'm sure I speak for all the folks watching, there has never been a pair who deserved punishment more than the two we have here tonight."

Wendi pulled me back on to the couch. I hadn't realized I was headed to kick in the TV. "Don't destroy the TV. We have to see what happens." Her face flushed with the anger, amplifying my own.

"Sorry."

A map of the Megadrome arena filled the screen. "The arena has been split into five zones for tonight's match. Each zone is fifty yards deep and two hundred yards wide. Plenty of room to maneuver. Zone one is open ground, but they are in for a warm reception."

"Five zones," Marcel muttered, flipping open his laptop, typing at a feverous pace. "Usually there are only three."

Jon snickered. "They must be really worried Abby will do some major damage."

"And there is the horn signaling the start of the match," Calloway said in his game show voice. He could have been talking about the latest car on *The Price Is Right* instead of a fight to the death.

Abby and Dad moved across the laser line marking the zone. Abby took a few quick steps more, but stopped, head half turned to listen. She slowly backed up to stand next to Dad as they waited for attack.

From the floor, eight robotic warriors rose. Each carried a kite shield in one hand and a whip in the other. A black band ran around their head horizontally, the optics tracking three-hundred-sixty degrees. Obviously, the designers had learned the hard way about robots with blind spots around Dad.

Abby crouched as a barrage of lightning streaked out toward the metal warriors. Each crouched neatly behind their shield, absorbing the energy with no damage. Abby leapt to her feet, watching the robots stand and ignite their lashes, the flames running the length of the weapon. As one they advanced. She nodded once and stood shoulder to shoulder with Dad.

"Oh, man," Marcel whispered. "They aren't taking it easy on them tonight."

"What do you mean?" Wendi said not taking her eyes off the TV.

"No one has ever reached the ninth match before, so this is uncharted territory. My guess is they'd want the finale to be the death match, so they'll let them get through. Those robots are basically immune to Cyclone Ranger's attacks, and the fire will do a lot of damage to the Gifted. The gloves are off, and there are still four challenges more to go."

The robots continued to move in, push in so their shields became a wall. Dad launched himself into the air, but two of the lashes wrapped around his legs, dragging him down. His suit had kept the fire off him, but he was grounded.

Abby screamed as a lash twisted around her waist. She grabbed the burning cord and tugged. The warrior lurched toward her. She pulled again while it was off-balance. This time it fell flat on its face. Still holding the burning lash, she jerked it back to the right, using the prone robot against its own teammates. They dropped, the pins before the robot-shaped bowling ball. The whip was a part of the robot, so it couldn't let go as Abby bludgeoned the fallen into pieces by slamming her attacker into the other over and over again like a giant game of Whack-A-Mole.

Dad attempted to roll away, but the two whips held tight, with two more robots closing in for the kill. Smoke rose from his legs where the flames tried to eat away at his suit. Launching himself into the air, he pulled the robots slightly closer, but they held fast. The crowd noise increased as he fought to free himself, lightning pulsing up and down his legs as he tried in vain to break the whips. The other two robots' whips joined the first two, snaring him around his arms. The robots crept backward, pulling Dad into a spread eagle.

Chip Calloway crowed. "And that's all she wrote, folks. I think we've seen the last of Cyclone Ranger."

Dad screamed as the whips pulled at his limbs, threatening to tear him apart. The audience shrieked for blood, flashes of blue flickering across the barrier above from all the thrown chains. Below Dad, a form grew, small at first, but growing quickly. The flames on the whips flared from the wind of the tornado taking shape under him. It swallowed him, the winds making it hard to see him. Slowly the robots slid to the right as the speed of the whirlwind increased.

Chip Calloway fumed. "He should be dead! Where the hell did that come from?"

We all cheered. The robots fell as the winds grabbed them, spinning them faster and faster. Suddenly a robot flew across the arena smashing into a wall, splintering to pieces. Shortly, the other three joined their brother against the arena walls.

"Such a waste of good hardware," Marcel muttered as we cheered.

The winds died down, depositing Dad on the floor. Scorch marks were visible where the whips had been. Abby ran over to check on him, but he climbed to his feet to a chorus of boos from the audience. After a brief conversation, they moved deeper into the arena.

"Well, that was an interesting way to dispose of the bots," Chip said. "Let's see what zone two has in store."

An air horn blaring signaled they had moved into the second zone. The cameras swung back to show two doors set into a solid wall that ran the width of the large arena.

"Oh, man," Chip said, excitement thick in his voice. "We have the maze. There are all sort of tricks and traps for our contestants."

After a moment, heads together, they each strode to a door, nodded to each other. Dad turned the handle, cautiously opening the door to peer inside. Abby ripped the door from its hinges, throwing it so hard it impacted the protective screen above. She rushed through the door as the cameras switched to an overhead view. Dad stepped through and jumped up, slamming into the barrier that enclosed the top. No flying over zones after the first time.

Abby turned the first corner, staying against the walls as she crept. Halfway down the second hall, she suddenly dove forward as three blades sliced through the air above her from the wall. She rolled and came to her feet on the far side of the trap. We all exhaled at once.

Dad strode down the center of the hall on his side of the maze, surrounded by a glowing sphere. The blades arced out, shattering against his shields, a new ability that no one knew about.

A camera swung back to Abby as she stalked down the hall. Lasers fired from concealed locations, and one clipped her shoulder, tearing her suit and leaving a large red welt. She spotted the laser, zig-zagged toward it, and with a mighty leap, pounced on it, smashing it on the floor. She looked wild, her two-toned hair tangled, a snarl permanently affixed to her face. Her suit compensated for her increasing size.

"Oh, this is going to be fun, folks," Chip said with a huge grin on his face.

Abby moved into a large room with a hallway leading to the next zone. The wall in the center shimmered like a mirage. As she entered, Cyclone Ranger stepped through the wall, striding toward her. She visibly relaxed, pointing to the door. Cyclone Ranger closed on her and threw a vicious punch at her head. Reflex took over as she pivoted, taking the blow on the shoulder. It knocked her off balance.

"Oh, my," Chip gasped. "Whatever could have happened to bring this about?"

Cyclone Ranger tackled her to the ground. He threw wild punches, only a couple connected, but Abby broke his grip and gained her feet. Her face twisted with rage, her mouth moving, though we couldn't hear it.

Again, Cyclone Ranger advanced, a rapid succession of punches driving her back. Abby blocked them. I could tell she didn't want to hurt her partner but had to defend herself. He connected with a nasty uppercut that snapped Abby's head back.

"What the hell is he doing?" Marcel yelled. "They are on the same team."

Abby lost it at that point. She screamed with rage, her eyes flared red, and she towered over Cyclone Ranger, her combat suit stretching as she grew. She swung and grasped the side of Cyclone Ranger's helmet, tearing it free of his body. Electric sparks erupted like a volcano. The android Cyclone Ranger took a few steps and collapsed.

"Well, no need to lose a head over it," Chip said. "These Dissidents take this so seriously."

The camera switched to the other side of the room, where an android Abby was attacking my dad with a series of massive punches. He staggered from a blow to the side of his head. He rolled before the double-fisted overhead slam could break his back.

He stood with some effort as the android turned to face him. He wouldn't fight back against Abby, but I'm sure he was just as confused as Abby had been on her side. Android Abby leapt into the air, fist back to deliver a killing blow. A black object streaked across the room, taking it in the side. Abby stomped through the shimmering wall, the Cyclone Ranger android's body dragging behind her. Her twin started to rise but met with her fellow android as Abby swung him like a sledgehammer, striking the android Abby full in the head. Abby continued pummeling it until both bodies resembled the after shot of the demolition derby.

Dad walked over, and Abby dropped her impromptu club to the ground. He reached up and hugged her. They put their heads together for a few minutes before heading to the long hall with the exit marked.

As they entered the hall, a new wall shot up from the floor, trapping them in the hallway. A loud crash announced the last of the obstacles. The wall holding the exit fell forward launching a massive spiked ball. It filled the whole hallway leaving nowhere to go.

"Wow, that would be two tons of spiked death," Chip cried in glee. "Indiana Jones, step aside, we have one huge ball."

The ball rolled forward gaining momentum as it careened down the hall. Dad fired a continuous bolt into the wall by Abby; sparks flew in all directions at the onslaught. The wall didn't give, but he created a good size depression in it. He shoved Abby toward the dent as he ran at the ball. At the last moment he jumped, flew, slamming his back into the corner of the wall and the energy barrier. The ball rolled past, one spike catching him in the center of the chest. His suit tore as the spike sliced a narrow furrow down the fabric covering his chest and abdomen before it rolled past him. Abby curled herself further into the divot Dad had made. The ball rolled harmlessly past her, slamming into the far wall. They had made it through the second zone.

None of us cheered this time as we watched Dad fall from the ceiling. With his helmet on, you couldn't see his face, but he had to be in pain. Abby rushed to his side and helped him up. He walked out of the zone on his own. I looked for blood, but there wasn't any. That was way too close.

"Dang, I thought we got Cyclone Ranger on that one," Calloway said, disappointment heavy in his voice. "But on the bright side, there are still three more zones, and he's weakened. We might finish him off tonight."

Zone three was the demented skateboard park, littered with concrete pipes, ramps, and bunkers, a skater punk's dream. The horn blared, and Abby and Dad ran for the closest pipe, readying themselves for the next challenge.

252

"The air force has arrived, folks," Calloway chirped. "We've got gunships to hunt them down."

The whirling noise announced the twelve sleek black drones as they swooped over the zone, lasers firing in a strobe of flashes.

"Wow," Marcel said, admiration clear in his voice. "The four props gives them stability and maneuverability. That's an impressive design."

Jon snapped. "Can you not drool over the things they created to kill our people?"

Marcel gulped. "Sorry, got carried away."

At the end of the zone, the formation broke down into four groups of three. The first two groups strafed the tube protecting Abby and Dad as they flew by.

"The bad part is wind won't work given the design; there isn't enough to grab on to." Marcel clicked away at the laptop as he spoke. "Damn!"

I jumped. "What?"

Marcel slammed the laptop shut. "I thought I'd be able to disrupt the ships or shut off the shields so they could escape, but I can't. When they broadcast, it should have exposed the core system for my hack."

I gasped, shocked to the core. "I thought you could hack anything now?"

"The systems in the Megadrome aren't physically hooked to the outside world. Everything is internal to the building—electricity, water, air are all run from a stand-alone system. It can't be hacked because it can't be reached. Even with the broadcast running, it's still true. Looks like they use an independent system to send the feed to a sub-station before it actually passes to the satellites. Best I can do is move the cameras."

I'd secretly hoped Marcel would find a way to shut down the systems so we could break them out in the confusion, but now that plan had been scrapped. "We'll have to figure something out later." I didn't add if it was still necessary since the drones had them pinned in the pipe.

The lasers flashing reminded me of Mom's Pink Floyd concert tape. Parts of the pipe crumbled and dropped to the ground, spewing dust in their wake. Suddenly, Dad shot out of the pipe, banking hard to the left, barreling directly toward the attacking drones.

The drones rotated and sped into pursuit of Dad. He flew, diving toward a halfpipe while weaving to avoid the rapid pulse of laser fire. He increased speed as he entered the end of the pipe, flying up the wall as he went. The drones matched velocity, easily following his maneuvers, lasers pocking the concrete surface around Dad as they flew.

At the highest of the pipes, Dad flew straight up and spun in a tight spiral as he unleashed an arc of lightning out in front of him. Three of the drones flew straight into the lightning buzz saw, their propellers smashed by the force of the energy.

"That's the first 720 Ollie we've had on *SNS* folks. Cyclone Ranger must have been a skater punk in his day," Calloway exclaimed.

The other three drones climbed sharply, lasers hitting the shield above the arena, as the crowd screamed for blood. Six drones near Abby kept up the onslaught of laser fire. Chunks of concrete rained down from the destroyed top of the pipe she hid in. The steel rebar structure the concrete had been built around showed like the bones of a long-lost creature. Abby ran full speed up the wall, planted her boot on the broken edge of the wall, and back flipped over the drones. She held a chunk of broken concrete in each hand. As she soared over the drones, the concrete missiles launched from her hands, destroying both drones they hit. Abby fell, but quickly reached out to grasp a steel pole, spun around it, and shot past the drones, touching down behind a bunker. The drones raced after her, but a quick roll and she slid into the concrete bunker as the lasers beat against it.

We all cheered as Chip Calloway remarked, "We haven't seen gymnastics like that since the Protectorate Games, though I doubt she could keep up with our pure Gymnasts without her powers."

Jon growled, "If we get a chance, I'm putting an arrow through that asshole."

Cyclone Ranger blasted across the intervening space, coming up on the drones firing at Abby from behind. He swerved right and dove through the center of the four drones, rocking them as he passed. The three trailing drones, attempted to follow, resulting in mass confusion.

Marcel laughed. "Awesome! Their guidance systems will overlap causing a special anomaly."

"What?" we all remarked in unison. Another major jinx moment.

One of the following drones slammed into a drone firing on Abby's location. The two locked and spun out of control, crashing on the floor.

The others collided but managed to stay aloft though out of the neat formations they had been.

Marcel pointed at the TV. "That is what will happen!"

Why he couldn't just say crash, I'll never know.

Calloway chimed in. "Looks like we've got us a pile-up on the interstate. Better call the tow truck."

The drones moved to align into a new formation. An arc of lightning flashed toward the drones, missing by a mile, striking the bunker below. Concrete flew in all directions but didn't hit the drones.

"Cyclone Ranger's getting sloppy, wonder if he's out of juice," Calloway commented.

In unison, the drones spun on axis to orient themselves, lasers firing wildly. Suddenly, one of the drones bucked, spun out of control, impacting the steel cage of the pipe. Another one suffered the same fate. The cameras swung around. Abby bolted between structures throwing chunks of the bunker at the disoriented drones.

The remaining three drones opened fire on her, but she'd already ducked into cover. Cyclone Ranger flew up from beneath the drones, a piece of the steel cage in his hands. He impaled the nearest drone, and sparks flew in all directions. With a heave, he bashed the first drone into the second two. They flipped upside down, wobbling as they attempted to right themselves. In a flash, Abby hurled two more pieces of concrete, and they plummeted to the ground.

Cyclone Ranger floated down to join Abby, and zone three was done.

The camera zoomed in on Abby. Her eyes were solid yellow, her face contorted and buckled in places. You could see her muscles straining against her combat suit. She threw back her head and screamed.

"Holy cow," Chip Calloway gasped in shock. "What is she? You can feel the evil from here."

We knew Abby was strong and fought better than any of us, but we were all shocked to see what the fight had done to her. The story she told me flooded back. How her parents had turned her in because she had lived in the forest hunting her food as an animal would. I didn't realize she meant it literally. Dad stood next to her, not even coming up to her shoulder. She must be pushing eight feet tall. As he spoke to her, she shrunk until she stood even with Dad. Her eyes were normal, as was her face. *Note to self, never piss Abby off.*

Marcel fidgeted as he watched. He'd open the laptop, start to type, then shut it in futile desperation. It killed him that he couldn't help. I noticed anytime Abby got into trouble, the laptop opened, and his eyes got a bit crazy. Marcel had two friends, true friends, and one fought for her life, and it wasn't sitting well with him.

Abby hung her head as Dad continued to speak to her. The horn sounded announcing zone four had begun. Dad lifted her chin, she nodded once, and then they moved to face their next obstacle.

In this case, obstacle fit the chaos before them perfectly. I've seen city junkyards with less stuff in them. The zone consisted of a huge pile of twisted metal. To get to the last zone required climbing over and through the junk.

Both glanced behind them before running toward the pile. The cameras swung around to show twelve huge metallic dogs bounding across zone three toward them.

"Who let the dogs out!" Calloway said, overly impressed with his own humor. "This one is going to be ruff."

I groaned. *Where did they get this guy?*

Dad reached the top of the heap first; he launched a bolt into the pile in front of the two lead dogs. As they hurdled over the new hole, a second blast hit overhanging debris next to them, burying them in a pile of metal beams.

Abby grabbed a long bar from the junkyard and shish-kabobbed the closest dog. She spun and threw it into the overhead shield where it exploded. The front row of spectators screamed in shock. Drifting motes of super-heated metal flakes floated away, the remains of the cyber dog.

The footing for climbing through the assorted junk turned out to be the biggest problem. Abby fell as the pile below her collapsed. In a heartbeat, two dogs were on her. One bit down on her arm, blood spurting out from its metallic teeth. The second dog took a boot to the head, sending it crashing down the pile, impaling its torso on a sharp piece of metal.

The surviving dog shook its head, dragging Abby across the metal. Blood flew everywhere as the attack continued. The cameras showed more dogs bounding toward the downed prey.

Dad leapt over a pile, landing on the dog who dragged Abby. He punched his hand into the vents at the dog's neck, and smoke bloomed from the vents as he fried it from the inside. Another dog pounced on

Abby, but she was ready this time. She rolled back, getting her feet under the chest of the dog as it crashed down on her. The force of her uncoiling legs launched the dog into the overhead shield, eliciting another round of screams from the audience.

"What a moonshot, folks!" Calloway said. "Fido would be in orbit if not for the shield."

Abby had taken a lot of damage. Her suit was torn in multiple places. Blood flowed from her arm as well as down her chin, courtesy of her split lip. Dad tried to help her to her feet, but how long could she last in her condition?

"Looks like the chew toy has had enough," Calloway said snickering. "I can't say she doesn't deserve it after what she did to those poor kids. I hope this helps the families get some closure."

The rest of the pack arrayed themselves around Dad, who stood over Abby. They circled, waiting for an opening. Dad raised his arms in front of him. The wind picked up, swirling around him. Pieces of metal spun, gaining speed. The dogs charged, the guys running the robots realizing too late what happened. Flying metal shredded the dogs like a flechette gun. The dogs had been dispatched in less than a minute by the metallic vortex of death.

Dad let the wind drop as Abby got up. They stumbled together over the last of the junkyard and sat down so Dad could bind her arm with a strip from her combat suit. Only one zone left. I really wondered if Abby would make it. Marcel told us Gifted heal faster than Norms, but how much could she come back from?

"Another impressive display from the Cyclone Ranger," Calloway said. "You can see why he has earned the infamous reputation of being walking death."

Jon growled from his perch. "They forget to mention he's defending himself."

"It keeps the people scared," Marcel said. "If they aren't scared of us, then why are we collared and imprisoned without a trial or ever committing a crime?"

I shook my head in disgust. "True, but when the Gifted were free, a lot of innocent people died in the crossfire."

Jon gaped at me, shock written all over his face. "So, what? It's okay we are denied our Gifts and locked away for no reason? At five, they clamped a damned collar on me. What the hell did I ever do to anyone?"

"I don't agree with it, but I could see why they would be scared of the Gifted."

"You kill me, Ward."

Chip Calloway saved me from replying. First useful thing he had done all night. "We are into the red zone. Sudden death or victory, you make the call."

Dad half carried Abby to the edge of the zone and sat her down. He walked across the line, and all hell broke loose. Explosions went off across the front of the zone, smoke obscuring the view. Three machines rolled across the zone placing themselves in front of the exit button. They looked like tanks, treaded for stability. A center gun mounted in the front. Arms stuck out from the side, spinning chains with hooks on the end. In order to complete the zone, they had to get past these to push the button. Abby slumped just outside of the zone, making it a three-on-one fight.

Dad launched himself to the right, avoiding the initial strafing rounds. The tanks turrets followed his movement, continuing to fire. They used actual shells. Smoke billowed out with every shot. The Cyclone Ranger dodged back and forth, his black suit blending into the dust cloud. He gave ground, forcing the tanks to move with him, their distance limited by the size of the arena.

Arcs of lightning flashed out, intercepting some of the shells. They burst like fireworks at a Protectorate Day celebration. The tanks closed in, firing the hooks, attempting to ensnare Dad and bring him down. Back and forth the fight raged: hooks and shells firing, lighting flashing through the smog.

The tanks had him pinned to the side wall. The hooks flashed in and out, trying to catch the leaping, twisting figure, more dancer than warrior. A deadly game of dodgeball. Then it happened. Dad landed and stumbled. A hook wrapped around his calf. The other around his waist.

"This could be the end for our contestants," Calloway crowed. "Cyclone Ranger has put up an admirable fight, but in the end, justice is served."

Another hook wrapped around his neck. Lightning arced along the chains, but they held. The tanks kicked into reverse, and the crowd swelled with excitement, waiting for Dad to be torn in half. Wendi screamed and covered her face with her hands, but I refused to look away. I couldn't believe my dad would die before I ever met him.

A loud blast sounded across the arena. The cameras frantically scanned the floor for what had happened. The tanks died, the chains going slack. Standing at the top of the stairs, bloodied, bruised, and exhausted was Abby, her hand firmly holding down the exit button.

"Oh my God," Calloway said, his voice tinged with panic. "The Butcher has triggered the exit, ending the match and saving Cyclone Ranger in the process. What an end to the match. I feel bad for the people who turned it off before the end. The finale is shaping up to be the greatest in *Saturday Night Showdown* history."

Dad walked over and hugged Abby. They had won against all odds. I had to find a way to get them out before the finale. The Protectorate couldn't allow them to live.

Desmond Roberts came back on the screen while Abby and Dad were taken off by Reclaimers. "Wow, that was a great match, but we have a sneak preview of what's next. We are having a special guest for the Gauntlet finale. Tell the audience about it, Chip."

"Sure thing, Desmond. The question you'll be asking all week is who is this woman and what role will she play in the epic finale of the Gauntlet? Find out more next week."

The scene changed to a long hallway, ending in metal bars. As the camera zoomed in, a slight blond woman in an orange jumpsuit sat on a prison bed, her hair concealing her face from the camera. Slowly, she lifted her head, a prominent black eye and a snarl on her face. Fire raged in her eyes. A fire I knew all too well.

Mom.

38

"Oh my God, Tommy," Wendi said, her hands over her mouth. "How did they know about her?"

I shook my head. This had been the worst week in recorded history. Abby captured and forced to fight, Waxenby bagged by the Syndicate, Dad almost killed, and now Mom imprisoned. I needed space. No, I needed something to hit. "Marcel, find me a way in, I don't care how."

"Tommy, I've looked there..."

"LOOK AGAIN!" Hot tears threated to spill from my eyes. I fled the room before I lost it. Through the winding halls and into the training room. Marcel had rigged up a special outlet I could charge from. I jammed my hand in and cranked it. The pain hit me like a freight train, but I savored it. This was all my fault, and one way or another, I would fix it.

Pure lightning surged from my hands, annihilating the targets across the room. Clouds of cinders drifted in the air, glowing brightly as they cooled. I cried and laughed at the same time. These bastards would pay. I had the ability. Mom wouldn't suffer for my mistakes—I would rip them limb from limb to get her back.

The electricity erupted from me until it was gone. I sank to my knees, and Wendi's arms were around me. The tears fell and wouldn't stop. She held me like my mom had a hundred times over the years. I felt safe with Wendi.

After a time, we sat on the floor, staring at the scorch marks on the wall from my fury. I wondered if I needed to become more weapon than man, but if it saved the people I loved, I would sacrifice anything.

The days wore on and nothing changed. Alyx and Gladiator scouted the area around the Megadrome some more, but nothing new presented itself. Marcel's bots couldn't penetrate the perimeter to connect to the system, getting fried before even getting close to anything useful. The Block would have been easy to break into compared to the Megadrome. After our failed attempt to rescue Dad, the Protectorate stood on high alert.

The guilt of my mom getting dragged into this mess wore on me worst of all. I still couldn't figure out how they had found her. In the grand scheme of things, it didn't matter, but I wanted to know. Losing a dad I had never met would hurt, but to lose the one person in the world who had always been there for me was unbearable. My knuckles and the walls bore the brunt of my frustration.

Thursday morning, I woke up, and I knew what I had to do. It made perfect sense. I got showered and dressed, packed my backpack with my combat suit and helmet. I thought about leaving the ring Mr. Fix-it had given me behind, but it had become a kind of good luck charm, and I would need all the luck I could get. I turned off the light and headed for the exit.

I didn't make it. Wendi stood in front of the door, her arms folded across her body. She tapped her foot as I approached. "Where are you going?"

"Wendi, there is only one way I'm getting my parents out, and that is to go in and take them."

"And you were going to do it all by yourself?" Her eyes told me there'd be hell to pay for answering wrong.

"Yes, they are my parents, and I'm not letting anyone else get hurt in the process."

"She's my mom, too," Marcel said walking up behind me. "Don't I get a say?"

"Look," I said. "I know how you feel Marcel, but you can't fight."

He grunted. "I can't fight, but I can still help."

"Man, you are our ace in the hole."

Wendi put her hands on her hips. "Well, obviously, you don't think you're going without us."

"Plus," Jon said as he entered the room. "I told you when you went after those creeps that I wanted in. I dare you to say I can't fight."

This was getting out of hand. "Of course you can fight," I said my head spinning from the unrelenting assault. "Guys, I appreciate you wanting to help, but I can't ask you to fight your way in with me. This could be a one-way trip. If you are going to go, I have to tell you something important first."

Wendi examined my face. "You sure?"

I nodded. "If you're going to fight and possibly die, you have the right to know." I took a deep breath. "The reason I want to save Cyclone Ranger is...well, he's my dad."

Marcel and Jon's jaws both dropped in unison. "Bruh, that is so awesome!" Marcel beamed. Jon didn't say anything for a while. "Why didn't you tell us before now?"

"I'm sorry, I should have. Mom made me promise I wouldn't tell anyone, that the information could be deadly if the wrong people found out, but if you guys are willing to go with me, you should understand why I'm going." I steeled myself for the backlash. It didn't come.

Jon regarded me for a moment. "I should have seen the resemblance. It makes more sense than running off after a random Gifted."

I exhaled sharply, the pressure subsiding. "Still, this is my fault, and I can't ask you all to fight. It's something I need to handle."

"Hmmm, last I checked, we could all make our own decisions," Wendi said, punching me in the shoulder. "We are a team, and we are all going or none of us. You didn't surrender when Grim Reaper had you, did you?"

"That's it!" Marcel shouted a huge smile on his face. "Wendi you're a genius!" He grabbed her in a huge hug.

The shocked look on her face was priceless.

"Okay, so explain it to the moron over here because I certainly don't understand."

Marcel laughed at my expression, which obviously rivaled Wendi's. "Give me your shoes and meet me in the war room in the morning. They'll never see this one coming."

"My shoes?"

"Yeah, give me your shoes. You'll understand tomorrow."

As I handed over my shoes, I had the feeling I was going to regret this.

I couldn't sleep. The sight of Mom behind bars tore at me when I closed my eyes. If they hadn't hidden my backpack, I would have tried to leave again, but I had the sneaking suspicion Gladiator guarded the exit. A light tap on my door roused me from my worries.

"Come in," I said, wondering who was still up at two a.m. Wendi slid in, softly closing the door behind her. I could barely make her out in the darkness of my room. I reached for the light, but her hand stopped me.

"Tommy, I love you."

I wished I could go tell my younger self Wendi would be my girlfriend. I would have gotten a lot more sleep. "I love you, too."

She kissed me, hard. I felt an unusual urgency flowing from her. She pulled back. I heard her bathrobe fall to the floor as she climbed into my bed. She kissed me again. "In case something bad happens, I want us to be together tonight." She slid in next to me, put her head on my chest, and sighed. I wrapped my arms around her, smelling her hair and wondering if we'd ever have a normal life together.

I fell asleep with my angel next to me.

I woke up. Wendi had gone, but the scent of her lavender perfume lingered on my pillow. The smile on my face wouldn't go away, not that I wanted it to.

I jumped when Marcel swung the door open. "Bruh, I've got a way to get Mom out."

The smile died. We had one more day to get Mom, Dad, and Abby out before they were killed. "War room in five," and he left.

I thought about just throwing on clothes and going until I realized I smelled like a field of lavender. I jumped into the shower, scrubbing vigorously so that Jon wouldn't smell her perfume on me. Guy has a nose better than a dog. I toweled off then threw on some clothes and headed down, grabbing a banana on the way. Wendi, Jon, Alyx, and Gladiator were assembled. My shoes sat in my customary chair.

"Okay, let's start," Marcel said from behind his laptop. The Megadrome popped up in the center table in three dimensions. "Alyx and Gladiator mapped the perimeter of the Megadrome during their reconnaissance, and there aren't any weak points into the prisoner area. But there is one way in, here."

The model zoomed into the heavily armored entryway. "This leads underground to where all the holding cells, the main frame, and comm array are housed. A nuclear bomb couldn't breach all the concrete and Carbinium they used. The internal lift moves the contestants from the cells to the arena floor. There isn't another way from the arena to the holding area."

"Okay, so we know this, Einstein, but how does it get us in?" Jon said from where he perched on the sideboard. He never sat in a chair since becoming fully Gifted. He looked like he could launch across the room in a heartbeat.

"Oh, there isn't a way to break in."

"What?" we all exclaimed in a major jinx moment.

"No way to break in. But what if you walk up and surrender as the rest of the crew from the massacre? They will escort you to the holding cells, and overnight, I pop the security system and you fight your way out. They'll never expect it."

"Okay, so what do we do once we are out?" I said.

"Just so happens Mr. and Mrs. Jablonski won a trip to Los Angeles to be on *Wheel of Fortune*."

"Good for them. How does that help us?" I asked. Marcel's smug grin appeared on his face. I seriously thought about slapping it off.

"They live here," he said as the model zoomed out. They overlooked the entryway we would be going in. "Alyx paid their apartment a visit last night; he'll be waiting with Gladiator to pull you out quick."

We had a plan, if you could call it that, but it's the best we could do in such a short timeframe. "So why did you need my shoes?"

"I didn't. I just didn't want you to leave before I could tell you the plan."

I dropped my head to the table to the laughter of my friends. Once, just once, I wanted to come out on the good side of the conversation.

The sun hung directly overhead as we approached the tunnel entrance. Marcel's description of the details sounded good, but actually walking up the Reclaimers and turning yourself in was more nerve wracking than listening to him talk about it.

Two guards approached, machine guns pointed at us. We set our backpacks in front of us, Jon laid down his bow as well, as we explained who we were. An officer stepped out the smaller entry door; the loading dock doors stayed closed. He frowned as he approached.

"What do we have here, Collins?"

"Sir," Collins said, his eyes never leaving us. "These three say they participated in the massacre with The Butcher. They want to turn themselves in."

The officer, Captain Wilker according to his name tag, barked a mirthless laugh. "Kids, you might think this joke is funny, but I assure you tha…"

Wendi stood behind the three soldiers with only the breeze to announce that she moved.

Wilker grabbed the radio from his belt. "We have a code 43, I repeat code 43 at the main gate." He pulled his pistol pointing it directly at Wendi. "By the authority of the Protector, you are under arrest."

We put our hands behind our heads as soldiers ran from the Megadrome like ants from a kicked hill.

I swallowed hard. I really hoped Marcel knew what he was doing.

The guards surrounding us, shoved us forward through the massive doorway. The concrete hallway slopped, reversing its course every hundred feet or so. I'd guess we were a couple of hundred feet below the Megadrome by the time we stopped walking. A guard station, situated between two massive concrete bunkers, blocked our path. The narrow entry forced you to enter or exit one at a time. An armed guard could hold off an army here.

They jammed orange jumpsuits at each of us. Shock wands hovered inches from us as we stepped into a clear chamber. Laser lights flowed over us, air circulated around us, and when a green light clicked on overhead, the glass frosted, and we were told to change. My clothes and shoes were confiscated as I exited the booth. One of the techs examined my shoes carefully, prodding at the sole a couple of times before they were deposited into a bag and tossed to the side. I sighed with relief in my head, glad to know Marcel's little joke hadn't been discovered.

A couple of the guards made comments about leaving the glass clear while the Wendi changed. Captain Wilker turned on them, teeth clenched. "How about I switch off the dampener and see how well you fair in there?" Both snapped to attention, and the other guards all found something to do.

After another long walk, I was placed in a room, a window separating me from the three military men. It couldn't make out details with the bright light focused on my face.

"Looks like our net caught a few more fish," one chuckled. "We should kill kids more often—we might rid ourselves of the Dissidents once and for all."

I wanted to break through the glass, but I held my tongue. For the next hour, they shot questions at me about why we had surrendered, who else was loose, and various other questions that I answered without giving anything away. A loud buzz sounded, and I was escorted to the holding cells.

The guards collected us, verified our restraints, and marched us through a maze of halls. Another station guarded the entrance to the holding cell. I saw on the video screens the cell consisted of a large room, separate sleeping quarters, and two bathrooms. A TV screen had been embedded into the far wall, and the Protectorate propaganda news station played on it. Gladiator would have felt at home in such a place. Surely the architect must have a thing for the Roman Coliseum since it could have been taken from there.

Each of us had our cuffs removed and then were shoved into the cell. Mom stood there, and I could tell she wasn't pleased to see me. The flood gates broke, and I raced over to hug her. She returned the hug with enough strength to crush a car. "What are you doing?" she whispered into my ear.

"We have a plan," I whispered back as much from lack of air as not wanting to be overheard. "I'm getting you out of here. Marcel is shutting off the security systems during the night so we can escape."

She released me, and I glanced around. Wendi, Jon, and Abby were huddled together talking. Mom took my arm and led me to the back of the room. Seated on the bunk in his cell was my dad. He glanced up as we approached.

"Michael, I would like you to meet Tommy," Mom said.

Dad stood up, and it shocked me to look him straight in the eyes. I'd grown more than I thought. I could see what Mr. Fix-it meant. His face mirrored mine, the same nose, the same hazel eyes. Bandages covered his arms. Waxenby had told me Dad's Gift burned him as he used it. He started to offer me his hand to shake, but then pulled me in to a hug. I couldn't believe I had finally met my dad.

He held me out at arm's length so he could see me better. "Tommy, I've waited a very long time to meet you."

"Me too, Dad."

He went on as if I hadn't said anything. "But you shouldn't have come here. What were you thinking?"

I recoiled as if he had struck me. "What?"

"You surrendered," he said, a bit of heat in his voice. "There is nothing you can do here but die. This is rigged, and you know it."

I could feel my face ignite with a mixture of outrage and embarrassment. *After all I've gone through to rescue him, this is what I get?* "Well, I guess it runs in the family, huh?"

His face flushed with rage. "I was protecting you and your mother. They stopped hunting for you after I surrendered. You were safe."

"Safe?" My tone would have made a polar bear shiver. "We lived in Redemption. I got beat up almost every day, and people spat on Mom for having a Dissident for a kid. We weren't safe. Powell tried to kill me and my friends. We were far from safe."

He sat down on the bed. "Powell was a good man at one time. He lost his wife and child when Titan destroyed the bus they were on. I hoped he would be able to find some peace after he brought me in."

"No, he hated you with a passion." I'd never pictured meeting my dad going like this. This reunion should have been epic, not us fighting.

"Hated?"

"He attacked me and my friends. When I told him about you, he went nuts and used jumper cables so he could ruin my face." I stepped carefully around the subject since Dad had burned him so badly. "My collar shattered, and I killed him."

"I'm sorry, Tommy," Dad said slowly. "I should have finished the job, but I couldn't kill any more people. We were losing, and I knew they would stop searching for you after I gave up. I should have been there for you and Susan all those years."

Mom put her arms around him, whispering softly in his ear. After a lifetime of her being angry that he left, it felt good to see her forgive him. I left them alone to make up.

An hour later, Mom and Dad joined us in front of the TV. The footage of the school bus massacre dominated the newsfeed. Dad stepped over and shook Jon's hand. "Nice to meet you, Jon."

For once, Jon didn't have the smug air about him. In fact, he might have been a bit awed. "Very nice to meet you, sir. You are amazing to watch fight, sir."

Dad smiled warmly. "Abby has told me a lot about you and your sister, Wendi, isn't it?" He held his hand out to Wendi, who took it. Dad patted the back of her hand. "I understand both of you are quite talented. It will be an honor to fight beside you both."

Wendi beamed. "Thank you. I wish we could have met under better circumstances."

"As do I, Wendi."

We sat together, the muted TV broadcasting propaganda. We talked about little things, and Dad and Abby spoke about the challenges they had faced in the Gauntlet. Soon the lights flickered, announcing lights out.

We each took a bed in one of the alcoves; I wisely did not follow Wendi to hers. The lights turned off as I climbed into the uncomfortable bed. I definitely preferred the previous night's not sleeping to this one. The hum of the dampening units droned on through the night. I had fully charged before we left, but I couldn't feel the power, so I didn't know if I'd have juice when my Gift came back.

I laid still, feigning sleep. I didn't want the guards wondering why I paced the cell and coming to investigate. The hours dragged by without the signal. I finally drifted off.

I sat up in shock as the cell doors slid open with a resounding clang. The night had passed, and the security systems were still running. Marcel had failed. Tonight, I would die on national TV.

39

Nerves were getting the better of me in the holding cells. The security system was not going down. When they came for Mom, they got her, but not without a fight. Abby had been shocked, but not before she had smashed in one guard's knee and another's teeth. Jon limped slightly. My ribs ached from where I'd been struck with the baton. They made sure not to hit us where it would show. Once the inhibitor field dropped, the injuries would heal rapidly.

I spent my time talking to Wendi, hoping at any moment the signal would sound and we could break out, but time passed, and nothing happened. Marcel must be going crazy since his plan hadn't worked. I should have never let Wendi and Jon come along.

They fed us stale chicken salad sandwiches and water. So much for our last meal before execution. After we ate, the guards showed up. Guards filled the hall, all in riot gear. As they called each of us, we stood with our backs to the door and handcuffs were put on. They left Abby for last. Instead of cuffing her, a guard shot her with a dart, and she tumbled to the floor. "That'll teach the bitch," I heard from one of the guards. Abby was carried out; the rest of us followed.

The others walked behind me as we were led down the silent hall. We walked through a door like we had back in the Air-Lock and entered wonderland. The place contained racks of clothes, props, barber chairs with lighted mirrors. The cuffs came off, and a small man with black glasses and a scarf around his neck came over. He pranced around me *tsk*ing the whole time. "They expect miracles with these deadlines," he muttered as he stood in front of me. "I'm Frankie, your stylist. We need to prep you for tonight. Now your friend there," he gestured as the four guards moved Abby off through the clothes and out of sight, "she made it hard on all of us. You can make this easy or hard. Your choice."

I noticed a series of tooth-sized scabs on his left arm. I guess hair and makeup didn't rank very high on Abby's list.

"I'm good."

Frankie nodded. "Take the pretty one to Darlene and tell her I want her to shine, unlike beast girl." He looked me over one more time. "Mmm, child, I have just the thing for you."

He went to a clothes rack filled with different suits. After selecting and rejecting ten different suits, he settled on one. He held it out for me. "What do you think? I wish I had time to design it from scratch, but the show must go on."

My suit had a blue center and dark red with extra armor at the shoulder. The legs were red on the outside while the blue continued down the middle. Solid gunmetal gray boots with a red stylized star burst on the side, blue gloves, and belt finished off the look. "Ummm, it's okay."

"Let's make you fierce," Frankie said with a laugh. "At least you'll be a beautiful corpse."

Great, I get stuck with the comedian.

I emerged from Frankie's grasp with my hair puffed up and wearing makeup. I got jammed into the suit, and while I'd seen more subdued clowns, I appreciated the carbon fiber plates that covered my hips, chest, arms and shins. Reinforced knee pads would come in handy as well. I figured the suits didn't have any other use than a costume. I was glad to be wrong. Frankie refused to let me wear my helmet. "No helmets in the finale! We must see your beautiful faces."

The guards shoved me down another hallway to the prep room. A gun butt to the back propelled me into the room. I could hear them laughing about us being dead men walking. We would enter the arena from here. Dad wore a new combat suit since the last one had been torn to shreds. This one had golden lightning bolts from his hips to his black combat boots. The center chest piece shimmered with the same gold, running from the edges of his shoulder armor and narrowing as it descended his torso.

"New suit?" I asked innocently.

Dad laughed. "I wanted my old one, but Taylor almost fainted when I mentioned it. I really want my helmet."

I mimicked Frankie. "No helmets in the finale!"

We both laughed.

"Dad, I'm sorry. I thought things would have worked out differently."

He put his hand on my shoulder. "Tommy, I am proud of you. Your mother pointed out to me I pulled the same boneheaded stunts back when I fought with Omega Squad. I guess the apple didn't fall far from the tree."

I felt a warm glow of pride well up inside of me. "Thanks, Dad."

"Let's make it the fight of the century. If they are going to take us down, we'll do it with style."

I started to reply, but Dad nudged me with his elbow. The door to the prep room opened, and Wendi sauntered in. Her suit was a deep red with yellow accents. Laces held the front of her suit together, showing a lot of skin. Her hair was curled into ringlets, and she had on a lot more makeup than normal. I couldn't take my eyes off her. She struck a runway model pose, spun around, and walked over to me.

"Wow!" All thoughts died in my brain.

A knife flashed under my chin as Wendi giggled. "Eyes are up here, Sport."

"Knives?" I asked, noticing matching sheaths on each hip.

"Darlene informed me I needed weapons to fight." She spun the knife around and reseated it in the sheath.

Dad stepped up. "Wendi, you should probably hang back during the fight."

She nodded. "Because if I stand back and we lose, they'll just let me walk, right?"

When neither of us answered, she continued. "I'm Gifted just like you. This is my fight as much as yours. I'm taking down whatever they put in front of me, even if I have to use my bare hands. Got it?"

Dad held his hands up in mock surrender. "Wendi, you remind me of Susan, which is the greatest compliment I can give you. I'm honored to have you fight by my side."

Wendi gave him a quick grin. The door opened, and Jon and Abby stepped in. She wore solid black, but Jon's suit was brown and green in the same design as Wendi's, minus the laces and the skin.

Wendi laughed. "I guess they took the twins thing seriously."

Jon seethed. "We had our combat suits."

Jon's hair was gelled into a ridiculous style involving a tidal wave of hair and a curlicue hanging over his forehead, but his bow was across his back, and he had his quiver and knife in place. "I want to fight, not walk the red carpet. How did you get a normal suit?" he asked Abby.

She bared her teeth at him. "I bite."

Jon rolled his eyes and looked at Dad. "Okay, you have a game plan for this?"

Dad shook his head. "Until we are in the arena, we won't know, though we should probably pair up and watch each other's backs."

"Um, there are five of us," Abby said. "How does that work?"

"Abby and Jon, you take the right side; Wendi and Tommy you take the left," he said indicating the sides. "I'm going after my wife."

"Abby and Tommy are the brute force. You need to protect your partner. Jon and Wendi, you take out targets and keep out of reach." Wendi scowled at him. "Your speed allows you to dart in, do damage and get away. Use it to your advantage."

I asked, "But why don't we group together?"

"Too easy of a target." Jon sounded more like a general than a teen going into a fight to the death. "We have layers and can flow with the fight."

Dad nodded, an approving expression on his face. "In between zones, we regroup quick, assign targets, and move away. They aren't going to let us live, but we can go down swinging. If one of us falls," he grimaced, shaking his head. "No lies. *When* one of us falls, keep moving."

Nobody spoke, the emphasis on "when" made all our faces grim. Wendi's hand slipped into mine. I squeezed it. At least she'd be with me until the end. A blast horn sounded, and the far door slid open.

"Okay, follow my directions, watch for the obstacles, weaknesses, and good luck," Dad said as he turned to go.

Two guards stopped us at the door telling us to wait. The noise was deafening. I could slightly make out the blue shimmer of the force field above us.

"Ladies and Gentlemen, I'm Desmond Roberts. Welcome to *Saturday Night Showdown!*" His voice echoed around the arena. "We are honored tonight to have another first in our history. The Protector will speak to us live from the Hall of Liberation."

The noise died as if the plug were pulled. A huge four-sided screen slid down from the ceiling, stopping inches above of the shield. The screen leapt to life, and the Protector appeared, standing behind a podium. He waved to the crowd, his silver collar glittering in the spotlight.

"Citizens all over the world have paid a terrible price at the hands of Dissidents over the course of human history until the day the Reclamation rid us of this menace. Many brave men and women sacrificed themselves to build a world where the Dissidents could be shackled, returning the world to its right place, in the hands of the human race."

The crowd roared its approval. The Protector basked in the praise of the crowd. He acted like he had done it himself. He held his hands up, and quiet resumed.

"Today marks another victory against a foe who knows no bounds. The Dissidents killed millions and destroyed cities in a quest to rule our world. We stood as one, defeating their evil. Now the Reclaimers have captured the band that murdered our children in cold blood."

The crowd raged, screaming for vengeance. The Protector paused, reveling in the hatred of the Norms above, whipped into a fury by his words. He raised his hands for quiet, and the crowd gradually subsided.

When he could be heard, he continued. "The Reclaimers paid a great price to capture The Butcher's accomplices." The screen split in half showing footage of the Reclaimers attacking a building. "Brave soldiers lost their lives to ensure you would be safe. We owe them a debt of gratitude, and tonight, we will see them avenged in the Gauntlet!" His voice rose at the end and the crowd swelled to match him. Sparks flashed along the shields as the audience threw silver chains at the arena floor.

The footage of dead soldiers and a blown-apart building incited the crowd to even greater levels of hatred. A tsunami of sound hit us, forcing us to cover our ears.

"This will be a fight to the death!" he said, continuing to pump up the crowd. "The Reclaimers asked for the chance to mete out the death sentence themselves, and I have agreed. So tonight, the soldiers who protect you and your families will put their lives on the line to see justice served. May God bless their actions and allow a swift and bloody victory."

The screens shut down, and a spotlight stabbed through the darkness stopping outside the door. "Thank you for gracing us with your presence, Protector," Desmond said in a pious tone. "Now we are here to witness the finale of the Gauntlet. First up, the vilest of all the Dissidents, Michael Ward, the Cyclone Ranger!"

My head came up sharply. They had never used Dad's real name before now. Something was seriously wrong. The guards pushed Dad out into the light. Head held high, he strode across the arena to the starting location. Hands behind his back, he could have been a statue carved of granite.

"Next, the first of the massacre perpetrators, The Butcher!" Abby jogged out next to Dad. Where he stood still, she bounced, building up for the upcoming fight.

"Now, this little beauty resembles an angel, but she's the devil's own. The Succubus!" Wendi looked over her shoulder, mouthing "Succubus?" at me. She strolled across the space, stopping, hand on her hips, waiting for the rest of us.

"Our next Dissident is as tough as they come. That bow of his killed quite of few before they took him down. Enter the Huntsman!"

Jon rolled his eyes at me and stalked out to join the team. I waited for my turn, hoping my manner read as cool, not scared boy. With my luck, I would wet myself on national TV.

"And finally, we have the worst of the lot. A multiple murderer by the age of sixteen and the son of Cyclone Ranger," Desmond said, pausing to let the crowd react to the news. They must have been listening to us in the holding cells yesterday. "Enter the arena Tommy Ward or, as we like to call him, The Executioner."

Man, where the heck did they come up with these lame names? I locked my eyes on Wendi and walked slowly across, the light dazzling my sight. I'd be blinking away the aftereffects for an hour.

As one, we took our spots, Wendi and I on the left, Abby and Jon on the right with Dad in the center. Badass didn't do us justice. I started to feel like we could do this.

Then the lights came on.

40

We were standing in the middle of a street. More accurately, the remains of a street. Concrete barricades, demolished cars, and debris littered the ground; the walls were painted to resemble a city block. At the far end, a collapsed building dominated the space. And at the very top, Mom stood, her mouth gagged and her arms tied over her head so she hung from part of the building.

"Ladies and Gentlemen, I would like to introduce you to our special guest for the finale," Desmond said. "Tonight, we have a living exit. Susan Ward, wife of Cyclone Ranger, mother of The Executioner, will share the fate of her boys. She has been convicted as an accomplice in the deaths of both the massacre victims and the Reclaimers who captured the perpetrators."

I heard Dad gasp. His face had gone white with shock. His eyes bugged out as he took it all in, and his bottom lip shook a bit.

"The scene for our final match of the Gauntlet. Baltimore 2012. Bravo Strike Team gets a tip Cyclone Ranger and Dominion are in the area. They move out to take down two of the most ruthless killers the Dissidents ever spawned. They neutralized Dominion with an inhibitor, but Cyclone Ranger breaks her free. In a fit of rage, he kills virtually every member of the Bravo Team. Tonight, we will settle an old score between Cyclone Ranger and the Reclaimers. In the role of Bravo Team are twenty members of the 55th elite Dissident Strike Force. Give a big *Saturday Night Showdown* welcome to the 55th."

The men entered with military precision and took up stations in front of the rubble. Each wore full gear, helmets, armor, and multiple weapons.

Jon whistled. "Wow, those are HKs."

How he knew that I'd never know. They appeared deadly from where I stood, especially since they were pointed at me. I glanced at Dad, and, well, he didn't look right.

I stepped closer and nudged him. "You okay?"

He shook his head. "Tommy, that was the worst day of my life. Dominion took control of me and killed everyone around us with my Gift. I swore I'd never kill another person again. I can't do this."

I couldn't believe my ears. We were all going to die, including Mom who didn't even have a Gift and he couldn't do this? "Listen," I shouted to be heard over the increasing noise. "Your wife, my mom, is up there. She is depending on us. We will save her, no matter what. They are messing with your head, hoping for an easy kill."

We locked eyes. I could see the panic fading. "Mom's life is on the line. We fail, she dies. We didn't ask for it, but it's what we've got to deal with."

I saw the steel return to his stance. A grim look of determination chiseled on his face. Cyclone Ranger was back and ready to kick some ass. "You're right. I need my head in the game if we're going to stand any chance."

The applause diminished. "Only one member of Bravo Team survived the day, and he single-handedly captured Cyclone Ranger. His son tried to avenge his father's defeat and almost did, but Lewis C. Powell is too tough to kill. So, let me introduce the Reclaimer's super soldier, who we like to call him the Vindicator!"

Powell. Alive. That's how they found Mom. I told the bastard.

I led them straight to her.

From behind the rubble, Powell emerged, more machine than man. Both arms and legs had been replaced with cybernetic pieces, as well as one of his eyes. Even from a distance, I could see his crew cut and the scars from his fight with Dad.

He held both arms up in victory as he crossed to the center of the line. He caught my eye and smiled. The shock on my face had to be plain as day. The left arm ended in a machine gun, the ammo belt fed over his shoulder. His right hand had been replaced by a metal cylinder.

Dad turned around. "Game plan, kids. You take down the soldiers. Powell is mine. It is time for me to put down that rabid dog once and for all." He stuck his hand out, and we slapped our hands on top. "We take as many of them as possible. No mercy this time."

We broke and spread out. "The Dissident team is ready to start. I'll send it up to Chip Calloway to kick off the finale!"

The crowd howled for blood as the soldiers moved into position. All the scattered wreckage provided plenty of cover for both sides. The dampening system dropped. A surge of power blossom in my chest, and the hair on my arms rolled with waves of electricity. The horn sounded, and the fight began.

Wendi and I slid in behind a cement pillar. I expected a hail of bullets, but none came. The real battle raged at the center of the arena. Dad launched himself on a vortex of wind as Powell charged toward him. Powell roared, "He's mine," as a couple of the soldiers moved to intercept.

I watched the ten guys on our side leapfrog from cover to cover, trying to surround our position. I noticed one signaling the moves as they advanced. When he left cover, I let loose a blast of lightning, taking him in the chest. He flew backward, his armor melted, and laid still. I dropped as they returned fire, the sound of the bullets on concrete intense.

I wouldn't be getting another easy shot like that, now that they knew what I could do. The robots had been immune to lightning, but not these guys. Peering around the edge, three guys flanked us. Wendi signaled we had two on her side. We needed to get outside their circle, or they'd have clean shots at us.

Wendi crawled over next to me as I concentrated on gathering the energy in my hand. I counted down three-two-one and threw the ball at the two as they crept around a broken-down Humvee. The ball detonated in front of them. As they recoiled from the blast, Wendi leapt on them, her knives flashing in a blur of motion. Blood splattered, and down they went. I jumped over a broken concrete pylon to the sounds of gunfire. I rolled and came up behind the Humvee.

Wendi still had the knives out, covered in blood. She turned and threw up on the floor. She had killed Brunner, but she had been pushed past her limits to cope that night. Now she had full control and realized what she'd done. Even though I knew I had zero choice in the decision to kill, I would be dealing with the ghosts of all the people I had killed for the rest of my life. I couldn't deal with it now, but lots more sleepless, guilt-ridden nights would be in my future. I could hear her getting sick, but now wasn't the time to be holding her hair. Not unless I wanted us dead while I did it.

I looked across to see Jon firing his bow at the advancing soldiers. One soldier down from an arrow and one crumbled against the side wall. Screams of fury reverberated as Abby tore into her enemies.

I couldn't worry about the others; there were seven more Reclaimers to deal with. The first set of flankers had gotten into position. With the left flankers dead, I had some room to maneuver, but not for long. I grabbed Wendi's arm, pulling her to the passenger side door of the Humvee.

"Can you fight?" I asked.

She nodded, but I could tell she teetered on the brink.

"Can you run down the left side and get near Mom? I'm going to try something, but it's dangerous. If it works, these guys will be done for, but you may need to clean up if it doesn't."

"I'm good. It just shocked me when I..." Her eyes drifted toward the gore.

"I know, but we have to focus," I said. "On the count of three, run for it."

"One, two, three." She sped away in a split second as I jumped up unleashing a low power fan of energy. Most it would do is static cling. Bullets slammed into the Humvee, and I ducked back down, but the important part happened: the driver side tires deflated. The vehicle lurched as it settled at a forty-five-degree angle.

A roar swelled up from the crowd, not a good sign. I needed to end this fast so I could help take down Powell. I stepped out from behind the Humvee, bullets flew around me, one clipping the back of my leg. I fell to the ground, part for show, part because, man, it hurt, but the surge of energy crackled through me. I dragged my leg, faking an injury. I reached down to find a welt where the bullet had opened a gash in my suit. I fell on my back and slid myself under the car.

The crowd screamed in delight. If I played it right, the soldiers would think I was down for the count. I kept still, playing possum. I concentrated on forming the shield Dad had used. Our Gifts were different, so I wasn't sure if it would work. From the corner of my eye, I could see soldiers stalking up to the Humvee. I concentrated as much energy as I could and fired it into the gas tank. The vehicle turned into a fireball. The shield kept the worst of the damage off me, but parts of my suit burned from the explosion.

I rolled away from the burning wreckage and stood up. Pain cascaded down my spine as bullets slammed into me, knocking me down. I could barely breathe, the pain consuming me. *I'm dying* was all I could think. I heard a grunt from over me. "One more Mutt down, sir," he said then paused. "Yes, sir, the rest of the squad is down after the explosion."

I'd gotten all but one. My plan worked. I realized my breathing came back to normal, and the pain, while still intense, slackened quickly.

I felt a foot wedge under me. With a push, I flipped on to my back. I opened my eyes.

Surprise and shock registered on his face as he realized I was still alive. "How? I nailed you good."

"You forgot one thing."

"What?"

"I'm not alone," I said with a smirk. Wendi hit him from behind at full speed with a two-by-four from the pile of rubble. He dropped like a rock, an armed and armored rock, but a rock none the less.

She knelt down, grabbing my face. "They shot you. I didn't see the last guy with the explosion until he had shot you. I'm sorry, Tommy."

I sat up to a chorus of boos and catcalls. "Wendi, I'm okay."

She pulled me forward to check where the bullets had hit me. "You aren't bleeding, but those bullets should have ripped through you."

"I'm certainly am glad they didn't." She helped me to my feet. "Go back by Mom. I'm going to go help Jon and Abby."

"No, I'm staying with you," she said hotly. "You could have been killed. I can't take that chance."

"My mom is defenseless. I need you to protect her. If this goes bad for them, they will go after her to stop us."

A grim smile touched the corners of her mouth. She understood, we had to protect Mom at all costs. "Gotcha." And she jetted away.

I moved toward the center of the arena. Jon lay still, blood flowing from his mouth and nose, slumped against a barricade. Abby crouched down behind a dumpster. Four Reclaimers had her pinned down. I called out, but too late. She screamed an animalistic battle cry and charged toward the closest one. A flash of light flickered as an inhibitor band wrapped around her leg. Suddenly, her Gift vanished. She dropped to the floor like a wet bag of cement. The soldiers punched her, nightsticks slamming down on her as she curled into a ball, trying to protect her head.

All I could see was Brunner standing over me, kicking me while I couldn't fight back. The arena fell away as I moved to intercept. The first guy didn't know what hit him. I jumped from the top of a nearby pylon, delivering a massive overhead punch to the back of his helmet. I felt the helmet give way as he crumbled.

The nearest soldier, startled, didn't fare much better. He swung at me, but I ducked under the club, shattering his kneecap with a punch and finishing him off with a massive uppercut that knocked him into the far wall.

The crowd screamed in disbelief as I dispatched the final two attackers by slamming their heads together. I knelt down to a barely conscious and bloodied Abby. I tried to free her of the inhibitor band, but it had fused to her.

"Thanks, Tommy." A small smile played on her lips. "I had them right where I wanted them."

"You made my job easy."

"Go get Powell. Kick him once for me."

"We're friends, I'll kick him twice." I laid her head back gently. I needed to find Dad fast. He'd been one-on-one with Powell the whole time, but something amazing happened. The shield above the arena cut off. The audience shrieked in panic.

Desmond's voice came over the PA system. "Please keep calm, we've had a technical difficulty with the shield. It will be restored momentarily."

Marcel. He did it. He shut down the Megadrome's security system. I needed a distraction, so they would have to handle it instead of getting the system back online.

I destroyed the unmanned cameras, targeting each in turn. The explosions turned the crowd into a fleeing mob. Screams of pain floated down as people climbed over each other to get away. I shot out a couple lights, the cascade of sparks adding to the panic until it was a full-out riot.

I barked out an evil-sounding chuckle and ran toward the sound of the last fight. I crossed over a barricade and jumped to the hood of a demolished car that overlooked the battle. Powell had fresh scorch marks on his arm and torso, but the damage appeared minimal. I'd seen corpses in better shape than Dad was. Blood dripped from multiple slashes across his body. Powell's right arm ended in a nasty, bloody, combat dagger.

Powell charged, swinging the knife in an overhand slice. Dad dodged, barely getting out of the way in time. Powell delivered a vicious kick to Dad's knee. He fell to the ground, clutching his leg, teeth gritted against the pain. A second kick struck as I ran. Dad's head jerked back as the boot connected with the side of his head, knocking him cold.

"It ends now!" Powell bellowed as he stabbed downward at his immobile target. I tackled him halfway through his swing, toppling him to the ground. I sprang to my feet, a move Blaze had spent hours drilling it into my head.

Powell smiled. "I've been wanting this almost as much as offing your old man."

"I torched you once, Powell." I gritted my teeth, biting off every word. "I'm back to finish the job. When I'm done, there won't be enough left to make into a Nintendo, let alone a cyborg."

His left arm machine gun fired without warning. A couple of the bullets hit me, but I was ready. I rode the wave of pain and fired a bolt of pure energy back at him. He moved faster than I would have thought; obviously the enhancements had increased his speed.

"I figured after the jumper cables didn't do the job, you were some sort of absorber."

I fired a second blast, knocking him down, but barely damaged him. "Carbinium exoskeleton. Gonna have to do better than that, boy."

He flicked his arm, and a spiraling disc hit just before me. The blast stunned me. I tried to run but stumbled and fell on a piece of debris. My balance failed me as the bullets started. A solid stream hit me in the chest. My suit shredded under the raining shots. The pain flared to an incredible level. I forced myself through it, but I had another problem. I absorbed the energy from the hits, magnifying it. It built up to the point where I thought my head would blow off like a shaken pop bottle. I wanted to fire it at Powell, but Mom hung directly behind him and I couldn't risk hitting her.

"What's wrong, Slag, can't handle a little extra energy?" Powell's mocking voice came over the noise from the machine gun. "Come on, Slag. Let me have it!"

I screamed as the pain intensified. I could feel the energy growing faster than ever before. I couldn't hold any more, so I shoved my hands straight up and unleashed every ounce of built up energy. The top of the Megadrome erupted as all the energy hit it, vaporizing about half and throwing the other half in every direction as chunks. The machine gun silenced as it ran out of ammo.

The energy ebbed as it flowed out of me. I laid there completely spent. I couldn't have powered a lightbulb with the power I had left. Powell knelt down over me. The knife hovered in front of my face. He smiled his sick smile at me.

"Impressive." Sarcasm dripped off his words. "Now I'm gonna end you, then I'm gonna kill your girl. After that, I'm gonna take your pretty, smart-mouthed mama and give her to my men before I slit her throat like a pig. Then we will be even."

I spat in his face. "I'm sure your wife and daughter would be so proud of what you've become."

Powell's smile turned into a snarl. "You shut your mouth, boy, or I'll make that little girl of yours suffer even worse."

A glint caught my eye. The seam where Powell's left arm joined his torso had torn in the fighting. The wires were exposed. I needed one more burst of energy, but I had nothing left.

"Burned yourself out, didn't ya?" He snickered. "I'll give ya this, kid, you're a scrapper. Too bad you bein' a Slag and all, I could use men like you."

Then it hit me. The ring. I pushed the ring Mr. Fix-it had given me into the exposed flesh on my leg. The shock zoomed through my depleted body. I grabbed the wires and sent a surge of power through.

Powell's face distorted in fear. His systems went haywire as the energy overloaded his circuitry. He lurched to his feet and fell over a fallen Reclaimer with a mighty clang. He jerked back and forth as the systems shut down.

"What did you do?" he screamed. "I won! I beat you all!"

I stood over him. I should do what he would have done to me in the same place, but I could see the broken man my dad had spared. I headed to set Mom free and get everyone out before reinforcements could arrive.

"You are gutless, Ward," Powell screamed, spit flying out of his mouth. "Kill me like a man."

"You aren't worth my time."

"They took my family, so I'll take yours!" he shrieked as a single gunshot fired.

The whole world slowed. The bullet streaked toward Mom. A blur pushed her aside. Instead, the bullet struck Wendi in the head. Her body had been speeding when the bullet hit; she careened out of control, bouncing down the pile of rubble.

"NO!" I ran to her. The bullet had punched straight through her head. Her suit had torn, and blood flowed, splattering the broken building pieces on the way down. "Oh my God, Wendi!" I pulled her into my lap, rocking back and forth. I should have killed him, and none of this would have happened.

I heard Powell's insane laughter from where he laid. "What's wrong, Tommy? Girlfriend lose her head?"

I laid her down. I should have killed him before. I wouldn't make the same mistake twice. I leapt onto a car headed to kill Wendi's murderer. A flash of light hit Powell in the back of the head, exploding it like an over-ripe watermelon. Dad hobbled into view. He looked tired, but he still lived.

I went back to Wendi, and Mom sat with her, holding her lifeless hand. She rose as I approached, hugging me fiercely. "Tommy, I am so sorry," she said. I wanted to cry, but the tears wouldn't come.

"Tommy," Dad called. "We've got to get everyone out of here. They are bringing in reinforcements."

I pulled gently away from Mom. I picked up Wendi's lifeless body and walked to where Dad waited to fly us out of the arena. We had won, but the cost had been far greater than I ever thought.

I stood in the middle of the field. The coffin suspended before us held the person I loved more than anything in the world. Her last act saved my mom, a debt I could never repay. Mom stood on one side; on the other stood my dad, still using a cane while his knee healed.

Abby, Gladiator, and Alyx sat next to Wendi's mom, who cried softly in the background. The priest had finished the service. We were the last of the small group of mourners to pay our final respects. Jon couldn't be found. Her own twin had deserted her, but my inability to kill Powell resulted in her death.

Mom and Dad laid roses on the lid of the coffin. I still held mine. As soon as I placed mine on the lid, she would be truly gone forever, buried in the land where she had been born seventeen short years ago. It wasn't fair. Mom rubbed my arm on her way by.

"Wendi, I'm sorry. I let you down. I failed. If I had only done what I should have, you would be here. I love you, and I already miss you more than I could ever believe possible. I'm sorry." Tears filled my eyes, rolling down my cheeks as I spoke. I set the rose on the lid and watched the coffin lower into the ground. Never again would I see her sparkling blue eyes, kiss her tender lips, hold her hand. The hole in my heart grew as I stood there.

Mom moved me away from the gravesite as everyone returned to the house. I headed up the stairs to what had once been her room and closed the door behind me. Her presence was still here, even though nothing in the room was hers. I sat on the bed, eyes closed, soaking in the last of her love. Remembering our time together, how she kissed me, the jokes we shared, our one amazing night together. I had accomplished what I had set out to do but lost the person I loved. I wondered, not for the last time, if it had been worth it.

Two envelopes sat on the bed. One had the word "Tommy" written in Wendi's hand, and the other was blank. I opened the one from Wendi.

Tommy,

If you are reading this, I am gone. I hope that we saved your mom and dad. I wanted to thank you. You were always there for me when things went bad. I have felt alone since I was sent to Redemption until I met you.

Please don't blame yourself for me being gone. Things happen for a reason that we can't always know. The thing to remember is I loved you more than I could ever tell you. Our time together meant everything to me. When you were gone, it was if the color went out of my world. I know we will be together again, that our love will never die.

Love,

Wendi

After I pulled myself together, I opened the second envelope, unfolding the letter.

Ward,

Wendi left letters for us in my things. She asked me to make sure it got to you. I would do anything for her, so I delivered it as she asked.

My sister is dead because of you. If you had taken care of Powell instead of walking away, she would be alive. In Wendi's memory, I give you this one warning. The next time I see you, I will kill you.

I folded the letters and laid back on her bed, feeling her warmth around me. I fell asleep, knowing I'd have a lot to deal with, but it could wait until tomorrow.

ACKNOWLEDGMENTS

The book you are holding is the fruit of many individuals that contributed their time and insight into taking a rough tale and turning it into a polished story. It was a long and winding road to finish this book.

The first person who helped set the foundation was Carol, who pointed out flaws in the structure of the book. Without her I'm not sure I'd have ever got the story down. Next were my Gifted team that beta read the book and offered frank assessments that helped strengthen the story. They are Chuck, Jon, Regis, Catherine, Cheri and Joe. If I've missed anyone it is completely unintentional. I'd be remiss if I didn't mention Mike M. has listened to book ideas since 9th grade and now it actually is here.

After a long search John Hartness of Falstaff books gave me the opportunity to have Storm Forged published. My Editor Erin Penn is simply amazing, pointing out oversights and places to add depth to the story that has taken it to the next level. Melissa Gilbert hammered it into the final book and Davey Beauchamp provided an amazing cover.

Most of all I'd like to thank my family. My parents always said you could do anything you set your mind to and were right. Emily and Nicholas have been an inspiration every day since they were born. Both have contributions to the story, some intentional, some not. Emily was my first beta reader and Nicholas was my teen age boy coach. Emerson, our dog, kept me company many a late nights. And last but not least is my wife and best friend Hope who has put up with late nights of writing/editing, had to listen to endless prattle over minor issues, deal with the stressful and grumpy days and yet still is amazingly supportive and loving.

ABOUT THE AUTHOR

Patrick Dugan was born in the far north of New York, where the cold winds blow. This meant lots of time for reading over the long winters. His parents didn't care what he read as long as he did. This started with a steady diet of comics and science fiction novels.

After two degrees and lots of odd jobs ranging from Blockbuster Video manager to Lab Researcher to running a video game arcade, Charlotte, NC beckoned. Packing up his dog sled he headed for warmer climes and a lot less snow. Still a voracious reader, he read all sorts of great books. Rothfuss, Butcher, Duncan, Sanderson, Hobb, Farland and Feist sparked his imagination and he started writing horribly. Bad short stories and worse novels would follow. Thankfully these are nowhere to be found.

A husband and father of two great kids and one opinionated dog, Patrick works as a software engineer by day before his author shifts on nights and weekends. When he's not writing, Patrick enjoys brewing and drinking craft beers, watching Science Fiction & Fantasy movies/shows and building things out of wood and metal for use around the house.

FALSTAFF BOOKS

Made in the USA
Middletown, DE
14 May 2020